Play With Fire

Cindy Davis

Cindy Davis (signature)

L & L Dreamspell

Spring, Texas

.d Interior Design by L & L Dreamspell

This is a work of fiction, and is produced from the author's imagination. People, places and things mentioned in this novel are used in a fictional manner.

ISBN: 978-1-60318-142-6

Library of Congress Control Number: 2009933063

Visit us on the web at www.lldreamspell.com

Published by L & L Dreamspell
Printed in the United States of America

Acknowledgements—my writers group, the greatest group of girls: Dee, Jen and Susan. Big thanks to Judy and Margi at the Olde Bay Diner.

Play With Fire

Dedicated to Bob—he knows why.

One

"That's a wrap, folks," Angie Deacon called. "Great job. *Checkmate: Love* will be the biggest thing that's ever hit the Lakes Region!" Overhead, the bright lights faded and then died out, officially marking the end of the final dress rehearsal.

Tyson Goodwell closed his script. "Nice job, everyone. Go relax a few hours. Back at five."

The actors filed past, their faces wearing various levels of anxiety. Angie and Tyson patted each shoulder and muttered words of encouragement. When the last person disappeared backstage, Angie tossed the script on the bed and collapsed beside it. "I am exhausted." Even though she spoke softly, her words carried to the furthest corners of the warehouse-turned-theater.

Tyson stepped to the vanity table and clicked off the lights around the mirror. He fell into an overstuffed chair much the same way she'd dropped on the bed. "You'll feel better after tonight. I think they—" he inclined his head toward backstage— "are holding up amazingly well. Most of them have never been in front of an audience."

She raised her head to peer at him in the dim light. "You were nervous as anything this morning. What caused the mood reversal?"

He laughed. "I was being supportive. Actually I'm scared to death. We've invested everything into tonight. I've been center stage, but it's nothing when put against owning the whole thing. Seriously, after the first performance the pressure will be off.

You'll see, everything will be smoooooth sailing."

Angie believed him, but the flurry of caterpillars in her nether regions didn't. "Can you believe the caliber of talent we found right here in the area?"

"They are pretty great." Pride oozed in Tyson's voice.

They had a darned great cast. Especially one man, cop by day, actor by night. Detective Colby Jarvis so surprised them with his ability they'd regretted not giving him the starring role. Not that he intended to try out for any role at all. He'd arrived to pick up Angie and tried out on a bet by his fellow officers.

"What a magnificent theater!"

At the unfamiliar and slightly accented voice, Angie lifted her head. Then she sat up. Tyson swiveled on the chair. A man stood silhouetted in the doorway leading to the lobby. He was tall and lean and holding a cane whose gold tip glittered in the house lights. He strode down the aisle, walking with an elegance that had to be contrived. He wore a long coat and a fedora like the one Bogie wore in *Casablanca*. His face was obscured beneath the tipped-down brim of the hat. An actor. Had to be. Come to audition for something.

The stranger stopped at the end of the first row and took off his hat. He was maybe seventy with classic Slavic features: high cheekbones, a finely chiseled nose, and brilliant blue eyes. He ran a gloved hand through fashionably styled white hair that immediately lay back in place. The hand moved to stroke the precisely trimmed beard. "I never would've guessed." Angie could tell now, the accent was Canadian. She stood and crossed the stage. She had to have this man in their next show. In passing, she threw Tyson a look that said this.

The man breathed deep and let it out before repeating, "I never would've guessed...that a splendid place like this existed inside such an unremarkable building."

He laid it on a bit thick—lowering her estimation of him.

Tyson joined Angie at the head of the stage. He gestured for her to precede him down the trio of steps into the auditorium.

The man shot long lean fingers toward Tyson, and then her. "My name is Carson Dodge." He smiled. And waited.

Should she know him? Her brain scurried for recognition of either the face or the name. He had hold of her fingers now. He brought her limp appendage up and grazed his beard across the back of her hand. *Sheesh.* "I'm very sorry, do I know you?" Angie asked.

"No need to apologize. I thought my son might've advised you of my arrival."

"Son?"

"Colby Jarvis."

Gulp. "But I thought—" Mr. Dodge didn't ask what she thought, and she didn't elaborate. "You've just missed him. I imagine you can reach him at the station, or at home."

"I'll do that. I'm sorry to have troubled you." Dodge settled his hat on his head and gave a tiny bow in Angie's direction. He shook Tyson's hand again, turned and caned his way up the aisle.

Part of her wanted to beg him to come back and read for a role right then. Another part of her said to let him go, they had to get through tonight's show first. After all, if tonight flopped, there might not be another performance. Besides, she could always reach him through Jarvis. Funny thing, she would've sworn Jarvis said his father was dead.

Behind her, a pair of stagehands clomped across the gleaming hardwood and began exchanging bedroom for living room furniture for the night's opening scene. Angie watched them roll that oh-so-inviting bed into the wings. Her eyes roamed back to the street door. She mentally compared Mr. Dodge and his son: different as, well, different as all those dumb clichés. Whether feigned or not, Carson Dodge was rich with culture. Jarvis was down-home all the way: hunter, fisherman, homebody. She squeezed her thighs tight and distracted herself by watching the stagehands move the bedroom wall panels and replace them with the fireplaced living room scene.

Tyson drifted to the first row of velveteen-covered chairs,

all two hundred salvaged from a defunct movie theater in Detroit eight months ago. He and Angie had driven a rental truck thirteen hours and loaded each seat themselves. During the trip, they worked on the script, a concept Tyson had already spent two years nagging his Broadway contacts to produce. Failing that, he'd proposed a partnership in a neighborhood theater and Angie jumped at the idea. What else would she do with her life? Her long-time marriage had fizzled. Her ER job lacked stimulation. Two friends had betrayed her. Okay, screwed her royally, if truth be known. Things like that could really suck the pizzazz out of a person.

"I wish John had been here for rehearsal," Tyson said.

"You did a nice job standing in for him."

"It felt good acting again, even if it was unofficial. Are you concerned about him showing up tonight?"

"No. Yes. A little. I'm worried he'll get so busy in his lab he'll forget to come. I can't help thinking we made a mistake giving a part to a scientist. He missed so many rehearsals—"

"But he's a great actor," Tyson said. "He told me he recites his lines to his plants."

"I wonder if they applaud when he's through." She pushed a stray hair off her face, realizing her fingers were frigid with nervous anticipation. She rubbed her palms together, then folded her fingers into fists. "I *am* concerned that he hasn't brought the plants over yet."

Tyson picked lint from one of the chairs and dropped it in his breast pocket beside an ever-present array of highlighters he used to mark individual lines of dialogue. "I'm going home for a shower and something to eat. Want me to bring something back for you?"

"No thanks. I'm going home. What did you think of that guy?"

"Guy? Oh, you mean Jarvis's father? I wonder why they don't have the same name."

She shrugged. "There's a lot of that going around these days."

"By the way, I know you were thinking of asking him to read. Get a grip. We need to survive this show first." He ran a doting palm over another chair then removed his coat from the back of the seat behind it. "I'll call John and jerk his chain."

Soft spoken John Bloom was the essence of tall, dark and handsome, and knew it. He wore the near-black hair a little on the shaggy side, probably not by design, but because he was so busy. John not only ran a wholesale nursery, he also bred irises in a laboratory attached to one of his rambling greenhouses. He spoke proudly of his work in iris genetics; he'd recently discovered something—Angie couldn't quite remember what it was.

That disheveled look meshed perfectly in the mild mannered, and somewhat flirty, leading man in *Checkmate: Love*, though. Not that she'd responded to the flirting. Not even once, but she couldn't help enjoying the attention. Another, tinier part relished the jealousy it inspired in Jarvis. As an actor John was a great find, and a total fluke. He'd come to see what sort of plants and trees were needed for the sets and ended up with the lead in the play. If he 'forgot' to come tonight…

"Angelina!"

Angie cringed. Her feet made two running steps toward backstage before she could stop them. Tyson's lips twitched in a restrained smile. He slung the coat over his arm, wiggled four fingers in the air, and whispered "good luck."

"Coward," she whispered.

He strode up the aisle; his wispy male form soon replaced by a feminine one in the doorway. A blast of icy air pushed toward Angie. Tiny hairs all over her body sprang to attention.

Gloria Farnsworth was still trim and shapely at the age of seventy-five. Her once-blonde hair had faded to platinum but neither physique nor hair color belied the woman's feistiness. Tyson stopped long enough to give her a hug and a peck on the cheek. He hurried out into the lobby without stopping to put on his coat. Angie remained standing in the orchestra pit—though there would be no ensemble for this performance.

"Angelina?"

Angie met her mother at the first row of seats.

"I thought I'd find you here."

"It's where I work, Mother."

Gloria bundled her coat tighter around herself and gave an elaborate shiver. "God, how can you stand living in this godforsaken part of the country?"

Angie jammed her fists in her jean pockets, managing not to offer a lift to the airport.

"When are you coming back to the apartment?"

"Probably some time after midnight. In case you've missed the perpetual string of ads and announcements, our play opens tonight. Putting on a show requires—"

"I know, I know, many man-hours and total dedication." Gloria repeated words Angie said many times over the past ten days.

"Mom, we've been over this."

Gloria heaved a sigh that must've emptied her one remaining lung. "I come to town once in ten years and you can't even spare a little time for me."

Angie didn't bother mentioning that the past two nights they'd stayed up all night talking. She was so sleep deprived she could barely hold her head up. God, when had her mother gotten so needy? All Angie's life, Mom held things together. When Dad went on his binges, Mom protected Angie and her brother. When Dad died, Mom got a job, a major feat for a woman whose only duty had been as housewife and mother for fifteen years. When Mom won the lottery three years ago, she took herself on a world tour—alone. Suddenly now, she breezed into town, needing every ounce of Angie's attention. A horrible thought eclipsed the annoyance. Her health. There was something wrong.

She smoothed a hand over her hair and took two steps: one forward and one back.

"Don't run away from me, Angelina. You've always done that. Haven't you changed at all?"

Angie wiped sweat from her palms onto her slacks. Yes, she'd changed, especially over the past year. She took her mother's arm just above the elbow and changed the subject. "What are you wearing tonight, that lovely teal sheath you bought the other day?"

Gloria's frown grew into a smile. "Yes. I think it would be perfect, don't you?"

"If you're not too busy, there's something you could do to help out. John couldn't make it to rehearsal, which means he hasn't brought the plants. Perhaps you could go get them?"

Gloria bent forward and kissed Angie on the cheek. "Happy to, darling. Back in a flash."

"Could you also remind him to be here at five? Don't let him make any excuses."

"Don't you worry, he'll be here if I have to drag him bodily."

Angie refrained from reminding her mother that John probably went one-seventy-five to her hundred pounds because if anyone could get him out of his laboratory, it was Gloria Farnsworth.

The door hadn't swooshed all the way shut when soft footsteps marched across the stage. She turned to see Colby Jarvis, a solemn grin on his almost-handsome face. He still wore the *Harry Temple* costume: blue jeans, black leather jacket and black baseball cap. A fifty-year old version of The Fonz. Three months ago, when Tyson suggested Jarvis for this role Angie fell into gales of hilarity. What a hoot, the local constabulary playing a burglar. The idea still amused her.

"I didn't know you were still here."

"Everybody stayed a few minutes to talk about tonight."

"You all right?"

"Just fine, ma'am." He leaped off the stage and swept her into his arms.

Her hormones fluttered. Angie stepped back to disburse the heat.

"Are you busy right now?" he asked. "Can I run through a

line or two with you? I don't feel comfortable with the confron-
tation scene. To tell the truth, my stomach feels like I swallowed
a handful of Mexican jumping beans."

"Just—"

"If you try telling me to imagine the audience is naked…"

She shook her head. "Imagine I'm the only one in the
room."

He made a strangled sound in his throat. Together they as-
cended the steps to the stage—now decked out as a living room—
the furniture all borrowed from the leading lady's house. A
Danish style sofa sat perpendicular to the right of the fireplace.
Two chairs faced it with a small cherry end table between them.
A Danish column lamp sat on the table. Jarvis took his place
near the fireplace. He drew a cloth bag from his left pocket and
a gun from his right. Angie stood near the bedroom door to the
far left, prepared to take the role of Roman Richards, the part
John would play later that evening.

"Okay," Angie said, "I walk into the room with my daughter and spot you putting my valuables into your bag. I ask what
the hell you're doing in my house. You take out a gun, aim it at
me, and say…"

He wiggled the barrel of the gun toward the couch. "Git over
there." His low, guttural voice made Angie shiver.

"I push my daughter behind me and walk toward the couch,
but I stop halfway and ask, 'What do you want?' Then you
say…"

"Kind of stupid question since I'm loading your stuff in this
bag, dontcha think?" Jarvis shook the sack at her.

"Take what you want and go away." Angie waved a hand to
encompass the room. "Now, my wife calls from the other room
and I take a step in that direction."

Jarvis aimed the gun at her. "That's far enough!"

"I push my daughter down behind the sofa. 'Look, my wife
is an invalid. She's fallen out of her wheelchair. She might be
hurt.'"

"If she was hurt she woulda said so."

"I'm going to her. Shoot me if you want."

"I mean it—stop where you are."

Angie kept walking. Jarvis ran up behind her and pretended to knock her above the left ear with the butt of the gun. She went to her knees then sprang back up. "Now we scuffle." They reached for each other but rather than scuffling he pulled her into a deep, impassioned kiss that sent flare-guns blasting into all corners of her being. They parted. Without skipping a beat, she said, "Then the gun goes off and I fall on the floor."

"I run for the door, leaving the sack on the chair."

"I get up and as the door slams behind you, I race in to help my wife and daughter."

Jarvis replaced the purloined crystal on the mantle, rolled up the sack and put it in his left pocket. The gun went into the right.

"So, what part of that has you nervous? You did great."

He shrugged, took hold of Angie's arm and spun her toward the stairs. She didn't ask the question again. In the past weeks she'd learned that actors' egos needed constant bolstering. Apparently Jarvis was no different.

"You look tired," he said. "I bet you've been here since day-break."

Almost. She'd left home at seven to escape her mother, whom she heard stirring in the spare bedroom. She had the books updated and the bills paid by the time Tyson zipped into the office at eight bearing croissants and coffee freshly made by his parents' housekeeper. After eating, which they did in the lighting booth, gazing down on the stage—their stage—Tyson climbed up and checked the rigging for the fly system that held the lighting. Then he went off to find a prop they needed for one of the sets. Angie put last minute touches on a costume and repaired a tear in the main drape that they'd gotten from a high school drama society who'd bought a new one. As owners of the low-budget theater, they each did some of everything.

"Come on, I'll change my clothes and take you to dinner," Jarvis said.

"Nice scuffling, by the way," she said as they headed backstage. "You don't plan on doing that with John, do you?"

Two

"I'm so freaking nervous."

Angie stifled a laugh. "Jarvis, I've seen you at gory crime scenes. You were so collected and cool I wanted to light a fire."

"This is different." He tilted his head at the curtain, the other side of which two hundred people buzzed with conversation.

John Bloom and the town clerk's six-year old daughter, wearing a pink flannel nightgown and fuzzy pink slippers passed. John raked a hand through his dark curls and flashed Angie a thumbs up. He bent and whispered in her ear. "Would you like to come to my place after the show?"

She was shocked, about to say that, no, of course she didn't want to do anything like that when John added, "I've invited Trynne and Blake, and Tyson and Jarvis too. I have an announcement—no, not an announcement, a wonderful discovery. I want you all to see it."

"In that case, I'd love to come."

Tyson's voice rang out in the theater announcing the start of Act Four. John poised his hand on the 'bedroom' doorknob and waited till the buzz of voices in the auditorium died. Angie grabbed Jarvis by the waist and pulled him close. "You'll be great." She kissed just under his left ear then nudged him forward. "Break a leg."

"By the way, you look gorgeous."

She gazed down at the satin gown Gloria insisted she buy for tonight. The long sleeved dress was a brilliant teal her mother said set off her eyes. Angie had to admit, it made her feel elegant and pretty. Jarvis planted a kiss on her temple, straightened his spine, drew the pillowcase bag from his pocket and stepped on stage. He crossed, almost on tiptoes, to the mantle and picked up the crystal figurine. As the curtain rose, he prepared to drop the statuette in the bag.

John and his little blonde 'daughter' entered the living room from the left. John said, "Okay, let's get your milk and get you back to bed." As they reached center stage, he spotted Jarvis. He thrust the girl behind him and held her there with both hands. "Who the hell are you?"

Jarvis reached into his pocket and pulled out the gun. He shook it at John, then waved it toward the sofa. "Get over there."

John, keeping the child behind him, moved in the direction of the couch but stopped half way. "What do you want?"

"Kind of stupid question since I'm loading your stuff in this sack, don't 'cha think?"

John shoved the girl. "Get behind the sofa. Lay down and stay there." To Jarvis he said, "Take what you want. Then get out."

From off stage, Brianna, played by Angie's friend Trynne Mc-Coy, called, "Roman, can you come here, I've fallen."

John, as though forgetting Jarvis pointed a gun at him, made a step toward the bedroom.

"Stop!" Jarvis shouted.

"My wife has fallen out of her wheelchair. She might be hurt."

"If she was hurt she woulda said so."

"I'm going to her. You can shoot me if you want." John took two steps.

Jarvis ran at him, tossing the bag on the chair as he passed. He came up behind John and clubbed him above the right ear with the butt of the gun. John dropped to his knees then sprang back to his feet, using the momentum to drive a fist up into Jarvis's chin. Jarvis raised the gun. John head-butted him in the chest. Jarvis lurched backward, but caught himself on the back of a chair. It looked so real Angie almost cheered.

The gun swung downward. It went off.

Something whizzed past her right shoulder. John dropped to the floor. Jarvis looked at him, at his bag, and back at John. Then he sprinted for the door.

Perfect! Angie wanted to applaud. Jarvis played the part to perfection. But why wasn't John getting up and going to Brianna? He lay on the green print area rug, feet splayed the way he'd fallen, arms clutching his chest. A circle of blood on the rug—and his tan cotton shirt—grew larger each second.

"Drop the curtain!" Angie screamed. She snatched the cell phone from a passing stagehand's belt and raced onto the stage dialing 9-1-1.

The curtain dropped. Wild applause sounded throughout the theater. Angie plugged one ear with a hand and shouted into the phone. "We've had an accident at Prince & Pauper Theater." She gave the address. "Someone's been shot."

She thrust the phone into Jarvis's hand and knelt beside John. Blood soaked the front of his shirt and the rug beneath.

"Gimme your shirt."

Jarvis threw off the leather jacket, fumbled with the top shirt button then gave up and wrenched the lapels apart. Buttons popped loose and flew everywhere. He handed the garment to her as he said into the phone, "We have a nurse on the scene."

Angie rolled John onto his back. His eyes were open, his expression puzzled. She pressed the shirt in his wound and leaned on it to staunch the tide of blood.

"She's doing that," Jarvis said then told Angie, "They said put pressure on the wound."

Even though one act of the play remained, the riotous applause in the auditorium continued.

Tyson crouched on John's other side. "What can I do?" The look on his face said he already knew what to do. Asking was a simple gesture of respect.

"Send the crowd home," she said. "Tell them there's been an accident. Then go wait for the EMTs. Bring them in the back way."

Tyson put a hand on John's arm. "Don't worry, everything will be all right." Then he stood, walked around John's slippered feet and parted the curtain.

Jarvis was dialing the phone as he turned his back to the commotion, calling authorities, the department where he worked way too many hours. After a muffled conversation, he pocketed the phone and disappeared into the wings where he gathered the cast and crew together. Ever the professional, he set right to work.

Two sounds in the auditorium, the rustling of coats being donned as folks moved out into the blustery January weather, and the hum of confused voices.

John's left hand flailed in the air. His fingers closed around her wrist. She brushed damp curls from his forehead with her free hand. "I'm sorry if it hurts, I have to keep the pressure on it until help arrives. Hang on, it won't be long."

John let go of her arm. "Doesn't hurt." She gazed into the face that a few moments ago was robust and fit. His expression went from puzzled to resigned. As an ER nurse for more than twenty-five years Angie had seen that look dozens of times.

He crooked a finger that implored her to move closer. He mustered a whisper. "Rhapsody. Take care of Rhapsody?"

Angie had no idea who Rhapsody was. A pet snake probably. "Don't talk like that. You're going to be all right. Just hang on."

"Please. She's my life. Please."

"Yes. Yes, of course I'll take care of her." What else could she say?

Groping fingers clenched the hem of her dress. "Make sure she's warm."

"Yes."

"She needs to be warm. Keys...in my bag." His eyes closed.

His jaw relaxed, his head tilted to the side, his fist released her dress and thumped on the blood-soaked carpet. Suddenly Angie's neck wouldn't support her head. She dropped her chin and released the pressure on the wadded-up shirt. Jarvis's hand touched her arm, urging her up. A pair of EMTs took her place.

Jarvis walked her several steps away and pulled her into a tight embrace. Her heavy head slumped on his shoulder. He smelled like Polo cologne and gunpowder. His palm drew comforting circles on her back. By the time she felt strong enough to stand on her own, John's body was being wheeled away. Jarvis dabbed a hanky on her eyes. He pressed it into her palm.

He led her to the front row of the auditorium, to a seat. He gestured for Tyson to come. "I've got to get to work. Stay with her." He kissed the top of her head and disappeared just as the NH State police major crimes unit swarmed in like flies to road kill.

Tyson took hold of her hand, but didn't mess up things by trying to speak. Together they watched the proceedings, which looked more like a botched dress rehearsal than a police investigation. What was there to investigate? The prop gun had misfired. She'd heard of it happening before. Wasn't a movie director killed the same way a number of years ago? A dreadful accident, but accidents happened.

She watched them dig something from the wall a foot behind where she'd been standing during the performance. A bullet. It had to be. Wait a minute. Prop guns didn't fire bullets. Her dismayed brain had trouble processing the information. A real bullet? The officer bagged whatever-it-was and moved away. The other investigators and forensics men were apparently done with their business on stage and moved to other parts of the building. She heard muffled, low-pitched discussions of people out in the lobby.

At some point, Trynne McCoy had slid into the seat on Angie's left. Trynne's arm linked through hers and she took hold of Angie's hand. The circulation had long ago been cut off by Tyson's grip, but she barely noticed the tingling. Trynne and Angie had been friends for many years, ever since that boring Alton Bay town meeting where they escaped into the hall and ended up learning they had much in common, most especially a love of the outdoors. The pair frequently hiked the mountains of the Lakes Region.

Trynne was tall and slim, a testament to her Danish heritage with pale blue eyes and platinum hair. In the late 70s her family had moved from Amsterdam to Oregon and opened an iris nursery with John Bloom's parents. Trynne and John grew up together. At one time, they were engaged to be married. Interesting, yet a total coincidence to their starring opposite each other in *Checkmate: Love*. When Tyson cast them, he had no idea they'd ever met before.

Jarvis and two policemen stepped to center stage. One wore a green and tan State Police uniform. Balding and paunchy, he looked more suited to a job as a pharmacist. He held up the baggie containing the evidence pried from the wall. The other officer whom Angie recognized as Sergeant Wilson of the Alton Bay police department took the bag from him.

Jarvis examined it, a perplexed frown wrinkling his vee-shaped eyebrows. He drew his prop gun from his right hand pocket. The baffled expression deepened.

"Oh my God, is there a bullet in that bag?" Trynne said. The men on stage turned to look at her.

"I guess so," Angie whispered so her voice wouldn't carry also. "They dug it out of the wall behind where I was standing."

"Are you shitting me? It went through John and—" This came from Tyson. "You could've been killed."

As though they were the audience attending the performance, the trio settled back in the seats and watched the exchange between Jarvis and the two cops. Jarvis turned the weapon over in his hand, tilting it one way and the other as though he'd never seen a gun before. The state cop held out his hand. Jarvis laid the gun in it. Suddenly his professional litheness wilted like a plant too long out of water as his confusion became replaced with dread realization: a pure and simple understanding that transmitted to Angie as if it were a solid object. He had killed John Bloom.

Misfiring prop gun or not, he'd killed their leading man. And had nearly shot Angie too.

She shivered. Her elbows jostled both Tyson and Trynne, who edged closer. Trynne tipped her head against Angie's. From her seat, she couldn't see the hole in the wall where the bullet struck. But the wound was as vivid in her mind as if she stood before it at that very second.

Jarvis nodded. "My keys are in my coat on the chair in the dressing room."

Sergeant Wilson bagged the gun and left the stage. The state police lieutenant and Jarvis held a whispered conversation, none of which she could hear.

As the small clock on the mantle chimed 3 a.m., four officers moved onto the stage. A bald one shouted, "You can all go home now."

Tyson and Trynne stood immediately. "You coming?" Trynne asked.

"I'll wait for Jarvis."

"Tell him good luck from me." Her tone suggested he would need it. She kissed Angie's cheek.

Just then, Jarvis appeared. He held out his hands, then hauled her to her feet and wrapped her in an embrace that confirmed the extent of his concern. "Come on, let's get out of here."

"You're leaving?"

"Since I'm involved, I can't work the case."

"They're not accusing you of anything, are they?"

Tyson stepped on the stage and handed down her purse and coat, which Jarvis helped her into.

"I'll finish locking up," Tyson said.

"Thanks."

With strong, confident hands, as though she were the one who'd suffered the grievous accusation, Jarvis guided her out through the front door. Sometime during the last few hours, snow started falling. Huge clumpy flakes blew at them from all directions on a wind that smelled like winter and stormy weather. Clods of snow punched down inside her spiked shoes. The parking lot was slippery under the five-inch cover. She and Jarvis supported each other as they descended the slight grade to his vehicle.

"You realize that if one of us loses their balance, we're both going down."

"No place I'd rather fall," he replied, pulling her closer.

Neither spoke again till he had her buckled in the passenger seat of his Jeep. "We'll get your car tomorrow." Besides her Lexus, there were two other cars still in this part of the lot: Tyson's Bronco and John's Jeep, the same year and make as Jarvis's but navy instead of red.

Jarvis started the engine and adjusted the heater knob. Cold air pushed into the cab and he twisted the fan button to lower the blast. Angie busied herself dumping snow from her shoes and wiggling her toes that had fallen asleep in the tight footwear.

"Are you all right?" she asked, leaving the shoes off.

"Why wouldn't I be? Are you?"

She didn't answer. He'd already shoved his emotions into the background and settled into protector mode. For once she'd wanted to take care of him.

"I got the idea they suspended you."

"It's standard procedure when an officer's involved in something."

"What actually happened anyway?"

"Somebody replaced the prop gun with a real gun. My service revolver."

"I don't understand."

He shifted the car in four-wheel drive and backed out of the space. The snow crunched like cellophane under the tires. He leaned forward, squinting through the curtain of white heaving itself against the windshield. The full moon that had shone with pure gold effervescence earlier seemed to have been erased from the sky. Before moving onto Route 28, he answered her question sounding tired and distracted, "I left the jacket—the one I wore in the play—on the chair in the dressing room while we were at dinner. The prop gun was in the right hand pocket. Somebody substituted my service revolver for the prop gun."

"Where was your gun?"

"At my house. In the top drawer of my dresser."

"Did the cops go to your house?"

"Yeah. They found the prop gun there, in the same spot where I'd left my gun." He slapped his palms on the steering wheel.

"How did they get in your house?"

"When I changed into the costume coat, I left my street coat on the back of the chair. My keys were in the pocket. Easy for somebody to take 'em go to my house and get my gun. After rehearsal when I changed back into street clothes, I hung the costume jacket on the chair. They probably switched the guns, then during the play, they took my keys and—"

"Put the prop gun in your drawer," she finished for him. "You don't appear on stage till the fourth act, which is well over an hour into the program."

"Plenty of time to do the deed. I only live five minutes away." The wheels spun. He let off the gas and then pushed more gently.

"But who?"

"No clue. No frigging clue."

The vehicle eased onto the road, aimed in the direction of her condo. "Why do you figure John invited us to his place? What do you think he wanted to show us?"

"No idea."

"Jarvis, I need to go there."

"It's late—"

"If you don't want to go, that's fine. Take me back to my car and I'll go on my own."

"I don't want you driving in this shit."

It took a minute to find a place to turn the car around, but soon they were plowing south toward John's *Northeast Nurseries* in Alton Village. The snow still drove with blinding force, as though a giant fan pushed it at them.

"Who is this—what's her name—that John talked about?" he asked.

"Rhapsody. I don't know what, or who, she is. With my luck she's some sort of lizard."

Jarvis laughed then. "Maybe she's a tall, sexy blonde."

"Jarvis."

"Have you considered how we'll get into his house?"

Angie drew a bundle of keys from her purse and jingled them in the air. He heaved out a long breath. "How did I know? How *did* I know?"

"I have a question: is there a difference in weight and size between a prop gun and a regular gun?"

"If you're asking whether I should have noticed the difference, the answer is no. Remember, I brought the prop gun from the office. It's exactly like our service guns but doesn't have a firing pin. I keep replaying it in my mind, and maybe in some deep recess, I did notice a slight difference in weight, but I'd walked on stage by then. And thinking only about my lines. The prop gun was in my pocket earlier, I had no reason to think it would be anything other than that when I took it out."

It made sense. He'd been dreadfully nervous. He wouldn't think about the heft and size of the gun; he'd be imagining the words he'd say as he pointed the thing at John. Angie didn't interrupt the long silence as Jarvis concentrated on maneuvering along the icy roadway. When he finally spoke, she wished he hadn't.

"So, how come you agreed to a perfect stranger's last wish? He *is* a stranger, right?"

She couldn't stop the wedge of anger that formed before her eyes. And she couldn't stop the word from squeezing between her lips. "You know what? I'm tired of your insinuating something is—was—going on between John and I."

"Shit, I'm sorry. It slipped out."

"No it didn't. You've been preparing that *speech* since we left the theater. And, your apology doesn't cut it."

As they passed the fast food joint, Jarvis swung in. The rear wheels slid sideways for several feet before getting traction in the unplowed parking lot. He growled into the speaker box at the all night drive-thru, "Two large coffees: one extra extra, the other just milk."

Angie wanted to demand he take her back to the theater to retrieve her car. Her fear of driving on treacherous roads kept her lips pressed tight together. She'd made a promise to John and would see it through in spite of Jarvis. Tomorrow she'd deal with him and his jealous streak.

Three

The six-foot rectangular sign for *Northeast Nurseries* loomed at the head of John Bloom's driveway. Snow capped the length of the top and caked in the lower corner of the frame obliterating the first and last letters of the word nurseries. The grass hadn't been mown around the posts, sad brown clumps poked through the snow like wayward corn tassels.

Jarvis swerved the vehicle to the right and they skidded to a stop. On the single garage door the headlights lit up flaked paint like tiny stars. The overgrown grass and peeling paint contrasted so radically with her impression of John that Angie had to close her eyes. When she opened them, Jarvis was already out of the vehicle and moving around the front, using the hood for support.

He pulled open her door. She didn't want him touching her right now, but if she said so it would start a row that was inappropriate to have here. Wind swooshed into the vehicle, biting her cheeks and snapping at her nose. She crammed her feet back into the unsuitable shoes and got out, only to have them re-fill with white stuff. Snowflakes tickled her eyelashes; she brushed them away with the back of a hand as they lurched and slipped to the three snow-covered steps leading up to the back door of John Bloom's house, a single-story ranch with siding of some dark color.

John had left the porch light on, but little of it trickled between the quarter-sized flakes. The scent of meat—hamburger probably—pushed out at them when the door opened. The light over the stove illuminated an immaculate stove and countertop. A dish drainer held a plate, butter knife and frying pan. Across the room, things weren't in such a tidy state. Piles of books and papers crowded the floor and every available surface, standing as tall as five feet in most places. Haphazardly atop each stack lay hand garden tools, trowels and such. The tabletop wore piles a foot high all around the edge except for an uncluttered path from where John obviously sat to eat—a drinking glass with something brown sat on a paper placemat—all the way to the window that overlooked the driveway.

Angie braced a palm on top of the closest mound and dumped snow out of her shoes. Then, stretching her thumb down, she flicked through the stack. "They're all iris related," she offered, not surprised.

"This pile has some catalogues from plant and tree companies, but you're right, it's all about irises."

"Irises are his life."

"Bo-ring."

"Rhapsody," she called softly, holding up her long skirt and bending to peer under the table and around the clean but cluttered linoleum. "I guess Rhapsody's not a dog. She would be barking by now."

Jarvis opened each kitchen cabinet in turn. "I don't see any kitty litter or pet food."

"There's no bird cage. Or water bowl. Or snake—what do they keep snakes in anyway?"

"Aquariums, I think."

The house was so silent she could hear the shush of snow against the windows. Jarvis flicked a switch, revealing a hallway with several closed doors. The first on the left entered a small dining room. The walls were nearly invisible behind stacks of cardboard boxes. It looked like he'd never finished unpacking. A long plastic picnic table sat in the middle of the room...piled with books and newsletters. Here though, interspersed with the books on irises were science fiction and fantasy novels. She lifted an eyebrow at Jarvis.

"Who'd a thunk it?"

They finished an examination of the living room, bathroom and two bedrooms, the second of which had no furniture, just floor to ceiling shelves—all bowed under the weight of books and papers.

"How long has he lived here?"

"I don't know," Angie said, then called, "Rhapsody! Chirp, meow or bark so we can find you." She squinted in corners. No tentative whisker poked out. She gazed into gaps between stacks. No wary eyes looked back. Nothing but silence greeted them in the congested living room. The far right hand corner held a floor-to-ceiling bookshelf. It had no iris magazines or brochures or newsletters—only novels. Angie slipped one from an eye-level shelf: science fiction.

There were two bedrooms; the only furniture in one was a desk dead center of the room, hidden under more brochures and magazines. The other bedroom was John's personal space. It too bore piles around its perimeter, framing the double windows like foot-thick wallpaper. The bed was made. The mirror shone with newly polished brilliance. A stack of folded laundry sat on the edge of the dresser. John wore briefs, not boxers. She didn't think it was the sort of observation she should mention to Jarvis.

"Rhapsody, are you in here?" Angie hiked up her gown, knelt and lifted the corner of the polyester—motel-type—spread. She got to her feet, shaking her head. "Where is she?"

Jarvis opened the closet. Angie stepped past him to examine John's clothes. Two dress shirts, one white one blue. Two plastic cleaners' bags, one held a velvet-collared tuxedo, the other a good quality suit coat and slacks. Side by side in the corner, a shiny pair of medium-quality dress loafers and well-used pair of Nike sneakers. Angie backed out.

Jarvis shut the door and joined in calling for the illusive pet. They were met with total silence until the furnace clicked on with a hearty thunk that shook the house.

"Furnace needs cleaning." Jarvis stepped into the hallway and pulled open the last uninspected door. The drone of the furnace increased. "Wait here." He flipped the light switch and went down, calling Rhapsody's name. In a minute he returned. "Nothing there."

"Packed with stuff, too?"

"Believe it or not, it's empty, just a furnace and water heater. Come on, Rhapsody's obviously not coming out for us."

"John said—"

"I realize that. But whoever Rhapsody is, she's obviously hiding. It's warm here. She'll be fine. We'll come back in the morning."

"It *is* morning," she said, stepping back into the kitchen. She couldn't smell hamburger any more. Now the scent was of musty paper, like a place long closed to fresh air.

Angie's eyes burned. Her back ached. She buttoned the coat she hadn't realized she'd unbuttoned. Before tugging open the door, she called Rhapsody one more time. She even pursed her lips to add a few squeaky sounds like she'd heard people use to call their cats or puppies.

"Man, this place is an arsonist's dream," Jarvis said.

"There must be stuff dating back to the beginning of the Printing Age," Angie said.

"I don't think there was a Printing Age."

No kidding. "Rhapsody. Come out come out wherever you are."

Together they stepped into the snowstorm and locked the back door. Angie bundled her collar against her nose and mouth to ward off the sting of the wind. Another inch of snow had fallen while they performed the wild Rhapsody chase. She stepped off the bottom tread. Snow poured into her shoes, wedging itself in huge clumps around her insteps and heels. A shiver, not entirely related to the weather, devoured her. Something wasn't right.

Jarvis took her elbow, sidetracking her from the worrisome thought and reminding her she was still angry. He aimed her toward the Jeep. A yellow glow to the left caught her eye. She stopped, nearly knocking Jarvis off his feet. A rectangular glow, a long narrow strip across the horizon about fifty yards away.

Jarvis took her arm again. "Let's go home. I have the feeling tomorrow—um, today—is going to be busy."

"Damn, why didn't I think of that?"

Angie plucked her sleeve from his grip and started toward the greenhouse. He cursed. Not only didn't John paint his garage, mow his lawn, or throw anything away, he apparently didn't shovel snow either. Throughout the season, the snow had been trod on, and frozen. Now and again, the moon shone through the storm clouds, casting light on ruts that showed as blue-black voids. Even with the newly fallen snow, some were more than six inches deep, regions where entire feet might be lost, and never seen again. The image almost made her giggle. For some reason, she found the thought of tottering around on leg-stubs funny.

"Angelina!" Jarvis's irritated voice broke through her thoughts. She stopped and gazed back at him, still standing in the driveway. A blast of arctic air whistled under her dress and stung her tender flesh through the skimpy panties.

"What!" she called.

He threw up his hands and started toward her. "Do you really think he'd keep a pet out there?"

She said, "She isn't in the house," but her feelings had suddenly led away from Rhapsody being a living being.

She stumbled in one of the crevasses. Thankfully, Jarvis got a grip on her arm and kept her from a plunge into foot-less-ness. She yanked her shoe from the abyss and giggled seeing the foot still attached. Surely the expensive shoes were junk by now. Ahead, the enormous glass hothouse shimmered like a beacon. Midway along its length, a tall yellow rectangle marred the sideways appearance of the structure. A tall rectangle meant a door. The color yellow meant the door was open. John's words shot into her head: "She needs to be kept warm."

Angie broke into a run, swaying and tripping on the irregular ground, a desperation to her movement that froze Jarvis in place. She covered the last fifty feet like a marathoner and launched herself through the door that flapped back and forth in the wind. Snow had blown inside and piled three feet high against the nearest obstruction, some sort of table with a row of shelves underneath.

She stood a second letting her eyes adjust to the light given off by a small watt bulb at the far end of the room. In other greenhouses she'd been in, the aromas had been pleasant, a gentle melding of warm, damp soil and sweet flowers. Here, the scent of soil stood out above the rest. As a matter of fact, she couldn't pick out the aroma of flowers at all. Neither was the air warm. It was downright freezing. The furnace blew hot air blew from a ceiling heater at the far end, not doing a bit of good against the January air driving through the doorway.

Then, her eyes allowed her to see. And Angie nearly dropped to her knees in dismay. The raging storm had destroyed everything in sight. Three rows of tables stretched the length of the building—one along each wall and one down the center. The tables were actually long boxes filled with soil that until recently held plants. Now, they lay like corpses on the snow-covered floor.

"Don't touch anything," Jarvis said, stepping up beside her.

That's when she realized—the storm hadn't caused this devastation. The plants hadn't blown over. They'd been lopped off! The place looked like an autumn cornfield after the chopper went through. Someone deliberately destroyed John's life's work. For a fleeting moment, Angie felt glad he was dead. If he were here, surely this sight would give him a coronary.

Her feet backed away, turned her around. Escape...such a cowardly thing to do, yet she couldn't stop herself from moving toward a wood door to the right. As if having minds of their own her feet stepped over downed plants. The big door was unlatched and open about an inch. Her right foot nudged it open, flinching at the high-pitched squawk of protest.

She found herself in John Bloom's office, on a cement floor

covered by a cheap throw rug in a deep green color. It didn't take Miss Marple to know whomever wreaked the havoc in the greenhouse had also been here. Except for a very new looking flat-screen computer and blotter, the desk was completely bare. All the drawers stood open and, except for jumbles of paper-clips and the like, empty. All eight drawers of the pair of metal filing cabinets along the right hand wall were open—and empty. Against the wall shared by the greenhouse stood a heavy, very old looking safe. Open, and empty.

Angie stumbled out of the room passing a pink plastic waste-basket lying on its side, also empty. The thief, or thieves, hadn't left a single thing behind. Except the computer. Strange. Computers were the first place people stored information. Why did the burglar bypass it? She backed out of the room feeling as forlorn as this place. She wished she could magically transport away to a time—before Act Four, before John's death, before Jarvis's jealous remarks.

His arm snaked around her waist and eased her from the room. He let go long enough to dial the cell phone. Angie faced the destruction and took note of details. The plants were all one type: long spear-like leaves, large-petaled flowers in many colors of the rainbow. Unless she missed her guess, they were irises. What had John mentioned about them in particular? For weeks, he'd talked endlessly about the things. Angie should recall *something* of what he said. A special discovery yes, but what about it? Try as she might, every time she tried to envision John talking about his flowers, she saw him lying on the stage, a river of blood spurting from his chest. Bloodied lips whispered, "Please take care of Rhapsody."

"Okay," Jarvis said, and put the phone in his pocket.

Angie pointed to the mess on the floor. "I think Rhapsody is a plant." She ignored his snort of disbelief. "John kept talking about a discovery. I didn't hear most of it because—"

"Because it was freaking boring."

"I think that *freaking boring* talk holds a clue to what's going on here. This wasn't a random act."

"How do you know that?"

Ignoring his cynical tone, Angie found a chair, brushed the scattered soil and leaves off the white plastic surface and sat. She took off a shoe and massaged her cold, wet, aching toes. "Because whoever did it, didn't bother going in the house."

Jarvis shook his head. "Maybe he did go in. And kidnapped Rhapsody." With a grunt, he crouched and picked up a decapitated stalk, shaking the soil from the multi-hued pink petals. He held it toward her. "Somebody must've been really angry."

He was right. Destruction like this signaled a very strong emotion. What? Revenge for something John did? He'd seemed so easygoing. Yes, but he'd also seemed tidy. What else triggered devastation like this? Jealousy maybe. The word sparked a flame of annoyance and she glanced at Jarvis, now on his feet.

"I think we should go back in the house," Angie said.

"To look for...?"

"A possible motive."

Moments later, Angie stood on tiptoe in John's kitchen looking through a stack of publications on top of the microwave. With thumb and forefinger—to keep fingerprints to a minimum—she sifted through dozens of Iris Society Bulletins. As the front covers flickered past, a familiar face caught her eye. She thumbed back through one at a time, examining each cover photo, seeking the face. One by one she discarded them. All the pictures were of men. Why then had she thought she'd seen a woman?

"You got something?"

"I thought I recognized someone on one of these covers." Angie examined the newsletter covers individually, moving each to a new pile. "I don't understand it. I thought I saw a woman but the cover pictures are all of men. Oh well. Guess I was seeing things."

Jarvis opened the refrigerator. Angie laughed. "What do you expect to find in there?"

He tossed her a scowl and bent to look inside. "Nothing

much in the way of food: a few condiments, a quart of milk and a cooked cheeseburger on a plate and covered with Saran wrap." He shut the door and turned around.

The tiny corner of something protruded from the pile about six inches from the top: a single sheet of white paper, tucked between the June 2003 and July 2003 issues. Angie plucked it out.

"Find something?"

"The header says Nielsen Nurseries, 1417 Kierkergaard, Amsterdam, Holland. It's dated the 30th of January 2003. 'Dear Mr. Bloom, This is in reference to your letter dated 14 December. I feel it would be best if we discuss this in person. A partnership of some sort may be profitable for us both. Please telephone at your earliest convenience.' It's signed, Pedar Sondergaard."

Angie laid the letter on the table, beside a glass of something that looked like flat cola. "What do you bet this guy also breeds irises?"

"Wouldn't surprise me."

"Did you know Donna Marks breeds irises? She has over three thousand."

"The florist? No, I didn't know."

"She told me John had twenty-three thousand." Jarvis's silence said his jealousy had reared up again. Angie ignored it. "She also said there's been all kinds of money spent developing a certain color, I think it's true red. Hundreds of thousands of dollars by one Oregon breeder in particular."

"Is she trying to get a red also?"

"That I don't know, but I'll find out."

He flung an arm around her shoulders and rotated her toward him. "Did I mention you look sexy in that gown?"

Angie ducked out of his embrace. "You aren't taking this seriously."

"I'm serious. It's just that the idea of spending so much money on a flower... when there's people starving all over the world."

A sound in the driveway brought both of them to the window. Two cruisers slid in beside Jarvis's car. Three officers got out. Angie and Jarvis went out to meet them. Jarvis explained the situation then took her arm as they started the long trek to the greenhouse again. She wanted to walk back out there about as much as she wanted to go home and wake up her mother.

The head officer, a short balding man with a narrow mustache, introduced himself as Sergeant Ralph Whitcomb.

Jarvis gave a quick run-down of the situation. "Apparently the thieves concentrated on the greenhouse and office. The house hasn't been touched." He told them about the letter from Amsterdam. "I don't know if it's related or not; we found it buried under a mile-high pile of Iris Society Bulletins. It's on the kitchen table."

Angie ducked into John's office amid warnings from one of the sergeants to not "touch anything." She used a fingernail tip to hit the light switch just inside the door. A single-bulb fixture in the ceiling illuminated the barrenness in frightful clarity. The computer was one of the newest models, a 17" flat screen with the works inside: no bulky boxlike thing taking all the space on the desk. Using the tip of a fingernail, she punched the ON button. Nothing happened. She hit the button again. Still nothing. She located the cord and followed it to the outlet.

"Something wrong?" Jarvis asked from the doorway.

"I think I figured out why the thief didn't take the computer. It's broken."

He strode to the desk and hit the ON button the same way Angie had. When nothing happened he said, "This machine is too new to be broken. Yeah yeah, I know they break but it's more likely they downloaded what they wanted and busted the thing so nobody else could use it."

"It doesn't look busted."

Jarvis shrugged. He drew a jackknife from his pants pocket and poked the tip in the slit where the back and front of the computer joined. He'd barely touched the knife to the opening when the back of the computer popped off and crashed to the floor. Jarvis bent to peer into the machine.

He wiggled two fingers at Angie. "I've never seen inside one of these things. Does everything look all right to you?"

She'd never examined the inner workings either. A guy from Nashua, Montez Clarke, maintained her home computer and the one in the theater office, plus he designed and maintained the Prince & Pauper web site.

Two officers raced in from the greenhouse. The officers bent beside Jarvis. With their tan uniforms framing Jarvis in his dark clothes, they looked like an inside out Oreo. God, she was getting punchy. She squinted to read the numbers on her watch dial: 5:12 in the morning.

"Well, that explains it then," Jarvis said.

"Explains what?" she asked.

"The hard drive is missing," replied the tall officer in a tone that implied he'd already said this. His nametag said Lieutenant Randolph Spicer. "That's why they didn't have to move the whole computer."

"I don't understand."

"They will install the hard drive into another computer," Spicer said as if everyone should know this.

"Why not just download it? Send it to—" Jarvis asked but Angie interrupted with, "Because it's traceable."

Jarvis took hold of her arm. "Come on, I'll take you home."

They stumbled and staggered back to his vehicle. The storm had dumped more than six inches, most of which felt like it was in Angie's shoes. Daybreak struggled to break through the dense layer of clouds still shrouding the area. The coldest temperatures of the day brought a series of bone-jarring shivers. A snowplow had cleared the roadway but left an eighteen-inch windrow of snow the Jeep pushed through as if it weren't there.

She folded her arms around herself and leaned her head back. "I guess there's no doubt John's murder is related to the mess in his place," she said, not opening her burning eyes.

Jarvis didn't answer. She raised her head to look at him, wondering if he'd fallen asleep. The dawn light showed him in profile, cheeks and jaw clenched tight, lips almost invisible.

Someone had wanted John dead. They lacked the courage to do it themselves and used Jarvis as the vehicle. How awful it must be to know you've killed someone. The urge to escape, not only the prevailing guilt, and thoughts of the victim's family, but the sleeplessness and resulting fallout had to be compelling.

Did John have family? Angie knew he'd once been engaged to Trynne, but not whether he had an ex wife or children, parents or grandparents. What must Trynne be feeling right now? A man she'd once loved had died. An event such as this would revive long-buried emotions. After some sleep, Angie would visit Trynne.

Neither she nor Jarvis spoke again till he stopped in front of her condo. The plow blade had cast a huge barrier of white stuff against the front door. The walks hadn't yet been shoveled. The porch light lit the area around the doors. No lights on inside; Gloria was probably asleep. Angie said a thank you for small favors. A slight wind whipped stray flakes off the roofs and swirled them in front of the car like albino autumn leaves.

"What do you think about all this iris breeding stuff?" Jarvis asked.

The inane question was intended to postpone something inevitable: he didn't want to go home. Probably couldn't face being alone right now. She could invite him inside. But Gloria would be up soon, and bombard them with insensitive questions. Angie loved her mother dearly, but these days she didn't seem to comprehend how her words affected people.

Angie half-turned on the seat to face him. He took her hand and absently played with her fingers, opening and shutting them like box tops, watching the action as though it were some momentous event.

Though he probably didn't expect an answer to his question, she said something part reply and part expression of her thoughts, "The topic of iris breeding is coming up too often to be coincidence." She extracted her hand from his and counted on her fingers. "First there's John, who's some kind of iris-genetic-aholic. Then there's Trynne." The mention of Trynne's name made Jarvis frown. "Remember, her parents and John's were partners in a nursery in Oregon. She and John were once engaged."

"I don't see how that's related."

"It might not be. I'm just pointing out the coincidences. Donna breeds irises too. What do you want to bet she's breeding for a red?"

"Nothing surprises me any more."

Angie would bet the substitution of his service revolver for the prop gun came as a surprise. She didn't say so.

"Everything comes down to money," Jarvis continued. "How much is spent, or how much something can make is all that matters these days."

"Not sure where you're going with this."

"That letter from Amsterdam talks about money. Well, it insinuates anyway."

"Is that how you interpreted mention of a partnership?"

"Why else would two strangers in different countries merge like that? I don't believe for a minute that it's all about the simple betterment of a flower."

"No. If someone spent hundreds of thousands on the development of the flower, then no, I don't believe it's enough. I agree with you that everything comes back to money."

Jarvis made a scoffing sound between his teeth. "Millions spent on stuff like freaking flowers. Nothing on feeding starving people or fixing global warming."

She let him ramble till he wound down looking totally deflated. "Want to come in?"

He looked about to say no, then changed his mind. "A quick coffee." They got out of the Jeep and met in front of it. Jarvis peered around. "Where's your shovel? I'll get rid of this snowbank for you."

"Don't have a shovel, the association clears it. Someone will be here soon. It's not even six yet."

He took her arm to help her over. She lifted her right foot. "By the way, your father's very handsome."

Jarvis dropped his hand and she nearly tumbled headfirst into the snow. She righted herself using the doorframe for support.

"What are you talking about?"

"I forgot to tell you, your father came to the theater yesterday looking for you. I told him where he might find you. I didn't know you were still in the building."

Usually that trio of lines over his nose gave him a thoughtful look. They'd bunched together now, wrinkling his whole face.

"How come his name is Dodge—not Jarvis?"

The wrinkles tightened. Jarvis' keys jingled as he jammed his hands in his pockets. He turned away and began marching across the parking lot. Walking like a man late for an appointment, he disappeared around the side of her building.

What did she do? Should she follow? No, probably not. He would come back when he got over whatever was wrong. She unlocked the front door and crawled over the hump of snow.

Cozy, vanilla-scented air greeted her. Home. Angie kicked off her shoes and hung her coat in the hall closet. Why would the mention of Jarvis' father upset him? Carson Dodge seemed nice enough, though she wondered about the dark circles under his eyes. At first she'd attributed them to the lighting in the theater. Now, she wondered. The circles coupled with his sallow skin color suggested something health-related.

The thought of health brought her mother to mind. Just what prompted Gloria's arrival in town? She hated New Hampshire. A metallic thunk in the kitchen said Mom was up. The absence of a coffee aroma said she hadn't been up long.

As Angie passed the hall clock, it began chiming. Six times. She'd now been up two straight nights. She should be exhausted. But only felt restless. What the hell was wrong with Jarvis?

Four

His fingers were stiff and stubborn, but one by one Colby Jarvis punched the six oblong wooden knobs through the loops down the front of his coat. Then he wrenched up the collar and thrust his hands in his pockets, the satin lining as cold and unyielding as his fingers. He strode out the end of the Alton Bay Condominiums complex and onto Route 28. He headed downhill—south—for no reason other than it was easier than walking uphill on the slick roadway.

Snowplows had passed; still an inch of snow clung to the pavement, hard as cement in some places, coarse as oatmeal in others. With each step he dug in his heels to keep from falling on his nose. The way things were going today the blade of the next plow that rumbled by would scoop him up and heave him into the woods. His body wouldn't be found till spring thaw.

A few cars had slogged by since the plow; their tracks were etched parallel to each other like lines of cocaine. Why think about coke at a time like this? Oh yes, yesterday's training film. Yesterday. A lifetime ago. He jammed his hands deeper and ducked his head against the breeze off the bay. What the hell was he doing still in New Hampshire? Hadn't he vowed at Liz's funeral that he'd ditch it all and head south?

Jarvis climbed over the mountain of snow along the shoulder of the road. He forged a trail, estimating the location of the narrow walkway that meandered here for the tourists. He passed the pavilion and cleared one of the benches positioned to afford the best view up the bay. How often he and Liz had huddled here, on this very bench, holding hands, reveling in each other's company. Liz. The single constant in his life.

He reached out his right hand, imagined her warm one gripping his fingers. "Damn it, Liz, I killed a man."

Okay, he'd said the words that had been circling in his brain since it all happened. Killed somebody. Another human being. All his years behind a badge and this had never happened. How did a person go on after such a thing? Every time he picked up his gun, he'd see John's surprised expression as he realized what happened. Jarvis wondered if placed in a situation where he had to draw his gun, would he hesitate to fire?

"I killed a man."

What would Liz say? That it's a terrible thing. Nobody deserves to die that way. So young. But she would also say, "It's not your fault.

Why hadn't he noticed the substituted gun? Because they were exactly the same, except one lacked a firing pin. Damn. He should've noticed anyway! Jarvis dropped forward cupping his frigid face in his hands. And for the first time since Liz's funeral ten years ago, he cried.

Then he felt like an idiot. Jarvis jumped up and kicked at the pile of snow he created when he brushed off the bench. He kicked and kicked until the entire area lay bare to the grass.

What about his good-for-nothing father? What the hell was he doing in town? Looking for a handout probably. Jarvis kicked at another snowbank and flopped on the bench. What kind of man discards his wife and three young sons like week-old fish? Worse than that, why come back? What the hell did the fucking deserter want?

Did the army still shoot deserters?

Across the bay, daylight urged pale shades of gray between the spires of dark emerald pines, their spiny branches bent under the weight of the new-fallen snow. Great wads of the stuff tumbled loose, bounced off lower branches and ruptured back into its original form. Gusting flake-clouds decorated the landscape like fog. Out on the road, the swoosh of cars slogging through the road crud brought a reminder that another day had arrived. He forced himself off the bench. Rear end wet and numb, he retraced his steps. Right then Jarvis realized why he hadn't escaped this place. Simple. Liz would've called him a quitter.

He never quit at anything.

He scaled the bank and trod up the road, feeling the splash of shit on his backside each time a car passed. Every barb of ice striking him was penance; he'd cheated on Angelina in his mind. Liz was dead. He had to accept it.

The lights were on in her condo. But he couldn't face her right now.

Four minutes later, he eased the Jeep down his unplowed street. His ranch house, the second place on the left, looked forlorn and violated. The driveway was a mishmash of tire and footprints. Out front, one of the major crimes vehicles swathed in an inch of snow had parked half on a snowbank.

They'd entered through the back porch, an inch of snow covered it too. That meant the investigators were done in the house and had set to work rousting his neighbors from their nice warm beds. Lights were on up and down the short street. "See anything out of the ordinary in the neighborhood yesterday afternoon?" "Anyone at Jarvis' house?" "Does he get along with everybody?" Yada, yada.

Jarvis stood in the kitchen doorway, leaning on the raised panel, waiting for the usual hominess to set in; the sense of well-being at returning after a long day. When Liz was alive, the place always smelled like cooking and furniture polish. That scent had been replaced by his own smells—aftershave and gun oil. But they were his smells, things he'd become comfortable with. Till today.

A stranger had violated his space, framed him for murder. Why? Sure, cops ruffled feathers, made enemies. The past couple years, things around town had been fairly quiet. The most recent thing, nine months ago, netted a gunrunning operation. The ringleader escaped capture. Had he come back for revenge?

Jarvis didn't bother removing his boots. The floor was already a mess. He hung his coat in the closet then trudged toward the bedroom. He stopped halfway down the hallway. Maybe the *why* of it had little to do with him. Maybe this someone simply wanted John dead and he was the vehicle by which the deed was accomplished. But why choose Angelina's theater? Between renovating contractors, hiring production and theater staff, interviewing potential actors, perhaps hundreds of people had been through the building. Possible for any crackpot to devise and set up something like this. Most likely, though, it was someone closely related to the place. Someone who walked the cavernous building at will.

Jarvis thumped along the bare wood floor to the bedroom. Black fingerprint dust dotted most of the flat surfaces. The dresser top was strewn with his underwear, t-shirts and socks, all the stuff from the top left drawer where he kept his service revolver. He slid it open envisioning the drawer as it had been earlier in the day: balled pairs of socks lined up across the back, briefs in two piles on the right side, t-shirts taking up the rest of the space, the gun nestled between.

With the back of his hand he slammed the thing shut, then marched down the hallway, shrugged into his coat and stormed out the back door. The clock neared seven-thirty when he let himself into Angelina's condo. Vanilla and coffee scents swirled in the air. He tried to take off the coat but his stiff fingers wouldn't work the awkward buttons. He crouched to remove his boots.

Angelina stood in the kitchen. Her bare toes poked from under the long robe as she glided toward him. He folded his arms around her, burying his fingers in the fleece folds, so soft and warm…and unyielding. She was still angry. He didn't blame her. The jealousy monster wouldn't stay hidden. That single entity that stood between he and Liz had now erected a wall between he and Angelina. He hadn't told her about the group counseling, even though they encouraged openness. He wanted her to think he was ousting the demons on his own. He sighed. Time to tell her, to let her know he was at least trying.

"I'm sorry. Very sorry," he whispered and felt her spine thaw a little.

They might've held each other like that all day if Gloria's voice hadn't burst them apart. "What time did you lovebirds finally roll in?"

Jarvis laughed, seeing a blush burst up the back of Angelina's neck. He slid onto the stool Angelina had vacated. She moved to pour two more cups of coffee and brought the cups to the center island counter. Jarvis took one with a nod of thanks. He closed his fingers around his cup, feeling the welcome warmth ease away the tingling sensations. He winked at Angelina. As she pushed the third cup across to her mother some of the hot liquid sloshed on the back of her hand. Jarvis plucked a napkin from the holder and dabbed it on her.

"Mom, what's going on?" Angelina asked.

"I don't know what you mean, dear."

"You're grinning like the Cheshire Cat," Jarvis said.

"Well…" she drew out the word. "I met a man last night." She plunged the spoon in the sugar bowl. "Jarvis, aren't you going to take off your coat?" Then she frowned. "Why is Angie wearing a robe and you're in a coat?"

He said, "I just got here" the same time Angelina accused, "You didn't see the show last night."

"I told you I'd be there, dear."

Angelina flew up and faced her mother. "I can't believe you could lie to me like that. You know how hard I've worked for this and you couldn't even bother coming to the performance."

Jarvis hopped up and took her arm. "Relax," he whispered. "You're overreacting."

"I am not overreacting. My entire life everything I did took second to my brother. She went to Robin's ball games, drove Robin to and from his friend's houses, was even a den mother for his scout group. Did she ever do any of that for me? Well, did you?" She flung off Jarvis' hands and whirled on Gloria. "And now you've ditched me for a perfect stranger."

Gloria's mouth literally hung open. She dropped back onto a stool as if she'd been pushed. Angelina threw him a *see, I was right* look. He wanted to kiss her pain away. He knew what *unwanted* felt like. Why else would a father take off the way his had? Jarvis urged her to sit, placed a mug in her hands, which he instantly thought might be a mistake. Was she the type to throw things?

He tried again to unbutton his coat, but still his damned fingers wouldn't work. Angelina stood again and helped. Her manner had thawed a bit. He liked that in her—she didn't stay angry for long. Right now, she had every right to be mad. How inconsiderate of her mother not to acknowledge all the hard work. The coat came off. Angelina disappeared to the living room with it. He took the opportunity to scowl at Gloria in hopes she'd mend the situation before it grew into a rift too big to heal.

But she didn't.

"We had some trouble at the theater last night," Jarvis said. "John Bloom…he died."

"How terrible! Now I see why you're so upset," she said when Angelina returned.

"Yes, and I'm doubly upset that you think so little of me."

Though he had no desire to expand on it, to diffuse a potentially dangerous situation he related the events of last night. He didn't mention being removed from the case, couldn't make the words come out of his mouth.

Gloria voiced the appropriate words about John's death, but ignored all her daughter's accusations, and left to shower and dress. She had a date for breakfast with her newfound friend whom she described as gallant and distinguished, and well off. Jarvis raised his eyebrows as Gloria kissed his cheek. "Take care," she said and left the room.

"So…" Angelina said, bending toward him. "Can we continue the talk about your father?" Then she leaned back and waited for him to fill in the blanks.

The image brought a smile. Liz was always the opposite. If she knew something bothered him, she pestered and nagged till he let it out. He took a breath. "Is there any more coffee?"

Angelina slanted her mouth at him, but got up and poured the last of the pot into his mug. She sat and busied herself pouring milk in her cup. He listened for the sound of the upstairs shower before speaking again. "I told you a lot about my childhood."

"You told me you and your brother grew up in a logging camp in Canada someplace north of Minnesota. You said your mother cooked for a hundred men in the camp. You said she was your teacher and mentor and she died ten years ago. I thought you said your father died when you were three."

He suddenly couldn't meet her eyes. "I got in the habit of saying that because the truth was too embarrassing. He ran off. Just up and left us one night when I was almost four."

"Why is that embarrassing?"

"I guess in the eyes of a kid, dying is better than being deserted. For a long time I believed he left because of me. That day I broke a window in the store. Which, to most people is no big deal. But glass was hard to come by at the camp."

"So now he's back."

Jarvis peered into the depths of the cup rather than at her. Not that she was passing judgment. She wasn't like that. "Yes, he's back." She waited, but he knew the question on her lips was *what are you going to do?* "I guess I'll meet with him; find out why he's chosen this time to come back." He drained the rest of the coffee and got up to put the cup in the dishwasher. Then he sat back down. "What's he like?"

"Good looking, polite. Canadian accent. Carries himself well—like an actor. I thought he'd come to try out for a part."

"Figures you'd be thinking of that."

"What can I say? Otherwise, he seemed nice. What about his name? Dodge."

He shrugged. "Not sure."

"Maybe Jarvis was your mothers' maiden name."

"It's possible." He stood up. "Guess he'll know more about that."

"Any idea where he's staying?"

"No, but I can find him." Jarvis strode to the hallway, picked his coat from the arm of the sofa and slipped into it.

Angelina moved close and began buttoning his coat for him. Her sleep smells melded with the slight aromas of fabric softener and coffee. Very erotic.

"Where are you going now?"

He backed a step away. "To the office. I want to see what they've turned up."

"I thought you'd been, um…"

"Relieved of duties," he finished, though the words literally hurt moving up his throat.

"Will they tell you anything about the case?"

"Don't know why they shouldn't," he said with more conviction than he felt. He pulled her into a hug, kissed the top of her head and then moved out into the chilly morning air.

8:04 am. Outside, a blue-serge gray sky doused rain relentlessly off car roofs. Water ran underneath snowbanks, thawing them from the inside out. Jarvis rubbed his eyes with his knuckles and waited for the printer to spit out the information on John Bloom and Pedar Sondergaard. He turned from the window, grabbed the pages and dropped in his chair to read. Bloom's info began with the most recent and worked backwards:

January '03—granted the right to erect a 100' X 30' greenhouse.

February of '02—granted permit to erect a 75' x 20' greenhouse.

March '01—granted permit to operate Northeast Nurseries selling trees, perennials, vegetable and flowering plants at the Alton Village location.

November 2000—purchased 34 acres, ranch house and

one-car garage in Alton Village with cash in the amount of $122,000.

No certificate of marriage ever issued.

NCIC—the National Crime Information Center—had no listing for John Bloom. That meant he had no arrest record, had never been fingerprinted, never been declared missing.

Income tax records wouldn't arrive till Monday.

Bloom's packrat habits had Sergeant Wilson all bleary-eyed, but turned up one lead—phone statements that went back practically to the day he'd moved in. All that interested Jarvis were the past three, three and a half, years; calls out of state or out of the country.

There they were, four international calls, all to the same number. He dialed information and could barely hear the operator's words over his pounding heart. "The number, sir, belongs to a Pedar Niels Sondergaard of…" He didn't hear the rest.

Jarvis set the Bloom folder aside and picked up Sondergaard's page of information. Pedar Niels Sondergaard, born in Arhus, Denmark in 1954. Parents Enok and Lisbet Sondergaard. Graduated University of Nottingham, England, '76, certificate in European Studies (Biosciences). In 1979, granted membership in EMBO (European Molecular Biology Organization). In 1982, opened Nielsen Nurseries, 1417 Kierkergaard, Amsterdam, Holland.

Jarvis pushed away from his desk, made a quarter turn to the left and tapped Nielsen Nursery Amsterdam Holland in the Google search square. The first hit: Nielsen Nurseries, owned by Pedar Niels Sondergaard. Page after page looked legitimate, a nursery specializing in irises. No mention of reds or research or anything like that, just irises available anywhere in the world. Six more pages of hits ultimately came back to the nursery or articles Sondergaard had written on iris genetics. Jarvis printed the Nielsen Nursery information then swung back to his desk.

Sondergaard had no arrest record. One marriage to a Clady Laila Madsen in 1985. No record of divorce.

Jarvis stood up and stretched out the kinks. He put on his

jacket and left the office, stopping at the dispatcher's station on the way out of the building. "Can you get me a phone number for the Danish police? I'll be at Bloom's. You can reach me on my cell." The dispatcher shot him a dubious look.

Well, until someone picked him up and bodily heaved him off the case, he would forge ahead. Jarvis looked at his watch but the time didn't register in his brain. "Wilson should be about finished by now." Jarvis pulled open the glass door and was assaulted immediately by driving rain.

He stopped at McDonalds for two large coffees, had the lid off one and half the contents drunk before getting out of the parking lot.

Wilson should be ready to wrap up the evidence gathering. As far as Jarvis had seen, the crook, or crooks, hadn't left much to examine but seventy-five feet of dirt and chopped up plants.

Three minutes later, wipers at full throttle, he slid into Bloom's driveway behind the sergeant's police car. He jammed the deerstalker on his head, grabbed the coffees, and trekked to the greenhouse.

He thought about Angelina warm and cozy in her bed. Sleep would be an illusive entity for a few days at least. Still he imagined himself curled up beside her. It would be hard keeping her out of this case. The guy, after all, died in her theater. Angelina would take this personally.

Jarvis stumbled in a snow-pit, said a thank-you for not dropping the coffees and kept walking. He had to admit it. Angelina Deacon was good…in more ways than one…not only beautiful and sexy, she had a logical mind that could sift through information in an unemotional manner.

He burst into the greenhouse, startling Sergeant Wilson to his feet. Ambrose Wilson was tall and thin with gaunt cheeks and bony knuckles. His longish hair the captain constantly nagged him to cut, hung down his forehead. The usual ramrod straight back was somewhat bent, the shoulders stooped. Wilson's requisite rubber gloves were coated in black potting soil.

He spotted the coffee in Jarvis's hands. He grinned, peeled off the gloves and heaved them atop the mound. "Didn't think you could stay away."

"How's Bennie?"

He grinned. "She had a long labor. Handled it like a trooper." Wilson laughed. "She's already talking about having another. Wants to keep going till she gets a daughter."

"What did you name the baby?"

"Richard Evan."

"Nice." Jarvis gestured toward the mess with the hand holding the nearly empty cup. "Find anything?"

"Not a thing. No stray fingerprint. No unrelated footprint."

"No red flower?"

"Got white and yellow. Got orange and pink. Got plain brown. Got about a dozen shades of red. But no red red." Wilson plucked off the lid and took a long drag. "I've sifted through a ton of this shit."

"Where did the perps park?"

"We found a set of tracks and a million footprints behind the building. Looks like they came up a log road, cut themselves a back door in that thick greenhouse plastic and took the stuff out that way."

"What's the road like?"

"Narrow, bumpy." Wilson drank again.

"Could a car drive on it without headlights?"

"Possible, but difficult. It leads to the paved road after a hundred feet."

"Tire tracks?"

"SUV. A big one. Footprints indicate at least three people. They all wore sneakers."

"You been in the house yet?"

"Not yet. Got a few minutes left here."

"Gimme the key."

Without hesitation Wilson handed the key across to him. "Sorry about the suspension. Damned low thing to do."

Jarvis shrugged. "Procedure." He launched himself out into the rain. Half way to the house, he stopped in his tracks. Water ran off the brim of his hat so hard he couldn't see. He started moving again, the key ridges digging into his palm.

Inside, the smell hit him almost immediately. The coppery aroma of fresh blood. The sick-sweet smell of death. His mouth went dry. His cheeks burned. Jarvis considered returning to the Jeep for his gun. To the greenhouse to get Wilson. To the phone—good idea. He used his cell to tell dispatch to send Wilson and backup to the house. He peered out the window in the door—to be sure his brain hadn't played tricks on him. No, just his footprints in the snow. And some full of fresh snow—had to be what he and Angelina made earlier. That meant whoever was in the house came in a different way. Damn, he'd only been here a couple of hours ago.

The place was dark. The morning light seemed absorbed by all the cartons. Jarvis stole a knife from the dish drainer. Senses alert, hands ready to use as weapons, he sneaked through the kitchen. Jarvis squinted into the shadows behind and between piles of boxes and books in the dining room. He did likewise in the living room, adrenaline shooting through his veins like lava.

In the hallway four closed doors. The two on the left, cellar and bedroom/storeroom. The two on the right were the bathroom and master bedroom. He pushed open and checked each room in turn, knowing the futility of it because every cop's instinct said the odor came from the master bedroom.

The door stood open about a foot. He could see the back half of the bed against the wall. Dark headboard. Bed neatly made. Bedside table with a lamp and miscellaneous stuff.

The whispered words, "What's wrong?" in his ear nearly gave Jarvis a coronary. Wilson shoved his gun in his hand. He used the barrel to edge the door open, keeping the knife in his left hand, ready too.

Then he saw the feet. White socks. Legs clad in dark denim. A male.

Gripping the gun in both hands, arms rigid and straight, Jarvis inched into the room. In one flash of thought, he thought of John and felt no hesitation in holding this gun.

The body lay on its side. Black leather jacket, much like the one Jarvis had worn in the play. The dead man's left arm lay wedged between two piles of books, right arm bent and partially under the bed. Caucasian, cocoa brown hair, wispy mustache. Brown eyes gaping wide. Whoever shot him had surprised the shit out of him.

"Who is it?" asked Wilson.

"Damned if I know."

Five

After a shower Angie stopped at the diner where Judy popped lids on two coffees. "You look tired."

"Late night."

"Awful about that guy who died." Judy slid onto a stool, rubbing the back of one calf. "It was a great performance till then."

"Thanks. Did you know him?"

"Not sure." Judy grinned. "Forgot my glasses last night. Couldn't see details. What's he look like?"

Angie untied the pile of early edition papers near the front door and handed one to her. Centered on the front page, John's photo, taken from an ad he'd placed when his Northeast Nursery opened in 1991. Judy pushed a hand through her hair as she gazed first at the picture, then swiveled on the chair to peer toward the back of the long, narrow diner.

"He came here, maybe a week ago. Sat down back," she gestured to the last table, "with a hunky looking guy."

"Hunkier than John?"

"Hunky, but opposite from John with reddish blond hair and a beard. And, pale pink skin."

"Pink?"

Judy laughed. "Pink like he hardly ever went outdoors. The best part was his accent."

"Accent?" Angie asked, drawing money from her handbag. Her excitement grew like Jack's Beanstalk.

"It didn't have the twangy syllables like Australians." Judy flung both hands to her chest and exaggerated a moony expression. "Ooh, Mel Gibson! I love Australian accents. I even like that Geiko gecko." They both laughed. "This guy's accent was smoother, kind of romantic."

"Danish maybe?" Angie ventured, dropping the bills on the counter.

"You know, that might've been it. Danish isn't one you hear all the time."

"How were he and John acting?"

Judy shrugged. "At first they were okay, talking kinda low, bending their heads together like some big-time secret. But as the conversation went on, this guy…" She tapped the newspaper. "He got upset, kind of like he wanted something the other guy wasn't willing to give, you know what I mean? John Bloom acted apologetic. You know what? I've seen him before."

"Which one?"

"This Bloom fellow. He's been in here." She rubbed a palm over her face. "With somebody." She shook her head. "Sorry, I can't place him."

The guy with the accent had to be Pedar Sondergaard. What could they have been talking about? Money? Information? A partnership had been mentioned in the letter. But that was three years ago. Maybe they already had a partnership. Maybe Sondergaard disagreed with the terms, maybe he wanted it all. Maybe he wanted the red iris.

"Earth to Angie!" Judy called. Angie snapped her handbag shut. "You're acting like this pink-skinned guy is important."

"He might be. Did you happen to see his car?"

The corners of Judy's lips twitched just before she shook her head. Angie slung the purse strap on her shoulder, picked up the cups and started for the door.

"Hello?"

She turned toward the voice. Carson Dodge sat alone in the first booth. She stepped close. His cheeks were reddened, as though he'd walked a distance in the cold. "Good morning. How are you?"

"I'm wonderful. Do you have time to sit a moment?" He tweaked his narrow mustache with the thumb and index finger of his left hand.

She didn't really have time, but couldn't pass up the opportunity to get to know Jarvis's father. She slipped into the booth and unbuttoned her coat. "You're up early."

"I could say the same about you. How goes the murder investigation?"

"I'm not inv—" Angie stopped herself as she realized he'd overheard her talking to Judy. "Going all right, I guess. Have you and Jarvis gotten to spend some time together yet?"

His blue eyes clouded over. "Not yet. I've phoned his house several times. He hasn't returned the messages."

"I wouldn't be surprised if he hasn't picked them up yet. He's very involved in the case."

Mr. Dodge frowned. "I heard he'd been suspended."

"When you get to know him, you'll realize that's not going to stop him. Besides, he's sort of personally related to this one."

"Do you think he'll be able to clear himself?"

"I believe so. He had no motive to want John dead." But as Angie said this, she realized that wasn't true. John's flirting had caused the ugly head of jealousy to rear up.

"Are you sure about that?"

Angie laughed. "Jarvis always tells me my thoughts are written all over my face. He doesn't have a motive, really. It's just that John's a flirter and Jarvis gets jealous. As far as I'm concerned, it's not a motive."

"The police might have other thoughts though, right?"

"You know how they are."

"Do you think he's avoiding me?"

"I couldn't say."

"Even if you knew, you wouldn't tell me."

She smiled and popped the lid from her cup. "I might. But I

honestly don't know. With all the stuff going on at the theater—Jarvis is a really open minded guy though. I believe he'll come around. I personally think he'll be anxious to talk to you."

"I have so much to make up for."

"So, tell me what you've been doing."

"Since I deserted my family?"

"I didn't mean to imply that."

"I know. Sorry. I am—was—a salesman. I retired eighteen months ago."

"Excuse me for saying so," she looked pointedly at his cashmere coat, "but it must've been quite lucrative."

He laughed, a delightful sound, deep and resonant. Judy stopped to smile at them. "I admit, I've done well for myself. I—" He looked away. His eyes glazed over a bit and Angie knew he couldn't help thinking about his demise—someone with sallow skin such as his, had to be in late stages. After a minute, he shook off the emotion and faced her. "I wanted to repair all my bridges. I amended my will and…well, I wanted Colby and his brother to know…"

Angie put her hand on his. The veins stood out so much she could feel them as taut ropes beneath her palm. He picked up his cup and downed the rest, then stood to leave. Angie waited, in case he needed help, but he maneuvered out of the building with her only holding the door for him. They stopped beside a black Cadillac Escalade. She watched till he pulled out and drove the big vehicle away.

In her car, Angie set the cups in the holder and navigated the slick road toward the theater. If Sondergaard visited Alton Bay as recently as a week ago, maybe he came here two days ago. Maybe he was still here. Sondergaard had to be the key to this case. Little hairs on the back of her neck stood on end. She rubbed them down and parked beside Tyson's car at the back of the freshly plowed lot. Condensation on the windows said he'd been here a while.

What would happen to the show? She and Tyson spent months

writing the play, slaving over every word. She'd spent every last dime of her money on the building, props, costumes and advertising—well…she'd paid for half of everything. Though cash wasn't an issue for Tyson, he'd placed every ounce of energy into this production. His every dream centered on the success of this business. He stood to lose more than Angie.

Just exactly what did protocol say in cases like this? It's said the show must go on but Alton, New Hampshire wasn't Broadway; the actors weren't professional performers. They were neighbors; they knew and cared for each other. After the death of a friend, there had to be a period of recovery. On the other hand, the patrons had purchased tickets. Schedules set, ads placed.

Early this morning Tyson had phoned with the same concerns: "Not to be disrespectful to John's memory, but how do we handle this?" They'd decided to broach the idea to the entire cast at rehearsal.

The lobby, done in deep, rich maroon, stretched two-thirds the width of the building. To the far right, rest rooms. Far left housed a space that would someday be a restaurant. Straight ahead, the ticket booth—with its requisite bulletproof glass—had the shade pulled down tight. Book-ending the ticket booth were swinging doors leading into the auditorium. Muffled voices filtered through. Angie crossed the low-pile carpet and pulled open the left hand door. Tyson, Trynne, and her husband Blake were seated on the edge of the stage, sneakered feet dangling. Only the ghost lights were on, casting them in silhouette.

Trynne and Blake slid off the stage and strode toward her. Six feet tall and rail thin, Trynne wore a green silk jumpsuit and a flowered kerchief headband around white-blonde hair that cascaded down her shoulders. Her light skin, high cheekbones and angular features spoke of a Slavic background. Her cheeks were flushed and though she wore makeup, it did nothing to disguise her red, puffy eyes.

The years hadn't been as kind to Blake. He'd gone totally gray; wrinkles decorated his face. Trynne pulled Angie into an embrace that felt awkward because of the difference in their height. At five-seven, Angie only came up to her shoulder. They stood back to look at each other. "You look like shit," they said at the same time.

"You okay?" Angie asked.

Trynne shrugged. "A little tired."

Blake wrapped one arm around Trynne and one around Angie. "I'm worried about you both."

Trynne unwound herself and went back to sit on the stage. "I just want to know who did this awful thing."

Tyson made a sound as though he tried to clear his throat and failed. "What if…did anybody consider that it wasn't an, er, accident?"

"What?" Angie asked. "You think Jarvis switched guns on purpose?"

"Why would he do that?" Trynne asked.

Tyson thumped his heels against the stage. "His jealousy of you and John." He turned palms up. "No secret."

"How can you even think that way?" Angie said the words but they echoed a thought she'd had after climbing into bed for an hour this morning—after Jarvis's mysterious disappearance. Though most of the time Colby Jarvis was as even-tempered and in control as a statue, he once showed that awful jealousy in front of the troupe. But he wouldn't kill. Never.

No. Someone trying to make a point perpetrated this murder. Someone angry with John for more than a little harmless flirting.

Tyson poured steaming cups of coffee from a Thermos on the stage. He pushed a cup into her hand. "It'll be all right."

The thud of many footsteps from out back signaled the arrival of the rest of the cast. Soon almost everyone stood around the front of the auditorium.

"Where's Jarvis?" Tyson asked.

"He's sort of working," Angie said.

"Sort of? I thought he'd been relieved of his duties—"

"Did they arrest him?" somebody asked.

"No," Angie replied, "it's standard procedure whenever an officer is involved in a shooting."

"We won't wait for him then," Tyson said. "Angie and I wanted your opinions about whether we should postpone the show."

"Frankly, Tyson and I don't know the proper protocol. If we do the show, will the crowd think we're callous and insensitive? Will nobody come?"

Someone laughed. "People will come—just to see if somebody else gets whacked."

A terrible thought, but he was probably right. After a lengthy discussion, everyone decided to continue with the scheduled performance, with Blake, John's understudy, in his place.

"For Blake's benefit, we'll do a walk-through," Tyson said.

Between scenes, Trynne and Angie sat in the front row. "You never told me why you broke your engagement to John," Angie said.

"Because of Blake." Trynne smiled. "John and I were taking preparatory classes at the Vo-tech. I met Blake in a horticultural class. I was sixteen. He was twenty-eight, and so handsome. I fell head over heels for him. When I broke my engagement to John—"

"You were engaged so young?"

"Not officially. You have to understand, my parents were from Amsterdam. They lived under traditional Danish ethics. They expected I would marry John to merge the family businesses. When I broke off with him, I practically slapped my parents in the face." She stopped talking to gaze at the events in the stage living room. "So, Blake and I decided to go to California. We enrolled in technical courses. I majored in genetics, Blake in landscape design and business management."

"You moved to New Hampshire in '01. I remember because that's when we met."

"At that bo-oring town meeting."

"Not boring for Blake," Angie said.

"No. That night they gave him the permit to open Lakes Region Yard Design. All those questions were like an interrogation. I sneaked out for a cigarette. You and Will just sneaked out. I saw the look in your eyes. Naughty naughty."

Angie didn't want to talk, or think, about Will. The wound from their breakup still ached. "Does John have any relatives in the area?"

"No. His parents were killed in a head-on crash in Oregon about ten years ago. He had no siblings. I guess Blake and I were all he had."

"What was he working on?"

"The same as when we were teens. He's trying to achieve a perfect red iris."

"What are you doing after rehearsal?"

"Nothing in particular, why?"

"There's something I want to check out at John's house."

When Angie didn't elaborate, Trynne asked, "Are you going to tell me what it is?"

"I don't know how to say it. See, as he…when I…oh damn." She took a breath. "John asked me to take care of Rhapsody. Jarvis and I went there, but couldn't find her. I want to go back and look again. She must be hungry by now."

Trynne laughed. "I doubt it. I suspect Rhapsody is an iris. Each iris, when registered with the Iris Society, is given a name."

"That explains why he asked me to keep her warm."

"I've never heard of—wait just one second!" Trynne must've spoken too loud because everyone on stage turned to look.

"Trynne, you're on," Tyson called to her.

"Tell you later." Trynne scurried to her feet and onto the stage.

Three hours later, Trynne and Angie were walking the newly shoveled path to John's greenhouse. The police and forensics teams were long gone. Angie stepped under the yellow crime scene tape and held it for Trynne to duck under. Angie watched her blink away some emotion seeing the devastation.

"Last night," Trynne said, "John invited Blake and me to come here after the performance. He said he had something to show us. Guaranteed it was a flower, probably Rhapsody. It's the only thing that would have him that excited. He never invites anyone here. We always got together at our place, or a restaurant. If John saw this, it would kill him."

"That's what I said to Jarvis last night. All those years of work gone."

Trynne knelt and picked up a handful of stalks and let them drop. "It would just kill him."

"Do you know where his lab is?"

"No, but we can probably find it." Trynne stood, brushed off her hands, gave a heartbroken glance at the mess, then walked to a wood door at the far end of the greenhouse.

Angie stepped into a room done in stainless steel motif. It looked like a lab belonging to any scientist. Well, it would have except that everything was tipped over, broken or otherwise ruined. "Any idea what might be missing?"

Trynne walked carefully amongst the broken test tubes and beakers. She opened a drawer and then another. "His journal."

"Journal?"

"He kept records of what he did every day. All scientists do."

"Would they be in his computer?" Angie asked.

"No, they would've been handwritten, notes he scribbled while he worked. I don't see anything."

"The thief probably got it. Which means we still have no idea who Rhapsody is."

"He must've registered her with the Iris Society. One of the things our families impressed on us—register every single new production, the cost of registration far outweighs the potential loss."

"So, if someone else tries to register a red, flags will go up all over the place."

"Not necessarily. There's nothing to stop the thief from registering her as a pink, or copper."

Angie's cell phone rang. She checked the caller ID and said, "Hey, Tyson."

"Are you close by?"

"Yes, what's up?"

"We can't find the box of costume jewelry."

"It's in the cabinet on—"

"No, it's not. I've torn the place apart."

"I'll be right there." She closed the phone. "I have to go back to the theater. He can't find the box of jewelry."

"Can't find?"

They left through a side door. Neither woman spoke until seated in Angie's Lexus. She rubbed cold hands together while the heater pumped out tepid air.

"Does Tyson think somebody stole the jewelry?"

"It's just costume stuff. Nothing of any value, we bought it all at a junk store. Somebody had to have misplaced it." She backed out of the yard and changed to the original topic. "All I can figure as a motive for the break-in…somebody wanted to steal the red flower—Rhapsody."

"We have no proof there *is* a red. But, knowing John as I do, I think it's safe to assume there was. What I don't understand is, why kill him too?"

"To keep him from talking?"

"What if he talked? Without a single shred of proof of its existence, he'd be just blowing smoke."

Across the street, in a farmhouse that had seen better days, a curtain moved. Surely the police already spoke to the residents. She'd ask Jarvis later. "I don't understand…" Angie maneuvered off John's small side road and onto Route 28, heading north. "All this commotion over a stupid flower."

"A *stupid* flower? Hundreds of thousands of dollars have been spent so far just *trying* to produce a red."

"Hundreds of thousands?"

"Here's how it works," Trynne continued. "You breed the flowers."

"Breed?"

"Yes, but not with penises—oh, never mind. You breed the flower, crossing selected plants together. Eventually you get what you want, longer blooming time, stronger scent, taller stems—whatever. But after that, it might take years to get that particular feature to reproduce successfully."

"Years?"

"I'm thinking John invited us tonight because he realized it *was* finally happening; the red had reproduced with the right percentages. Perhaps the newest batch of blossoms opened. The red lived up to all expectations. That's also why I'm sure he registered it. Let's go to my house. I know the iris society president. She'll be shocked to hear about John. I'm sure she'd be happy to do some checking."

Angie eased back onto the road for the short ride to Trynne's ranch house. She thought about the letter found in John's kitchen, from a man named Pedar Sondergaard: "A partnership may be profitable for us both." The letter was dated three years ago, possibly around the time of John's initial development of *Rhapsody*. Did he and Sondergaard have any further contact? If so, how deep did their relationship go?

Angie pushed the questions to the back of her mind, reminding herself not to get involved. Problems closer at hand needed attention. First off, her fledgling theater business. What consequences would a murder at their very first performance produce? It might just be their first, and only, show. Angie didn't want to think about that. Second, her mother, which she didn't want to think about either.

"Damn!" Trynne shouted. "I forgot the marker genes!"

"What?"

"Marker genes are deliberately set into the gene 'mixture' where they remain forever—through all successive reproductions. Generations later, a DNA sampling can identify that marker gene and trace the plant back to the original plant."

"Assuming John remembered to put marker genes—"

"Right," Trynne said, "it could eventually be traced back to him. Trouble is, that might take years too."

Angie couldn't keep the excitement from her voice. "I think you've just stumbled upon the motive for his murder."

"You might be right. Even if he reported what marker gene he put in, there'd be no proof it was his."

Tall snowbanks made Trynne's driveway extremely narrow; somehow Angie wedged the car between Trynne's blue compact and Blake's SUV with the logo for Lakes Region Yard Design.

"Man, I'm ready to be done with winter," Trynne said, getting out of the car.

Angie squeezed out so her door didn't scrape on the frozen bank. "I thought you loved winter."

"When I can get out to enjoy it. I've been cooped up in my lab since September. If you hadn't coerced me into doing the play, I might never have seen the light of day. Poor Blake's been doing housework and shopping."

"So, what's got you so cooped up?"

Trynne pushed open the front door. "Monsanto has me researching color genetics in sheep. They want to isolate new genes so they can produce more natural colored wools."

"Sounds boring."

"Genetics is never boring."

Angie followed Trynne through a small hallway lined with brick on the left—the back of their fireplace. The small kitchen seemed even smaller because of the wrought iron pot rack hanging from the ceiling. The wall clock chimed three times.

"I'll get you that phone number." Trynne went to a sideboard at the end of the long living/dining area—one of the only pieces of furniture that hadn't been moved to the theater—and began rummaging in a drawer. "Mention my name to the president. She'll be happy to help out. Ah, here it is." Trynne copied the information and handed it to Angie who pocketed the slip of paper, drove back to the theater and stopped beside Trynne's car. They hugged. Trynne headed home. Angie went in to look for jewelry.

Tyson stood in the foyer with his arms crossed. She felt like a teenager coming in past curfew.

"I'm sorry," he said.

"For what?"

"Calling you before exhausting all possibilities. Well, I thought I had but—"

"You're saying you found it."

"Somebody put it in the wrong cabinet."

Together they went through the left hand door into the auditorium. Angie stopped at the top of the aisle and breathed in the scent of furniture polish. Tyson put an arm around her shoulders. "I love this place."

"Yeah partner, so do I." She stepped away and walked down the sloping walkway. The stage floor had been cleaned, the blood-stained rug heaved in the dumpster. The hardwood floor shone with new-wood brilliance.

"I really hope people show up tonight."

"And that everything goes smoothly."

They left some words unsaid—that nobody else dies.

"What were you and Trynne up to anyway?"

"We went back to John's place, looking for…oh, I don't know what we were looking for. Something to take the heat off Jarvis, I guess."

"You are going to stay out of the investigation, right?"

He was the second person to warn her of this. She gave a tired nod.

Gloria wasn't at the condo. Angie would be glad for some private time. She'd been running on high for several weeks. She toed off her boots on the plastic tray and threw her jacket on the arm of the sofa.

The telephone rang. Angie answered it. "Hello Ms. Deacon,

this is Rachel Spofford of the *Concord Monitor*. I wondered if I could ask you a few questions about John Bloom's death."

"I don't think so," Angie said.

"Wouldn't you like to see the story reported correctly?"

"I'm hanging up now." And she did, then sighed, and went to the kitchen.

As tea brewed, the air filled with the soothing aroma of orange blossoms and springtime, fresh air and happy times. Two hands wrapped around the big, heavy mug and soothing sniffs of the sensations evoked by the steeping tea leaves, almost relaxed her to sleep on the stool.

She dialed the number Trynne had provided. A woman answered on the third ring. "Mary Grayson here."

"Hello, my name is Angie Deacon. Trynne McCoy gave me your name."

"My goodness, how is Trynne? I haven't heard from her in ages."

"She lives—we live in New Hampshire, but I'm afraid I have bad news." Angie told of John's death and the theft at the nursery.

Mary Grayson said, "What an awful thing to happen. I knew John well. He's scheduled to speak at the conference at the end of this week."

"Do you know anything about him having developed a red iris?"

"He developed a red?" Real interest crept into her voice now.

"We think it might be the reason for his murder. Does the name Rhapsody mean anything to you?"

"There's a Rhapsody in Bloom. Developed by the Ernsts, I think in '93, though I'd have to look it up to be sure."

"What color is it?"

"Pink. And then there's Rhapsody in Peach—I'm into the computer now. Hold on while I bring it up...Yes, this one was developed in 2000. I don't see anything else by that name."

"So, that means John didn't register it."

"Not under the name Rhapsody. If it would be any help, I could search all his registrations over the past...what do you think, year?"

"Could you go back to January of '02?"

"All right, though it'll take some time. While I do that, why don't you contact the registrar? Maybe something in red has come in the past month or so—something not yet entered into the system." Ms. Grayson recited the number for Angie. Then she took Angie's contact information. "I'll email you whatever I come up with. Will you let me know when funeral arrangements are made? I'd like to be there."

"I will do that. By the way, do you know anyone named Pedar Sondergaard?"

"Pedar?" Her tone softened. "He's the keynote speaker at the conference this weekend."

"How well do he and John know each other?"

"I couldn't say. The iris world is a close knit group, though."

Angie said good-bye then dialed the registrar. He expressed as much surprise as Mary Grayson to hear about John.

"You know," he told Angie, "if I were John—or even the person who stole the red—I'd be less interested in registering its pedigree than I would be in patenting the actual process I used to produce it. You don't know how important the discovery is to the world of genetics. It could open doors in a hundred other fields."

"Would the marker genes be recorded along with it?"

"You know about marker genes? Yes, they'd be included too."

Excitement roiling through her veins, Angie phoned Jarvis.

"Hello." He sounded tired.

"Did I wake you? You sound tired."

"I have company."

"I see. Well, call me later then."

"I will." And he hung up.

Was there a full moon? She'd heard rumors that it made people act weird. First her mother, now Jarvis. Angie gave up thinking about everything. She reheated the tea, took it to the living room and settled on the couch. Her eyes closed.

The front door opened. Plastic rustled. Something thumped on the hall floor. Footsteps clicked on the tile. Gloria appeared bubbling with bright chatter. The chatter ceased when she saw Angie lying there.

"Are you sick?"

She sat up. "I haven't been to bed in two nights. I'm tired."

"Well, wake up. Look at what I bought." Gloria dragged in the bags and displayed the contents of each one. Still holding a white leather purse, she dropped into the chair next to the sofa. "I'll have a cup of that tea, it smells wonderful."

"Teabags are in the cabinet, cups next to it. The water's probably still hot."

Gloria made a face but left, hauling her packages behind her. Angie lay back down. This time she actually fell asleep. When Angie next looked up, Gloria sat in the chair three feet away, and in the middle of a sentence. "...so handsome. He took me to lunch at Double D's. Then he drove me to Meredith so I could do some shopping."

Angie shook the fuzzies out of her head. "Who? Who took you to lunch?"

Gloria frowned. "Why, Carson Dodge, of course."

She came alert. "You had lunch with Jarvis's father?"

"He's Jarvis's father? Well, isn't that interesting. He said he was here visiting his son."

"You didn't ask about this son?"

"Why would I? I don't know anybody around here."

"How come he hung around you instead of Jarvis?"

"Carson figured, with the murder and everything, he would be busy all day, so he took me shopping. He was going to see him after dropping me off."

Angie stood and took her cup to the kitchen. "I'm going to do some research on the computer."

"What sort of research?"

"I want to check to see if John recorded a patent for his flower."

Angie went into her office/den and shut the door. Soon the Iris Society web site blinked onto the monitor. She learned nothing new. Angie Googled *red iris* and found two articles published in old issues of the iris society newsletter. The first featured a nursery in Oregon that predicted they'd unveil a red the following May. The date of the paper was two years ago. That meant the red should've been announced more than ten months ago. Angie dialed the phone number at the end of the article and was put through to the nursery owner. He showed concern about John's plight but had no suggestions different from Mary Grayson's.

A Jan Van Blozend Bloem wrote the second article, dated six years ago. It was filled with Latin words, but basically the color red could not be attained and people were wasting their time and money trying.

Angie brought up the US patent office site. It didn't take long to learn that patent registrations were public information after all.

"I once knew somebody who invented something."

Gloria's voice over her shoulder nearly made Angie fall out of the chair. Gloria pulled up a chair and sat with her elbow touching Angie's.

"They said it took three months just to fill out the application."

Angie sat up straight and kneaded the kinks from her back. "Good point."

"Besides that, it's only been a day." Gloria counted on her fingers. "Sunday evening they steal the stuff. They spend most of the night and today boxing and shipping to wherever it's going. Then, when the stuff finally gets there, they have to unpack it, sort it, and read everything."

"There has to be a ton of information. Trynne said he's been working toward this his whole life." Angie found the phone number for some low person on the patent office totem pole, and dialed.

"What are you doing?"

"Trying to find out if John filed a patent for the flower."

No answer. That's when Angie realized it was after four o'clock. She shut down the computer.

"You're done?" Gloria asked.

"I'm going to take a bath and get ready for tonight's perfor-mance."

"So, we aren't spending time together *again* tonight?"

"You were the one gone all day." Gloria didn't have to know Angie had been away too.

Six

Angie wore a long sleeved white gown and her hair twisted into a bun at the nape of her neck. When she opened the door Jarvis first whistled and then laughed. "We look like the quintessential Odd Couple." His police issue nylon jacket and blue jeans definitely contrasted with her outfit.

Shipley's Restaurant was crowded with people of the same mindset as he and Angie—dinner before the theater. They stood in line waiting for a table. "So, where were you all day?" Angie asked.

"Well, one thing...I met with my father."

She tilted her chin up to him, watching his face for signs of his mood. Had he punched out the gentle old man in retaliation for his desertion so many years ago? Or raced into his arms, crying tears of joy that they were finally reunited? Angie suspected reality to be somewhere in between.

From his back pocket he drew out his wallet and handed her a sheet of paper. A photocopy of a very old black and white Polaroid. The edges were frayed. The images blurred. But Angie could make out a young couple standing on the lawn in front of a gargantuan stack of logs. The man, in his twenties was tall and lean, with curly hair, high Slavic cheekbones and a well-trimmed goatee; a young version of the person who'd visited the theater a day or so ago. Carson Dodge, in jeans and plaid shirt, pointed at something in the distance. The pregnant woman, wearing a flowered sundress, had shoulder length hair and big wide eyes.

She stood stiffly beside the man. Neat cursive penmanship under the picture said *Rena and Carson 1951.*

"Your mother looks scared to death. Well, I assume that's your mother."

He nodded. "I was born nine weeks later, and my brother almost three years later. Dad took off two weeks after that."

"Speaking of your brother, have you told him about Bud's return?"

Jarvis gave a sardonic chuckle. "Called him right away. He said, and I quote, 'Tell the bastard to get lost again.'"

"Really? You think he'll come around in time?"

Jarvis shrugged. "Probably not. He can be pretty stubborn."

"So, how did your meeting go?"

"He was there when you called. It was...It...I learned a lot of things. About him. About my mother. About why he left. After he left, I called my brother. Dwight wants nothing to do with him." He shrugged. "Can't blame him, I guess."

The hostess led them to a table. Jarvis settled with his back to the wall, as he always did, so he could watch the goings on. He ordered drinks for them both. Then he leaned forward, lips pressed into a straight line. "I found a body in John's bedroom early this morning."

"A body? How come I didn't see it?"

"Got there sometime after you and I left. ID puts him as a Lonnie "Sticks" Lawson. Twenty-seven. Resides in Manchester. That's where I was most of the day. He's got a long sheet: B&E, petty theft, small stuff. Nothing so far relates him to Bloom. He's got three buddies he's been in trouble with. I figure whoever hired him sent him back alone to one, look for more information, or two, something missing from the previous night's haul."

"John's journal."

Now Jarvis laughed. "Journal?"

"Trynne said scientists make meticulous notes detailing *every* process they do."

"I bet that's why that Lawson guy was there."

"Makes sense."

"It also makes sense that he wrote in it at night. You know, expanded all the things he did during the day while they were fresh in his mind."

Jarvis grinned. "What makes you think he didn't do it *before* going to the greenhouse every morning? You know, sit at the table with his morning coffee—or tea—and write down what he *planned* to do that day."

"First off, he was a coffee drinker."

"How do you know that?"

She gave an exaggerated sigh. "Because the coffee pot had brown stains. He used it a lot. And because there was an inch of coffee—not sludge—in the pot."

"Why do you think he wrote at night rather than in the morning?"

She couldn't resist a superior smirk. "Because of the arrangement of the kitchen chairs. John's chair sat so he could look out the window. If he's doing serious writing, chances are he doesn't want to be interrupted by what's going on in the neighborhood."

Jarvis rolled his eyes and put his elbows on the table, tenting his fingers together. "Is there anything else you didn't mention?"

"He sat at the right end of the couch to watch television and quite often slept there. He liked to read in the bathroom. He didn't smoke. He slept alone—at least most of the time."

Jarvis stretched his arms on the table in front of him. "Okay. Tell me how you figured all this out in one walk-through."

She gave him an I-can't-believe-you-asked look and changed the subject. "Question: why didn't John tell Trynne and Blake about the flower? He knew them both for years, knew they'd been involved in iris breeding."

"Whoa. Go back. They were into irises?"

"Sure, when they were young. Back in Oregon." Angie related Trynne's past. Jarvis's eyes grew wider with each word. "Anyway, knowing how dedicated the McCoys had been to the field, he should know he could trust them to keep the secret quiet. So, why didn't he tell them?"

He gave a thoughtful nod. And a slow head shake.

"Did you learn anything about Sondergaard?"

"How fast do you think we can work? The case is only…" he pulled up his sleeve and looked at his watch. "…twenty hours and eighteen minutes old."

"I know."

"We can't work as fast as on television."

"You aren't supposed to be working at all."

He touched a finger to his lips to sign for her to be quiet, and smiled. "I'll stay till they throw me bodily from the building."

"By the way, John had allergies."

Jarvis laughed. "I don't suppose you want a job on the force?" He leaned back so the waiter could deposit their drinks on the table. "I do actually have news about Sondergaard. People at the nursery in Amsterdam say he's out of town. We thought they were lying, protecting him so we put in a call to the Amsterdam Police."

"Sondergaard *is* out of town." Angie let a few beats pass. "He's here in the United States."

Jarvis's eyebrows unfolded and raised high.

"He'll be in Philadelphia on Thursday." She explained about her call to Mary Grayson and handed him the paper with the woman's information.

"How the hell do you do it?" Jarvis shoved the paper in his breast pocket without reading it. At the same time, he drew out several sheets of what looked like fax paper.

"Do what?"

"Get information before authorities?"

She shrugged.

"There's more, right?"

"Sondergaard met with John at the diner last week."

"Shit, woman. You are amazing."

She sipped again, letting Jarvis' compliment flow over her in warm undulating waves. "Judy said at first they were talking low with their heads together. As the conversation went on, Sondergaard got upset. Not raving mad or anything like that, just sort of disturbed. Then John acted apologetic. Maybe you can tweak more information out of her."

As their meals arrived, Jarvis slid the fax pages across the table. "I got this from the police in Amsterdam just before coming here."

She picked at the food as she read. Page one: childhood/family history. Page two: education. She set both pages aside. Pages three and four were the history of Nielsen Nursery from inception in 1982. She set this aside also. Page five held a short but concise financial report. Pedar Niels Sondergaard was in the black, but just barely. This had been status quo for most of his life. The last page was a letter from an Axel Dyhr from the Amsterdam Politie.

To Detective Colby Jarvis,

Attached find information on your suspect, Pedar Niels Sondergaard. Except for a printout from the airline, which you'll receive under separate cover, it is complete. Sondergaard has led a quiet, though busy, life. Nothing illegal or out-of-the-ordinary that we can determine. Most of his life has been spent researching irises. We've found nothing to suggest he might be involved in your case.

We hope this is helpful to your investigation and please don't hesitate to contact this office should something more be required.

Regards,

Axel Dyhr

"I have more stuff at home: newspaper articles featuring the nursery. A couple of articles from Iris Society bulletins. He married in 1985. No record of divorce."

Angie pushed her plate away.

"Nerves?"

"A little…Okay, a lot."

He reached across and put his calloused hand on hers. "If we thought there was any danger of a repeat of last night, you would've been closed down." He picked at some of her leftovers then set down his fork. "Come on, let's go."

Angie went through the motions of putting on her coat, walking to the car and making her way into the theater, but her mind lay awash in thought. Why were they so focused on Pedar Sondergaard? Because no other name had surfaced in relation to John Bloom. Because he was a geneticist. A red iris seeker. And seen with John just a week ago.

Still, they could be chasing the wrong person. The iris bulletins in John's house were fat with information, pictures and articles, and potential suspects. Question: how had it all touched small-town New Hampshire? Why did John chose Alton Bay as a home base? Yes, conditions were good for growing irises but so were thousands of other places.

"Oh yeah, forgot to tell you something. A search of Bloom's bank records showed he had just under three million dollars."

Angie stopped walking. Jarvis bumped into her, the stage door slapped his backside. Angie turned; he folded his arms around her. Their breaths mingled as she asked, "Three million? Dollars? As in a three and a bunch of zeroes?"

"Six zeroes. Deposited in his account twenty-eight months ago."

Months after the letter from Sondergaard to Bloom. Months after mention of the partnership. She took a sharp left turn and unlocked her office door. He followed her inside.

"We're still working on it. We'll find out where it came from."

Jarvis helped Angie off with her coat and hung it on the back of her office door. He used his fingertips to smooth the fabric of her dress. She slapped him away. "Stop that. I can't go out there looking like I stored pencil erasers in my dress."

"Looks nice to me." He laughed and stuck out his hand, pretending to pinch the peaked nipples.

She sought a subject that would keep her from thinking about shoving him on the long, hard sofa and tearing his clothes off.

"I really wish you could find that journal."

"Like looking for a flea on a sheepdog."

"I suspect he carried it everywhere with him. Back and forth to the greenhouse to have it always available for notes." Suddenly she spun around and pointed a finger at him. "I know where it is!"

"Okay, wiseass, where?"

"In his car."

Jarvis's face broke into a wide grin. "Damn woman, you're good."

"You did impound it from our parking lot, didn't you?"

"Yup. We didn't do anything with it because it didn't seem related to his murder." Jarvis whipped out his cell phone and called Sergeant Wilson. When he finished, his mood was a lot lighter.

"You didn't finish telling me about your father," Angie said.

Jarvis heaved his jacket on the arm of the sofa and flopped down. "He said my mother had another man. Shit, Angelina, I just can't imagine that of my mother. You know?"

She stood on tiptoe to kiss his cheek. "There are two sides to every story. You don't know. Your mother might be totally innocent. Or, she might've had good reason to cheat."

"What the hell kind of reason—"

"Don't let it destroy your memories of her. I'm sorry to have to break this up, but I have a lot of work to do." She kissed him again. "I'll see you after the performance."

She strode from the office, careful in her spiked heels, along a narrow hallway. No light squeaked from under Tyson's door. A great hubbub came from the common area, a large room with numerous rooms stemming from it like spokes: costume rooms, makeup rooms, dressing rooms. Chopin played in one of them, but only the occasional snatch of it could be heard. People in all manner of dress and makeup rushed from one place to another. Angie stopped to say hello, give encouragement, and bolster egos on her way to the ticket office. First, she had to make sure everything was ready for the second performance—a sellout since the day the tickets went on sale. She and Tyson had decided to do two shows tomorrow, the second to honor last night's disappointed patrons.

Angie retrieved the vacuum from the tool room and did a quick cleanup of the mud on the lobby carpet. As she closed the door and turned to check on the stage lights, she bumped into Tyson. "How's it going?" she asked.

"It's a madhouse. Mostly nerves."

"Are you nervous?"

"As a night crawler at a fishing tournament."

In spite of the nerves, the Saturday night show went off without a problem. Afterward, the cast gathered in the common area where long tables overflowed with food and champagne that Tyson had so considerately provided for the opening performance of the night before. Rolling Stones music blared from a boom box set like a centerpiece. The walls seemed to vibrate with the sound.

The reviewers were smiling. Ten members of the press were present. Tyson looked about ready to burst with enthusiasm when a reporter took him aside and a cameraman snapped pictures. The first step toward his Broadway career.

Jarvis, still in makeup and costume, approached. By his sides were his father and Angie's mother. Jarvis handed her a flute of champagne and introduced her formally to Carson Dodge. Mr. Dodge took Angie's fingers. Did he just bow? How gallant! No wonder her mother fell for him. But, there were those dark circles and sallow skin. Not the color and tone of someone his age. Her thoughts about the short-term-ness of Gloria's and his relationship were cut short when he dropped her hand. She realized he was speaking.

"…your mother and I."

Angie had no idea what he'd said and was too exhausted to ask him to repeat. Jarvis, Gloria and Carson chatted, but the voices were blurred, like they were talking through cotton batting.

At two a.m. Gloria and Carson said their good nights. As they left she told Jarvis, "I think my mother's smitten."

"He won't let it go too far." Then he said the words she'd been expecting, "He's dying." He sighed. "Come on, I gotta get out of here. Can't hear myself think."

Jarvis tugged Angie down the dark hallway and into her office. He kicked the door shut and shoved her back, thumping her head on the panel that vibrated to the Stones. His first kiss stifled her gasp of surprise. He leaned in, crushing her breasts with his chest. The thick bulge of the prop gun pressed into her hip. And became the most erotic sensation she'd—his tongue drove deep in her mouth—ever experienced. As the final pulse-pounding bars of *Wild Horses* shook the walls, Colby Jarvis rode Angie with the pulse-pounding fury of a stampede.

Seven

Damn. How could someone get so out of shape that sex hurt? He had to start exercising again. Get rid of this bagel around his waist. Angelina was worth it; his health was worth it.

How many times had he dreamed of their first time together? How many times had he planned his moves, imagined how great it would be? Forget about the bullishness of his moves—never had those plans or fantasies included agonizing leg cramps or shortness of breath so severe that twice he'd nearly passed out. Had she known?

Jarvis buttoned his shirt and finished tightening his belt— two holes bigger since last fall. Angelina's attention focused on his hands, which made him hard all over again. God, if their relationship progressed from here, he'd be dead within a month. From the small couch along the wall, a cell phone rang. He groped in the jacket pocket, then checked the caller ID. "Jarvis here. What's up, Wilson?"

"Thought you might want to take a gander at some new info. I left it on your desk."

"Thanks." He slapped the phone shut and tucked it back in the jacket pocket. "Gotta go to the station."

"I thought you were suspended, Angie said."

"Wilson keeps me in the loop."

"Will he get in trouble?"

"He *accidentally* leaves stuff on my desk. It's my responsibility to retrieve it."

She slipped those long, slender feet into her sexy spiked heels, then tilted her head to look up at him. "Maybe you should let them handle the case."

Jarvis gave a sharp laugh. "Yes, just like you are."

"Yes, but I care about you and want this off your shoulders."

"Well, I care about me too. And my career."

Angelina bent forward to peer into the mirror over a battered dressing table. She fluffed her hair with both hands, used an index finger to wipe smudged mascara from an eyelid and then straightened up. Damn, she was beautiful. He squeezed his buttocks together and picked up her coat to drape over her shoulders. They both laughed seeing the wrinkled gown. He made a deliberate show of buttoning the coat over it.

He kissed her in the parking lot and waited till the Lexus disappeared up the road before climbing into his car and driving the half-mile to the station. His stomach growled, and he smiled. Sex always made him hungry. Suddenly guilt punched him with an almost solid force. What the hell had he done? A beautiful, elegant lady like Angelina, and he'd plowed her up against a wall and taken her like…like a bull in a field. He punched a fist into a cupped palm and yanked open the station door.

Behind the thick glass window, the dispatcher's desk sat empty. He used his keys—nobody had thought to confiscate them—to open the security door and strode down the hallway hoping his arrival would go unnoticed. He unlocked his office and slipped inside. A small stack of manila folders sat on the desk.

Jarvis stepped around the desk and grunted seeing the floor carpeted in white. A dozen or more pages had missed the fax machine's in-tray. He gathered them, not worrying about numerical order then slipped everything into a Walmart bag he found in his bottom drawer.

The dispatcher, back at her desk, threw him a sly wave as he passed.

Yellow-gray shades of dawn were poking between the pines

lining the parking lot. Looked like it might be a nice day. A few more with blue-sky sunshine and the snow should be gone. The sound of a diesel engine had him looking street-ward. Headlights of the town sand truck turned in the parking lot. Jarvis waved to the driver.

At home, he dropped the folders on the kitchen table. All the folder tabs were blank, giving no indication where Wilson wanted him to start. While coffee brewed he changed into pajamas. Angelina's scent wafted from his clothes and the guilt returned like a bad virus. One thing was sure; she would never want him to make love to her again. Make love! Shit, what he did wasn't making love, it was a coarse, selfish act perpetrated by an over-age, oversexed—

He slapped both palms on the counter. He'd really messed up this time.

Jarvis sloshed coffee; a lot of it missed the cup. He didn't clean it up, just flung himself into the chair. The first folder: Wilson's personal report. He'd spent yesterday in Manchester chasing down friends, relatives and cohorts of Lonnie Lawson. All he'd learned was that Lawson habitually traveled with three others: Ramon "Grunt" Ramirez, Bradley Short and a Victor "Halfway" Dench. All three had mile-long rap sheets. Wilson had made a huge asterisk next to *Mr. Short has a small blue car.*

Lawson still lived at home with a mother and two sisters. None seemed too broken up about his death. One sister had confided that her brother was nothing more than a leech, sponging off his hard-working family. No one had seen him since Wednesday. Near as Wilson could determine, they hadn't stayed in any motel within a ten-mile radius. Whoever staged this job knew what they were doing.

The next folder held Bloom's credit report. He had a good rating—over 700. Jarvis started to set the page aside then stopped. Weird…nothing at all before '99. He got up and went into the living room, to the coffee table piled high with work related stuff. He drew a notebook from the bottom of the left pile and returned to the kitchen. Finding a fresh page, he made a notation about the date.

The next folder held bank statements from the last four years. Jarvis didn't care about every single detail right now. He first checked the most recent three months. Nothing unusual. Regular bill payments: electric, phone, water, etc. Regular deposits, in varying amounts. Jarvis thumbed back two years and four months, to the deposit of three million dollars…ten months after the letter from Pedar Sondergaard suggesting a partnership. Ten months—just enough time to get together, discuss red flowers and dicker on a price to—what? To buy the rights to the plant? To fund laboratory work? He didn't know yet, but would bet his pension that the three million came from Sondergaard. A sticky note inside the front cover of the folder said in Wilson's handwriting: *have petitioned for Sondergaard's bank records.*

The third folder held John Bloom's phone company records for the past four years. Wilson had notated the origin of each number and highlighted the frequencies in different shades. Either John Bloom had no relatives—Jarvis made a note to ask Trynne—or he didn't keep in touch with anyone because the only long distance calls were to nursery suppliers, laboratory supply companies, or iris related people. Several in the last two months were to a Mary Grayson, whom Jarvis recalled was President of the Iris Society. The calls were probably related to his upcoming speech in Philadelphia. Another note from Wilson: *have petitioned for Sondergaard's phone records.*

Jarvis had to give Wilson credit; he was busting his ass on this case. Probably hankering for a promotion, which would mean Jarvis' job. The thought made him laugh. Some job. No advancement, shitty pay, and endless hours. Of course, by the end of this case—some case, a stolen freaking flower—he might not have a job anyway. He might be in jail.

He tilted the chair back against the wall. Eyes closed, arms behind his head, legs crossed—his thinking position. An ideal case closed in forty-eight hours. After that, clues grew cold, physical

evidence deteriorated. This case had counted down thirty-two
hours and they hadn't turned up any new suspects. Just the Danish guy and the florist. The most logical suspect, Sondergaard,
they couldn't find. The local suspect, well, Jarvis just couldn't
wrap his mind around Donna Marks for murder.

Jarvis maintained the thinking position. This time John
Bloom, Pedar Sondergaard, or Donna Marks didn't pop into his
brain. It was Ms. *Soon to have a finalized divorce* Angelina Deacon. She'd be free of that cheating ex who kept trying to worm
his way back into her life. The guy couldn't let go. Well, fuck him,
he cheated on her. How anyone could cheat on her was more of
a mystery than this Bloom case.

He slammed the chair legs to the floor, bumping his abdomen on the table. A sheaf of paper-clipped witness statements
lay on top of the pile. Bloom's two employees, whose statements
pretty much agreed in all respects; Bloom was a strange but nice
guy who, to their knowledge, had no close friends or girlfriends.
He rarely left the property; they did his shopping and banking
without, it seemed, animosity for such requests. Otherwise they
tended to customers. Neither had ever been inside the back two
greenhouses, nor, in particular Bloom's laboratory.

Bloom wasn't registered at the video store. He didn't get pre-
scriptions. He'd never ordered flowers, or pizza. He had his mail
delivered to the house.

Since the nursery opened, six of Bloom's neighbors had filed
complaints with police. Five were related to parking. From Me-
morial Day to mid-July, cars parked all up and down the road,
sometimes on people's lawns. The fourth complaint had come
from a Frank Chute. He lived directly across the street and had,
so far, been unavailable for questioning.

Except for Blake and Trynne McCoy, there were no family statements. Jarvis checked in the other folders. It wasn't like
Wilson to be lax. He dialed Wilson at home, knowing the man
would be asleep but he answered on the second ring sounding
wide awake. He checked the wall clock—4:58 a.m. People angling

for other people's jobs answered phones sounding wide awake. Then his little voice interrupted to say no, people with newborn babies were up this time of day.

"Jarvis here. I can't find the statements from Bloom's friends and family…Everybody's got somebody, Sergeant. Schoolmates, ex girlfriends…"

"We can't find anyone."

He bounced the chair back and then forward. "Isn't that interesting. Where did he go to school?"

"Community College, Salem, Oregon. There's a curious fact—he attended with someone from right here in town. Mrs. McCoy."

"Uh-huh."

"You don't sound surprised."

Jarvis picked up a pen and stabbed the tip into the blotter. "He and Trynne McCoy grew up together. At one time during their teen years, they were unofficially engaged."

"That right?"

"What about women?"

"You mean, besides the one in the blue hatchback?"

"Yeah, did you check Donna Marks' registration?"

"The car is definitely registered to her. Whether it was the one seen in Bloom's driveway…"

"It might be time to bring Ms. Marks in for questioning."

"I was thinking the same thing."

"Three to five months a year, Sergeant, Bloom's place has to be knee-deep in women. Didn't he hit on a single one? More than ten years is a long frigging time to go without sex—" Damn, it had been that long for him! Jarvis launched himself from the chair and began pacing, his other thinking position.

"Jarvis, you all right?" From Wilson's tone, it wasn't the first time he'd said the words.

Jarvis realized he stood in the living room. He dropped in the red leather recliner—Liz's chair. "Yeah, just thinking."

"Care to share?"

"Not yet."

"What's up next?" Wilson asked.

A sound in the background. Jarvis attributed it to a bedspring creaking. "Gotta do that matinee. Afterward I'll shoot over to Bloom's place again. I want to talk to that neighbor, Chute. Then…I don't know…I guess I'll go back in the house and see if I can turn up anything from under one of those mountains of paper."

"Okay. Keep me posted."

As Jarvis hung up the phone, he got another scent of Angelina's perfume. He sniffed his arm, the backs of his hands, unable to locate the source. Angelina Deacon, the only redeeming element in his life in a very long time. Unfortunately their relationship was a lesson in futility. Forget the way he'd slammed into her at the theater. Forget his jealous streak; that online counseling group had been a tremendous help. Forgetting all that, they were still polar opposites. She was beautiful. He was paunchy, and balding. She was always on the go. Damn, she jogged every day. Well, chimed his little voice, you go outdoors too—from the house to the car. Shit, he was no better than Bloom, holing up like a mole.

Profound understanding dropped Jarvis in his chair, slamming it off the wall. The reason she kept a distance between them these long months; till just now, he chalked her aloofness up to emotional strain over her broken marriage. It wasn't that at all. She'd been waiting—for him to show some balls, to take initiative and make something of the relationship. He sat straighter and slapped his palms on the pile of folders. He'd show her the real Colby Jarvis; the one who got lost so long ago. The *not a jealous bone in his body* Jarvis. The fit and trim Jarvis. He'd take her on a trip. Out of town, where ex husbands, dead wives and police work couldn't breathe on them. As soon as the case was over. Paris. Or London.

No, too overwhelming. Start smaller. Boston. There's a great symphony. He hadn't been to the symphony since a year before Liz died. Liz, whose flaming red hair matched her personality.

They never sat home watching television. Sadness clutched his throat and for a moment he couldn't pull in a breath. After she died, he'd hidden in this cave called Alton Bay, watching Celtics games.

Jarvis swallowed sadness big as a watermelon. He slapped his palms on the chair arms and stood up. The past was the past. Life went on.

Where the hell were those barbells?

At home finally, champagne sleep pulling at her eyelids, Angie undressed and climbed in the shower. She leaned her forehead on the tiles and let sleep fairies play lullabies in her brain while the throbbing shower massage alleviated what tension Jarvis hadn't already pounded from her body.

The memory of Jarvis in her dressing room…what a surprise that had been. She'd expected sex with him to be conventional and routine. None of her fantasies included the passion that rose up in that somber man. It put a whole new light on their relationship.

Glowing with after-sex memory and carrying a brimming snifter of brandy, she turned on the television, propped pillows and crawled between the cold sheets. Nothing on TV looked interesting and she shut it off. The apartment was quiet. Maybe she should check on Gloria. But no, Angie couldn't face another night of girl talk.

She lay there watching the red digital numbers click past— the technological age's version of counting sheep. Sleep wouldn't come.

At four, she kicked off the blankets and went to the den where she booted up the computer and checked email. One from Mary Grayson said, *Good evening Angie. It was nice speaking with you earlier. I'm very sad to hear about John Bloom. You mentioned Pedar Sondergaard and I didn't really elaborate on his importance to the iris world. He's a world-renowned iris geneticist. Ten years ago he produced a brilliant, fire engine red flower—the most beau-*

tiful thing I've ever seen. But he was unable to get it to reproduce.
Such a disappointment. He once told me he's still got descendants
from that plant.

Angie replied to the email then typed Pedar Sondergaard's name in the Google search box.

How it must feel to have a dream fail so radically...with the whole world watching. Did that failure end Sondergaard's research? Angie doubted it. People dedicated to something rarely gave up completely. Especially when someone like John Bloom wrote to you.

Sondergaard's reply said that a partnership of some sort might be profitable for them both. Question: had John told of his success producing a red? Or merely hinted at his interest in producing one? If Sondergaard still had descendants of his red—maybe melding iris genes *was* the partnership. Then again, maybe the partnership entailed a dollar sign, a three, and six zeroes.

Several pages of Pedar Sondergaard hits appeared on the screen. First, Nielsen Nurseries. Sole owner: Pedar Niels Sondergaard. No mention of John Bloom. No mention of a partnership of any kind—not even with a wife. Many Google hits linked back to his site. Others led to articles he'd had published in predominant Iris publications or Danish newspapers, most regarding the futility of breeding for the red. A person could take that to mean he was trying for one.

Angie typed in John Bloom's name but it produced too many unrelated results. How odd to have the name Bloom when you're a horticulturist. She wrote another email to Mary asking if John Bloom was his real name. Then she shut down the computer. It was five a.m. Another sleepless night.

She dressed and went for her morning jog south on Route 28. Jogging presented time to relax, to let life's pressures be neutralized by the scent of the air, the beauty of the scenery, the rhythmic slap of shoes. A time to void things like divorce, the tribulations of leaving a good paying job and starting a business with hardly any capital, and mounting pressure of a relationship with a cop.

Today, errant thoughts invaded that void. After ransacking John's place and stealing his life's work, why go to the trouble of killing him? Trynne and Blake spoke of him as a quiet, unassuming and private man. Nobody's description called him abrasive, one to create trouble, a person someone would wreak revenge upon.

At the top of Bay Hill Road Angie turned and retraced her steps, her shoes slapping muck on her sweatpants.

What if John and Sondergaard spent the last three years negotiating—or arguing—about a partnership and John ended up turning him down? Sondergaard came a week early for his speaking engagement at the conference and used the time to convince John in person. From Judy's description of their meeting, Sondergaard had been unsuccessful. Had he been so angry about this failure that he perpetrated the theft? Possible. Sondergaard's own discovery of a red sort of cemented the idea of a motive. Still, why kill John afterward? And where did that three million dollars come from?

By the time her shoes slapped back to the condo, Angie was soaked from the knees down. She dropped her clothes in the laundry. Then she picked up last night's gown and underthings from the floor. The dress, though not ruined, desperately needed dry cleaning. She buried her face in the soft material and inhaled the essence of Colby Jarvis. The aromas of aftershave and sex sent her juices flowing. Angie turned on the hot water and nearly leaped into the shower.

Afterward, sex drive not the least bit thwarted, she headed for the kitchen for something to eat. Movement in the second bedroom said Gloria was awake. In a totally uncustomary move, Angie grabbed up her keys and escaped to the diner where Judy had two coffees waiting on the counter.

"You're late today."

"Didn't get home till dawn."

"I hope that means the show was a success. Girl, you and

Tyson outdid yourselves. It was suspenseful and funny and romantic. Jarvis was fantastic as a thief."

"I hope the critics agree with you."

"Let's check, the papers just got here." Judy undid the strap on the bundle and returned carrying two. They'd made the front page again—this time the headline said *Local Theater Pulls off a Winner.*

Angie's fluttering heart smoothed to a more sedate rhythm though it still tripped with energy. She read: *On Friday night, Prince & Pauper Theater's first performance was marred by the death of their leading man, John Bloom. Night two went off without a hitch. Bloom's understudy, played by Blake McCoy. All this critic can say is: fabulous. It makes one wonder why he wasn't cast in the part in the first place. Checkmate: Love is funny, romantic, and thoroughly entertaining.*

Angie paid for several papers and the coffees. "Tyson's probably already seen this, but I'll bring some for the cast."

"How long is the play running?"

"Friday and Saturday nights and Sunday matinees all month. We switch to *Ruckus in New York* for next month."

"I'm so happy for you two." Judy used a marker to write on the lid of one coffee. "This one's Tyson's, cream and three sugars."

Angie started to leave.

"By the way," Judy called, "Jarvis came in this morning. He brought pictures of that guy I saw meeting with John Bloom."

"So it *was* him."

"For sure. Peter somebody."

"Pedar—P.E.D.A.R."

"Romantic. Hey, something else. Remember I said that Bloom guy had been in her before? I remembered who he came with— Blake and Trynne."

Angie nodded. That agreed with what Trynne said—how he never invited them to his house. She'd never thought to ask how often the three of them 'went out'. Or whether Blake and John ever did things together, guy things.

"Well, I've got to run. It's going to be a zoo today. We're doing two shows to make up for Friday night. Did Jarvis say where he was going?"

"He mentioned something about Manchester."

What could be in Manchester? She hoped it didn't keep him past matinee time. Perhaps she should prepare the understudy just in case.

Angie had no sooner buckled the seatbelt when her cell phone rang. "Hey Ange." The familiar voice sent ripples of emotion—both good and bad—through her. A question burst onto her tongue but didn't leave her mouth—what did her ex want?

"Hi Will."

"I just wanted to congratulate you and Tyson on *Checkmate: Love.*"

He saw the show? With whom? "Thanks."

"I really liked Blake. Better than Bloom."

He saw both shows?

"You think so?"

"Yes, I thought Bloom was a little stiff."

She didn't reply. Opening mouth right now might mean inserting foot because she really wanted to know...who Will had gone to the show with. It was none of her business. That part of her life was over. His cheating broke them up.

"Probably just nerves," he was saying. "I know how I'd feel in front of that crowd. Blake is a natural. Will you be using him in another production?"

What the hell kind of conversation was this?

"I don't know."

"Jarvis was great too."

Okay, so that's where it was leading; to her relationship with the cop. "Um, maybe. Will, I have to be getting to work now."

"You punch a time clock these days?"

"No, but it's freezing out here."

"Where are you?"

"Thanks for calling, I'm glad you liked the show. We're doing

Ruckus in New York next month. Seeya." She flipped the phone shut and threw it on the passenger seat.

The theater parking lot had been freshly sanded. It was March, when the snow melted during the day but at night refroze into sheets smooth enough for ice-skating. Tyson's car sat just outside the front door. Sometimes she wondered if he slept here. If she had to live with his overbearing mother, she'd move in here too.

Gloria's face popped into her head. During this visit she hadn't been much less domineering than Tyson's mother. Thank goodness for Jarvis's father keeping her occupied. Still, Angie thought, if he's dying, perhaps it's not a good idea for Gloria to get too attached. The thoughts brought Gloria's health to mind—they really did have to talk.

As she neared the door, she heard the hum of the vacuum. Tyson pushed it across the carpet near the ticket window. "Good morning," she shouted.

He shut off the machine and began winding the cord. "Hi."

"Are you still here, or back already?"

"Party broke up bout three. I went home for a couple hours shut-eye but I couldn't sleep."

"Neither could I. Have you seen the reviews?"

A smile erupted onto his good-looking face. "Saw the Monitor. But I see you have the Telegraph." He pushed the vacuum into the closet, shut the door and came back to take his coffee.

"How were the reviews in the Monitor?"

"Awesome." They walked into the auditorium where Tyson set his cup on the arm of a chair. He rustled the pages looking for the review. Angie waited while he read. "Awesome," he said again. "This is great!" He folded the paper and tucked it under his arm. Angie followed him down the aisle and up the stage steps. "I think we should frame these and put them on the wall in the lobby," he said over his shoulder.

"Good idea."

In the common area out back, they tossed the newspapers on the long table.

"How come you and Jarvis don't move in together?"

Tyson was twenty-five, half her age. He lived in a world of *now,* everything done in a hurry. Meet somebody, move in with them, get married.

She avoided his eyes. "I'm not ready for that. I—"

"You're not over Will yet."

"I'm not in love with him any more. I just—"

"Don't want the responsibility."

"It's not that either. To be honest, I don't think Jarvis is over losing his wife."

"When did she die?"

"Ten years ago. I'll get started cleaning the auditorium."

"Good. Avoid the subject."

"I'm not. Sometimes things are just out of your hands."

"So, if you were convinced Jarvis was over his wife, you'd fall into a serious relationship with him?"

"I didn't say that. Hey, let's talk about your love life for a while."

He plucked off the coffee lid and took a long drag of his coffee. Then he set the cup on the table. "My mother will be here soon."

"Okay, so you change the subject too."

He grinned, showing straight, perfect teeth. "I sent her out to have that script copied. We should probably look at it before the author comes in. The title is *Ring of Muddy Water.* It's about a woman who gets a late night telephone call from an old friend. This friend asks if she'll meet him out on the bridge. When she arrives, there's no one there. The cops suddenly arrive and arrest her for murder. They all peer below to see the body wedged in some shrubs along shore. There's a hate note in the pocket, supposedly from the woman."

"Sounds intriguing. I love mysteries. Speaking of plays, want to get together Wednesday to work on ours?"

"Sure. You remember we're going hiking tomorrow morning, right?"

"Right." He shoved one of the mismatched hardback chairs under the table and used his thumbs to straighten it. "My mother will be here at noon. She's bringing lunch too."

Angie cleaned the auditorium then sat at the table in the common room to make a shopping list that included props for the next month's show. Much of what they used had been borrowed from the casts' homes. Angie smiled remembering the echo of voices in Trynne and Blake's empty living room. Maybe that's why Blake's acting was so natural—he felt right at home.

A pounding came on the back door. Tyson ran to let his mother in. He took the huge basket of food from her and let the big metal door whoosh shut with a resounding thud. Agnes Smith Goodwell entered, bringing the aroma of hauteur and Donna Karan's *Cashmere Mist*. She laid a pair of thick manila envelopes on the table, out of Angie's reach. "Good day, Miss Deacon."

"Hello Mrs. Goodwell. How are you today?"

"Fine." She leaned down and waited for Tyson to kiss her cheek. The dutiful son. "What time will you be home?" she asked Tyson.

"Probably not until after midnight." Tyson shoved one of the envelopes at Angie and opened the lunch basket. Agnes Goodwell took that as her cue to leave.

Tyson pulled out the recently-straightened chair and drew the basket closer. While he unpacked lunch, which included wine glasses and chinaware, Angie opened her copy of the manuscript. "Your mother still hates me."

He laughed, twisting the cork from the bottle of wine. "She still thinks you're after the family money."

"Do you think she poisoned the food?" she asked.

"And take a chance of harming her precious son?" Tyson shrugged. "Can't help it if she thinks I'm God's gift to mankind."

Jarvis shut off his Jeep in the Jiffy Mart parking lot and stretched his legs as straight as he could. He'd had a devil of a time staying awake on the trip to Manchester from Alton Bay. Not that distance-wise it was very far. The pressures of the last few days had taken a toll on his stamina. Only one vehicle in this lot, looked like it had been here for several days. None of the shops along this stretch were open for business yet. His watch read 7:25.

He had no idea where to start looking for Sticks Lawson. His experience in the city of Manchester, with a population of over a hundred thousand, had been limited to trips to the shopping areas with Liz. That's why he'd phoned the local cops and asked for a tour guide.

It wasn't long before a black, fifteen-year-old Ford Fairlane rumbled up. A man of about twenty-five, with unkempt hair and wild beard climbed out. He wore jeans with both knees torn out, and a denim jacket with patches sewed all over it. Jarvis had time to identify Harley Davidson and Budweiser logos as the man raced around the front of the vehicle. He jumped in and shut the door. Jarvis was suddenly surrounded by the smell of cigarette smoke, so strong he had to fight the urge to open the window.

The newcomer stuck out a giant, hairy paw. "Detective Gordon Lewis. Call me Lew."

"Colby Jarvis. I'm investigating the death of a man named Lonnie 'Sticks' Lawson."

"I know. I also know you're on suspension."

The damned suspension. Because of it, this guy would refuse to help, wouldn't want to chance getting his balls chewed out. Jarvis reached down to twist the key.

"I think the suspension policy is crap," said Lew. "Guilty before proven innocent. Makes all kinds a sense, don't it?"

Jarvis resisted breathing a sigh of relief. "Any idea where this Lawson creep hung out? Where he lived? I tried the place listed as his home address but—"

"Lemme guess, nobody there ever heard of him."

"On the contrary, his mother and sister seemed almost glad to have him out of their hair. The sister called him a leech. 'Twenty-seven years old and never held a real job,' she said. Neither knew the people he hung out with. Except their street names: Grunt and Halfway."

Lew nodded. "Grunt is Ramon Ramirez. The other is Victor Dench. There's a fourth guy too: Brad Short. He's not a bad kid. Comes from a stable home environment. So far, he hasn't got a record." Lew pointed to the left. "Drive that way."

A myriad of twists and turns took them to a dark back alley. At its end, a long-abandoned warehouse with pocked bricks and broken windows. "This is their meeting place." Lew pulled on the door handle so Jarvis did likewise.

But the effort was for naught. Oh, the guys had been here, no doubt about that. The big echoing space contained worn furniture and a corner full of cast-off beer cans and take-out containers. Jarvis had the impression the group had cleared out for good. They performed an examination of the place anyway. He slid his hands between cushions while Lew kicked aside the piles of containers. They found nothing that could even remotely tie this place to the Alton Bay case.

Eight

The matinee ended at four. Angie changed from dress clothes to jeans and sweatshirt, and called the florist. "Hi Donna. Can you make me up a colorful vase of carnations?"

"The stage ones wilted already? Must be the lights."

"No, these are for my apartment."

"Uh-oh, you need cheering up. What did Jarvis do now? Or, has Will been hasseling you again?"

Angie laughed. "Nothing like that. I'm feeling spring-like. I'll be there in a few." She considered phoning Jarvis to see if he wanted to see Donna's irises but he'd acted so strange at the theater. Like he was avoiding her. Probably regretted making love to her. She'd been too easy, hadn't resisted one inch when he hefted her dress and jabbed his—

"Angie, are you okay?"

She found herself standing inside the florist shop, surrounded by the scent of roses and humidity and a very serious looking Donna Marks.

"Um, yeah, I'm fine."

"You look a little pale."

"I had to get out of the theater. Claustrophobia."

"In that huge, echoing building?" Donna laughed. "I know how you feel though. Sometimes I want to close this place up and go romp in a snowbank."

"I haven't been sledding in years," Angie said wistfully.

"Too bad about what happened Friday night."

"Were you there?"

"No." She smiled. "I thought I'd go toward the middle of the month...after you got the kinks worked out. No offense."

"None taken."

"Besides, I kind of had something to do."

"Something to do, huh? Did you know John?"

"No. Well...I've been to his nursery before."

A bell over the door clanged as a customer entered. A gust of cold air rushed in too, but soon became absorbed in the humidity of the shop. Donna called good afternoon, then lowered her voice, "I went there once in a while, for outdoor bedding plants. I can't remember who I dealt with, might've been a salesperson. That seems more likely, doesn't it? I'll be right with you," she said to the customer, then continued to Angie, "A friend said the cops have been all over the neighborhood asking questions: did you see any activity over there; did you hear anything; how well did you know him?"

"*Did* your friend know anything?"

"Only after the fact. Lots of commotion around one a.m. Turned out to be the cops." Eyes on the customer who'd picked up a vase of cattails, Donna told Angie, "I'll be right back."

Once the customer left, Donna gestured at a vase on the far end of the counter. "Colorful enough for you?"

"Beautiful. By the way, the next show is called *Ruckus in New York*. I'll need sunflowers for that. Can you get them this time of year?"

"Sure. How many?"

"A couple dozen a week. And also, something subdued for a dining room arrangement. Maybe nine inches tall."

"Consider it done."

Angie paid for the carnations. "By the way, can I see your irises again? I haven't been able to stop thinking about them." The truth.

"Uh, sure." Donna peeked onto the sidewalk to make sure no customers were coming in.

Her hothouse was just as neat and orderly as Angie's visit two days before. Just as aromatic. There were a lot of red flowers; she surveyed the long aisles: brown-red, orange-red, rose-red, reddish edged in other colors, but not a single red-red. And, no overcrowding from the addition of red plants. How many might that be anyway?

Angie tried to recall the placement of the irises from her last visit. Hadn't there been a tall, rose-color Donna had called *Gingersnap* in front? Yes. They had talked about scents: how some were strong and some nearly absent.

In the left aisle, hadn't there been a cranberry-brown called Fire-something? Yes, *Play with Fire*. The flower was gone. She mentally kicked herself. Donna could be no more involved in this than her. To move a plant from a spot to mate or debug, or whatever else had to be done, wouldn't be unusual. Besides, it would be stupid of Donna to put the red on display just days after stealing it.

Donna's eyes were on her. Angie leaned forward, wrapping both hands gently around the nearest bloom and giving an exaggerated sniff. "Mm. Very nice. What's the name of this one?"

"That one's one of my favorites. It's called Spiced Custard."

Angie made a show of reluctantly releasing the flower, and straightening up. "How's the breeding program progressing?"

"Er...Not very well right now. I guess in the long run it doesn't really matter. I love the flowers so much, I'd have them anyway."

"Maybe you wouldn't have so many though?" Angie offered.

"I don't know. I think I'd still have a lot. I have very little outlay since I've bred most of them here. They don't cost much to keep."

"Record keeping must take quite some time."

Donna's grass-green eyes lit up. "Definitely. I have a log on each flower. The logs are cross-referenced several times, both on paper and in the computer. Then, of course, there are extensive pedigrees…"

Finally a glimpse into the magnitude of John's theft.

"Could I see a pedigree?"

"My office is really a mess. I'd be embarrassed."

"It can't be as bad as mine and Tyson's," Angie said with a dismissive wave of her hand. "I have stacks this high in every corner. I'm curious about your filing system; I haven't got a computerized one at Prince & Pauper yet."

Donna stepped forward, white Converse sneakers showing below too-short jeans. Angie had a glimpse of brown socks before the foot moved back. "You should call Montez Clarke, he does all my computer integrating."

"I know him," Angie said. "I hear John was breeding for a red iris."

Donna's glance shot toward her. Then it moved away. She put a hand on the doorknob—the tour had ended. "Is that right? Wish I'd known. We could've traded pointers."

"The other day, you talked about cloning. Have you done any of that?"

"Gosh, no. I haven't the education. I'm just a backyard breeder." Donna stepped into the hallway and crossed her arms. "Did John do cloning?"

"I have no idea. I know two things: he's been breeding for several years, and he's been in touch with a guy from Amsterdam, who's bred irises for a long time."

When Donna made no comment, Angie changed the subject and moved back into the shop. "So," she put a sly tone in her voice. "What *did* you do this weekend? Have a date?"

Donna's eyebrows scrunched. "Why are you asking so many questions?"

"Oh goodness. Sorry if I've overstepped. I was just making conversation." Angie picked up her vase. "I will see you Friday for the weekend's flowers. Thanks."

Angie left, blinking in the bright sunshine. Even though it

looked like winter, the smell of spring peppered the air. The revelation put a jaunt in her step in spite of the mood instilled by the dramatic change in Donna's attitude. What prompted that change? Just two days ago, she'd invited Angie to see the greenhouse. Shown her around like a mother parading a newborn.

Which brought up the question, was there another reason Donna hadn't come to the show? Because she waited for John to leave his property she could break in and steal *Rhapsody*? She had the means and the opportunity, and a smallish motive.

Not a small motive, really. The red would be worth millions. Every breeder in the country—no, the world—would breed it. Sell it. Love it. Want the process for other genetic work. Which led her to think of Trynne. Angie shook off the notion and stuck with Donna for now. Why didn't she didn't want Angie in her office? Maybe she told the truth about the messy conditions. But it could also be a mess from an overload of files and laboratory equipment, a red iris—and a hard drive. What did a hard drive look like?

Had Jarvis considered Donna as a possibility? Angie took out her cell phone, but as she fingernailed the buttons, a strange sensation oozed into her. Somebody was watching. A slight tilt of her head revealed Donna standing in the window between two bushy plants, arms crossed, the corners of her mouth turned downward. Angie waved. Donna didn't.

Angie put the phone on the seat and realized someone else was waving…from the window of the shop beside Donna's: Will's real estate office. Angie waved to her soon-to-be ex and drove a few hundred feet to the Downings Landing parking lot. Jarvis didn't answer either his cell phone or his home phone. She dialed the station and learned he was out. The tone suggested he'd been reminded of the same thing. In Alton Village, she turned right onto Barr Road. Most of the houses were older but interspersed between were newer ones, many of them modulars. Middle-income cars.

Jarvis's red Jeep sat alone in the yard. She pulled in beside it.

Icicles the size of pencils dripped like broken faucets from the garage eaves. Rivers of salty sludge puddled in the driveway. Earth thawed, pooled. Mud season had begun. Meanwhile, brown grass lay bedraggled and limp, but ready to erupt to green with very little encouragement from the sun. Daffodils and crocus waited to push green points through mulch and dead leaves, and bring hope to even the most downcast cabin-fever victim.

Her side-view mirror sent a reflection of activity across the street. In the rearview mirror where objects didn't "look smaller," a stout elderly man stalked down the circular driveway of the aged Victorian home, painted a harsh green. He didn't even look both ways before crossing the road. Not that there was any traffic, but Gloria's voice shouted in her head, "No sense taking chances."

Angie got out of her car, the open door pinging indignantly, and faced the oncoming man. He was of medium height with thick jowls and a too-high forehead. Bits of gray hair poked from under a bright orange toque, boots splashed in the mud. He breathed hard, from anger more than exertion, Angie thought. His face might have been pleasant at one time, but something had forced his mouth into a permanent frown.

Angie said a bubbly, "Good afternoon."

He stopped walking…a foot away. She stepped back a foot and a half. He stabbed a finger in the comfort zone she'd created. It poked the air in her direction, and jerked toward Jarvis's car. "I want you police people out of here. My wife is very ill and this is too much. Just too much."

"I'm not from the police."

The man lurched toward her. She opened her mouth to shout for Jarvis. "You gawkers are even worse. Can't you let this go? Let the dead man rest in peace. My wife is ill, we can't have this commotion."

She'd seen this behavior before; the man was grieving. "I'm very sorry. I didn't mean any harm." She shuffled her feet acting uncomfortable with her new knowledge. "Terrible when some-one we love is ill."

The wrinkles around his mouth twitched. The ones around his eyes softened—a little. "Not your fault." He pulled off the toque and raked a blue-veined hand through his hair, flattened by the heavy hat. "We've been married forty-seven years."

"You don't see many long-term marriages any more," Angie said, thinking about her own. Twenty-six years.

"Nothing they can do for Edna."

The face of Carson Dodge superimposed itself on this man. "I'm very sorry," Angie offered, laying her hand on the coarse sleeve. Then she reached back and pushed the car door shut, silencing the energetic pinging.

"I'm trying to make her last days as peaceful as possible." He waved a gnarled hand at John's house where a kitchen curtain moved. Jarvis. "And now this," the man said.

"My name is Angie Deacon."

"Frank Chute."

Angie stuck out her hand, a small amount of physical contact helped put people at ease. "Nice to meet you." His hand was soft, the hand of an inactive person. The creases at the corners of his eyes smoothed.

"Are you the girlfriend?" He glanced over her shoulder at the Lexus. "No. No, you're not."

"Did she look like me? Was she tall? Short? Fat? Thin?"

His eyebrows knit. "One night the porch light came on. I got a peek before she got inside. I'd say she was more tall than short. Thinner than fat, if you know what I mean."

Angie gave a shrug. "An impression is better than nothing at all."

"So, you're not a policeman, er, woman?"

"No, I'm sort of a…"

"A detective?"

"No. Mr. Bloom was a friend. I'd really like to find out who did this to him. Would you mind telling me what you told them?

You never know when something new will come from a simple conversation."

"They say that on TV all the time."

"Talking helps jog the memory. Can you remember what kind of car the woman drove?"

Frank yanked his hat back over the gray curls and eyed Angie's car. "Nothing like yours, that's for sure. Hers was one of those small jobs with five doors."

"A hatchback?"

"Yes. That's right. Blue."

"Did she come here often?"

"I don't want you thinking I spend all my time watching my neighbors but at night, the sounds carry our way. Don't know why that is. Top a that, I don't sleep well." He stopped for a breath. "I'd say she came a couple times a month."

"Did John go out much?"

"Never at night. Sometimes during the day."

"Did you hear, or see, anything the night he died?"

"Around midnight I heard a lot of door slamming. Muffled voices. Turned out to be the cops."

"What about before that, say around nine or ten?"

He looked toward his house, probably thinking he'd been gone too long, wondering if Edna was all right. "Most weekend nights there's activity down there." He pointed past Bloom's driveway. "Old log road kids use. Probably to smoke dope."

"There's more, isn't there? Something you didn't tell the police."

Frank Chute looked at her, as if assessing her integrity. He smiled, revealing well-made false teeth. "I didn't mention the other car."

"Car?"

"I got up to—well, a car inched very slowly along the road. At the time, I thought it was just some kids, you know? That's mostly why I didn't mention it before. But I've been thinking maybe it was related because it *could* have been pulling out of the driveway.

I say could have because I didn't actually see it doing that."

"Was the car small and blue?"

He grinned again. "*That* I would have mentioned. As you can see, there's no streetlight, and neither of our porch lights were on. We don't get much company in the middle of the night." He shrugged. "One of the reasons we bought on this road."

"The moon wouldn't have been much help either," she said, recalling the sliver of moon and the minimal light illuminating the snow on their way to the greenhouse.

"This car was bigger, and a dark color. Navy or black, maybe. The weather was clear and cold. The heat came on. Shakes the house a little." He gave a chuckle. "That's how I know when we need a furnace cleaning."

"Can you remember the time?"

He pursed his thin lips. "I can only guestimate that it was between nine and ten."

"How did you get along with Mr. Bloom?"

The lips flattened. "That yard brings down property values for people trying to sell their house." Anger and frustration welled up inside him again.

Over his shoulder she saw the sign, jammed into the ground near the front walk. "Are you selling because of Mr. Bloom?"

In that short instant before he spoke again, Angie knew the reason the house had been put on the market. "Edna's bills...we have no insurance. I hate to do it; she loves the place so. But what choice do I have?"

"Where will you go?"

"With one of our kids. We have four. I didn't tell Edna, I've been worried that if the house doesn't sell in a few weeks..." He shrugged. "When the snow melts, buyers will see the mess."

"I guess that's moot now, isn't it?" Angie stopped talking, letting the implication behind her words sink in, but he either didn't get it, or chose not to. "Did you know Mr. Bloom personally?"

Chute jammed his hands deeper in the pockets of his wool coat. He took them out, then put them back in again. Something had happened between the neighbors. Chute didn't volunteer anything.

"Do you know what he did for a living?" Angie asked.

A light flickered behind his brown eyes. "I see what you mean. He was doing something on the side. Drugs?"

"No, nothing like that. He bred irises."

"Irises?"

"Red ones in particular." She watched, but saw no reaction. "Has anyone ever come around asking about irises in relation to Mr. Bloom?"

"This trouble related to that?"

"Maybe."

"No, the only talk was about the traffic on the street."

"Do you have a computer?"

He laughed and shook his head. "Kids keep saying we should have one, to do something called E-mail with the grandkids. Why?"

"No reason."

She ducked inside her car, wrote her name and home phone number on the back of a Prince & Pauper business card, and handed it to him. "Would you call me if you think of anything else?"

"Else? Did I say something helpful?"

Angie touched his arm. "I really appreciate you trusting me. Please give your wife my best."

Frank nodded toward the house. "Who's inside?"

"Police Detective Colby Jarvis. He's one of the good guys."

Frank's face finally smoothed out. "I get it. You and him."

"Go home to your wife," Angie said, playfully.

This time Chute looked both ways crossing the street. She headed for Bloom's house feeling a bit gloomy. A tiny part of her wanted Chute to be a suspect. Physically he probably couldn't have ransacked the nursery. What motive would he have anyway? To get Bloom out of the way, so the house would be sold, and property values rise again? Much too uncertain.

Bloom's door opened. Jarvis gestured for her to come in. She followed him to the dining room where he'd obviously been sitting amid mountains of papers and pamphlets. Jarvis sat and picked up a stack. "Sometimes this job is really boring."

She sat in front of him, crossing her legs Indian fashion and leaning forward, elbows on her thighs. "Find anything worthwhile?"

"Nah. The big guys took everything yesterday."

"Nothing about Sondergaard?"

"A few mentions in newsletters." He thumbed through a pamphlet with bold black letters saying International Code of Nomenclature for Cultivated Plants. He wiggled it in the air. "Mucho boring-o."

His attempt at humor made her laugh.

"I'm sorry about last night," he said.

Sorry that she was too easy?

"I didn't mean to force myself on you. Well, I guess I did mean it because otherwise I would've stopped. I guess what I mean is—"

"I liked it."

Their eyes met, lingered. Jarvis broke away first. "What did Chute say?"

"A woman in a blue hatchback visited a couple of times a month. His impression was that she was taller and slimmer rather than shorter and fatter." Jarvis didn't say anything, but his eyebrows wrinkled. "Also, between nine and ten p.m. a large dark color or vehicle might have turned in, or come out of, the driveway."

"You sure you don't want a job on the force? You could probably have mine."

"Cut it out, you'll be reinstated, though I wonder what they'll do if they catch you here."

"Don't know. Don't want to find out." He slapped the book to the floor and put out a hand to help her up. "Come on, let's go."

On the way out, Angie told about Donna's about-face attitude. "She's a dedicated breeder. Won't admit to breeding reds but she owns a little blue car."

"You think she's the girlfriend? After here, I thought I'd head over to talk to her."

"She'll never speak to me again."

"I'll keep you out of it."

"How you going to do that, I was only there an hour ago."

He walked Angie to her car. "I'll figure something out. But there will be a price."

"There always is."

Angie slowed as she passed Donna's shop. A narrow driveway, framing two long patches of muddy looking garden, led around the right side of the building and greenhouse. Between the rectangles of garden sat a car, identical to the one Frank Chute had described. Angie couldn't tell the exact make from her location. Behind, Jarvis waved and pulled into a parking space.

Could Donna be John's illusive girlfriend? A mutual interest in something like iris breeding could really spark a relationship. Angie pictured long, boring conversations and marathon laboratory sessions. And yet John's neighbor said the girlfriend only visited a couple of times a month. Trynne said John never invited anyone to his home. Wouldn't she be surprised to hear about this?

Maybe it wasn't a romance between John and Donna; perhaps the relationship was business. The pair met to compare progress, tell lies, chat about the industry.

Angie realized she'd driven past her condominium complex; she whipped the car into the pull-off area across from the ledges overlooking the bay. The vehicle following gave an irritated honk and sped past. Pulling her jacket tight against the perpetual breeze off the water, she got out and went to the guardrail, taking in great breaths of cold air that shot chills into every cranny. Below stretched the long narrow bay that, from here, might be mistaken for a river. She couldn't see its abrupt ending at Downings Landing. Across the water, the homes and seasonal cottages were lined like pickets. Upstream was the gaping mouth of Lake Winnipesaukee.

Why couldn't she extinguish the urge to find killers? What if her marriage hadn't broken up and loneliness didn't drive her emotions, would the investigative compulsion ever have surfaced? Or was there some inbred desire for danger? Granted, the feeling of bringing a murderer to justice brought great satisfaction. And she had to admit, that fleeting fame garnered interest in the theater. Angie shivered, climbed in the car and headed home. She drew two newspapers from the tube and pushed open the door. Warm smells oozed out—Gloria was cooking dinner. Beef stew maybe. A cupboard door shut.

"I'm home!" She hung up her coat and bustled into the nice, cozy kitchen. Her mother, in bathrobe and slippers, stood bent over, looking at something in the oven. Angie slipped onto a counter stool and set the newspapers in front of her. "Smells great. What prompted your Suzie Homemaker impression?"

Gloria shut the oven and smiled. "I felt like it. I invited Jarvis and his dad."

"Mom…about Mr. Dodge…"

Gloria stopped smiling and dropped onto an adjoining stool. "What about him? What is it about him that you could possibly dislike? He's considerate and kind, he's—oh, I get it, you hate him because he ran off on his family forty-something years ago."

"No. I like him a lot. It's just that…are you sure you should get involved with someone who's…"

"Who's what, dying? Angelina, I know all about death. People my age face the possibility every day. Everyday I read of friends who have left us."

"Okay, okay. I just don't want you hurt." And, heaven help her for being selfish, she didn't want a grieving woman clinging even tighter.

"Don't worry. I'm fine. I'll *be* fine. So, where have you been all afternoon?"

While her mother brewed cups of chamomile tea, Angie outlined the events of the day. She opened the previous day's newspaper, the phone rang. Gloria groaned. "The thing's been ringing off the hook. Reporters."

Angie let the machine pick up. A man's voice identified himself as a reporter for the *Union Leader* and asked her to phone when she came in. Yesterday's *Concord Monitor* headline screamed *Prominent Alton Bay Nurseryman Dies*. It featured a picture of John standing beside his sign, one hand extended as though to say, see what I have! His smile was wide and welcoming. A pang of sadness drove through her. What a waste. Angie pushed the paper away. As the hall clock chimed six, the doorbell added its chord.

Angie almost laughed seeing Jarvis and his father standing there. If two men ever looked less excited to be on a date, she hadn't seen it. Jarvis's face was tight and somber. Carson Dodge looked tired, the gray circles under his eyes more pronounced. Jarvis kissed Angie on the temple.

Mr. Dodge laughed. "Son, even I'm more romantic than that! Go on, give the girl a real kiss."

Which Jarvis did, hauling her in close and bending her over backward, like dancers dipping. She came up laughing. "Good evening, Mister Dodge, can I take your coat?"

"Please, call me Bud."

Jarvis helped him off with the coat then handed the garment to her. Gloria appeared in the kitchen doorway. Bud went to her and planted a kiss on her temple. Angie nearly threw out a sly comment about kiss placement but thought perhaps their relationship hadn't progressed to that stage yet.

Dinner was delicious. It had been a while since Angie had a home cooked meal. They chatted about politics, weather, sports, and more politics. Everything but murder.

Prompted by his father, Jarvis related a story from his childhood. "Dwight and I were playing behind the cookhouse. The snow was as deep as I'd seen it. And cold, god, the cold could freeze the insides of your nose before you could get off the steps. We took a couple of old burlap bags out of the trash bin and climbed the bank behind the shed. It was roof high, great for sledding. After twenty or so trips down, it got pretty slick and had extended a good ways from the building." Angie watched the animation on his face, and hand gestures. She wished he could be this way more often. "Well, long story short," Jarvis continued.

Gloria broke in with a "too late" that made everyone laugh.

He threw her a fake scowl. "As I slid down that last time, face first, I decided to blaze an even longer track and pulled the bag left. It went up over a small ridge. I couldn't see anything on the other side, but wasn't worried." He laughed. "Not till I went over. And down. Into the well. Took them an hour to fish me out." Jarvis shivered. "Never been so cold in my life."

Bud turned serious. "I should've been there for you."

"That's not why I told the story."

"I know."

"I actually only remembered bits and pieces of the story. My mother repeated the *Colby falling in the well story* anytime company visited."

Jarvis then told of a fourth grade spelling bee he and the other logger children participated in. He'd won on the word nausea. This was the first time he'd really opened up. On a roll, he then told how he'd broken his wrist in a basketball game.

"I bought you a football for your second birthday," Bud said. "Caught hell from your mother. She didn't want her little boy getting hurt." He smiled. "Worked out in her favor though. You didn't like it. You went out the next morning and stole…well, I should say traded without permission—the football for a neighbor's kid's basketball."

"I always dreamed about being a Boston Celtic. I wanted to be Larry Bird."

"You sure did, it was all you talked about. Finally I took you to a game in Boston. You had the time of your life."

Angie waited for Jarvis to agree, but beneath the mustache

his lips had dipped into a frown. "I don't recall ever leaving that logging camp. Not to go anywhere."

"Funny how the brain erases some things, isn't it?"

"Yeah, funny."

"So, why didn't you become a basketball player?" Angie asked.

"After Mom died, I came back to the states and played through high school. I was pretty good, averaged twelve points a game, coupla blocked shots." Jarvis shrugged. "When I was a senior, some scout came and watched one of our championship games. When one of my teammates—a guy who averaged less points, re-bounds, *and* blocked shots—got the call, I hung up my sneakers. I know it sounds petty, but it broke my spirit. Anyway, a couple weeks later, a career counselor came and talked to all the seniors. I got hooked on police work."

"I think you chose well," Gloria said.

While Jarvis talked, Angie watched Carson. His demean-or was sad, wistful. She felt bad for this man who'd missed his children's exploits, their accomplishments. Angie set her utensils across the plate and pushed it away.

"I guess that's what it takes to get you to eat right," Gloria said, "home cooking."

With stalled breath, Angie waited for the bomb to drop: Glo-ria's suggestion that she stay on permanently. But she merely rose from the chair and walked to the refrigerator. She returned with a pie, said, "apple," and began dishing out slices.

"Mmm," Bud and Jarvis said at the same time.

She watched the men. They were nothing alike. Even though seriously ill, Bud Dodge presented an image of energy and socia-bility. She'd rarely known Jarvis as anything more than somber and steadfast. He was brave and determined; if he got his teeth into anything—like this murder investigation—there was no dragging him away. Then again, as time passed, she saw different sides to the serious man. Last night, for example. And tonight, when he related stories about his past. His manner became much more like his father's.

"Pie, Angie?" Gloria asked.

"No thanks," Angie said.

"Come on, you can eat a piece." Gloria slid a huge hunk onto a plate and pushed it in Angie's direction.

Jarvis and Bud dug into theirs and ate in silence till the last crumb of crust disappeared. Jarvis hauled Angie's untouched plate toward him and ate her slice too.

Bud stood up and began clearing the table. "You two go get ready to leave, Jarvis and I can handle this," he told Angie and Gloria. Gloria smiled like a schoolgirl just asked to her first prom.

Jarvis gathered the paper napkins, crumpled them in balls and heaved them into the trash container. Then he took her elbow and escorted her down the hall. They stopped outside Angie's bedroom door. "I wanted to tell you the news. Sergeant Wilson called as I was going out the door. He found cameras in John's lab and greenhouse."

"So, the theft wasn't a random act. Someone carefully planned this. Any way to determine when the equipment got installed?"

"Maybe. Wilson's having the stuff checked by an expert."

"Any way to trace where the camera signal is going?"

"I wondered the same thing. I'd guess yes because they can do it with cell phones. We'll know in the morning. The expert is coming up from Nashua first thing."

She put a hand on her doorknob. "One more thing," Jarvis said. "I did as you suggested and called the registrar of the iris society. He said he didn't know John personally, but knew of him. He has…had…a good reputation in the industry. The registrar said unfortunately there's no proof John ever produced a red. There's no application for registration, he's published no articles, given no symposiums."

"What about the theft? Did he have any theories? Any suspects?"

"No. But he did tell me one interesting thing. He said every day he gets claims by people saying their 'discovery' has been stolen. 'The simple fact is,' he said, 'it's easy to steal pollen. I'm in your greenhouse. All I do is distract you a moment. I already have a Q-tip cupped in my hand. I knock some pollen onto it and stick it in a baggie. Then I take it to my host plant and deposit it…' I forget where he said it goes. Anyway, poof, you've got off-spring." He chucked her under the chin. "I prefer the good old fashioned way of breeding."

Angie laughed. "There was nothing old fashioned about last night," she said and ducked into her room.

Nine

"Okay, thanks for your help." Jarvis clicked off the phone and then slapped his palms down on the table. He flung himself into the worn kitchen chair and bent his head into cupped hands. What did it take to get a break in the case?

Across the table, Wilson's feet scuffed the floor. Jarvis looked up. "You look tired."

Wilson grinned. "Haven't slept in four nights. Not since Bennie went into labor Thursday at midnight. Had the baby Friday afternoon. Came home last night."

Typical Ambrose Wilson. He'd play football with the other two sons all day, visit Bennie in the hospital and then work till he dropped.

"So, why *do* women wait till the middle of the night to go into labor?" Wilson asked.

"Because that's when their men are home from work." Jarvis counted on his fingers even though he had only one item on the list. "Here's what we have. Sondergaard left Amsterdam via United Airlines. Destination Logan Airport in Boston. That was ten days ago, which matches with what we've got from the waitress who saw him and Bloom at the diner. And that was seven days before the theft." Jarvis added more fingers. "Coupla questions based on what we know. One: if Sondergaard planned to visit Bloom in Alton Bay, why not fly into Manchester? Two: he's keynoting a conference in Philly where John Bloom is also scheduled to appear. Why not wait and see him there?"

"Maybe he wanted to visit Boston. You know, see a Bruins game. Take a duck boat ride."

"Duck boats don't run this time of year."

"Very funny," Wilson chided. "Maybe Sondergaard didn't plan on visiting Bloom until after the reservations were made."

"Or, Bloom contacted him once he was in the US."

"At least someone could find him."

"Damn." Jarvis got up and grabbed a box of 'Nilla Wafers from the top of the file cabinet. The wall clock said 7:22 a.m. He leaned against the counter and ate two. "The airline said Sondergaard arrived in Boston on Tuesday. Our next move is to trace his movements from the airport." He handed Wilson his cell phone and a Massachusetts telephone book. "You check car rental agencies. See if anybody rented to a pink skinned man with a Danish accent."

"You think he would've used his own name?"

"No reason he shouldn't. At least not till he got to Alton Bay." Jarvis picked up the cordless phone. "I'll check hotels. His flight arrived at 11 p.m. Chances are he spent at least one night in Boston."

"Isn't there a Hilton right beside the terminal?"

"Yup. First place I'm checking."

Two hours and a pot of coffee later, both men set down their phones.

"Damn," Jarvis said, "all we've got is that Sondergaard spent one night at the Hilton. He didn't rent a car, buy a bus ticket or hire a cab, that we know of."

"Not under his regular name. Hey," Wilson added, "what if I go to Boston and flash the guy's picture around? That's got to do more to jog memories than over the phone."

"I have a better idea. Why don't we set the Boston PD on it? After you leave here, stop at the station and fax 'em Sondergaard's information. Then call and make sure somebody's on this." Jarvis scribbled a name on a sticky note and stuck it on Wilson's sleeve. "Speak to this man. We went to the academy together. Besides, he's bucking for promotion."

Jarvis stood up and opened the refrigerator. He ducked inside. "I was so sure Sondergaard drove that dark SUV the neighbor spotted on Bloom's street that night."

"What did you say?"

He repeated what he said as he pulled out bins looking for something to eat. He spotted a green plastic bowl. Couldn't remember what was in it. "You'd think Sondergaard would have a cell."

Wilson fumbled in his shirt pocket and came out with a folded slip of paper. "I got it from the Danish police. I've called about a hundred times but nobody's answering." He dialed the number.

Jarvis let go of the refrigerator door and set the bowl on the counter. He opened the container, sniffed the contents and flinched back.

Wilson laughed, then clicked off the phone. "No answer."

Jarvis heaved the bowl in the sink and Wilson laughed again. Jarvis scowled at him and went back to the fridge. This time he found eggs and a hunk of cheese without too much green. He made omelets while Wilson read from one of the folders of information.

"Donna Marks was born in the area, Ossipee, to be exact. Attended Ossipee area schools, graduated in '79. Married Paul Zimmerman in '84, she was twenty-two. They bought the florist shop fourteen years ago. Tax records show it was a long road, but the place is finally making money. She and Paul divorced last fall. She's been attending a lot of conferences. Most recently April in Albuquerque. She spent a lot over the last four years buying irises from around the world, mostly from two places in Oregon: one called Cooleys the other, Shreiners."

Jarvis punched down the lever on the toaster. "That is the second time Oregon has been mentioned."

"What's your point?"

"Trynne McCoy is from Oregon."

"Think there's a connection?"

"Dunno. Question: does Donna Marks have any genetic background or education?"

"Far as I can see there's nothing beyond high school."

Jarvis set a plate in front of Wilson who went to work spreading grape jelly on a slice of toast. The toaster popped up and Jarvis slathered butter on the dark slices of wheat bread.

Wilson's cell rang. He listened several moments, making notes on the back of a file folder. Then he hung up and took a bite of omelet. He wadded the food in his left cheek, pointed the empty fork at Jarvis, and said, "John's three million has been traced to a trust account in a London bank."

"Lemme guess, there's a mile long paper trail they're trying to unravel."

"Whoever is at the heart of this did a lot of planning."

They ate in silence. Jarvis played with scenarios in his mind. None would gel into anything worth discussing with Wilson. Afterward, he instigated Wilson's help moving the red leather chair from the living room to the garage.

Wilson flopped in the chair, breathing hard. "Why you getting rid of this? It's nice."

"I…need change."

As if with sudden understanding, Wilson nodded. "You want me to take it?"

Jarvis thought a moment. Yes, Liz would want them to have it. He nodded.

"Okay," Wilson said, hefting himself from the cushion. "I'll come back with my pickup."

"After you get some sleep."

"Can't…I have to take the boys to their karate class."

"Why don't you get a couple hours shut-eye? I'll take them for you."

"Thanks, but I'd like to do it."

"Wouldn't due to fall asleep on the road."

"It's not that far. I'll be fine."

They shook hands. As Wilson folded his lanky frame into his wife's station wagon, Jarvis said, "Hey, see if you can get a number for Sondergaard's wife."

He remained standing with his hands in his pockets a few minutes. Then he went in the house and carried the barbells from the cellar to the spot where Liz's chair had stood. Outside the window, a neighbor walked by leading a small dog who obviously hated getting his feet wet. The little animal alternated between tiptoeing and hopping with one foot off the ground.

The barbells glared at Jarvis as if daring him to pick them up. He did and, after several minutes, his limbs and lungs achieved a rhythm. He thought about Angelina, and the decision made yesterday—to invite her on a trip. So they could get better acquainted. So he could show her the man he really was.

Lifting felt like it had in the old days. Though every part of him burned with the exertion, he felt fantastic.

Yes, a trip would be just the remedy, for their lives and their relationship. Not to Boston as he first thought. Not when the case was over. They'd go to Philadelphia, the site of this weekend's iris society conference. Sondergaard would be there.

Jarvis stopped to catch his breath. Damn. How could he have gotten so out of shape? The barbell thumped to the floor. Head down, palms flat on his thighs, he pulled in a labored breath. Sooner or later exercising would feel good again.

Most important, sexual stamina would return. He hoped.

Jarvis inhaled and lifted the barbells. In the old days, exercising grew rote. Barbell up. Barbell down. A mindless activity that allowed his brain to sort out problems.

But the case's problems were multiplying like rabbits. He pushed them away for a glorious five minutes of hot shower. Then he dressed and made a sandwich from past the sell-by date ham. While wolfing it down, he called Manchester airport and bought two tickets for Thursday afternoon. Then he drove to the theater to tell Angelina the news.

Angie, Tyson and Trynne stood at the base of a very soggy Mount Major. Melted snow raced downhill in small paths following no rhyme nor reason. Angie hefted her bag on both shoulders.

A well-trod hiking trail, once an old logging road, wound ahead for about a dozen feet, then disappeared between the trees. She gestured for Trynne to lead the way. Trynne carried a walking stick, a lopsided length of oak that Blake had carved and varnished at least ten years ago. She carried a backpack with water, cell phone and first aid kit. Tyson followed and then Angie, her pack loaded with veggie sticks and finger foods.

"How's the investigation going?" Trynne called over her shoulder.

Angie kept her eyes glued to the slippery trail for roots or downed limbs. The sun was bright but the brisk breeze countermanded its warmth. "Slow. Where's Blake today?"

"At his office. He's trying to find another wholesaler."

"Another wholesaler?" Tyson asked from ten feet behind.

"Oh, you probably didn't know. John Bloom supplied the shrubs and plants for Blake's company."

Trynne stopped and waited for Angie and Tyson to catch up. "Isn't it beautiful here?"

Below, the grey of the bare hardwoods glimmered stark against a backdrop of dark green pines and cedars. Mountains stretched as far as the eye could see. The ski slopes on the distant Presidential Range looked spiderwebs. As they stood, the mournful hoot of a bear echoed across the valley. Angie waited but no answering call came.

Trynne turned from the late winter vista and pushed her hands deep in her pockets. "What a waste of human life, but also a gifted scientist."

Nobody had to ask what she meant. Tears stinging her eyes, Angie started walking again.

"There's a fork, which way should we go?" Tyson asked.

"Left," answered Trynne. "In about a half mile there's a plateau overlooking the lake."

They hiked the rest of the way in silence, their boots making slapping sounds on the wet ground. The plateau, an area about thirty feet across, did indeed look out over the lake, and the surrounding valley. The mountains lay in tiers before them as though placed by some enormous hand.

"No matter how many times I see this…." Angie said, not bothering to finish her thought.

"I love the way the air smells," Trynne said.

"Like pine and cedar and—" Angie groped for the word she wanted, but Tyson said it simply.

"Cold." He took a sheet of plastic from his pack and spread it on the ground. They sat. Tyson poured soup into Styrofoam cups.

Trynne spoke as she opened bags of veggie sticks. "Jarvis said you called the iris society."

"Yes," Angie replied. "If I were the thief, I'd be anxious to register it—to let the powers that be know about my new creation."

"John didn't do that?" Tyson asked.

"Apparently not. The iris society president said something I hadn't thought of: John, or even the thief, could register the flower as dark rose or some other color. The fact that it *is* red is all that's important in the end. The important thing is the registration."

Trynne waved a stick of celery as she spoke. "And that it reproduces."

"That goes without saying. She also said a good scientist would back up his data off-site."

"What's off-site?" Tyson asked.

"On CDs or something he can store off the property," Trynne said. "I keep mine in a safe deposit box at the bank."

Tyson used a napkin to wipe his mouth. "Does anybody know for sure whether John backed up the data?"

"No."

No self-respecting scientist would *not* keep records. It just wasn't done. Angie wondered if John emailed the information to Sondergaard and he did the backing up. She considered mentioning Pedar Sondergaard, to see if Trynne knew of him in the genetic world, but if Jarvis hadn't said anything yet maybe he didn't want the name to be public knowledge.

"If developing the red is such a big deal," Tyson said, "I mean, I don't know much about genetics, but wouldn't something like the discovery of the red benefit the whole genetic world?"

Trynne dumped the last of her soup on the ground then dropped the cup into a paper bag with the rest of the trash. "Absolutely. It could open doors in a hundred other fields. The new color possibilities could be amazing."

"Did you and John ever talk about this?"

Trynne shook her head. "No. At least not in specific terms. We talked about how nice it would be if it happened, but I didn't have the idea John was any closer than I was with my ovine work."

"Donna said there are several ways to propagate irises."

"There are the normal ways via seeds or pollen," Trynne said, "which is pretty much grade-school biology. You snip off the tip of the anther and stick it in—"

"Anther?" Tyson asked, standing and settling his cap tighter to his head.

"The anther is the filament in the middle of the flower. All flowers have them. They hold the pollen."

"Then this pollen is used to breed with other flowers?"

"Right. But then there's genetic splicing. The process is being used more and more often. I'm using genetic splicing for Monsanto."

"What the hell's genetic splicing?" Tyson asked.

Trynne stood up and brushed off the back of her jeans. "It's combining the genetic material, the DNA. The process allows us to identify specific genes, remove and clone them to be used in another part of the same organism, or in this case, an entirely different one. It makes the genetic material capable of performing new functions."

Angie made a scoffing sound. "Technology."

"The process is far from new. The technique became possible during the fifties when Francis—"

"You're getting too technical now," Angie said.

"Oh, sorry."

"Come on, let's get started back."

"I'm sorry," Tyson said, "but the whole genetic thing feels wrong to me."

"In what way?" Trynne asked.

"No offense Trynne, I know it's your life work and all that, but messing with animals' insides is just wrong."

"What's wrong with making things different colors?"

"What's wrong with being happy with the way things are?"

Trynne zipped her pack and slung the wide straps over her shoulders. "I thought hiking up here would help get my mind off all this—"

"You brought it up."

Angie's cell phone rang. She almost laughed at the irony of being saved by the bell, dug it from her pack by the fifth ring and checked the caller ID. "Hi Jarvis."

"Where are you?"

"On top of Mount Major, where else?" She grinned. "Where are you?"

"At the theater. I came here to see you."

"It's Monday, we took some time off."

"Who's we?"

"Trynne and Tyson. Hold on a second." She held the phone to take a picture of the three of them and the surroundings.

Jarvis remained silent for several seconds. Angie wondered if one of two things was happening: the picture hadn't arrived or his jealousy had kicked up its ugly head again. Finally he said, "Nice view. When are you coming back?"

His voice sounded tight. "What's wrong?" she asked, knowing.

"Nothing."

"We should be back within the hour. Are you sure everything's all right?"

"Yeah."

"Okay." Angie shut the phone and put it away.

"Anything wrong?" asked Trynne.

"He says no. But he sounded tense." She shrugged. "He's probably just tired."

"Haven't you checked out his sleeping habits firsthand yet?"

"She has," Tyson said with a grin.

Angie turned a questioning gaze on him and he smiled wider. "You rattled the door."

"No."

"Well then, we were having an earthquake."

She stood and stretched, bending forward and back, and then side to side. She lifted two edges of the plastic sheet and shook off the dirt and leaves. Trynne helped fold it and slip it into the pack.

"I just had a thought," Tyson said. "What if *John* trashed his own place?"

"Why would he do that?" Trynne's tone suggested it was sacrilege to suggest such things.

"What if he couldn't produce the flower? What if he ran out of money? What if all those years, while dedicating himself to one flower, he let everything else go, realized his life had gone by, he had no family, no friends."

"You think he used the play as an alibi?" Angie asked.

"He wouldn't do that," Trynne protested.

Tyson kept on, undaunted. "You both said he hardly ever left his property. But in spite of that, he agreed to be in the play."

"He wouldn't—" Trynne said again but Angie interrupted.

"He's got a point. You said you and Blake got together with John either at your house or a restaurant. The night of the play, he specifically invited five people to his place."

Trynne stumbled and almost fell back to the ground. "John

wouldn't—Angie, he was a reputable businessman. He was my friend."

A morning breeze blew up from the valley raising goose bumps on Angie's neck. Or maybe it had nothing to do with the wind at all. She zipped the parka a little tighter to her chin.

Trynne did likewise but stopped mid-zip. "There's something you're both forgetting. It's fine and dandy to think John staged the whole theft thing—maybe he did, maybe he didn't. But he sure as heck didn't shoot himself."

"No," Angie had to agree.

"Trynne," Tyson said, "you might want to cover your ears but, isn't there the remotest chance John committed suicide?"

"What!" Trynne's voice echoed across the valley. They all stood listening as time after time her shocked word ricocheted back at them.

"You're thinking he substituted Jarvis's real gun for the prop gun," Angie offered.

The trio started walking, retracing their steps downhill in complete silence. Tyson's idea had merit. John arrived late to the last dress rehearsal. He had as much opportunity as anyone else to have gone to Jarvis's house and switched the guns. But the hypothesis didn't feel right. John wasn't the dramatic type. He wasn't one to kill himself in front of an auditorium full of people. He'd be more likely to do it in the privacy of his laboratory: the place that betrayed all his dreams.

They arrived back in the parking area. Angie's calves were stiff from the downhill trek. Tyson's breath came in short bursts. When he saw Angie looking at him he chuckled. "Really out of shape."

Trynne patted her backside. "Same here. We should do this more often."

Angie didn't think that Tyson, after Trynne's reaction to his theories, would be too apt to want her along next time.

He dropped Angie at her condo. The odors of last night's dinner were stale in the air. She lit a candle, took a shower and dressed, then made a call, to the US patent office. The woman who finally came on the line sounded winded, her voice raspy, as though she had either run a great distance to answer the phone, or was a heavy smoker. It took quite some time to explain the situation. Angie asked if anyone had applied for a patent for the process of developing a red iris.

The woman laughed. "An iris? You mean a flower?"

"Yes. A red bearded iris. A man in Alton Bay, who's dedicated most of his life to developing one, has been murdered. His greenhouse and laboratory were ransacked. We think they wanted to steal his life's work."

"You from the cops?"

"Indirectly."

"What's that mean?"

Angie didn't want to lie but didn't want to sacrifice a chance for a clue. "It means that I work closely with them, but I'm not one officially."

"Oh, you're like a detective." Angie didn't reply. The woman went on, "What a shame about the guy dying. Not sure what I can do to help though."

"I need to know if the thief has registered the process yet. Or, better yet, if I can find out that Mr. Bloom actually had time to register it himself.

Angie heard typing in the background and hoped it meant the woman was helping and not calling the crackpot line direct to the FBI.

"There's nothing in the system to do with irises. At least not for several years. The last one I have here is a long-stemmed variety with purple flowers. Hold on while I keep looking." A minute and several more clicks on the keyboard and she returned. Her hoarse voice turned rife with excitement. "I found a red!"

Angie sat up straighter in her chair.

The next time the woman spoke, she sounded deflated. "This can't be the one. This is dated ten years ago."

"Was the developer a man named Pedar Sondergaard?"

"Why yes. Wait—why didn't I think of this earlier? I have a stack about a mile high of applications waiting to be entered into the computer." There was a squeak, as though she'd shoved back her chair. "Hold on. I'll put you on hold while I look." Next came a giant sigh. "God, I didn't realize how many there were. Why don't I take your number and call you if I find something."

Angie didn't want to hang up. Once untethered to the phone, few people actually returned calls. In spite of her reservations, Angie gave the woman her number then took the woman's name. "I appreciate the trouble you're taking, Tory. I hope I'll hear from you soon."

"Okay. I'll call. I promise. You have me really curious about all this. Talk to you in a few."

"Bye."

"Wait!" Tory called. Angie froze. "I think I found it. No, this can't be the right one. This application is dated January 15th. Sorry to get your hopes up." Silence on the line. Then, "It must be the wrong one, the name on the application is a…wait a second while I figure out how to pronounce this. You wouldn't believe some of the screwball names people have. Like this one, the name is Jan…that's easy enough. But the last name is Van…Blozend… not sure how to pronounce it. I'll spell it, B-L-O-E-M."

"Did you say the date was January 15th?" Angie asked.

"Right. When did you say this guy died?"

"Friday night."

"Then this couldn't be his flower cuz this is almost March. Not if they applied for the patent three months before his death…"

"Was the flower named Rhapsody, by any chance?"

"They name the things?"

"Yes. Just like when you register dogs or cats."

"Hold on while I look for it. There isn't a place specifically for naming things Yes, it's called *Rhapsody in Scarlet*. What a pretty name."

"Can you spell the guy's name for me, please?"

"Why don't I just fax this to you."

"If it's not violating any rules."

"Patents are public information. Besides, if this guy *stole* that flower and *murdered* your guy, this thing will probably never go through."

Angie gave Tory the only fax number she knew, the one at the police station, thanked the woman and hung up.

So, the development process for *Rhapsody in Scarlet* was applied for three months before John's death. Three months ago. What the hell? It was possible someone stole it and John had spent the last three months trying to get it back. Without calling in the authorities? Without at least notifying the Iris Society? They were the quintessential group for anyone involved with irises.

A third party could be involved, this Jan Van whatever. Jan and Sondergaard put up the money and John did the actual work. That made sense.

Angie dialed Jarvis's number. Jarvis said hi then they both spoke at the same time, "I have news." They laughed and Jarvis said he'd pick up a pizza and be right over.

While she waited, Angie Googled Jan Van Blozend Bloem. She found iris articles, all related in one way or another to the pursuit of the red. Apparently he led the quest. She did a search for *true red iris*. On the web site of a breeder from Virginia she learned that not only were iris breeders having a difficult time producing a red, rose breeders faced equal challenges developing a blue.

The doorbell rang. She pulled open the door with a *welcome Jarvis* pucker to her lips, but it was Bud Dodge. His grin of understanding made Angie laugh and her face burn. "Mom's not here but come in anyway."

He stepped in and shut the door against the chill wind off the bay. "I'm not looking for Gloria."

"Where is she, by the way?"

"Shopping down in Concord."

"But she doesn't have a car."

"I offered to let her take my Escalade but she said it was too big. I called her a cab."

Angie didn't want to think of the cost of a cab ride to and from Alton Bay. No matter. Gloria could afford it. Angie took Bud's coat: cashmere. Somehow she resisted the temptation to bury her cheek in its soft folds. She hung the garment in the closet.

"I hope I'm not interrupting anything."

"No, I was just doing some research."

"On the Bloom case?"

"Sit down, won't you? Yes, the Bloom case. I'm really worried they're going to somehow blame Jarvis."

"So am I. That's why I'm here." Bud lowered himself in the center of the sofa. He clenched gnarled fingers in his lap and leaned forward. The man's watery blue eyes were bright today. "I want to help."

"Help?" she asked, sitting in her usual chair.

"Yes, give me some investigating to do."

Angie laughed. "All I do is follow hunches. Sometimes they pan out."

"I heard they frequently pan out for you. Give me a hunch to follow. You're busy with the theater. I have all kinds of time."

"All right, when Jarvis gets here, we'll talk about it."

Bud became occupied with twisting a big onyx ring on his left ring finger. What was it he didn't want to tell her? Finally he said, "Jarvis is being overly protective."

"He told you to…enjoy your retirement."

Bud's smile revealed lots of teeth. Angie would bet money they were still his own.

"So, you came to me thinking I'd aid you in doing something behind your son's back?"

"Not quite so blatant, but, yes."

"Did you have the nickname Bud for a long time?"

He thought a moment. "My father gave it to me because I was a small child. Rena never called me by it though. She liked the name Carson." His eyes flickered toward the door. "So, give me a job."

What sort of job could she give that wouldn't be dangerous? That would satisfy Bud's yen, but wouldn't put her in a bad light with Jarvis. "How about this? Would you drive around to the car dealers and get brochures on hatchbacks?" She told about John's neighbor's identification of the nighttime visitors.

"What'll you do with the brochures?"

"I'll go to the neighbor to see if he can identify them."

"Great idea." He leaned forward. She reached out to help him rise, but he got up on his own. "I'll be leaving before Jarvis arrives. Wouldn't want to spoil your evening."

"You couldn't spoil anything." Angie followed him to the hallway and retrieved his coat. "I'm glad you and Jarvis were able to get back together." She held the coat while he slipped his arms into the sleeves.

He turned and kissed her on the cheek. "I'm glad too. I'm especially glad he has you. He's wallowed in Elizabeth's death for far too long."

Angie had just enough time to fix her makeup before Jarvis punched the doorbell. He planted a kiss on her left temple and nudged the door shut with his hip. In the kitchen Angie poured chardonnay for herself and popped a beer for him. He flipped open the box and separated the slices of pepperoni pizza. The air filled with the luscious aroma. She sat and threw the pizza a disdainful glance.

"I thought you liked pizza," Jarvis said, sliding slices onto two plates.

"It doesn't like my hips."

"I like your hips." He held a slice with both hands, ready to take a bite. Instead, he said, "Sometimes I can't tell how you feel about me though."

"I like your hips."

"That's all?"

She avoided his gaze. She'd known this discussion would come up eventually. He took her plate and set it on the counter. "I care for you very much." She opened her mouth to say she cared for him too, but he put a finger to her lips. "I'm tired of being alone. And I'm tired of dating. I want a long-term relationship. Maybe marriage...someday." He shook his head as though discarding things to say. "The break with Will wrecked you, I know that. In a way that's a good thing. If you'd left that relationship without a backward glance, I'd be thinking twice about us. You know what I mean?"

"Yes, you're saying the fact that I suffered makes you happy."

He squeezed her hand. "It makes me glad you're a sensitive and caring person." A warm glow pulsed up her arm and into her heart. "I just wanted you to know how I felt."

Which was how? A cop experienced at interviews with reporters—almost like a politician. Saying a lot, but saying little. Angie stifled a grin and squeezed his hand. "I learned some things today."

Angie told what Trynne had said about the methods of breeding irises. "She says it's easy to steal pollen to propagate new varieties: go into the competitor's greenhouse with a little container. It doesn't have to be any bigger than this." She tapped a fingernail on a paper packet of salt that came with the pizza.

"Marvelous way to change the subject."

Angie sighed. "I'm not ready to talk about it yet. I can't think about a permanent future."

He kissed her cheek. "I understand. Sorry I brought it up."

"I'm glad you did." Then she palmed the salt packet again. "It's easy to hide in your hand. All you do is pluck off the tip of the anther and stick it in—"

"Anther?" Jarvis unfolded a napkin and wiped his mouth, taking particular care around his mustache.

"That's the filament in the middle of all flowers. They're what hold the pollen."

"This pollen is used to breed with other flowers?"

"Right."

He shook his head, as if it was more than he could comprehend.

"Let me guess, there's more."

"There might be another person involved." Angie told him about the call to the patent office.

He got up and went to the sink, speaking over the sound of running water as he washed his hands. "Okay, so you think Bloom, Sondergaard and this Van Whatever were partners?"

"I think it's a possibility."

He grabbed the towel hanging on the oven door. "Something went wrong with this partnership and Sondergaard and Van Whatever got together and ripped off Bloom."

"It's possible."

"Yeah, but why kill him?"

"I haven't worked that out yet."

Jarvis sat back on the stool. "By the way, John's journal wasn't in his Jeep."

"Damn. I thought…"

"The car had been jimmied. Very expertly. Nothing seemed missing. The CD player was intact. Coins in one of the cup holders. I figure the journal was there."

"That's why they broke in. I bet they did it the same time they switched guns."

He nodded, somber, and took another beer from the refrigerator. Angie refilled her wine. They carried the drinks to the living room and sat on the sofa. He crossed one leg over the other and put his arm around her shoulders. She leaned into the crook of his arm. He brushed her hair with his lips. They tilted their heads together. They interlaced fingers; he stroked the back of her hand with his thumb.

"Tyson had an interesting theory this morning," she said without looking up. "He wondered, what if *John* trashed his own place, and then invited us all to there so he could discover it."

Jarvis didn't speak.

"Tyson also wondered if John committed suicide."

After a long silence, Jarvis said, "I can't accept suicide."

"Neither could Trynne. She got pretty upset with Tyson for

mentioning it. Had you ever met John before the play?"

"No. There's no record of Bloom prior to when he appeared in Alton Bay. No income tax records, social security, school. Nothing. Neither can we find any record of his birth. Wilson's working on the idea that Bloom might be an alias."

That agreed with what Angie had emailed to Mary Grayson yesterday. Angie repeated the conversation to Jarvis. "I haven't heard back from her yet. One more thing: did you know John's nursery was the wholesale supplier to Blake McCoy's landscaping company?"

"No. That's interesting though. I talked to Blake this morning and he didn't mention anything about it."

Angie raised her head and kissed the left side of Jarvis's jaw. He smelled of Ivory soap. His stubble chafed her lips. A spark of static electricity clicked between them making them both laugh.

"Have I told you how much I enjoy your company?" he asked.

"Not today."

He removed his arm from her shoulder and backed a little to look in her face. "I—god, I'm awful with this kind of thing."

"You did pretty good in the kitchen."

"We've been seeing each other for almost nine months. Our relationship is good, but…I'd like it to move faster. Don't say anything, I know my jealousy has kept things on hold. I suspect that's the real reason you can't commit. Anyway, I want you to know I'm working on it. For the last six months I've been in counseling."

Counseling? He must really be serious about her.

"It's an online group. Hey, funny thing. My father went to counseling too." Jarvis shrugged. "Guess it runs in the family."

Suddenly he gazed at something over her right shoulder. When people couldn't meet your gaze didn't it mean they were lying? No, Jarvis wasn't lying; he was embarrassed. But desperate enough about their relationship that he had to open up. A rush of emotion pushed into her limbs and she squeezed his hand.

"I tried to see a psychiatrist. I—" He shrugged. "Made two appointments. But I couldn't make myself go into the office. I tried the group and…I think it's working. I care for you so much. Someday I'd like…Someday maybe we can…Damn. I can't make the words come out right." He sucked in a breath and said, fast, "I want our relationship to lead to marriage."

Marriage?

"Once your divorce is final. And I can rid myself of this jealousy thing."

Marriage?

He dropped his foot to the floor and shifted on the cushion. The kiss was slow, the hands gentle, the touch sure. Angie let herself be carried to someplace far away, where desire swirled like tidal pools and passion soared like eagles.

Ten

In the dim stripes of moonlight squeezing between the mini-blinds Colby Jarvis eased from under the covers and dressed. Angelina slept like a baby curled on her left side, one hand under the pillow, the other dangling over the edge of the mattress. She wore a smile, like she'd just sampled Godiva chocolate. His groin twitched and nearly talked him into getting back in bed.

Money jingled in his pockets and he quickly silenced it with a hand cupped around the outside of his pants. He caught a glimpse of himself in the mirror and looked away. A balding middle aged man with the beginnings of a paunch, and a job that occupied more hours than he'd noticed before she came along. What could he offer someone like her?

In the living room, he sat to put on socks and shoes. Her wine glass and his beer were still on the coffee table and it made him smile. For the first time since they'd met, she'd neglected to clean up. He took them to the dishwasher, then measured grounds and water into the coffeemaker so all she'd have to do was push the button when she got up. He tried to write her a note, something that said he'd enjoyed himself without sounding like a school kid. *Did you like it too? Check yes or no.* After seven tries he settled on *Will bring you pizza any time. J*

The Jeep's motor rumbled loud in the still of the night. He stopped at the twenty-four hour drive through for a bucket of coffee and sucked down the life-giving power on the way to the office. Jarvis's stomach growled and he almost turned around and went back for an egg sandwich.

Jarvis picked up the folder from his desk, skulked to the car and drove home. Within minutes he was seated on his couch, coffee in one hand, autopsy report on Lonnie "Sticks" Lawson in the other. He leaned back, sock-clad feet crossed on the coffee table.

Victim died of a gunshot to the back of the head. Probably from a .22. Powder burns and blood spatter put the barrel less than half a meter away. Entry angle suggested he'd been kneeling. The side table cabinet door stood open. Lawson had probably been searching inside. Final evaluation: homicide. Time of death: approximately 4:30 a.m. No one had seen or heard anything more than what sounded like a car backfiring. Made sense, John's bedroom was at the back of the house. Most of the sound would've been muffled by all those cardboard boxes that lined the walls. Jarvis knuckled his burning eyes and thought about Angelina sleeping snug in her bed. And wondered if he should come right out and ask her to marry him. Jarvis drank down the rest of the coffee and resumed thinking about the case because if he lost himself thinking about Angelina, nothing would get done—not that anything productive was happening.

The second page in Wilson's packet was a statement from the neighbor Frank Chute. Wilson called him cantankerous and got little out of him except that a dark SUV had come from, or turned around in, Bloom's driveway about nine-fifteen the night of Bloom's death. Jarvis grinned at how much more Angelina had gotten from the man. That finesse, that smooth way of relating to people; that's what made her so good at ferreting out information.

"Damn." Jarvis flung the paper. It fluttered away, scuffing off the surface of the coffee table and wafting to the floor. More than three days and nothing new in the case.

Okay, look at things from another angle: John Bloom's arrival in town in 1999. Except for Blake McCoy, the man didn't seem to have any male friends. So far not much attention had been focused on that relationship. Today he'd seek out McCoy for a long, enlightening chat. If Bloom *had* trashed his own place and/or committed suicide, maybe he'd let something slip.

But Jarvis couldn't stop wondering about the women in Bloom's life. During May, June and July, his nursery had to be knee deep in female gardeners. Hadn't he hit on a single one? Which led him to think again about the number of years he'd been celibate. Jarvis slammed his heels on the table. Liz died in '98. He made love—if what he did could be called that—to Angelina on Saturday. He launched himself up and stomped to the kitchen for something to eat. But the cupboard was bare. When had he last shopped? Okay, never mind the food, never mind the sex or the length of time between. He flopped on the couch. Think about the case.

What about the compact car the neighbor spotted at Bloom's house? Could Donna Marks be the girlfriend? Shit, there were dozens of blue hatchbacks out there. But not dozens whose owners were iris breeders.

The clock chimed. He sat up and blinked it into focus. Eight o'clock. What time had he fallen asleep? How did he sleep through the thing chiming so close without it waking him?

Jarvis showered and phoned to ask Blake McCoy to meet him at the diner.

By eight-forty, the two men were seated in a booth at the Olde Bay Diner with coffees and orange juices. Blake wore a houndstooth jacket over a yellow button-down shirt, open at the throat. His clothes were of good quality, well pressed. His hair needed trimming but he was shaved and smelled like Polo cologne. He seemed at ease as he dumped four sugars into his cup. Wasn't he curious why Jarvis had asked him here?

"I wanted to ask about your relationship with John," Jarvis said finally.

"Your sergeant has already questioned both Trynne and I at length."

"I know. I wanted to follow up on something your wife said: that John never invited you to his place. Didn't you think that unusual?"

Judy arrived to take their orders. When she left, Jarvis repeated the question.

"No. John was a very private person."

"Did he share any of his work with you?"

"Not the iris stuff if that's where you're going with this. He didn't talk about irises. He did talk about the nursery."

"Seems funny. You two being friends and all."

Blake shrugged.

"How long had he been your wholesaler?"

"Since I opened the business last year."

"Tell me about John's girlfriend."

He drew off his heavy-rimmed glasses and regarded Jarvis a moment with deep blue eyes. "I didn't know he had one." He pointed the eyeglasses at Jarvis. "Wait just a second, you aren't insinuating Trynne...and him." He shook his head hard.

"How can you be so sure?"

Blake slipped the glasses on, carefully fitting the stems over his ears. Then he drank. Jarvis waited, returning the same intense gaze he'd received before asking the question. Finally Blake replied, "Because I kept a very close eye on them."

"Because..."

Blake gave a one-shoulder shrug.

"Did you have reason to think they might be back together?"

"I just wanted to be sure it didn't happen."

"How exactly did you keep a close eye on them? How do you know what your wife does while you're at work?"

"I don't. But I know how dedicated they both are to their work, so they're probably in their labs. Besides, I know when her car's been used."

So, Blake McCoy spied on his wife. How trusting. "Okay, so let's get back to—"

Judy brought their food and a refill on coffee.

"Your questions are starting to sound very much like interrogation."

"Sorry, force of habit. Just see if you can think of any other men who might've gone fishing with John, met him for coffee. A friend. A woman who might've been in his life."

"Look Jarvis…" He sighed. "Blake wasn't my friend. We didn't hang out. I don't know who he hung out with. The only reason I even spoke to him was because of Trynne. When we went out, they talked, I smiled and listened, and answered if either of them directed something at me."

"I guess I'll have to talk to your wife."

"If anyone knows, she will."

"So, when you ordered shrubs from him, you never shot the breeze. Never spoke about anything but business."

"Shit. We talked about the weather, about politics. We talked about wholesale stuff. But we never talked about his friends, either male or female." Blake pushed his half-full plate away, stood up and left. He didn't even attempt to pay for the food.

Jarvis watched him march to his office, attached to the diner building. He dialed Wilson's number. "It's Jarvis. I just had an interesting discussion with Blake McCoy. I assume you did a full background on him?"

"I did. It's on your desk."

"Thanks. What's on your agenda today?"

"I'm on my way to talk with Donna Marks. Hey, I found the agency where Sondergaard rented his car. It's a white Buick Riviera."

"Doesn't fit any of the vehicle descriptions. Damn. I really thought we were on to something." Jarvis finished his breakfast and telephoned Angelina. After nine-thirty, surely she and Gloria were up. The house phone rang unanswered. Angelina was probably out jogging. But where was her mother?

A movement out the corner of his eye brought his attention back to Blake's office. Angelina strode up to the door.

Blake's grand opening of Lakes Region Yard Design last fall had been a great success. The three desks in the small room were overloaded with charts and architectural designs. Angie peered in through the sliding glass doors. Her target sat behind the center desk. He had a pencil in his hand, but his chin was lifted toward the ceiling. He gazed into space. She pulled open the door and stepped inside. The place smelled like wet paper and she couldn't help wrinkling her nose.

Blake shook himself alert. He stood up from his chair and approached, wearing a sunny smile that looked forced. Too many teeth were showing.

"How's Trynne?" she asked.

"Okay, I guess." He pushed an index finger under the bridge of his glasses and rubbed his nose. "I seem to have gotten mighty popular in the last hour." Before she could ask what he meant, he asked, "You didn't stop by to ask about Trynne. You probably see more of her than I do."

"I'm worried they're going to pin John's murder on Jarvis."

"So, you and he thought you'd see what you could do to pin it on me."

She almost asked what he meant, but didn't bother. She did ask, "How long have you known John moved back to town?" The question took him by surprise. He spluttered a moment, and she stopped him. "How long?"

"Look, I'm not telling you anything. You'll just turn it against us."

"You think I'm going to intentionally make one of my best friends look guilty?"

"If it'll get your lover out of trouble. Yes."

"Well, I wouldn't. Look, Blake, I don't think either of you are guilty of such a terrible thing, but if you don't help me sort things out we might never get to the bottom of it."

Blake lowered himself into the chair, laying both forearms

across the architect's drawing he'd been working on. "I knew John was here from just about first the day he got in town. It was April '99. I was getting gas down at the Mobil station. I turned at the sound of grinding transmission gears. I wasn't sure; hadn't seen the man since Trynne and I left Oregon."

"Did you talk to him?"

"No."

"Did you tell Trynne?"

"No."

Getting information was like picking up mercury from a broken thermometer. When did she find out he was here?"

His eyes narrowed. He removed the black-rimmed glasses and squinted at her. "It was November—seven months later—when he went before the zoning board for a permit to open his place. You already knew, didn't you?"

Angie shrugged. "Every time John's name is mentioned your eyes glaze over. Question: why use John as your wholesaler? Seems like there should be some animosity on his part."

Blake put the glasses back on. "Guess you should've asked him. I went to him because his prices were better, he had good selection and—"

"And because Trynne would've been suspicious if you hadn't."

"There's that too."

"How much did you plan to inherit by marrying Trynne?"

His eyes widened. His eyebrows disappeared into his curly hair. When they dropped back in place, his mouth was scowling. He stood up and strode close. "Is that really what you think? Friends all these years with you and that's how you felt?"

"I suspect you were friends with me the same way you were friends with John—because of Trynne and nothing more."

In one rush of motion, Blake whirled toward the door and wrenched it open. "I've had enough of your insinuations."

"Jarvis will be asking the same questions."

"If he's got warrants, then I'll answer." He waited till she stepped outside, slammed the door and clicked the lock in place.

Angie smiled. She loved making clear water turn muddy. Someone knocked on the diner window. Expecting to see Judy's grinning face, she was surprised to see Jarvis. She walked inside. As she passed Judy, the waitress tilted her head toward Blake's office. "What's wrong with him?"

"I'm not quite sure," Angie said, meaning it. "Could I please have a diet Coke?" She headed for Jarvis saying hi to some folks Will had sold a house to a few years ago.

"I just tried to call you," he said as she set her handbag on the back edge of the table and made herself comfortable.

"I was on my way to the theater. Tyson and I are meeting a playwright."

Blake came out of his office and stormed toward his shiny new Chevy pickup. He didn't glance toward the diner.

"Looks like you kinda pissed him off," Jarvis said.

"Looks like."

Judy brought the drink in a tall glass with lots of ice. Angie said no thanks to the offer of food. While she tore the paper off the straw and rolled it into a wad, she told Jarvis about the meeting with Blake.

"How do you think this is related to John's murder?"

"I'm not sure it's related at all. It's just curious the things you find out when you start asking questions."

"I bet that's not what pissed him off," Jarvis noted.

"No. I sort of accused him of marrying Trynne for the potential inheritance."

"That right?" Jarvis slipped his arms into his jacket and picked up her purse from the table. "Come on, let's get out of here."

Outside, they linked arms and walked along the sidewalk to the promenade overlooking the bay. Humor touched Jarvis's voice when he said, "I suppose you had reason for accusing Blake of being a gold digger."

"Do they really call men that—oh, never mind. What I can't

figure out is why he stayed with her all those years."

"Not sure what you mean."

"She had a falling out with her father. He disowned her. After so many years, you'd think Blake would see the futility of waiting for a reconciliation."

"Could be because she was supporting him. Far as I know he never held a job until he opened the company."

"Can't see how it relates to the case. By the way, Sondergaard rented a white Buick."

"Darn. I was so sure it would be a dark SUV. What about the guy you found dead in John's house? Is it possible he or one of his buddies rented one to come up here?"

"We checked. Nothing."

Angie kicked at a solid pile of snow. The hard outer shell broke and wet snow went flying in all directions. "I keep thinking about Blake and Trynne's relationship."

"They've been married what…thirty-something years? If he originally married her for the family money, and they disowned her when she ran off with Blake, shouldn't that be the end of it? Wouldn't he dump her the minute it looked like he wasn't getting a piece of the inheritance?"

"Maybe it's like you said, he stayed because she didn't make him get a real job."

"Then again, maybe she did."

Angie stopped walking. "You think she finally gave him an ultimatum?"

"Any indication that the time just preceding the business opening, there were problems?"

"Not really. They never were that close—you know, no hugging and squeezing in front of people. They didn't argue in front of me. I don't recall tense moments between them; nothing I could use to gauge the status of the relationship. I'm going to have a chat with Trynne this afternoon."

"If Blake hasn't called and forbidden her to see you any more."

"Not sure she'd listen if he did." They walked a moment longer sidestepping puddles and muddy spots.

"What kind of man takes a woman away from her family?" Angie asked.

"Not sure what you mean—oh, that Blake got Trynne disowned. Did you ever think it was her doing? That being a headstrong teenager she let things go too far? That maybe he wanted her to go back and make things right, but she refused?"

"He would try to repair things, though, wouldn't he?"

"She didn't go back. Which means what? That she suspected all along he wanted her inheritance?"

"I'm just throwing out ideas."

"I think you're choking on this one."

"I'm afraid you're right. I have to go meet Tyson now."

The playwright and Tyson were seated in the common area, at one end of the long table. She had long blonde hair—obviously colored by an expert because it looked natural. Angie joined them, draping her coat over the back of a chair.

Tyson performed introductions. "Angie, meet Sally Pruit, author of *Ring of Muddy Water*. Sally, this is Angelina Deacon, my partner."

Angie and Sally shook hands. "Nice to meet you," Angie said, "I love your hairstyle."

"Thanks, I get it done at a little place in Meredith." Sally's face was too long and narrow for her to be called pretty, her brilliant green eyes too close together. But she had a soft voice, a gracious manner. And Tyson was smitten. His attention remained fixed on Sally, even when Angie spoke.

"So, you're from around here?"

"I grew up in Laconia. I own a Condo in Meredith now."

Angie pulled out a chair and sat, pushing the stack of manuscripts to the center of the table. "I assume writing plays isn't your full-time occupation."

"No. I really love the theater, but I'm a ski slope designer by profession."

"Interesting. Do you ski?"

"As often as possible."

"Tyson skis too." As if by mutual consent, the preliminaries ended and they got down to business. Angie began, "Your play is very good. Neither of us guessed the ending." Sally beamed with pleasure. "That said," Angie continued, "there are a few scenes that don't work for us."

"I appreciate that," Sally said. "I'm open to any changes you suggest."

While Sally spoke, Angie watched her eyes. She seemed sincere though a bit lifeless. Angie would like to see more excitement, more animation about her characters and story. The trio spent two hours discussing and dissecting the play. In the end they decided to ready it for the May production. All three stood up.

"I'll have our lawyer give your attorney a call," Tyson said, "And get contracts written up."

"I can't tell you how happy I am," Sally said, looking at both of them. "So many years of rejections and dozens of 'it's not quite right for us'."

Tyson laughed. "This isn't exactly Broadway, you know."

"Not even Off Broadway," Angie added.

"I know," Sally said, "but at least it's a break. If just one of the right people were here…"

Angie had heard those same words from Tyson many times. What would she do if Broadway called him away? She scrunched her eyes shut till the burning went away. She'd deal with it if the time arose. For now, things were going well. The first weekend's cash receipts looked good.

As Angie said good-bye and left the building, she thought she heard Tyson ask Sally out for lunch.

At home, Angie slipped the mail from the box outside the front door. She had to work at removing a large brown envelope. It was from Mary Grayson.

In the kitchen, Angie leaned one butt-cheek onto a stool and tore open the envelope, careful not to rip the return address label. The envelope contained a copy of the previous year's iris society bulletin. A yellow sticky note with scribbled handwriting that said *see page 17.*

The bulletin was printed in black and white, bound like a magazine. She thumbed past the articles and graphs, looking for photos, and stopping on the page Mary had indicated. Angie didn't have to read the caption to know the tall man leaning on the podium was Pedar Sondergaard. Even though in black and white and not very sharp, Judy's description of the man who'd met John at the diner fit him to a T: tall and lean with very light skin. The lightish hair and beard could definitely have been red in color. High cheekbones and streamlined nose belied his Danish heritage. He had a finger in the air, obviously driving home a point to the assemblage.

He looked like an ordinary man. Handsome, clean-shaven. He didn't seem like a thief or a murderer.

Had he done the heinous deed? Sondergaard looked intelligent and self-confident. Stealing a person's entire life took both those qualities. An entire life. A big load. Suddenly Angie sat up straighter, she pulled herself completely onto the stool, the words *a big load* echoing in her head.

The thief couldn't exactly drive to the airport or UPS office and ship the stuff. Such a large load would draw attention. No, not if it was sent from one business to the next. That sort of thing was probably commonplace. Some of the shipment would require special packing and shipping. Temperatures in the hold of a plane would kill *Rhapsody in Scarlet.*

She got the phone book from her desk drawer and opened the yellow pages. Starting with Alstar and ending with Quasar, she called all the storage facilities in the area, asking if they'd rented a heated container to anyone around the middle of March. Most were suspicious, but once Angie explained that the questions were related to a murder investigation, two became very helpful. No one specifically asked if she was a police officer. Too bad none of the inquiries yielded anything useful. One company had rented to a man during that time period, but he'd been elderly. The person at Orion Storage said, "We rented a container during that period. The person was a tall woman with red hair and glasses. I can check the exact date if you need it."

Sondergaard was tall, but not elderly. John's female visitor was tall and slim but didn't have red hair. Angie asked the next obvious question, "Could the tall person have been a man in disguise?"

The woman thought a moment. "It was evening and not the best lighting. I didn't think of the person as a criminal or anything so I didn't concentrate on their features, but now that you mention it, I suppose it *could* have been a man. The voice was deep enough to be a male trying to talk like a woman."

Angie thanked the woman and hung up. Of the two suspects, Sondergaard was the only one who could have rented the compartment. Donna was definitely not tall and slim. But why would Donna steal *Rhapsody*? If she were John's girlfriend, surely he shared Rhapsody's discovery with her.

Then again, maybe he wouldn't have revealed his secret. Donna was a competitor, a fellow carousel rider vying for the same gold ring.

Something was missing. Probably something important. But darned if she could get a grip on it. As an afterthought, Angie called motels within a fifteen-mile radius asking if anyone renting a room over the past week and a half had loaded a large number of cartons into the room. The perishable plant and lab things definitely couldn't be left in the vehicle because some nights the temperature still dipped below freezing. It was a long shot that didn't pay off.

Angie poured a glass of milk and got two chocolate chip cookies that Gloria made during her Susie Homemaker phase. She took her 'lunch' to the living room and flopped in her favorite chair.

Why might Donna steal Rhapsody in Scarlet? Because she thought she was close to producing her own red by pollen, and couldn't allow the discovery via genetic splicing? Or maybe she craved the notoriety. No. Someone so dedicated to beauty and the love of flowers couldn't wreak such destruction. Could they?

Maybe Donna destroyed *Rhapsody* as revenge. The destruction at the greenhouse was a good indication that revenge, or its accompanying emotion, anger, guided the act. What had the iris society registrar said about pollen theft?—that it was very easy to do, they had frequent complaints about it.

What if John was the first thief; what if he stole pollen from one of Donna's plants and she was exacting revenge? Angie hadn't seen a red in Donna's greenhouse, which didn't really mean anything. If she herself had stolen something she certainly wouldn't leave it for just anyone to spot. Secondly, maybe Donna sold the red.

No, stupid idea, who'd buy a stolen plant?

Stupid question. You could always find someone to buy stolen goods; you just had to know where to look. Conferences. You might find somebody at conferences. You might also learn about genetics and cloning conferences.

Was Donna planning a trip to Philadelphia?

Eleven

Angie's front door opened. Gloria and Bud entered, laughing. "I can't believe you said that to him," Gloria said.

"I just made sure he was listening to you."

They laughed again.

Angie rose from the chair and went to greet them. She took two plastic bags from her mother and set them on the hall table. She hung Bud's coat in the closet. He held the door open with a spindly leg clad in sharply creased Levis, while he hung Gloria's coat. He wore a blue flannel shirt, open at the neck, a fluff of white hairs protruded from the vee.

Had the dark circles under his eyes deepened since yesterday? Did he look a little frailer? She took his arm. "Come sit down. Mom, will you make us some tea?"

While Gloria busied herself with the request, Angie spoke softly in Bud's ear. "I think you should be in the hospital. I can take you there and introduce you to—"

"No!" His sharp bark brought Gloria whirling around. "No more hospitals."

"I already tried to get him to go," Gloria said.

"I don't want to die connected to tubes and wires."

Angie couldn't blame him. "What about the pain? They can make you feel better."

"I have everything I need. Thank you for your concern."

"Where were you two last night? You weren't here when Jarvis and I got back."

"We went to a movie and dancing," Gloria called from the kitchen. "This morning he dropped me in Meredith so I could shop."

With a smile, he gestured at the pile of bags bearing names of different stores. "I hate shopping," he whispered. "This way, I don't have to pretend I'm having a good time, and she doesn't have to rush."

Gloria laughed. It was nice hearing her happy.

"Always worked with my wife."

The whistling kettle had her mother scurrying back to the kitchen. Angie and Bud followed. Gloria poured water into three cups. She plopped teabags after it and moved them to the table. They sipped tea while Bud and Gloria regaled her with their exploits of the previous evening. Bud's pale blue eyes shone whenever he looked at Gloria.

At one point he asked on the progress of the case.

"It's not moving. All we have a lots of suppositions."

"I don't understand why you all can't leave it be, and let the authorities handle it," Gloria said.

"I can't expect you to understand, Mom. It's personal."

"I know you're worried about Jarvis, but really, aren't the cops trained for things like this? Besides, they carry guns; they can handle the bad guys."

"One bad guy is dead. The others have left town," Angie said.

"You can't know they're gone. They could be living in the next apartment. Smiling to you every morning, but watching …waiting for a chance to—"

"Gloria," Bud said sharply.

"Sorry, I got carried away." Gloria concentrated on squeezing water from another teabag.

"She's got a point, though," Bud said, "People are rarely what they seem on the surface."

He was right. Angie changed the subject anyway. "What are you two up to today?"

Bud swallowed and set the cup down. "There's a concert in Boston. We thought we'd stay the night and go to the aquarium before returning here tomorrow. Unless there's something you need us for."

"You two go along and enjoy yourselves." One less thing for her to worry about. She wanted to ask Bud if he felt well enough to go, but didn't.

"Why don't you go get packed? I'll clean up the tea things," he told Gloria.

She kissed him on the cheek and left the room. He watched her and, as soon as her bedroom door clicked closed, said, "Will you please go into the hallway and bring the large envelope from the breast pocket of my coat?"

She did. He sat on a stool, opened the envelope and slipped out a stack of color printouts that Angie recognized as automobile models.

"I got these off the Internet," he said. "I thought it would be quicker than going around to each dealer."

"What a guy."

He'd printed copies of hatchbacks, of every make and model over the past five years. Each displayed from several angles. He'd even used a special program and made every car a bright blue color. She kissed him on the cheek. "These are wonderful, Bud. Thank you. You've saved me and Jarvis a lot of time and energy."

"Are you going to see if John's neighbor can identify them?"

"Yes."

"Wish I could be here to help."

"You've done plenty."

"Bah, this is nothing."

"You've saved me hours of legwork because I never would've thought to use the Internet."

"What else are you doing today?"

"I'll check on Trynne, to see how she's holding up."

Just then, Gloria came from the bedroom toting an overnight bag and makeup case.

"That was fast," Bud said. "My wife always took forever to get ready to go anywhere."

"We have a tendency to do that." Angie patted his arm. "We like everything to be nice for our men."

Bud took Gloria's bags to the hall. She and Angie followed.

After they left, Angie retrieved her keys, digital camera, and Bud's printouts and went in search of blue compact cars. First thing on the agenda: see if she could determine the exact make of Donna's car. But the vehicle was pulled so far into the driveway she couldn't tell.

Will, on his way into the adjoining shop, spotted Angie and waved. She pulled up to the curb and got out. The scent of spring wafted in the air. Colorful narcissus, tulip, daffodil and crocus decorated Donna's window. A trailing vine of green wove around the pots and up the frame.

The window of Will's real estate office rarely looked any different. Pictures of available properties dotted the glass at eye level, replaced as properties sold or became available, but never changing the basic motif. She hoisted the purse strap higher on her shoulder and ducked under his arm holding the door open for her.

"It's nice to see you," Will said, setting some paperwork on his desk.

His slacks and shirt were neatly pressed, his tie straight. In all the years of their marriage, he hadn't been able to get it right without help. She wondered who had helped him.

Will grasped her elbow and pointed her toward a chair. "Sit?"

She remained standing. "Could I ask you a couple of questions?"

"This about the case you're on?"

"I'm not on a case. I'm just—"

"Just helping Jarvis out of a jam."

She gave a one-shoulder shrug and started for the door.

"Don't leave. I'm sorry."

She sighed. "Look Will, I don't want to get into a discussion about getting back together. It's not going to happen."

He grinned. "Can't blame a guy for trying."

"Can it, will you? You're sorry you cheated on me. I'm sorry you cheated, too. Look, I just wondered if you knew what kind of car Donna drives."

"Something blue, and small."

"Make? Model?"

He dragged two chairs together and sat in one. Angie took the other, noticing he'd put them so close their knees would touch. She backed her chair a foot and sat.

"I don't have any idea. Sorry. Why do you need to know?"

"A car matching that description was spotted a number of times at John Bloom's house. Do you know if Donna's seeing anyone?"

Now Will shook his head. "I haven't seen a man around there. Not since Paul."

"Darned if I can remember his last name."

"Zimmerman."

"Of course. Do you happen to have his number?"

"What's he got to do with this? They think he got jealous and killed the guy?"

"Of course not. Did you know Donna breeds irises? Well, John Bloom was also an iris breeder. I thought I'd see if Paul could provide anything."

"I see. You think that's what might have gotten them together?"

"It seems worth looking into."

Will spun his chair around and scrounged in the drawer. He came up with a square of Post-It notes, wrote, tore one off and handed it across. It was a phone number. "I don't know his address in Portland."

"Thanks." She slid the paper into the inside pocket of her handbag. "Bloom owned a navy blue older model Jeep Cherokee. Have you seen it next door?"

Will gave her question serious thought. "I don't spend a lot of time looking at cars parked out front." He shook his head, slowly at first, then more rapidly as he made up his mind. "Can't say I ever did."

She stood up. "Thanks."

Outside, Donna pushed a broom on the sidewalk. Angie switched on the camera.

"What are you doing?"

Angie spoke as she tiptoed to the window. "I want to show it to John Bloom's neighbors." She focused and clicked. The flash went off. Donna glanced up. Angie hid the camera behind her back and waved. The way Donna held the broom made her look like that old farmer on Corn Flakes boxes. She stopped looking like him when her expression of mild surprise changed to a glare.

Angie stepped away from the window the same time Donna flounced back indoors, dragging the broom through the pile she'd just swept.

"She's not happy with you."

"I can't help it. She's been acting weird. Two days ago, she practically dragged me into her greenhouse to show me her irises. When I asked to go again yesterday, she became very curt, and just about threw me out."

"How did the picture come out?"

Angie checked the clarity. Donna's arms were a blur of motion and a cloud of dust swirled around her feet, but her face was clear and aimed straight at the camera. "It'll do." She clicked the camera off. "Thanks for your help."

He held the door and followed her outside. "Be careful with this investigating, okay?"

"I am."

"It was nice seeing you."

"By the way, you should get more sleep, you look like hell."

"It's this headache. I've had it for two days."

Angie set down the camera on the front seat, opened her purse and handed Will a bottle of acetaminophen. He tapped out two then recapped the container. When he tried to pass it back to her, she told him to keep it. "Wash them down with something, they'll work faster."

"I will."

"And go lie down. Let the pills work."

"Yes, Mom," he said wryly, and strode back into the building.

Angie got into her car and sped away. In the rear view mirror, she thought she saw Donna on the doorstep of the flower shop. Her hand hovered in the air. Had she been brushing hair out of her eyes or waving for Angie to come back? Or flipping her the bird?

She drove to Frank Chute's but the car wasn't in the driveway and nobody answered the door.

As Angie entered the theater, she thought about the manuscript *Ring of Muddy Water*. Perhaps, with Gloria out of town, tonight would be a good time to settle down and give it another read. Tyson called the cavernous room spooky, but she loved the boom of her voice through the auditorium. She loved thumbing through playbills, roaming the costume room, sifting costume jewelry through her fingers. Today though, something didn't feel right. As though she wasn't alone.

Cell phone at the ready, she tiptoed through the auditorium, turning on lights and systematically checking every corner and cubbyhole. Near as she could tell, the place was empty. The only two rooms she hadn't checked were she and Tyson's offices. Tyson had the only key for his, and it was locked up tight. She eased the key into her door, trying not to make a sound. In one rapid motion, she flung it open and flicked on the light switch.

And laughed. Of course nobody was there. How could they

have gotten in? Angie closed the door, leaned on the thin panel, and laughed again. The last time she'd leaned against this door, Jarvis had been leaning just as hard.

She shook off the image and pushed away from the door. The manuscript lay in the middle of her battered wood desk. She took five steps and picked it up. A white sheet of paper slipped from inside the cover page and fluttered to the beat-up hardwood floor. She smiled. Tyson had left a note. Probably something about the playwright.

Angie stooped to retrieve the page. Not from Tyson. She didn't recognize the handwriting. It said: *Leave the case alone or you'll be sorry. Dead sorry.*

Knees trembling, Angie hurried from the theater, manuscript and note tucked under one arm. She headed next for Trynne McCoy's. No car in the driveway. Angie remembered Trynne's car was at the shop, so, taking her purse and the envelope from Mary Grayson—and ignoring the ominous note lying so innocently on the passenger seat—she went up the brick walk and poked the doorbell.

The door opened almost immediately. Trynne smiled. "I'm glad you came, I'm going stir crazy. I keep expecting the cops to come back."

Angie stepped inside. "I thought you might be working."

"I can't work. Every time I look in the microscope, John's face materializes on the slide."

Angie followed Trynne through an arched doorway and into the living room that, through a wall of windows to the left, overlooked Lake Winnipesaukee. To the right, an enormous flagstone fireplace. The floor, tan Berber carpet. The stucco walls, white. The only notable furnishings were a sideboard at one end of the long room and a stereo system at the other. All the regular furniture would remain at the theater until the end of the month. Trynne sat on a folding chair in front of the fireplace. She patted a second chair to her right.

As Angie sat she recalled Blake's reaction to her rather pointed questions, and warned herself to choose words carefully. "I can't stop thinking about John either. The whole thing…" Angie clasped her hands and twisted the ring on her right hand, a silver filigree band with an oval turquoise stone. Will had given it to her on her thirtieth birthday. It seemed like so long ago. Then she smiled. It *was* a long time ago, almost twenty years.

They chatted about nothing for a while, each seemingly eager to leave behind the events of the past few hours. Finally Angie brought up the reason for her visit. "You never told me how you met Blake."

Trynne smiled. "Sounds a little cornball now, but we were in the same biology class at the Vo-tech. I felt sleepy, and tried to stay awake by gazing at things around the room. Blake sat across the room. I even remember what he had on: tan chinos and a brown and red plaid shirt. Our eyes met just that one time. I felt him looking at me the rest of the class. You ever get the feeling somebody's watching you and every hair on your body stands on end? It's creepy. This is going to sound really silly, so you have to promise not to laugh."

"I promise," Angie said, knowing that if it really was silly, she couldn't hold it in. Trynne had known her long enough to know the same thing.

"I kept envisioning he and I on horses, riding up a mountain trail. The image was so vivid, I still recall the autumn leaves— even though it really was spring—they were brilliant reds and oranges. The air smelled like apple cider and bonfires. The horses were both white. Big stallions." She stopped talking a moment as though to gauge Angie's attitude. Angie smiled, not in condescension but nostalgia. She had similar memories. "Next," Trynne continued, "we were lying in a field of daisies, the horses untethered, grazing nearby. Now here comes the silly part: I saw us walking out of our yard pushing a baby carriage to the park. When I close my eyes, I can still see that picture."

Didn't all young women picture themselves in similar scenes? Didn't it mean the nurturing hormone was growing and forming? "You should keep thinking about that scene. Maybe it'll push away the other one."

Trynne nodded. "When class ended, I gathered my things and left. Passing the row where he sat, I saw he'd already gone. I can't describe the emotion I had right then. It felt like someone told me all the people I cared about had died in some horrible catastrophe. He wasn't in the hallway either. Though our eyes only met that one time, I felt like we'd formed an unbreakable bond. I pulled myself together and went to my car. And there he was, standing beside it."

"Why hadn't he approached you prior to that day?"

"You wouldn't believe it, but he was painfully shy. He's changed since then." She smiled.

"So, what happened at your car?"

"He didn't have a car then. We took mine and went to the pharmacy, one with a soda fountain—whatever happened to them anyway? We had cherry Cokes."

"Where was John at that time?"

"In some agricultural class, I think. You have to understand, John and I were like an old married couple by that time. Yes, we were young, but remember, being brought up together we knew each other inside and out."

"Literally?"

Trynne laughed. "God yes. We'd been sleeping together since we were thirteen."

"So, you started seeing Blake."

"We managed to keep it quiet for a few months. When it came out, you can imagine the uproar. Since Blake was so much older—twelve years—my father *knew* he had a wife and seventeen kids stashed somewhere. He hired a man to investigate Blake. I can imagine his, um…disappointment when he found Blake was squeaky clean. I'm going to make some tea." Angie followed her to the kitchen, gleaming with copper-bottom pots and Danish design cabinets. Trynne filled the teapot and set it on the stove. "I didn't find out till just the other day that my parents talked John into being patient and giving Blake and my relationship some time to fizzle on its own. When it didn't happen, they threw out monkey wrenches one after another, doing things to keep us apart." Trynne leaned back against the counter, arms crossed.

Angie slid onto a stool.

"Did I ever tell you, my father tried to pay Blake off?" Trynne turned to the cabinet getting out ingredients for tea. "That's when I talked Blake into running away."

"It was your idea?"

"Yes. You probably thought Blake wanted my money." She set a pair of mugs on the granite counter and faced Angie. "Don't say you haven't, it's only natural. I even wondered for a long time." She shrugged. "After all these years…"

"Before everything blew up in your faces, did you ever talk to your father about bringing Blake into the family business? He was in the same field, after all."

"Several times, but my father swore Blake was up to no good. I tried my mother, but she wouldn't stand up against father's stubbornness."

Trynne poured boiling water over the teabags. The steam rose then dissipated, sending the rich aroma of Earl Gray into the air. For a second, the steam hid her face. She set the mugs on the center island counter. She was smiling. "So that's the saga of Trynne and Blake."

"And John."

"And John."

"Did you ever speak to your parents again?"

"Yes. Blake talked me into calling. The first time, John answered and hung up on me. The second time, my mother answered. We had a long tearful conversation where she begged me to leave Blake and come home. I gave her our phone number in case my father changed his mind. No one called."

"Did Blake ever work with genetics?"

Trynne paused from the up and down dipping of her teabag. "No. Though he's mad about plants and growing things, he hates the idea of messing with their basic makeup. That was one conflict between us all these years. He couldn't ask me to give it up, though; my work supported us.

"I suppose, a really good wife would've offered to move to another part of the country where jobs were more plentiful and higher paying." She gave a wistful sigh and settled onto the stool across from Angie.

"So, you would've quit working for Monsanto if Blake had a higher paying job?"

"It wouldn't have been easy, but yes, I guess I would have."

Angie wondered how strenuously Blake had objected to Trynne's work. Trynne seemed to read her mind, because she said, "Things between us haven't been bad. It's just…there's always this tension between us. You know what I mean?"

Angie did know. She'd felt it often with Will. The times she overspent her budget. Most especially the time she bought the Lexus. She sipped her tea then put up a finger for Trynne to wait. She went to the living room and retrieved the iris society newsletter from the envelope and opened it to the Sondergaard photo. She pushed it across to Trynne. "Do you know this man?"

Angie watched her friend's face giving the picture serious consideration. There was no recognition, no twitches that might indicate subterfuge.

"Who is he?"

"A geneticist. His name is Pedar Sondergaard."

Sondergaard: one of the premier geneticists in the world. Trynne: tops in the US. She should know him. Angie trained her senses on the woman sitting so innocently across the table. "He's from Amsterdam." Still no reaction. "He and John were seen at the diner a few days before his death."

Trynne leaned forward, her elbow banging the cup. Some tea sloshed onto the counter. Absently, Trynne slipped a napkin from the holder and dropped it on the liquid. Her eyes were on Angie. "Do you think he's the one who—"

Angie nodded. "Far as I know he's the only suspect."

"You said his name is…what?"

"Sondergaard. Pedar Sondergaard."

"The name sounds familiar. If he works with genetics, I should know him." She scrunched her eyes shut, rubbing both temples with her index fingers. "In my files, I have almost as much industry information as John. Except mine's in much neater condition. I'll see what I can dig up on this guy." She thumped the newsletter with her palm.

The doorbell rang making them both jump. Trynne stood up, her height especially obvious with the copper-bottom pots dangling from the wrought iron rack just a hair's width overhead. "Excuse me."

Angie peeked out the kitchen window and was surprised to see Jarvis' Jeep parked behind her car. Trynne led him and Sergeant Wilson into the kitchen. Jarvis sat on the stool Angie had vacated. He motioned for Trynne to sit too. Wilson leaned against the brick wall, arms crossed, his demeanor all business. Angie's heart began to pound. Thump thump, so loud she barely heard Trynne ask, "Is this an official visit?"

"Sort of," Jarvis said.

A lightheaded sensation swept over her and she dropped back, letting the sink cabinet support her weight. "Do you want me to leave?" Angie asked, a small part of her wishing he'd say yes.

"You can't, we're parked behind you."

"Would you care for a cup of tea? I think the water's still hot," Trynne's voice had lost that self-confident air.

Both Jarvis and Wilson shook their heads. Slowly, Trynne slid her rear end onto the stool, her eyes darting back and forth from Jarvis to Wilson's faces. Angie attempted to remain nonchalant, but with her throbbing heart and dizzy head, it became increasingly more difficult as the moments passed.

"I need to ask you about your work in genetics," Wilson began.

"It's a very complicated field," Trynne replied.

"So I'm learning. Tell me what you do exactly."

"In a nutshell, I examine ovine color genes. My job is to isolate specific colors which Monsanto can aggrandize, thereby creating alternative colors which occur naturally in the sheep."

"Where do you get these genes?"

"From a number of sheep farmers in the state. Monsanto pays them to work with us." She waited a second, her eyes still jumping from one cop to the other. "I've confused you," she finally said. Angie didn't miss the humor in her voice.

"Maybe you can demonstrate in your laboratory," Jarvis suggested.

Angie had only a side view of her friend's face, but the flicker of annoyance was unmistakable. Trynne didn't like anyone—even Blake—invading her private space.

Even so, wordless, she stood and opened a door just off the kitchen. She led everyone down the steps. To the left was a large den. Though the only windows were tiny rectangles near the ceiling, Trynne had achieved an open and airy feeling with low, Asian style furniture, colorful carpets and wall hangings. At the far end was a pool table, the cue sticks crossed in an X on the green felt cover.

Trynne opened a door at the foot of the stairs and flipped on a light. A long narrow room came into brilliant focus. The laboratory looked exactly like ones on television: all white and bright. Walls of cabinets. A very long, shiny black countertop, broken only by a huge stainless steel refrigerator that took up a whole corner. The counters were decorated with test tubes and Bunsen burners. In the center of the room was a rectangular island counter atop cabinets.

Jarvis crossed his arms and strode around island, his eyes working like video cameras. Wilson stayed in the doorway, content obviously, to let his ex-boss head the discussion.

"As you can see, it's nothing unusual," Trynne said, her hand remaining on the doorknob.

"Who pays for this?" Wilson asked.

"Monsanto. Of course, I have some things of my own. This microscope, for example." She gestured with her free hand, to an enormous piece of equipment on the right-hand counter.

"Looks expensive."

"It cost as much as this house."

Angie wondered if Blake knew.

What brought Jarvis here?

He walked slowly around the counter and stopped in the far corner. He picked up a black object about the size of a pound of hamburger. An electrical cord protruded from one end. It was plugged into a wall socket.

"Just some laboratory equipment," Trynne said, finally letting go of the doorknob. She crossed to him and put out her hand.

Jarvis held it just out of reach. "It looks like some high-tech video camera."

"Of course it's not a camera. What would a camera be doing in a lab?" Trynne reached again. "It's a complex piece of equipment. Be careful with it."

But Jarvis wouldn't relinquish the thing so easily. He set it on the counter with a gesture that said *don't touch*. Wilson moved finally, ambling across the shiny tiled floor to stand beside Jarvis. For several moments, it was quiet while Wilson examined the find.

Trynne's demeanor changed then. Her eye darkened to navy-blue slits. Her cheeks grew circles of red. Sharp claws snatched at his sleeves. In one motion, he pinned Trynne's arms to her sides and walked her backwards to the counter. And let go. "Stay."

He began opening cabinets. Trynne obeyed the growled command, her eyes avoiding Angie and shooting barbs at the men. "You asked to see my place, not inspect it."

Jarvis became a cop version of the Energizer Bunny. He opened cabinets, pushed aside jars and bottles, peered into the dark recesses. Trynne took a half step from the wall, her eyes flashing like lightning. Jarvis spun around and halted her with a look.

Angie stepped between them. This search violated Trynne's rights. Jarvis and Wilson had to know that. They were leaving themselves open for two monster lawsuits: one from Trynne and a bigger one from Monsanto.

Angie whispered in Jarvis's ear, "You've got to have a warrant—"

But his arms and head were already buried in a corner cabinet. His shouted, "Aha" stopped Angie mid-sentence.

He moved aside three Hamburger Helper sized boxes and a large jar of some neon yellow liquid. Angie nearly wept because his hands were clutched around something that looked exactly like a television. He eased it forward to the shelf edge and twisted a knob on the front. The image on the screen was fuzzy, but not too blurred for her to recognize a laboratory similar to the one where they now stood. Except this lab on the screen looked like a tornado had struck. Angie's heart stopped beating.

Jarvis unhooked his radio from his belt and flicked a thumb on a red button. "You there?"

Angie swallowed something desiccated and sour. On the screen, two State Policemen moved into sight. One gave a big smile and a thumbs-up.

Angie spared a glance at Trynne who'd slumped against the wall looking like a wilted flower.

Jarvis clipped the radio back on his belt. Wilson strode to Trynne, took hold of her arms and pulled them, none too gently, behind her back. "Trynne McCoy, I'm arresting you for unauthorized entry of John Bloom's property, and criminal trespass. I soon hope to have evidence to arrest you for the theft by unauthorized taking. Might even be able to add stalking to the list.

And…" he drew out the word, "maybe even murder." He recited her rights.

Throughout, Trynne stared at him. Her eyes were glazed, but no tears leaked loose. "You can't do this. My lawyers will eat you for breakfast."

Wilson let go of her, whipped a folded piece of paper from his inside breast pocket and wiggled it in front of her eyes. "Search warrant." He nudged her up the stairs, keeping hold of the short length of chain between the handcuffs.

Angie followed, stopping to throw Trynne's coat over her shoulders. By the time Angie retrieved Trynne's handbag and locked the front door, Trynne sat in the rear passenger seat of his car.

"It's not what you think," Trynne said, meeting Angie's gaze for the first time.

Jarvis stretched the seatbelt across her chest then stepped between them, edging Angie away from the vehicle. "What is it exactly?"

"I just… I wanted to watch his process. I thought I could apply it to what I've learned in ovine genetics. You know, to help my work."

The men waited. When Trynne didn't say anything else, he moved to shut the door.

"Please, you can't do this. I didn't kill John. I didn't steal his work."

"Did John follow you to New Hampshire?" Jarvis asked.

Trynne's eyes darted toward the street, as if she expected Blake to show up at any second. "I-I thought so, for a while."

Angie wanted to warn Trynne not to say anything without her lawyer, but if her friend was innocent, there should be no reason not to talk.

"Did John try to renew your physical relationship?"

"H-he tried to talk me into leaving Blake. We had no…no physical relationship."

"Did you think about leaving Blake?" Angie couldn't help asking.

"No. Well, not seriously. I wondered—a person can't help wonder—what it would be like not to—" Trynne sagged back against the seat.

"You obviously knew of John's obsession with the red."

She gave a weary nod. "My parents got him into it. I so wanted to be a success for Monsanto. I knew after twenty-five years, John had to be close to discovering the red. I couldn't sleep for thinking about it. I had to know. One night while Blake slept, I sneaked over there and set up the cameras. In case you haven't found them, there is also one in the main greenhouse and one in his office. I-I also linked our computers."

Jarvis nodded.

Now Trynne talked over his shoulder, at Angie. "That's it, I swear. I didn't want to rekindle our relationship. I've been happy with Blake, really. I just wanted the genetic information. I was ecstatic for John when he produced the red—"

"Wait a minute!" Angie exclaimed. "Did you keep the tapes?"

"Yes. In the safe, in the lab."

"Why didn't you give them to the cops? The crook must be on there."

"Oh god, I never thought of that. I was so worried you'd find the cameras and—"

Jarvis straightened up but didn't speak; neither did he move to shut the door.

"I couldn't let anyone know what I'd been doing. Angie, you have to believe me. Jarvis. Sergeant Wilson, please. Look, I'll tell you the combination, go in and get the tapes."

Wilson shut the door and somberly moved Angie away from the vehicle. She couldn't take her eyes from Trynne, who'd been transformed into a small child, pleading her case to be allowed a new toy.

The groping fingers of surrounding trees reached out, clutched at her, just the way Trynne had grabbed Jarvis's sleeve. A desperate act of a desperate woman. A desperate thief?

No. Angie wanted to scream the word to the heavens. Trynne was not a thief. She couldn't be! She felt herself being shaken, and blinked several time to right herself.

Jarvis had hold of her shoulder, prepared to shake her again. "Are you all right?"

"Yeah. Yes, I'm fine," Angie said as they rounded the front of his vehicle. "Aren't you going to get the tapes?"

"We don't have a warrant."

Twelve

Jarvis and Wilson stood in the long hallway between security doors, watching an officer lead Trynne McCoy to the cell area. The look she gave him just about brought tears to his eyes.

Wilson shook his head. "I can't figure this thing out. I never woulda pegged her for the spying type. And I sure as hell can't take her as a murderer."

Jarvis hated to admit it but neither could he. Not that he was close to either she or Blake, but they spoke a lot during rehearsals. You get a feel for people in basic conversation. And something about all this stunk. Know Trynne McCoy or not, through the years he'd gotten to know human nature pretty well. He could press his imagination to believe she was desperate enough about her career, to set the cameras, but like Wilson, couldn't wrap his mind around her as a murderer.

The captain's office door opened and the short, middle-aged man strode into the hallway. He crossed his arms over an ample stomach and cast his gaze from Trynne and the officer disappearing through the back security door, to Jarvis, hand on the knob of the front security door. Jarvis didn't stop his forward motion. Even after the door swung shut behind him, he still felt the buzz of the captain's glare.

He took a few steps into the lobby, hoping his face didn't portray the apprehension swirling inside him. Angelina rose from the bucket chair and hurried forward. He tried to gauge her mood but could get nothing more than concern for her friend.

"Can I see her?"

"You'll have to ask Wilson," Jarvis replied, one eye on the security door. Any second the all-powerful captain could just choose to invoke some of that power and have Jarvis heaved bodily from the premises. The fact that he'd uncovered the McCoy cameras and tracked them to Trynne wouldn't count for anything.

Angie knocked on the bulletproof glass and asked the dispatcher to summon Sergeant Wilson. Then she returned to Jarvis. "I have a couple of photos to show you," she said. "One is of Sondergaard, the—"

"Where in hell did you get a picture of him?"

"The iris society president sent it. I took one of Donna that I'm sending to her. I want to know if Donna's been as prominent in the events as she insinuated."

"What would that tell you?"

Angie shrugged. Just then the security door opened and Wilson appeared. Angie finished her thought, "I want to know just how interested Donna is in the red iris. The greater her interest in iris genetics, the stronger her motive to murder John."

Wilson, in his sharply pressed uniform and shiny badge, stepped toward them. He smoothed a hand through perfectly neat hair and looked at Angie. "You talking about Trynne McCoy?" Wilson asked.

"No. Donna Marks."

"You might have a good point," Wilson said, "I was just at her place. Wanted to have a little chat. See if she'd give me a looksee in the greenhouse. But Ms. Marks seems to have left town. Closed sign on the door. Nobody answers the apartment door." He paused a second, then added, "I looked in the window. There's a heaping bowl of cat food on the floor. The ironing board is set up in the kitchen and empty coat hangers hanging from it."

Apprehension wiggled itself up Jarvis's spine. He reached around and attempted to scratch the sensation away.

"She is gone," Angelina offered, "but only to Philadelphia."

Jarvis's anxiety smoothed itself out and he felt himself heaving a sigh of relief. Why hadn't he thought of it?

"Do we have enough to get a warrant to search the Marks place?" Wilson asked.

"Doubt it. All we have is that she breeds irises and some-body—we assume her—in a small blue car, visited John now and again. We have more evidence against Ms. McCoy."

In his peripheral vision, Jarvis saw Angie shaking her head in a dubious manner. She wouldn't let herself accept Trynne's guilt, even with the evidence staring right at her. He almost smiled—fi-nally, a flaw in the pretty amateur detective's personality.

"Can I post Trynne's bail?" Angelina asked.

"Of course," Wilson said, "I need an hour or so to prepare the paperwork."

"Has she called her husband yet?"

"Yes, and her lawyer."

Angelina jiggled her car keys, an unconscious habit. She found the desired key, then said, "I'll be back in an hour. Oh, by the way, I have some pictures you might be interested in: Pedar Sondergaard and Donna Marks."

Wilson's eyebrows lifted. "Together?"

"That sure would bring things into focus, wouldn't it?" She told Wilson about the pictures.

Jarvis was impressed, especially when she said, "I made some phone calls this morning. I called every motel within a fifteen mile radius."

"We've already done that," Wilson said.

"I know, but Jarvis said you were asking about Sondergaard and that guy Lawson. I asked for someone who brought an ex-cess amount of baggage. Think about it. There had to be a lot of containers, boxes and boxes. Some of what they stole would be very breakable. It would need to be wrapped and packed care-fully for shipping to wherever.

Wilson shook his head, but Jarvis wasn't surprised. She did this to him all the time.

"The motels didn't pan out. But then I started wondering if

maybe the thieves rented a storage facility."

"Big job, there are dozens of them," Wilson said.

"Yes, but there aren't that many heated ones." She pulled in a breath and let it out in a long whoosh between her lips. Beautiful lips. Lips that just a few hours ago—

"Too bad it was a dead end," Wilson was saying.

"Maybe not completely dead. When you search of Donna and Trynne's places—I assume you're going to search them—keep your eyes open for possible disguises they might've worn," Angelina said, then added, "I'll get the photos from the car."

Both men watched her leave. Wilson's sharp laugh made him jump. "Does she know how bad you got it for her?"

For several seconds, Jarvis didn't speak. Then he said, "We have some things to work through."

"Your decision or hers?"

"Both...I guess."

Angelina returned with the iris society bulletin and a digital camera, which she handed to Wilson. She punched a few buttons and Donna's image came on the small, flat screen. The florist holding a push broom and staring at the camera with a look of disdain. Jarvis had to grin. Where did you take this?"

"Will's shop."

What had she been doing visiting her soon-to-be ex? For months Will had made a nuisance of himself, insinuating himself into her life whenever he could. Once. that Jarvis knew of, he'd begged for reconciliation. Did Angelina's presence at his office signal her consideration of the idea? An ember of jealousy flickered. He swallowed it down. But she'd noticed. Damn. Her smile of pride straightened out. Her lips twitched and she turned off the camera with a severe wrench of the thumb on the tiny button.

Wilson took the camera and passed it through the hole in the bulletproof glass. He bent forward and spoke to the dispatcher, "Can you make several copies of the cover of this, and download the last picture and make some copies of it for me? Thanks." Wilson turned to Jarvis and Angelina.

"I'll pick up the camera and newsletter when I come to bail Trynne out." She turned and walked to the door. Jarvis didn't move. She was angry; it was better to let her cool down a while. She stopped at the door and addressed him, "You should try and convince your father to go into the hospital. He looks awful."

"I tried. Last night and again this morning. He's completely against the idea." He shrugged. "Except for picking him up and taking him there bodily, I don't know what to do."

Angelina left. Jarvis watched her through the window in the door as she climbed into her Lexus and drove away.

"What's she pissed off about?" Wilson's question made him flinch. He'd forgotten the sergeant stood next to him.

"Damned if I know," he lied.

Angie drove home at speeds well over the speed limit, part of her wishing a cop would stop her.

Who broke into the theater? Why couldn't the note just be sent through the mail? Or slid under her windshield wiper? Obvious. They were making a point. They could do anything they wanted, when they wanted.

Three suspects: Trynne, Sondergaard and Donna. The only one with access to the theater was Trynne. Her good friend. Maybe best friend. It just couldn't be her. Angie entered her condo with all the caution of a pit bull on sentry duty.

Everything looked all right. The vacuum lines in the carpet were unmarred. The furniture gleamed. No breeze rippled the curtains. Most of all, she had no sense of intrusion. Of course, her sense wasn't infallible, but it had warned her at the theater…

Even so, Angie inspected the five rooms with tedious care.

Who felt threatened enough by Angie's simplistic investigation to leave that note? Far as she knew, none of the clues pointed anywhere. Except Trynne.

All afternoon Angie asserted to Jarvis, you have no real evidence pointing toward her being the thief. That was until Angie drove her friend home from the police station because, in the driveway, looking proud and shiny as a new penny: Trynne's car. Back from the brake shop—the Honda Sport—a hatchback. Blue.

Angie dialed Tyson's cell phone. He answered on the first ring. Loud music shook the background. She raised her voice, "Where are you?" He named a club in Meredith. "Should I ask who you're with?"

He laughed. "No."

"What time did you leave the theater?"

"I don't know what time it was but it wasn't five minutes after you left. Why?"

"I went back to get the manuscript I left on my desk. I found a note inside."

"Do I need to ask what it said?"

"No. What I wanted to know was whether anyone came in after I left."

"Nobody." He went quiet a moment. Angie felt the boom of the bass through the phone. "I'll have the locks changed tomorrow."

"I doubt if it'll matter."

"Do you want me to come over?"

"No thanks. I'm fine. Have a good time, I'll see you tomorrow." Angie shut the phone before he could insist on coming. She dropped the phone into her purse, then tucked the menacing note in too.

Angie had left the theater around one-thirty. And returned between three-thirty and four. Time enough for anyone to go in and leave the note. Just as someone had sneaked into Jarvis's house and switched guns.

God, the night John died, had they taken her keys too? Copies could be made fast enough at any hardware store. There was one in town…on the way to John's house. If they had her theater keys, they also had her house keys! She hurried around double-checking locks and windows. At least Gloria and Bud were out of town; two less things to worry about.

Angie put the unanswered questions aside. Best to let her brain work on the problem during the night. She took the manuscript from the hall table and settled into her chair to read. A knock on the front door nearly knocked her off the cushion. She remained there, still as a stone. Another knock, and a youthful voice. "Ms. Deacon? It's Arnold. I came to collect your newspaper money."

"Be right there, Arnold." She counted money from her purse, unlocked the door and paid the boy. He handed her a paper. "Thanks," they said at the same time.

She shut the door and leaned back against it. What a day. Except for the meeting with the playwright, it had been a total and complete mess, topped off with her admitting to Jarvis she'd been with Will. What had she been thinking? Damn Jarvis and his jealousy. He said he was working on it. How long did it take to purge negative emotions from your psyche? Years probably. Was Jarvis worth waiting years for?

Without a satisfactory answer to the question, she returned to her chair and opened the manuscript. The first words she read were: but Richie spotted Daisy going up the walk. Angie put down the pages. Was Trynne the woman Frank Chute saw? If so, that would mean Trynne not only betrayed Blake, but Angie too. Best friends didn't do that to each other. They huddled in corners sharing secrets, trusting each other. What a mess. Two relationships in one day shot to hell.

A car drew up outside, and stopped near the front door. Not again.

The chime peeled through the condo. Angie remained in the chair until a familiar voice called out, "Are you there?" Angie opened the door to Trynne—wearing a totally out of character outfit: jeans and NY Jets sweatshirt—standing there holding a white handkerchief to her nose. Angie opened her arms. Trynne came into the embrace. They stood for a long time, Trynne several inches taller, slouching to lay her head on Angie's shoulder.

They broke the awkward embrace. Angie took her arm and

helped her to the living room where they settled side by side on the sofa. Trynne's eyes were red, her knuckles white. As Angie traced a circle with her palm on Trynne's back, a multitude of questions peppered her brain, the biggest and most troubling: how could Trynne cheat on Blake? How could she have so little faith in her own talents that she had to steal John's work?

As if reading Angie's mind, Trynne spoke. "I've made a terrible mess of things. No, terrible is too mild a word. It's important that you believe I didn't intend any harm. Honestly, I only wanted to further my own career. Selfish. Unthinkably selfish. But that's all, I swear."

"One of John's neighbors told me about a blue car and a woman who came around once in a while."

Trynne shook her head. "Not me. I was at John's house three times. Just three. Each time I parked down the road and walked there."

The words squeezed between Angie's lips before she could stop them: "Carrying boxes of video equipment?"

"Three cameras and a roll of wire fits in a backpack. I dressed like a hiker." She shrugged. "I didn't think anyone would notice a hiker. Once, I went in the middle of the afternoon."

"Where was John at that time?"

"In the driveway, checking in a truckload of trees. It took only twenty minutes. In and out before he finished."

"You were very brazen." Trynne had always seemed so down to earth, so logical. Scientists were supposed to be logical, weren't they? Not brazen and bold.

"Not really. I planned to string wires out back of the furthest greenhouse. There wasn't much chance he'd go there to mow or anything. As you saw, he didn't care much for esthetics."

"You still were very bold," Angie repeated.

"Very un-Trynne-like, you mean." A smile remained on her lips only a second, and was replaced by the same sad expression she'd worn most of the day. "That's what Blake said. 'I don't know you at all,' he kept repeating. I didn't mean for anyone to get hurt. It's important to me, if you believe nothing else of all this, believe that."

"I do," Angie said, meaning it.

"How do you think I feel knowing John might be dead because of my actions?"

"Not sure I follow you."

"I can't help feeling like, if I'd minded my own business, stayed the predictable Trynne everyone knew—"

"And loved."

A trace of a smile creased her face. "If I had, maybe the thieves wouldn't have…" Her voice trailed off. Angie waited for her to finish the thought. After a minute, she did. "Wouldn't have found out about the red."

"Who did you tell?"

"My boss."

"He knew what you were up to with the cameras?"

"She. Yes, I told her."

"Was she in favor of it?"

"She brought up the idea." Trynne blew her nose into the big hanky.

"You think she's involved in all this?" The notion opened a whole new kettle of fish. "Don't worry over it any more, I'll tell Wilson and Jarvis and set them to work on it. Relax. Okay?"

Trynne pushed her damp platinum hair from her face. "I love—loved John. I didn't realize it till I saw him at the town hall that day. Something inside me snapped then." She sighed. "I never should have gone off with Blake. Never should have broken with my family."

"John only asked once for you to get back together?"

"I swear Angie, just once. I guess I figured he was happy loving me from afar. Sounds dopey being put in words, but that's what I thought. I should have stayed around and become Mrs. Jan Van Blozend Bloem."

Angie nearly fell off the couch. "What?"

"That I should have stayed around and become Mrs. Jan Van

Blozend Bloem. Funny name, isn't it? I always thought it was poetic. He hated his name."

As Trynne rolled the syllables off her tongue once more, Angie lowered her head into her hands. Jan=John. Van Blozend Bloem=Bloom. How stupid of her not to have noticed the similarities. No wonder John Bloom's history didn't begin till he moved to Alton Bay. Prior to that he was someone else.

"Are you all right?" Trynne asked.

Angie raised her head, rubbed her eyes and peered at Trynne. "Yes. Fine."

"So, you think John followed you to New Hampshire?"

A small nod.

"How did he find you?"

"That wouldn't be hard. My name's all over the world of genetics. Shouldn't be that hard to get my address." Trynne stood up. "I've taken up enough of your time. See how self-centered I am lately? I didn't even ask about your mother. Is she doing all right?"

"She and Jarvis's father have gone to Boston for the night."

"I heard he's got cancer. Terrible thing." She buttoned her coat all the way to her chin. "By the way, Blake left me. He said he had thinking to do."

Angie hugged her friend and voiced sincere apologies. Then she followed her friend outside. "You aren't going to do anything foolish, are you?"

Trynne shook her head. "I'm done doing stupid things. I have some making up to do, to a lot of people."

Angie remained in the driveway, arms folded. The sun had set. Dusk had fallen. She waved until Trynne's car was out of sight then went inside to pour a gallon or so of brandy. Did she have a large enough glass in the house? Angie ridiculously searched a moment before settling in her chair with a tumbler and the bottle of Disaronno.

An hour passed, during which she thought about everything, and nothing. And came to not one new conclusion. The brandy made her woozy. She threw on her coat and boots, and after locking the door and inspecting the parking lot, walked to the park. She stepped carefully over the lumpy sidewalk avoiding tree roots protruding through the old tar along the promenade. She chose the bench closest to the water and farthest from the street. Wind was brisk here except in the most humid days of summer—the Dog Days. Other than that, even the smallest of breezes picked up velocity as it funneled down the long narrow bay from Meredith to Alton. If it collected enough momentum, it slammed against the Downings Landing buildings and rebounded back on itself; in winter, lifting whirlwinds of snow off the ice; in fall, stealing leaves from nooks and crannies and turning them into spinning rainbow kaleidoscopes. Today, there was nothing to be picked up and moved except for a Coca Cola cup that skittered across the grass and dropped onto the still-frozen bay.

Trynne had said: "Something inside me snapped then." She spoke about seeing John at the town hall and realizing how much of herself she'd left back in Oregon. Trynne's main focus had been herself, the same as most people. When Angie discovered Will cheating, something inside her snapped too. She kept telling herself she wouldn't go back to him because she couldn't trust him, but that wasn't the absolute truth. It was she who couldn't be trusted—to feel secure about her looks, her job, her relationships. Feelings of inadequacy lay deep inside, waiting someday to resurface. Eventually she'd return to the one-upsman-ship she'd had with herself. So long as depending on herself for a living was a priority, that eventuality would remain in remission. She hoped.

"Penny for your thoughts," came a voice from behind that nearly had Angie leaping over the embankment.

She swung around, wrenching her back on the hard bench. Donna smiled. This was a good thing. Angie stole a glance behind her then patted the bench. "It's nice to see you. Sit."

"I was on the way past and saw you walking." She wrapped her arms around herself, and sat, giving an exaggerated shiver.

"How you can enjoy being out in this weather...I came to apologize...for yesterday."

"I thought you were feeling sorry for bringing me into your secret garden. I'm sorry if I stepped on your toes."

"You didn't. You're welcome to visit my kids any time." Donna wore a bulky sweater with a big turtleneck that almost swallowed the entire lower half of her face. The yarn was mottled shades of green that, in the waning light, set off the color in her eyes to perfection. Her cheeks were flushed from her unaccustomed trek. "Paul had just left."

Paul Zimmerman, Donna's ex-husband.

Thirteen

Angie walked back to the condo wondering about Donna's appearance at the park. Was it simply to apologize for rude behavior? Or talk about Paul? Or maybe…follow up on a threatening note?

Most of their conversation had been about him. Not the complaints or rebukes exes frequently have for each other; he lived in Portland, he was happy in his new job, he'd taken up fishing. Not a single complaint, or anything that even remotely connected to the John Bloom case. So, why did Angie's brain keep trying to do just that? Could John and Paul have any link? Paul had been a plumber by trade. John was a nurseryman. Could the two careers have crossed at some point? The greenhouses had plumbing.

But what difference could it make?

She reached the condominium complex slightly out of breath, and having made the decision to call Will once more. Before she could talk herself out of it, before the coat even came off, she dialed her old phone number. "Hi Will. Sorry to bother you."

"You're not. I was just writing out an order for office supplies."

"How's your headache?"

"Pounding like a jackhammer."

"Take two more of the painkillers I gave you and go lie down."

"Yes, Mom."

Angie laughed. "Don't say it like that, you obviously didn't listen when I said it earlier."

"I had to return some phone calls."

"And an order for office supplies that just couldn't wait."

Now Will laughed too.

"Hey, have you heard from Paul Zimmerman? What's he doing now?" She picked up a pencil and twirled it between her fingers.

"He's still a plumber. Some company in Portland offered him more than twice what he made from the place in Wolfeboro."

"When did you see him last?"

"Let's see. Man, it's hard to think with my heading throbbing." Same old Will. "Almost a year ago. Why?"

"He was in town yesterday. I wondered if he'd come to see you."

"No. I went to Manchester all day…closing a deal." There was a clicking sound on the other end then Will said, "Doesn't look like he called here; nothing on the caller ID. Maybe he came to the office. Bummer. Would've liked to see him."

"Eat a few crackers so the medication will settle better on your stomach. Then go rest a while. Talk to you soon." Angie hung up and looked out the living room window. The parking lot was quiet.

Paul and Donna always seemed like such a well-matched couple. They were both quiet and unassuming, hardly noticed in a crowd. Their breakup had come as a surprise to even their closest friends. Donna said they'd just grown apart. Angie wondered if Paul's explanation would be the same.

Why had he driven ninety miles back to Alton Bay? Ninety miles wasn't so far these days, but people didn't make a trip like that just for the scenery, especially in April when the scenery was slush, dirty snowbanks, and bare trees.

Angie put her elbows on the back of the sofa and lowered her head into her cupped hands. Something wasn't right about the meeting with Donna. Angie rewound her mental recording of their conversation. Donna came to apologize for being rude. Her excuse was that Paul had just left, which insinuated his visit upset her, yet nothing in what she said revealed a reason for turmoil.

Angie took off her jacket and put it in the closet. Then she walked around the condo pulling down shades. She sat at the kitchen counter and dialed Paul's number in Maine. No one answered, not even a machine. She reheated some stew Gloria made the other day and sat at the counter to eat. Yesterday's newspaper lay atop the mail pile. Someone had read it, probably Jarvis. She wondered where he was right now. Probably investigating the case he'd been suspended from. She smiled. Nothing could keep him from business.

A twinge of anger surfaced. What to do about his jealousy? Though he'd said it was his problem, technically it was both their problems. If they were to have a serious relationship maybe she should be in counseling with him. She sighed and gave her attention to the newspaper. The headline was about a fire in Moultonboro. Two photos took up half the front page: one of the burning building, one of the landlord, a pudgy woman wearing a knitted cap.

The thought of photos rekindled the memory of Donna sweeping the sidewalk outside her shop. Angie retrieved her camera and downloaded the picture into the computer, then sent it to Mary Grayson with a note: *do you recognize this woman?* Afterward, Angie reheated the soup and took it to the living room to watch the news.

Why didn't Donna ask about Angie taking her picture? She sighed. Why did she feel like the case was a lot simpler than she was making it? That the answer lay much closer to home than appeared? She cleaned up the dinner mess, refolded the newspaper and took a glass of wine and a book to the living room.

Angie curled in the chair to read and relax. Nice that Bob had taken Mom away. Peace and quiet…just what the doctor ordered. She hoped Will's headache was gone. A clunk, then a rasp sound brought her head up. Ears perked, head tilted, Angie listened. Another clunk: metal on metal.

At the sound of grating footsteps near the condo, she settled back in the chair and began breathing again. Just a neighbor coming home. She picked up the book, folded her legs underneath her and removed the bookmark.

A thump against the front door brought Angie out of the chair; book and glass toppled to the carpet. Had she locked it? The act was so automatic the memory was impossible to recover. She leaned around the corner. The security chain hung limp and worthless—like a used-up erection.

A shuffle like footsteps outside the door. Another thump. For several ticks of the wall clock, silence.

Movement though, as her fingers braced on the smooth painted wall between the living room and hall. Eyes riveted on the gold doorknob. It was moving!

Fingers probed the table behind her, seeking the figurine that had been there when she dusted, finding nothing. The knob continued moving, turning, turning. The door swung open.

Angie ducked back, tucking herself into the tiny space between the table and wall. Her thigh jostled the table and there was motion. Not movement really, just that indefinable sensation that something was about to tip over. She groped blindly to steady that stupid figurine, but too late. The crash of glass on wood revealed her hiding place.

Feet scuffed on the hallway carpet. Something rustled; that unidentifiable rasping sound she'd heard outside the door. Plastic shopping bags!

"Angie, come help me, will you?"

Head pounding with the unwarranted terror, she stepped from her hiding place.

"What the hell happened?" Jarvis asked.

"I dropped something."

Angie took two of the bags to the kitchen. Jarvis set the remaining bags on the counter and then took the bags from her fingers where she stood dumbly frozen to the tile floor. He took hold of her shoulders and maneuvered her into a chair, then peered into her eyes. "What's wrong?"

"Nothing. Why didn't you knock?" He had on that blue plaid shirt she liked. The top two buttons were undone, darkish hairs peeked out. A finger under the chin tilted her head up and she had to look at him. His usual early-evening stubble was scraped smooth. He smelled of Polo. She didn't speak.

"Since you were expecting me, I didn't think it was necessary."

A glimmer of memory: as she'd left the station, he'd offered to come make dinner. Feeling like an idiot, she went to clean up the broken statuette, clearing away the broken pieces from the table and floor. She held the shards in her hand, recalling the day Will had bought the abstract artwork. They'd been at some museum in New York City. She couldn't recall the name. Angie closed her eyes and concentrated. She could see the glass and marble entryway. She could hear the echoes in the lobby, smell the lacquer and oils in the main room, but she could not remember the name of the place.

A stab of pain in her hand made Angie look down. Manicured fingers were wrapped tightly around the shards. Blood formed a map in the palm of her hand. She plucked the pieces from the flesh and went to the kitchen. Jarvis saw her coming and held open the trash bin.

"You're bleeding." He washed and dried the wound, kissed it, and returned the hand as though it wasn't attached to the rest of her.

"Thanks," she said softly and went back to the living room. The snifter lay unbroken on its side, empty, its brown goodness absorbed by the white pages. Angie set the book on the table, open so it could dry.

Jarvis's head poked around the corner. "Everything okay?"

"Yes. Fine." She couldn't tell him about the note. He'd drag her to a safe place. She wouldn't be allowed at the theater. Tomorrow, rehearsals began again. They planned to introduce the cast to Sally Pruit and *Ring of Muddy Water*. Thursday would be taken up with dress rehearsals for not only *Checkmate: Love*, but next month's play *Ruckus in New York*. It wouldn't be fair to leave Tyson to do it alone. No, for now she'd keep the note a secret. Probably only meant to scare her off anyway.

She followed the pungent scent of garlic and onions to the kitchen. "What can I do?"

He didn't look up from the cutting board where the pile of onions and peppers grew with amazing speed. "You can make a salad. Lettuce is in one of those bags."

"I have lettuce in the fridge."

He laughed. "I couldn't know that standing in the supermarket, could I?"

Angie prepared the salad. "What kind of dressing do you want?"

"I'll make some in a minute." He drew out a clear plastic bag of tomatoes and a long, suggestive looking sausage. "Sit."

To busy herself, she took the rest of the things from the bags: angel hair spaghetti, a wedge of Romano, a box of frozen tiramisu.

Jarvis stirred the ingredients bubbling on the stove then took plates from the cabinet. He bent and kissed her cheek in passing.

After dinner, they sat on the couch, Angie's head in that familiar, comfortable spot between his head and shoulder. "Did you get the tapes from Trynne's safe?"

"We're still waiting for the warrant. Should have it by morning."

"I thought she said you could have them."

"She did, but Blake won't let us in the house."

Angie peered up at him. "You had me worried for a while."

"You mean about the warrant?" He lowered his head and gave her a sly grin and a peck on the temple.

"What made you suspect her?"

"Genetics."

"Doing the same work as John was enough for a judge to give you a warrant?"

"'Course not. We have other stuff."

"And you're not going to tell me, are you?"

"Nope." He gave a droll chuckle. "How about making some coffee. I'll cut the dessert."

They sat at the counter and ate tiramisu while the coffee maker gurgled and dripped. He rose to pour the hot vanilla-scented drink but instead pulled her into an embrace. "Again I apologize for today. The jealousy…"

"I know. We've got to talk about it."

"I know."

After dessert they ambled to the living room, arm in arm. He sat and she knelt, wedging herself between his legs. She stretched up and kissed the tip of his nose, his throat, the space between his nose and cheek. She feathered her lips against his, poking her tongue inside his mouth, tasting the garlic and tomatoes, and wine. While her lips worked, so did her fingers, undoing buttons, pulling shirttails free, unzipping Levis.

Later, Jarvis grunted and said, "Devil woman."

He sat up and kissed her on the cheek, then stood and walked down the hall to the bathroom, dangling shirttails hiding the curve of his buttocks, but not the musculature of his thighs. Angie curled in a ball on the sofa.

She heard Jarvis scuffing from the bathroom to the kitchen where the sounds of pot lids and spoons rent the air. She didn't open her eyes until he poked her with something. She sat up and forced her eyes to focus on the newspaper ad, and not the revived erection punching through his shirtfront.

The paper was a grainy photocopy of John's opening day. *New Nursery Opens in Alton Village*, the headline said. Wearing neat new-looking jeans and a long sleeve shirt, and standing in front of the big sign at the head of his driveway…John. He stood beside the nursery sign, smiling, wide and prideful.

"Nice," Angie said, not seeing his point.

"Look to the right."

The photographer had set the angle to show John, the sign and long rows of plants and potted trees stretching from driveway to greenhouse—the same area that, just the other night, had been nearly impassable with frozen snow. People milled everywhere.

Angie examined the picture, squinting to catch every detail, afraid to admit she didn't see what Jarvis wanted her to see. Suddenly, the words "Oh God" squeezed between her lips. Trynne half-hid near a lilac bush. Not browsing for plants, not selecting a tree. Watching John. Even with the ambiguousness of the photocopy, it was clear Trynne knew who he was. Angie picked up the photo again and held it under the light. "You think he knew she was there?"

"I'm sure of it."

"I realized something this afternoon. She has a blue car too."

He nodded. "Wilson sent me the DMV report about an hour ago. It doesn't look good for her. Sorry. I know you two are close."

"Obviously not as close as I thought."

"Now might be the time to tell you the rest of the news. She and Blake are having money troubles."

She tilted her head to gaze at him. "That's not unusual for someone in a new business."

"We're still checking on it, but it appears to be an escalating state of affairs not related to his business."

"What are you thinking, that the money troubles happened because Trynne gave John three million dollars?"

"No. There's no indication they ever had that kind of money."

She handed him ad and leaned her head back on the cushion. She squeaked one eye open and said, "Trynne and I had a long talk this afternoon. She stressed she'd been to John's only three times; all three times recently—to set the cameras. Twice she went at night and once during the day."

He wiggled the newspaper ad in the air. "This could be the daytime trip."

"No. First of all, that picture was taken the day the nursery opened in…in 2001, right? You said yourself the cameras are new. Secondly, Trynne said that while she was stringing the wires out behind the greenhouse, John was unloading trees from a truck in the driveway."

"Damn, she's got balls. Where's your cell phone?"

"What are you going to do?"

"Have her picked back up."

Angie pulled in a sad breath. "In my purse."

He returned with the phone in one hand and the anonymous note in the other. "Where's *your* phone anyway?" she said, in a vain and senseless attempt to distract him from the anger brewing.

"Home," he said. Then, "Explain."

"I found it tucked in a manuscript at the theater." Then she told a whopper of a lie. "A few days ago."

Jarvis eyed her for several seconds without speaking. She saw irritation building and thought it would be a good idea to squirt water on the blaze before the irritation became full-fledged anger. "The thing could've been there for ages, for all I know. Maybe it wasn't even meant for me." Angie stopped talking and waited for God to strike her down.

"Let me have it and go get an envelope." She handed him the note and did as ordered. If ordering her around were the worst of the storm, she'd gladly take it.

He used just his fingertips to place the thing inside the envelope. "Probably destroyed any prints," he grumbled. He left her sight a moment, ostensibly to store the envelope in his jacket, hanging in the hall closet, but returned holding the envelope, which he handed to her.

Up close, Angie realized it wasn't the same one. She lifted the flap and drew out two airline tickets. To Philadelphia.

"The conference is this weekend," Jarvis said. "Thought you

might want to go with me."

She set the tickets on the coffee table. "I can't. Did you forget I have a theater to run?"

"No. Sorry I didn't clarify. We'll leave early Thursday morning and be back for dress rehearsal Friday afternoon." She gave a slow nod. "Besides, it'll get you out of the way for a while so Wilson can find that murderer."

Unless he was in Pennsylvania.

Since her thoughts were too often visible on her face she looked away. "Do you believe furthering her career was the only reason Trynne set the cameras?" she asked.

"Originally yes, and I also think she rekindled the relationship for the same reason. Then I think one of two things happened. Either he told her what she needed to know. She knew that when Monsanto tried to patent the exact same process, he'd figure out what happened, so she killed him. Or secondly, maybe he found out what she'd been up to and threatened to blow the whistle. Faced with the ruin of her career, and marriage—"

"Which has happened, by the way. Blake moved out."

"Where is he now?"

"I don't know. Probably at his office."

Jarvis got up and stretched again, arms high, back arched. "I have to get going." He pulled Angie close and fluffed a kiss across her brow. "Marry me."

What did he say? She lifted her head from the comforting scents on his shirt and looked into his eyes. He nodded, affirming she hadn't been hearing things. She opened her mouth. He put two fingers to her lips. "Don't answer now. Think about it. We could have a great life together."

"I—"

"Think about it." He kissed her once more, then whispered, "Oh yes. Don't think you're off the hook over that note." With that he left.

Angie leaned against the doorframe and listened till she couldn't hear his car any more. Tears trickled down her cheeks.

She raced to the bathroom and threw up. After washing up and brushing her teeth, she went to bed, cuddled in the down comforter.

She didn't want to be married right now. What was the big deal about marriage anyway? Look at the McCoys. They'd been married more than half their lives. Hiding secrets. Neither had enough faith in their love to just spit the stuff out and go on living. The delicate tendrils of their relationship were stretched out of proportion. How long before it stretched beyond endurance and exploded into millions of tiny pieces?

Look at her parents. No, better not look at them.

Look at she and Will. She'd thought they were happy. Then learned he'd been cheating. To her mind, cheating was the ultimate betrayal. Angie pounded her fists on the mattress to either side of her.

The telephone rang. Who could be calling at midnight? Had to be Jarvis. Probably couldn't sleep either—for the anticipation of her reply to his question. She grinned. When he said take time to think, she expected hours, or days. The number on the Caller ID was unfamiliar.

Her head began to ache. The anonymous letter writer? Don't answer.

She had to know. "Hello."

"Good evening Mrs. Deacon, sorry to bother you so late. I've called several times and you haven't been home. My name is Justin Masters. I'm a reporter for the—"

"No comment." She hung up and walked away, ignoring the blinking light on the answering machine. The phone rang again. She waited till it stopped ringing then took the phone off the hook and started for the bedroom. A sound outside the door... just a scrape, like a footstep. She stopped, and listened. No other sound. No doorbell.

The sound came again. Not a scrape this time. A small thud. Except for the lamp on the hall table, the condo was dark. Slow and careful, she slid the security chain into the slot on the doorframe. The sound came again, like a pebble tossed against the glass to get a lover's attention. She shut off the light and went to kneel on the couch, peering between the mini-blind slats. If kids were playing around her car...

Kids? This late? The parents should be flogged.

The single streetlight at the far end of the parking lot only accentuated the deep shadows between the vehicles. For a long time, she squinted into the darkness. Nothing moved. No kids playing hide & seek. No dogs chasing cats. Nothing.

Angie tiptoed to the kitchen for some wine, drawing the glass silently from the cupboard, uncorking the bottle in slow motion, all the while keeping her ears trained toward the front of the condo. The sound came again; this time at the kitchen window—not three feet away. Goosebumps jerked to attention.

The sound came again, a small tink against a window. Call the police. And look like a fool when it's just kids playing a game? Kids should be asleep now. Very few children lived in this development; condos were rented mostly by people like Angie, halfway between one life and the next. Probably teens with nothing better to do than torment people. Her grandmother's voice entered the back and forth discussion: "Better safe than sorry."

"Oh shut up, all of you," she growled, finished pouring the wine, grabbed a magazine and went to the bedroom. She set down the glass and shut the blinds as tight as they'd go. In the dark, she undressed and pulled down the comforter. Instead of climbing in nude, the way she always did, she dug through the dresser to find a baggy t-shirt. Prepared for an emergency dash outdoors.

Angie fluffed the pillows against the headboard, got into bed, turned on the bedside lamp, and anchored the comforter under her arms. She took a long swig of wine and opened the magazine, listening hard before beginning to read.

Something woke her. The bleary face of the clock said 3:12 a.m. Damned kids. Not kids. She tiptoed to the living room and parted the blinds a quarter inch. God, it was cold in here. Dawn hadn't yet oozed over the mountains. Frost-coated cars dotted the parking lot like giant marshmallows in a mug of hot chocolate. She pressed her forehead against the window, squinting, but the shadows remained constant, unmoving.

Probably cats. Frequently they yowled in the middle of the night: the high-pitched squabbles continuing until someone heaved water on them. She listened until her ears grew numb, then finally scurried back to bed. Shivering and tugging the comforter up tight, Angie heard nothing else.

At 3:57 she sat up with an annoyed slap to the feather pillow. No sleep tonight obviously. Blue dawn squirted between the slats of the blinds, making arrows on the carpet. No sense trying to sleep now. A jog would clear the cobwebs. She untangled the unwieldy t-shirt and made the bed. The room was cold. Goosebumps ran sentry duty up her arms, the chill centering in her nipples, so taut the shirt scratched painfully. Angie ducked into her heavy chenille bathrobe and pulled the belt tight. Why was it so cold? The baseboard wafted nice, cozy heat. Probably leftover nerves from last night.

She dressed in a gray sweatsuit and headed out the back door off the kitchen. The smell of spring laced the air. Morning light filtered between the mountains. The dusky gray sky made foretelling the weather impossible. Angie strode around to the parking lot. Gloria's car sat in the visitor's lot, covered in ice. A feeling of guilt halted Angie's first jogging steps—she hadn't thought of her mother since they left for Boston. Hopefully they had a good time. Angie really liked Bud. Not because he diverted Gloria's clinging, not because he'd encouraged Angie's involvement in John's case. He was gentle and sensible; Jarvis was so much like him. Immediately Angie erased thoughts of Jarvis for now. If she allowed herself to think of him, she might have to think about the question that loomed so close.

Time to get the blood pumping.

Angie slipped in the back door at 4:38 sweat cold against her skin. A hot shower chased away any lingering nerves. At five o'clock, hair still wet, she climbed back into bed. The alarm blared at 7:00. Angie got up feeling only marginally better than before the jog and shower. The room was still freezing. She opened the blinds and morning flooded the room. Heat from the register oozed up under the robe, and felt great. Outside, bumps of snow and dead grass stretched endlessly across a field that, in summer, grew thick with wildflowers and timothy. Not a footprint marred the surface of the field. Angie raised the blinds halfway and locked them in place. Directly below, the snow wasn't so even, or unmarked. Angie opened the window and screen and peered out. A set of fresh footprints traced a path from left to right, stopped below her condo, then turned and tracked around the building. She shivered, unable to take her eyes from the oval cavities.

Kids playing.

Sure. Leaving one set of not-at-all-kid-sized footprints.

Her body screamed for caffeine. The hallway was colder than the bedroom. The furnace must be out, she thought, then realized stupidly that she had electric heat—and it was working in the bedroom. Maybe a blockage of some sort. How did one check these things? Jarvis would know. The thermostat setting said 69°, the same as always. As in the bedroom, the baseboard was warm. Passing the hallway table, she replaced the phone in the cradle. Then she punched the answering machine button, expecting to hear the voice of that reporter, Justin somebody. But the first caller was Mary Grayson: "Hi Angie. I received your e-mail photo of the Marks woman. Sorry to say she doesn't look familiar. I've forwarded it to the conference steward. Perhaps he'll recognize her. If I can be of further help, please let me know."

Then Will's voice. "Ange. I was sorting through some boxes and found a few things you might want." She hit the delete button.

In the kitchen she started the coffeemaker. The phone rang. She leaped toward it, hoping to hear Jarvis' voice. Come for coffee, she'd urge. Can you figure out what's wrong with my heat?

"Hello...Hello?" No one there. She scowled, then hung up and watched the coffeemaker until the drip drip into the carafe stopped. She poured the hazelnut scented brew into the largest mug from the cabinet. She started for the living room, to savor coffee from the big, comfortable chair, and stopped short—

The front door was open, the gold security chain stretched to the max.

Angie ran to it, sloshing coffee everywhere. She pushed the door shut, twisted the lock and waited for the familiar click as it shot home. She'd done that last night. Right?

Locking the door, such an automatic thing. Like turning off the coffeepot or unplugging the curling iron—mindless actions, that, once done, couldn't be recalled.

Maybe the door hadn't clicked all the way shut. A breeze or something popped it open—one of the noises she'd heard.

But, she'd locked it, she was sure. Almost sure.

Angie concentrated, trying to feel the smooth roundness of the little gold knob between her fingers. To recall turning it into place. To remember that little click. And finally did. At the first of the noises, she'd slipped the security chain quietly in place. The door had been shut at that time. She hadn't double-checked the latch—Jarvis always made sure to lock behind himself—but the door had definitely been closed.

Call Jarvis. He'd just say it was kids playing. But at least he'd come over. She dialed four numbers before hanging up.

What if it wasn't kids playing around? What if the anonymous letter writer loitered out there? She ran to the kitchen and dumped the coffee into the sink. Shut off the coffeemaker. Without washing out the pot, Angie shrugged into her coat, grabbed purse and manuscript, slid back the chain lock and twisted the knob lock. A thin skin of frost covered the automobiles. She'd made two steps toward her car when the breath expelled all in one whoosh. She didn't have to bend down to see the front drivers' side tire was flat. Angie reached for her cell phone. She'd stuck a finger on the speed dial button for AAA when she spotted the second tire. Stomach shriveling, she walked around the vehicle.

Fifteen steps later, she was seething. An insistent voice called from inside the phone and she put it to her ear. "Yes, yes I'm here. I have four flat tires…Yes, I said four." Angie gave her name and address then slapped the phone shut. By now, her hands were trembling.

Fear replaced anger. Suddenly the morning didn't seem so bright. Spring didn't seem so near. Life didn't seem so wonderful. She strode back inside her condo and called Jarvis. His voice wore the unused quality that invades vocal chords during the night.

"I need you," she said. The line went dead.

The blinds were still shut and she spun the knob till they opened enough for her to see out without being seen. No movement, even in the deepest shadows. Whoever did this must still be out there, gloating.

She laughed. How could they know four flat tires were nothing compared to the other things going on?

Perhaps this *was* a continuation. First, noises and an open front door. Second, flat tires. Would Step Three be in the form of another prank, or would someone—namely, her—actually be hurt?

In the parking lot, each car looked familiar. All bore the same layer of frost. No footprints etched a path through the whiteness on the ground. Angie hammered the arm of the chair with both fists.

A car pulled in with a whoosh of unrestrained urgency, tires stopping too quickly, cold engine racing, door slamming as its occupant launched himself out. Jarvis's breath puffed in clouds. He'd already noticed her tires, and knelt beside the left rear. He wore the same jacket as last night, but had thrown it over striped pajamas.

The AAA truck arrived. Jarvis spoke with the driver who nodded and sped away.

Jarvis came in the condo. The baseball cap did little to disguise the tousled sprouts poking from underneath. He strode toward her, folding his arms around her, enveloping her in security. He talked into her hair, "He'll get tires when the shop opens, then come back and check the car mechanically, too."

She leaned into him, smelling his house, yesterday's aftershave, and morning breath—and liking it. As if reading her thoughts, he pulled her tighter. Was this what it would be like, he as her protector? Maybe protection and security were the most important things at their age. To be able to care for each other.

She stepped back. His arms loosened, but didn't release her. She looked him in the eye. "This isn't the first thing that's happened."

Anxiety appeared first as a slight hollow below his cheekbones, then in a trio of wrinkles at the corners of his mouth. Jarvis took hold of her arms and backed her into a chair. He knelt between her legs, enfolding strong arms around her waist. She felt his fingers intertwine behind her. Angie told him of the odd noises and footprints.

"Why the hell didn't you call me?"

"You would've said it was just kids playing around the building."

He remained quiet, peering from under the brim of his baseball cap. He leaned his head against her abdomen, dislodging the cap. She combed her fingers through his hair, brushing it back from his forehead. He rose and took her hands, pulling her up. "Come on."

Fourteen

Jarvis walked Angie outside. "Where are we going?" she asked.

"I'm putting you under protective custody." He swung around and took hold of her upper arms. "Don't bother arguing with me. I'm not taking any more chances with your safety. I've let this go on long enough."

"You'll take me to the theater, and that's not negotiable. Everyone—and that includes you—will be there for rehearsal."

Jarvis pushed out a heavy sigh, which Angie ignored. How much safer could she be amongst all those people? The thought was soon joined by one that said, *yes, and the note appeared there by itself.*

She hurried to the passenger side of Jarvis's Jeep and waited for him to open the door.

"What time is rehearsal?" he asked once he settled in the drivers seat.

"Noon, but Tyson and the new playwright will be there—should be there right now. Can we stop for coffee at the diner first?"

"I hope you mean to-go because I'm not exactly dressed for eating out."

Her eyes slid down to the striped pajama bottoms. She smiled. "Flannel jammies?"

He rolled his eyes and drove the few hundred feet to the diner. Angie went inside. "Help, I'm being held hostage."

Judy peeked over Angie's shoulder and grinned. "Looks like a dangerous situation to me. Should I call the SWAT team?" She passed Angie's usual coffee across the counter and prepared one for Jarvis. "So, when are you two gonna—" She wiggled her hand in the air in a motion that Angie could take in several ways. She chose not to elucidate and simply laughed.

When she returned to the Jeep, Jarvis had the phone to his ear. When he said, "I know. I'll be happier when they're both safe," Angie realized he was talking about she and Gloria. He could have been talking to Wilson, but more likely Bud was on the other end of the line.

Angie slid the coffee into the cup holders, Jarvis stowed the phone in his jacket pocket and put the car in gear. "So, what was so funny with you two?"

"Funny?"

"You and Judy were laughing like hyenas."

She said, "I don't recall any hyena-laughs," but Jarvis's expression said he didn't believe her. "Getting a little paranoid, aren't you?"

"No," he said, sounding defensive. "Only curious. Hasn't been much to laugh at lately."

"You have a very sour attitude."

"Would you expect anything different right now?"

Thankfully they arrived at the theater because the conversation needed an attitude adjustment. Jarvis insisted on examining the building for intruders, anonymous messages and booby-traps. Satisfied finally, he stopped at the long table where Tyson and Sally Pruit were seated.

Tyson introduced them. Angie knew the case had taken a toll on him when he barely reacted to the pretty woman's presence. "Angie received a threatening note yesterday," Jarvis said. "Here in the theater. I need you to keep a close eye on things while I'm gone. Don't let any strangers in the building. If anything even remotely out of the ordinary happens, telephone Wilson immediately."

"Where will you be?" Angie asked.

"Out of town a couple of hours." He turned back to Tyson. "Don't take any chances. I've alerted Sergeant Wilson of the situation." Jarvis jerked a thumb in Angie's direction. "If it were up to me, she'd be in a safe house somewhere."

He let the sentence hang. To cover the awkward silence, Angie became defensive. "We have a lot of work to do."

Jarvis pulled in a breath. "I can take a hint." He left through the back door, even though his Jeep was parked out front.

Angie, after explaining in detail about the note, her open front door and slashed tires, finally convinced Tyson and Sally to settle down to work. They spent more than two hours making notes, rewriting and fine-tuning the manuscript for their specific needs. Sally took the suggested changes with good humor, and even had some great suggestions for scenes Angie and Tyson hadn't envisioned. It seemed as though the relationship with Ms. Pruit might be quite beneficial. Especially after she mentioned having two more plays in the works.

The trio broke at ten for some leg stretching. Angie went to her office to scrounge for something to eat. But no food showed its face, not even a stale cracker. She took her cell phone from her purse and flopped on the old sofa bought at a yard sale last summer for $25. Paul Zimmerman's phone rang five times. She was about to hang up when a tired sounding voice answered.

"Paul? Hi, it's Angie Deacon." She waited for him to process the name and heard his pleased response.

"It's been a long time."

"Yes, it has. How've you been?"

His voice took on a more alert tone. "Not bad. Not bad at all. How's Will?"

"Fine. He mentioned you just yesterday as a matter of fact. He said he hadn't heard from you in a while. Anyway I thought I'd call and see how you were."

"I'm opening my own plumbing business here in Portland. Hardly any time to think straight."

"What good news. Not that you haven't time to think—that you're finally achieving your dream. How's that affect your love life?"

Paul laughed. "What love life? Speaking of that, how is Donna doing?"

Angie didn't know how to respond. Hadn't Donna said Paul came to town yesterday? "I saw her yesterday. She's doing well. The flower shop seems quite successful. She showed me her irises."

Paul made a scoffing sound. "Those damned irises."

"They're very pretty."

"And expensive."

"Expensive?" Angie asked.

"You can't believe the money she's spent trying to, what's the word." He thought a second, then said, "I know this isn't right but it's all I can think of—she's trying to breed the things. As if they were living, breathing creatures."

"I've had some trouble adjusting to the idea, too."

"What's your connection?"

"Not sure you know that I am co-owner of a small theater. During our first performance, one of our major players was killed, right on stage."

Silence, as though Paul searched for the appropriate words. Angie continued, "The guy who died—well, his regular job was as a nursery owner, where he bred irises. It's become quite the talk of the town."

"His name wasn't John Bloom?" Paul asked.

"You knew him?"

"She talked about him all the time. Him and some guy from Denmark. A Peter somebody."

So, John hadn't kept his iris affiliation a secret. Did that mean he also talked about his quest for the red?

"Angie!"

The way he called her name said it wasn't the first time he'd spoken. "Sorry. I—" A knock came on her door. Tyson said, "Angie, Blake is here. He wants to see you."

She cupped a hand over the phone and said, "Okay, tell him I'll be right out." To Paul she said, "I have to go. It's been nice talking to you. Please keep in touch. Will said he misses talking with you."

So, she thought, standing and going to the door...had Donna's extravagance with irises been part of what split her and Paul? Angie pulled open the door and started to walk through, but slammed up against a wall of muscle. Blake McCoy held his ground and didn't reach out to keep her from falling. Momentum carried Angie backwards. He stepped into the office.

"You're early for rehearsal."

"I wanted to talk to you first." He crossed the tiny space and dropped on the couch, almost sitting on her handbag. She planted her feet and crossed her arms, wishing she could move further from the angry missiles launching from Blake's eyes. With every second that he glared at her, the pounding between her ears increased. It was all she could do to say, "To what do I owe the pleasure of your visit?"

He bent forward, forearms on his thighs. "What have you got against us?"

"Huh?" For something to do, she poked hair behind her ears.

"I thought we were friends."

"We—what are you talking about?"

"You sicced the cops on my wife."

At last Angie knew where the conversation headed. "Blake, I had noth—"

"You told them Trynne was cheating on me with John."

Angie gave an emphatic headshake that only rekindled the throbbing. "Trynne wasn't—" *She swore she wasn't.*

"You made the cops search our house."

Angie couldn't contain her temper any longer. She stepped forward, hands clenched at her sides—after all Tyson was just a shout away—and leaned toward Blake's face. "*You're* the one who put your wife and John back together. *You're* the one who hired

John as your wholesaler. *You're* the one responsible for him having a part in the play. Not. Me."

Blake shot to his feet, for the second time in five minutes, nearly knocking her down. "I'm not the one who told everyone about her cheating on me."

"If she's cheating, I had no knowledge of it."

"You brought Jarvis to search her lab."

"How can you accuse me when you weren't...even...there?" Angie unclenched her hands and pressed them against her thighs. "All right, now I'll throw your words back at you: I thought we were friends."

"We were."

"Then how can you think I'd do any of what you just accused me of?" Angie took a breath. Her sentence structure really suffered when she was upset. "The way you're acting, I hardly feel like wasting my time talking to you, so I'll say one thing before I ask you to leave. I went to see Trynne, to make her feel better, which, by the way, is what *you* should have done. Jarvis arrived—all on his own—and, as long as we're throwing stories around, why don't we talk about the fact that Trynne's the one who set up video cameras."

Deflated, Blake flopped back onto the worn-out cushion. He bent his head into cupped hands. So there! Blake's guilt for running out on Trynne was eating away at him. He would focus blame anywhere else he could. Anywhere but on himself.

Angie marched to the door and yanked it open. "Go to your wife. Tell her you're sorry for losing your temper. Tell her you love her and will stand by her through this horrible tragedy." When he didn't move, she repeated, "Go."

Blake stood up, arms dangling at his sides, chin to his chest. He stopped in front of her. "I'm sorry, Angie. I don't know what got into me."

She put a hand on his arm. "Go see Trynne. Make up. Be back by noon for rehearsal."

Blake stopped again in the doorway. He opened his mouth.

Closed it. Indecision wrinkled his face. Angie wasn't about to ask questions. The door closed and she fell onto the couch, head really hammering now. Angie dragged her purse across the cushion and rummaged through the contents twice before remembering she'd given Will her bottle of acetaminophen. Food. That would help take her mind off the headache. A quick sandwich from the diner. Perhaps someone could deliver it. Spur-of-the-moment meals: another thing abolished from her life if she married Jarvis. Not that fast foods were good, or healthy, but not having the responsibility made things a lot easier. The opposing sides of Angie's brain renewed their discussion. Shirts to iron—money for a new wardrobe. Busy with his job—things to talk about. Fighting for the bathroom, sharing the hot tub.

The door opened and Jarvis stepped inside, wearing the silly Sherlock Holmes hat. She couldn't help smiling even though her mind scrambled for a reason for his sudden appearance.

He strode to the couch and picked up the jacket. She stood dumbly while he held it in the air. Finally her brain made the connection: he wanted her to put it on. Angie slipped her arms in the sleeves. Lunch. He planned to feed her before rehearsal. He handed her purse from the dressing table and propelled her out the door.

They were backing out of the spot before Jarvis said, "Will's in the hospital." Jarvis sped toward Lakes Region Hospital on Route 11A. While he outlined what he knew about Will's emergency, Angie sat with her back stiff, gazing at, but not seeing the road ahead.

"Will phoned 911 at 6:42. He didn't answer the doorbell and officers had to break in. Wilson found him lying on the upstairs bathroom floor in a pool of vomit and diarrhea. He was just barely conscious, but couldn't speak. Wilson called me and I called you. Gloria's meeting us there."

The urge to cry became too strong to ignore; sobs wracked her body. She folded her arms tight around herself. Jarvis reached across and squeezed her hand. As they squealed around the turn onto Highland Street, and the hospital came into sight, she finally developed the ability to speak. "Is he…is he going to die?"

"I don't know anything about his condition. I'm sorry."

She leaned her head against the window. Angie had never been very religious, but now seemed like the time to pray.

She came alert when they skidded into the ambulance bay of the hospital. Before he could come around to get her, Angie leaped out and raced through the automatic doors. Gloria stood near the nurse's desk, wringing her hands. She pulled Angie into an embrace.

Angie's ex-supervisor, Zoë took their arms and steered the two women to a corner of the waiting room. "Sorry to see you under these circumstances, hon. It looks like Will's got a severe case of gastroenteritis."

Angie's professional training kicked in. She asked, "Symptoms?" as Jarvis slid up behind them in a blur of denim.

Zoë counted off on her fingers. "Headache, stomach cramps, vomiting, diarrhea. We've got him on normal saline, oxygen and a cardiac monitor." She gave Angie a hug, her nylon uniform crinkling between them. "He's in good hands, you know that."

Angie gave Zoë a weak grin. "He had a headache yesterday afternoon. I gave him acetaminophen and sent him home to sleep. I talked to him later in the evening and the headache still hadn't eased up." She should've called this morning to check on him. She could've gotten him here hours earlier. Her legs buckled. Zoë and Jarvis gripped her elbows and lowered her into a chair.

Jarvis knelt in front of her. "You all right?"

Zoë showed them to a small cubicle where they could wait in private. When Jarvis spoke, his voice was tight with emotion. "He'll be all right." He settled Gloria and Angie in a loveseat under the television. Then he sat in a hard looking chair facing it, and repeated, "He'll be all right."

"Of course," said Gloria. "He's Will Deacon."

Angie gave them both a strained smile. "By the way, where's Bud?"

"Jarvis phoned and told Bud to get me to his place and stay there. He said somebody threatened you." She frowned. "And we'll talk about that later. We went to the condo to pick up clean clothes. By the way, did Blake catch up with you? He came while we were there. Anyway, we'd drove to Jarvis's. Bud wasn't feeling well. I sent him to bed. That's when Jarvis got the call about Will."

Zoë entered then, stepping soundlessly in white shoes. She wedged her ample behind on the seat between Angie and Gloria. "Will's been taken to a room on the second floor. We've been able to ease some of his discomfort, but there's been no sign of recovery as yet."

"You don't know what's wrong?" Jarvis asked.

"This early, we're assuming it's something he ate."

Gloria voiced the words Angie couldn't say. "Is he going to be all right?"

"We should know more by morning, why don't you go home and—"

"No!" Angie and her mother said at the same time. More calmly, Angie added, "I'm not leaving. Can I see him?"

"Not yet," Zoë said, and left saying she'd be back as soon as she had anything more to report. She returned in less than five minutes. Three people flew to their feet. She gave a sheepish grin and pushed an armful of pillows and lightweight blankets at them. "Sorry if I scared you. I thought you might be more comfortable with these."

Angie curled up as snugly as she could in a chair. Jarvis jammed the pillow behind his head and stretched out, arms crossed, in another chair. Gloria folded herself in the fetal position on the narrow loveseat, one hand under her chin, the blanket tucked around her shoulders. She already looked asleep. Now and again, Jarvis peeked at Angie and smiled. He reached over his left shoulder and flicked off the light switch.

The light from the television made the room glow blue. Hospital sounds faded into the background. Angie felt herself rising into the air, weightless. Below, on the gorgeous green New Hampshire terrain, she and Will hiked up Gunstock Mountain. They were laughing. They stopped for a picnic lunch on a rock outcropping. The scene changed, fading in mottled shades of blue. Now they stood on tall scaffolding, painting their raised ranch. Both of them were dappled in yellow paint. What fun they'd had scrubbing it off each other. Another scene change, they were on Valerie and Nolan Little's fishing tour boat. Will's fiftieth birthday. The day her life fell apart.

Angie woke to a buxom nurse jiggling her arm and came instantly awake. "Is he all right?"

"He wants to see you."

On the way out, she gave a quick glance at the still sleeping Gloria. Jarvis's chair was empty.

"You didn't answer me," Angie said, hurrying to keep up with the energetic woman. The energy transferred to Angie's nerves, she took hold of the back of the light blue uniform and made the nurse stop. "You didn't answer me."

The nurse tilted her head, waited till Angie let go of her clothes and then said, "I don't work on that floor. I'm only a messenger."

"Oh. Sorry."

"Go to the second floor, take a right out of the elevator. It's room 227."

"I know where it is. Thanks."

Odd that Angie was alone in the elevator this time of day.

Standing outside his room, she raked numb fingers through her hair, took a breath and willed herself to be strong.

Will lay flat in the bed, tubes leading from his left arm up to the dripping IV. Though the drops were silent each echoed with the volume of thunder. The heart monitor made a blipping sound and scorched a jagged yellow line across a tiny screen. She let out the breath she hadn't realized she held in. Angie approached the bed.

Will's eyes were open. They were on her. "You look like shit," they both said in unison.

Angie laughed, Will didn't.

His hand was cold and clammy. Angie stifled the instinct to drop it back on the sheet. Instead, she pulled up a chair and enveloped his hands in hers. She laid her head on their clasped hands and prayed again.

When she woke, morning lit the flowered broadcloth drapes. 8:30.

"Time flies when you're having fun," Will said, his voice raspy.

They smiled the smiles of long-time lovers and friends.

"Why do I feel so bad?"

"What did they tell you?"

"Nothing. They come, they poke me, and they leave. A while ago I woke to somebody plucking out my hair. Ange, what's going on?"

Angie couldn't speak. A hair sample meant they suspected poison. A list immediately formed in her mind. The possibilities were endless, the results rarely good. They couldn't do a generic test for poison; they needed a clue, an idea what to look for, a place to begin.

"What's going on, Ange? And don't tell me you don't know. I saw your face."

"It means they think you were poisoned."

"With what? Who?"

All she could do is shake her head.

"Guess."

"It wouldn't do any good. I worked in the ER, I didn't have experience with poisons. Did they ask what you ate yesterday?"

The word "Yeah" came out in a rush of air. He was getting tired. "Hard to remember. How long does the test take?"

"Depends whether they can do it here or have to send it out."

He gave a great heaving sigh that must have cleared his lungs. He winced and didn't inhale for several seconds. "What's the difference?"

"They don't have facilities to test for the more obscure things." She lifted his hand and kissed the palm. He folded his fingers around hers; his grip strong and firm. She traced the outline of his veins with an index finger remembering how she always laughed at the design: the state of Texas. Somehow she managed to hold in the gasp of concern because Will's skin held a definite yellow/green tinge. She papered a smile on her lips and let her eyes move to his face. As she'd feared, his face was also jaundiced. Tears played against the back of her eyes.

Angie stood up. "I'm going to find someone who can tell us what's going on." Without a backward glance, she raced from the room. Before the door swooshed closed, tears were rushing down her face. She let the cold hard wall hold her up. A nurse scurried from behind the desk. She bypassed Angie and ran into Will's room. Angie mustered enough energy to pull herself away from the wall, go to the elevator and push the button for the fourth floor. She walked the route by long-dormant memory.

Will, her one-time beloved, had been poisoned. He might be dying.

Horace Smith's office was at the end of the hall. Angie didn't bother knocking on the door of the hospital director, her ex-boss. The hefty man sat behind a massive oak desk. He looked up frowned at the interruption, then removed wire-rimmed spectacles and squinted past his bulbous nose.

His expression erupted into a smile. He rose and came around the desk. "Angie, so nice to see you." Then he noticed her tears and spread beefy arms wide. Suddenly her knees folded. Fog swallowed her. Firm fingers took hold of her upper arms and guided her into one of the leather-upholstered chairs in front of the desk.

"I'm sorry to bother you like this, Race."

"No bother at all my dear."

"It's Will…"

"I know, I heard about your divorce. I'm sorry."

"No." Her mind swirled with confusion. She struggled to find words to convey the situation.

"Something else," Race prompted.

She managed a nod. He went to the desk and plucked a tissue from the box on the corner. She blew her nose and tried again. "Will's sick. Maybe dying." After that, her words came in a rush.

Race's demeanor shifted. His voice became soothing, like a father to a daughter. He picked up the phone, dialed two numbers and spoke in short, curt tones—that of a boss to an employee. When he hung up, his manner had changed once more. Now he was anxious, as parent to a small child, he used her name as a buffer for the bad news. "Angie, they suspect he's ingested arsenic. Sorry, I worded it wrong. They think it's…"

"It doesn't make sense."

Unless…this had something to do with her. Had someone tried to get to her through Will? Angie's brain scrambled to connect the day's events: the anonymous note, the open front door, flat tires. It didn't make sense. Everyone who knew her knew about the divorce. They also knew she and Jarvis— Wouldn't he be a more likely target?

Race's fax machine pulled her away from the harsh thoughts. He drew out the single sheet of paper, read it, then handed it to Angie. "This is a list of what he ate yesterday. See if there's anything you can add."

"I only saw him for a minute in the afternoon." She told Race about his headache and how she'd given him her bottle of acetaminophen.

He took the page from her fingers and scanned the contents. She'd never before noticed how deep brown his eyes were, nor how little crinkles appeared at the corners when he was serious.

"There's no medication of any kind listed here. Where is this bottle?"

"He didn't give it back to me. It must be at the house."

Race dialed one number, waited for an outside line, then dialed seven more digits. He didn't have to wait long for someone to answer. "Hello, Alton Bay police, this is Doctor Horace Smith at Lakes Region Hospital. I'm calling in regard to Willis Deacon, brought in about an hour ago. I need one of your people to retrieve a bottle of—" he cupped his hand over the receiver and asked Angie, "What brand?"

"Exedrin. Green bottle. Capsules."

He nodded knowing, as she did, those pull apart capsules were one of the easiest ways for someone to insert poison. Angie leaned her head in her hands.

"—a bottle of Exedrin from Will Deacon's house. Can you get it to us ASAP? Thank you." The next words must've been directed at her. She peered up through her hair.

"Are you all right?" Race returned to "concerned friend" mode. His face grew blurry. She blinked. He didn't get any clearer. This time Race didn't attempt to comfort her; he sat on the edge of the desk and put his glasses on. "Want to tell me what's been going on?"

When she finished, he handed her another tissue, eased her upright and tweaked her under the chin. "The nurse said he's stable and sleeping. Go home. We won't know anything for hours. I'll tell the nurses you went home for a few minutes and leave your number. I'll call as soon as I know anything about the poison. Have faith."

"Thanks for everything."

Angie hurried to the waiting room to wake Gloria, but found her mother standing in the hallway talking to the same nurse who'd come to wake Angie. "How is he?"

"Sleeping."

Angie thanked the nurse and steered her mother into the waiting area. Gloria sat in stunned silence as Angie told about the arsenic, not mentioning that her bottle of acetaminophen might be the culprit. Who would have—could have—spiked her painkiller? When at the theater, the bag was always locked in her office. At home, she left it on the hall table, within anyone's reach.

Gloria's hand touched Angie's then reached down and turned up the car's heater. "Can we go now? I want to check on Bud."

Angie shook her head, hard, trying to dislodge the tangle of thoughts. She didn't remember leaving the hospital. Didn't remember taking her mother's keys or getting into the drivers seat of the rental car. Surely the chilly air should have shocked her alert. The digital clock on the dash said 2:03, but the dark clouds looked as though they'd been set atop a glass dome only a few feet overhead. Flat wads of multi-colored gray moved across the dome. Between the wads came glimpses of bright blue sky.

"Can we go now?" Gloria repeated.

"Huh? Uh, yeah."

"Do you want me to drive?"

"No, I'm all right." Angie reached down to turn the key, but the ignition was empty. Gloria got out of the car, came around and flung open Angie's door. "Out."

Gloria drove the thirty-minute trip and stopped in the theater parking lot. "Are you sure you're all right to drive? I assume you're changing and going right back to the hospital."

"Yes. I'll call and let you know how things go."

At the condo, shoes dropped on the hallway floor. Purse and jacket landed on the arm of the sofa. Bedroom closet door bumped open. Clean clothes were laid on the bed. Yesterday's clothing fell in the hamper. Angie oozed into the shower. She leaned against the tiles and let the scalding darts flush the toxins from her mind. The musky scent of shampoo filled the cubicle. Suds sluiced down her skin. The water turned tepid and she reluctantly twisted the knob.

Had someone put arsenic in her acetaminophen? How? She always had a bottle in her bag. Probably a lot of people knew that. But how many had access to it? How many murderers skulked around her on a regular basis? Substituting the capsules had to be planned in advance. The capsules had to be filled with poison. They had to be stored in someone's pocket waiting for one of the infrequent moments her handbag was left unattended. After doing so, the job still took time—open the clasp, hide the bottle at the bottom.

At 3:30, wearing a tailored pants suit, Will favorite, and a pink satin blouse open to the third button, Angie reentered the hospital. The elevator doors whooshed open. Zoë, holding a clipboard, grasped Angie's arm and pulled her aside. "Good news. It's arsenic poisoning. We've begun treatment and Will's already responding." Angie heaved a sigh that made Zoë's smile widen. "He's asking for you."

Angie hugged Zoë. "Thanks. That's the best news."

The curtains in Will's room were open a few inches. Late afternoon sun lit a long narrow triangle across the bed. "Want me to open the curtains a little more?"

"No, light hurts my eyes."

She sat in the chair and checked out Will's skin color. Zoë told the truth, he'd responded to treatment. Already his skin had lost some of the yellow tinge, and his eyes were brighter. He put out a hand. She took it and sat, her knees jammed against the metal bed frame. "You look better."

"What have I missed?"

"Nothing much."

"You haven't already tracked down who did this to me? You must be slacking off."

"Stop it, Will. How do you feel?"

He turned serious. "Better. For a while, I thought I'd spew my whole insides."

"The doctor said arsenic was in the pills you gave me. Were you trying to get rid of me, to get my millions?" He laughed, winced and turned serious. "Why would someone want to kill you?"

She didn't say anything. What was there to say?

"I heard the cops asking for you a while ago."

"They probably want a list of people who had access to my purse."

"Any idea…" Tiring, he paused for a breath.

"None at all." Somewhere inside Angie, a tremor began. Just a tickle at first, but it rose through her organs spreading up and out, growing like a cancer.

Will's fingers closed around hers. "What's wrong?"

"I just realized how close you came to dying. And I would've been responsible." Angie untangled her fingers from his, stood and bent to kiss his forehead. It felt cool and dry. Will reached up his right hand and pulled her down, folding her against his chest, squeezing the breath from her lungs. "You rest. I'll see you in the morning."

She said her thanks to Zoë and received a "be careful" warning in return. So, word had spread about Angie being the likely target of the arsenic.

Automatic doors swung wide, admitting the cool afternoon air. She stepped between some cars near the building, a single word echoing with each clip-clopped step on the pavement—target. Yes, a target. With a bright red and white circle painted on her coat.

She stopped a moment, listening, watching. Then felt ridiculous. Nobody but Gloria knew she'd returned here. Nobody could have a rifle zeroed in on her. Angie shook off the bizarre reaction and started walking, with only a small glance around to see if anyone had noticed her behavior. The Lexus sat three rows away, its navy blue paint glistened in the sun beside a low, red coupe.

A man with his back to her, stood up between the two cars. He had on a tan trench coat and round-topped hat. He brushed off his slacks and walked toward the opposite end of the parking lot. Angie's tongue felt like it had swelled to three times its size. It filled her mouth, her head, made her senses swim. She laid a hand on the nearest car, letting the sun-warmed metal keep her from falling on the pavement.

What had he done to her car? Strapped a bomb there? Cut her brake line?

Stop him.

No.

Call the cops.

It'll be too late.

Then, catch him.

Angie started after the man. It was nearly impossible, to run in heels. Especially hard not to make any noise. But she ran.

He was almost across the lot now, walking fast, weaving between vehicles in a parallel line to her, right arm held tight against his side. Probably keeping the bomb components from clanking against each other.

Three rows away. Then two.

He stopped. He turned.

Angie stopped too. Her knees buckled and she sagged against the nearest car.

Fifteen

Jarvis grinned. She looked fabulous in that suit, like the thing was painted on. Significant parts of him twitched to attention—until he remembered…she'd just come from seeing Will. Had dressed to impress her ex.

Angelina didn't speak. He knew that pinched look; something had gone wrong. Something happened to Will. But…just an hour ago they said he was out of the woods. Jarvis closed the space between them. "Is he all right?"

"He's going to be fine." Jarvis helped her lean away from the car, and pulled her trembling body close. If Will was all right, then what had happened?

She eased back to peer up at him with eyes the color of sapphires. Jarvis's insides melted. "What are you doing here?" she asked.

"Looking for you."

"You were leaving."

"I…er, figured I'd catch up with you at the theater." He inhaled. "Okay, I admit…I didn't want to interrupt you and Will." He exhaled. "Is he really all right?"

"Recovering."

"How is he otherwise?" Jarvis took off his hat, ran a hand through the thinning hair, remembered how thin it was getting and planted the hat hard in place.

"Not sure what you mean."

"Not very subtle, huh? Can we sit somewhere so we can talk?"

"I really have to get back to Alton. I've been away from the theater all day."

"I know. I missed rehearsal too." They linked arms and strode toward her car.

"Will said the cops were looking for me," she said.

"State police wanted to ask you about the arsenic."

"They think I did this?"

"No. They wanted you to outline your movements over the past few days, so they could figure out how the stuff got in your bag." He unlinked their arms and stretched his left across her back, cupping her shoulder with his palm.

"That's what you were doing near my car. Checking for b-bombs—and things."

So that's what upset her! He laid the side of his head on hers and didn't answer. Couldn't. Sensing her trepidation, he released his hold. "The car's fine. The dirt around it hasn't been disturbed. Somebody would really scuff up the dirt if they were trying to get under there."

"Under the hood?"

"Again, no footprints. Besides, you have an alarm, don't you?" He grasped handfuls of jacket fabric and yanked her close, kissed her on the lips and wanted to linger there forever. He swatted her backside. "Let's go." His cell phone stopped him mid-sentence. "Hello."

"Wilson here. Just an FYI, the McCoy woman swears her husband used the rat poison at a job site. I sent someone to pick him up for questioning."

"Good." There were several seconds of silence on the line. Jarvis thought he'd lost the connection when Wilson said, "Um, there's one more thing. Dispatch received an anonymous tip—remember that missing computer part?"

"From Bloom's office?"

"Yeah. Well, we got a tip it's in Angie's condo. Behind the sofa."

"No way." Jarvis turned and walked several paces away, anxiety clenching his gut. After a moment he said, "Okay, I'll check on it," shut the phone and stowed it in a pocket. His fingers had grown clammy, acid churned liquid inside him. What the hell would Angelina be doing with Bloom's hard drive? No reason he could think of. Sure as shit, the thing had been planted there. By whom? The same person who spiked the acetaminophen?

Angelina stood two feet away, squinting in the sun that poked through thickening clouds. She groped in her handbag for sunglasses. "Come on," he said, "I'll follow you to your condominium."

Her expression changed from curiosity to one of bewilderment. "I thought you didn't want me there."

"We're going to pack you a few things. Then I'm taking you to a safe house. With your mother."

She sighed, drew keys from her bag and touched a thumb to the unlock button. "Stay back so when the shrapnel flies, you're out of the line of fire."

He took his own keychain from his pocket and handed it to her. "You drive the Jeep, I'll take your car."

She laughed. "If you say my car is fine, I trust you."

He could see in her eyes that she did. "Oh yes," he said, knowing the following news would ruin what good mood she'd regained. "There's something…I want to tell you before you hear it from someone else. Trynne's been re-arrested."

She'd started to get in the car. Stopped and turned raised eyebrows on him. "What on earth for?"

"They found arsenic in the garage, in the form of rat poison. By this afternoon, we'll know whether it's the same stuff as in your pills."

"Why didn't they wait till the tests came back?"

"Wilson went there with a warrant to retrieve the tapes.

There was a suitcase on the kitchen floor. She said every couple of months she goes to the Monsanto headquarters in Mystic, Connecticut…for a meeting."

Angie nodded. "She does."

"Thing is, we couldn't find flight information."

"It wouldn't surprise me if she planned to drive. One, her car just came back from being serviced—she always has it checked out before a trip. Two, she and Blake are having problems, she likes to drive, to think. Three, she'd better not have been planning to leave my play in the lurch."

Jarvis laughed at Angie's joke. "Anyway, Wilson just said they're picking up her husband for questioning."

He leaned down and kissed her on the ear. He shut the door and walked back to his car. Only the Lexus's roof showed. For a long time, the car didn't move. A multitude of things raced through his head: it wouldn't start, someone had tampered with it, she didn't dare put the key in the ignition—damn, why hadn't he insisted on driving? Jarvis started the Jeep and wove in and out of the lanes, toward her. He stopped at the head of the row. Her car moved finally. It fell into line behind him.

A half hour later, he took her keys from her fingers and opened the condo's front door. Angelina stopped in the foyer. Chin raised, listening, sniffing—the same thing he did every time he arrived home—checking the home's wellbeing. Everything must've been in order because she removed her suit jacket and flung it over her arm. He wanted to tell her that the *radar* had missed the invasion of at least one person into her domain.

"We're alone now," she said.

"We are at that."

"So, what did you want to talk to me about at the hospital? I assume it was something besides Trynne's arrest."

He took off his hat and urged her to the living room, to sit on the couch. He could feel the hard drive's vibes searing through the cushion. On the way to the hospital, he'd decided to donate some total honesty to their relationship. Yesterday, his lips did what his brain had been unable to do—asked her to marry him. He'd spent half the night lying awake thinking how great marriage to her would be, and the other half imagining how awful it would be if she turned him down. "When I saw you coming from the hospital, I got scared."

"Because…"

"I thought that," he stopped. The words wouldn't come the way he wanted to say them. "I was afraid you would realize you still loved Will."

"And that we'd reconcile?"

He fiddled with the lining of the hat.

She leaned over and kissed his cheek. "We're not getting back together."

"Don't tell me he hasn't asked."

"He's asked me to give him another chance."

"Today?"

"Weeks ago."

"You didn't mention it."

"Trynne didn't do it, you know."

He tried to connect the statement to the topic of Angelina and Will. And couldn't. "Didn't do what?"

"Try to poison me. She's my friend. Friends don't kill each other."

Jarvis leaned his forehead against Angelina's and said softly, "Sometimes they do."

"Not Trynne." She eased away from him. "I don't know what to think any more. If you came to me saying she'd put video cameras in John's lab, I would have said you were insane. But that happened. So now…" She left the sentence hanging and disappeared down the hall and into her bedroom.

Angelina returned carrying two bags and three coat hangers laden with evening gowns. Jarvis took the hangers and propped them over the hall closet doorframe. "Personal opinion: do you think Trynne took the iris?" Jarvis asked.

She set down the bags and opened the closet door, careful

not to knock off the hangers. She took out two pieces of outer-wear, one sporty, made of down and nylon, the other long and dressy, in an emerald color. She handed him the dressy one and said while slipping into the other, "Like before, considering the video cameras, I guess I can believe she stole *Rhapsody in Scarlet*. With it, she'd have direct evidence for her genetic work. But why would she trash the place afterward? It goes against my image of what a horticulturist is. What they work *for*. They're supposed to grow things, nurture them. So much destruction can't be in their nature."

"You said you thought anger drove the action."

"I believe so. That's why I can't imagine Trynne as the perpetrator."

"Using that same theory, I assume you think Blake isn't responsible either."

"Blake's a lot of things. He's impulsive and quick-tempered. But he's also concerned about other people, quick to apologize. So, yes, by the same theory, I don't think he demolished the greenhouse. Are we leaving soon or should I take off my coat?"

"I er…have some official business to take care of." Her brows flexed into a big wrinkle that he wanted to smooth with lots of kisses. She said something that sounded like "wa-ha." Jarvis wanted to hug the confusion away.

Then she regained the ability to speak. "Official business?"

"The phone call from Sergeant Wilson…"

The wrinkle deepened. She tilted her head and pursed her lips and said something totally unexpected. "Don't tell me I'm being dragged into this along with Trynne? Are you going to put us in adjoining cells?"

"Wait, I'm not accusing you of anything."

"No, you're letting Wilson do it."

"Angelina. You've got this all wrong."

"Get out."

Man, this was going all the to hell. "You're—oh shit. I can't leave you here, it's dangerous."

"Seems like the danger is coming from a most unexpected arena. I want you to leave. Now."

"You should lower your voice. You don't want the neigh—"

"How can you know what I want? Maybe I want them all to know what a rude, insensitive beast... What is it? Are you seeing my arrest as a way to get reinstated?" She stopped and for a moment. Happily, he realized she was reconsidering her words. Till she said, "I never thought you were capable of some-something like this. I think I can answer your marriage proposal now."

"You're making a big mistake. Come. Sit down. Please." He went to sit on the sofa. She remained a moment in the hallway. Finally, she followed and sat on the edge of her chair.

"All right, Colby Jarvis. Tell me what's going on."

How to do this without alienating her all the way? He leaned forward, elbows on thighs. "Wilson had an anonymous phone call. Someone accusing you of being the iris thief."

He'd expected further anger. Instead, she broke into sudden high-pitched laughter that made him wince. When he didn't echo her humor she turned serious. "Before last week I'd never heard of a red iris. I'd never even heard of John Bloom. In case you know less about me than I thought, I don't much care for plants."

"I know—the mess." He warned himself to tread carefully. "I'm not saying I believe Wilson's caller. I'm just repeating what was told to me."

She blew out some breath. "Get on with it."

"The caller said he's got evidence you were Bloom's lover."

Angelina laughed again, this time wrapping her arms around herself. Finally she stopped for a breath.

He didn't reply—couldn't—for fear of bursting into uncontrollable laughter himself.

"What are you grinning about? Oh, never mind, don't answer that. Let's just say I took the flower. What motive did I have?"

"I don't know. I'm just repeating what Wilson said."

"I'm serious. You're making wild accusations."

"I haven't made a single accusation."

"Okay, pretend you're Wilson, what would he be saying right now?"

"He doesn't think you're guilty either."

"In light of the poisoning, the DA probably will."

He shrugged. "I can't say where this is going. I'm not privy to any of it."

"Just tell me. How will they pin this on me?"

He sighed, then ventured into treacherous territory. "They might say Bloom confided his secret to you, about *Rhapsody in Scarlet*. They might say he took you to the lab, showed you the results of his life's work. Then, for whatever reason, you two argued."

"And I took out my revenge by cleaning out his lab, trashing what was left, then going to your house, switching guns and—" Angelina rocketed to her feet, face red, lips in a straight line.

"You asked."

"You'd better leave before I say things I'll regret."

Jarvis didn't move. He couldn't. What had just happened?

She pointed toward the door. "Either arrest me this second or get the hell out of my house."

Maybe better to go and let things cool down a while. "Okay. If that's how you want it." Jarvis stood up. One thing to take care of first. He stepped around the coffee table, squeezed between the sofa and end table and leaned over the back, propping his elbow on the couch-back, denting her meticulously fluffed cushion. He groped down near the baseboard. And nearly groaned. He'd really hoped the anonymous call was a joke. Jarvis took hold of the plastic with thumb and index finger of his right hand and lifted. About the size of a videocassette, wrapped in black plastic, he wiggled the object in the air near her face.

Her expression evolved from dark to puzzled. She followed him to the kitchen. He set the package on the counter. "Got a pair of scissors?"

"In the middle drawer."

He retrieved the scissors and carefully cut away the covering. It stood open now, like flower petals exposing fertile pollen. But this wasn't a flower.

"What is that?"

"John Bloom's hard drive." Jarvis picked up the plastic wrapper with fingertips and examined it. She stood behind him. Even so, he felt the anger rolling off her in waves. Minutes passed. She said nothing.

He pulled up the pair of stools. "Sit."

From under the kitchen sink he retrieved two white shopping bags. He shook one of them to separate the sides. The plastic gave a harsh crack that made them both jump. Jarvis chuckled. She didn't. Her hand suddenly slashed the bag from his fingers. It fluttered soundlessly to the floor. "Either arrest me now or take your evidence and get out of my house. I want you out of my life."

Knowing his next actions would influence the rest of their relationship—if there was any left—he didn't move, or speak. She picked up the plastic and shoved it into his gut. "Please go."

Careful of fingerprints, he eased the hard drive inside one bag, and the black plastic wrapper in the other. As soon as he'd closed the bags safely around his trophies, she pointed at the door.

"We've got to talk."

"I've been framed. You *are* smart enough to realize that."

"If you recall, I distinctly said you weren't accused of anything. Let's hash this out. Who else has been in your apartment?"

"Nobody but you and me, your father and my mother."

She'd answered quickly; she'd obviously been thinking about this. But as she spoke, Jarvis saw realization hit. "What did you remember?"

"Blake came here this morning. I didn't see him; I was at the theater. My mother said he asked for me. I don't know how long he stayed or whether he had a chance to do this. But he couldn't have put the poison in my bag because Will already had the bottle." She made tracks toward the door. Damn, after all that, she was still throwing him out. "Take all that stuff and see if you can get some DNA or fingerprints, or whatever it is you do with evidence. But go away for a while, my head is pounding."

Jarvis nearly kicked up his heels with joy. She wasn't heaving him from her life. "I want you to come stay with me a few days. This thing is heating up. It's dangerous for you here."

"You can drop me at a hotel."

He switched off the lights and locked the door. "Out on the steps, he took the baggage from her too-tight fingers and laid them in his back seat.

"My car."

"I'll send someone for it tomorrow." He held the door for her then ran around to climb in. As he started the engine, he said. "Duck down, make yourself inconspicuous."

"For heaven sakes. This is ridiculous."

"Humor me." He put his right palm on top of her head and pushed. With a great sigh, she slid down low. Then she leaned back and closed her eyes. And imagined herself a kidnap victim reporting to the authorities after her escape—we turned right out of my apartment and went for about a quarter mile to a motel parking lot. A quarter of a mile. Funny how distances seemed longer when you weren't actually looking at landmarks. Angie let almost a minute pass then opened her eyes. They were still on Route 11, but far beyond the motel.

She didn't need to ask where they were going. Jarvis, leaning slightly forward in the seat, eyes scanning in all directions, was taking her to his place in spite of his promise of a motel. Jarvis's tiny ranch house only had one bedroom that, far as she knew, Bud occupied. What the hell, this was all Jarvis's idea, let him worry about where he would sleep.

His back door squeaked on aluminum hinges. She got propelled into the little ranch. Scents rushed out—lasagna—and her stomach rumbled. When had she eaten last? Gloria, at the stove, turned when they came in, and waved a large spatula in her direction. Jarvis disappeared with the bags.

"You a prisoner too?" Gloria asked.

"Guess so," Angie replied, pulling out an oak captain's chair and sitting. She asked, "How's Bud?" the same time her mother asked, "How's Will?" They both laughed and replied in unison again, "Sleeping."

"Will's out of the woods. He's exhausted though."

"The same with Bud. The trip to Boston did him in. We never should've gone." Gloria laid the spoon on a paper towel and took a chair. "I tried to tell him, but…he's so stubborn. He says he has no intention of laying in bed, waiting to die."

Jarvis clomped down the hallway and into the kitchen. "Mmm, smells great. What time's dinner?"

"The rolls have about five more minutes."

"Okay, I'll be in here." He ambled into the living room, the sofa creaked as he sat; the television came on to WMUR news.

Angie hadn't acknowledged his presence. Gloria whispered, "Trouble in paradise?"

Angie shrugged. "He's so pigheaded."

"Like father, like son."

Suddenly Jarvis stood in the kitchen door, boots dangling from his left hand. He dropped them on the mat near the door and came to kneel before Angie. "Can't you get it through your head, I'm trying to take care of you? You've got a great memory, so I know you haven't forgotten how I feel about you. That I asked you to marry me."

At this, Gloria's eyebrows shot up. Angie ignored her mother. "Don't try to soften me up, Jarvis, I'm still angry with your caveman behavior."

Bud arrived then, gray hair tousled. He leaned against the doorframe on spindly legs clad in sharply creased, though rumpled Levis. He wore a blue flannel shirt, open at the neck, a fluff of white hairs protruded from the vee. He looked happy. "Son, you didn't mention you asked her to marry you. Good decision. Been wondering what was taking you so long."

"How are you feeling?" Angie asked.

He wiggled a hand in the air, indicating okay. Gloria threw him a concerned look but said nothing as she bent to remove the rolls from the oven. The circles under his eyes had deepened. His skin was grey/yellow, his cheeks hollow. He should be in the hospital receiving fluids and painkillers. Pain etched his steps, but in spite of his physical well-being, Bud remained a wonderful dinner companion. He steered the conversation well away from murders and anonymous threats.

After dinner, the men went to the living room. Angie and Gloria cleaned up to the comforting sounds of father and son getting acquainted; so much to catch up on after forty-odd years apart. They brought coffee to the living room where Bud regaled them with more tales from Jarvis's childhood.

"You talked about being a salesman," Angie said.

"I traveled all over Canada selling everything from books to garden implements."

"You never remarried?"

"No." He looked at Jarvis. "Never found anyone like your mother."

By eight thirty everyone voiced a need for sleep. With a small smile, Angie watched Gloria and Bud retire to the spare bedroom. "Seems weird, them sleeping together, doesn't it?"

Her smile grew and she nodded. "Hard to think of parents in that way."

"Come with me." Jarvis took her hand and led her down the hallway, and into his bedroom. He urged her to sit on the edge of the bed then sat beside her.

"You were very somber tonight."

"I have a lot on my mind."

"And I'm not making things any easier on you."

Humored, he said, "No, but I'm learning to deal with you." Then he added, "Bud and I have just met and I'm going to lose him. When I was six, I cried myself to sleep at night thinking I'd done something to make him leave. By the time I was ten, I was pissed at him for not being man enough to face whatever troubles he had. At fifteen I was sure another woman had taken him away."

"And now?"

"I just wished I'd gotten to know him."

"You got your wish." She reached for his hand, warm, un-calloused.

"I watched Liz die. Afterward I prayed never to have to see anyone go through that torture again." He leaned over, kissed her on the forehead and whispered, "Try and get some sleep."

He went out, shutting the door behind him. Angie remained there a long time, part of her wanting to invite him back, part of her needing to be alone. He'd known that, and, as much as he needed her right now, had put her needs first. Facing Angie was her reflection in the mirror above an outdated dresser. She looked quickly away. But that one glance had left an image etched in her mind—the image of her mother. Angie had never noticed a resemblance to either of her parents before.

Most of her mother's emotional decline took place during the fifteen years of Angie's childhood. During that time, Angie blamed her father's alcoholism for Gloria's retreat from reality. As Angie grew older, she realized that maybe it would have happened anyway, that possibly the horrific things her father did while drinking weren't the entire cause of Gloria's emotional downfall. Gramps always said that life had a way of throwing things at you, and you either ducked or got hit by the pitch. Instead of ducking, Gloria gave up. Until Bud's appearance in their lives. Bud's strength and determination rejuvenated everyone, including Angie.

A wide irrepressible yawn and a vision of it in the mirror jolted her back to reality. She stood up and moved closer to the mirror. The image of her mother disappeared. Angie saw a fifty-something year old woman, who had been as her grandfather used to say, rode hard and put away wet. Angie raked her fingernails through the billowy blonde hair. After a shower, feeling a little better, she crawled into bed and lay on her back. The ceiling had been painted recently. Funny Jarvis hadn't mentioned doing any redecorating.

Movement in the kitchen. The sound of cabinets shutting and water running lent an air of domesticity to the tense situation they were all in.

She'd spoken out of anger saying she wouldn't marry him. She tended to blurt out things like that during stressful times. But did she really want a life with someone who could accuse her of such heinous things? You don't do that to a person you love. Angie buried her face in the pillow so Jarvis wouldn't hear her crying.

Bright sunshine flooded the room around the edges of the shades. The LCD clock on the side table stood out clearly—7:30. Couldn't be. Unfortunately her watch said the same thing. She'd slept the entire morning. Angie strained her ears but couldn't hear movement anywhere in the house. She dressed, pulled her hair into a ponytail, and went to find someone.

Fourteen or so hours had dulled her anger, but hadn't changed her mind about marrying him. She couldn't spend her life with someone who could so easily change his allegiances.

The door to the spare bedroom was open. The bed made. Empty. The living room was empty too. But Jarvis had been there. A blanket and pillow were folded at one end of the couch. How would he react when she told him they couldn't be married? Would he still feel inclined toward friendship? Probably not. Men's values were different than women's. If he couldn't be her husband, it was unlikely he'd want to continue the relationship.

Where was everyone? The scent of bacon was in the air. The room was neat and clean. Breakfast dishes were propped in the dish drainer. On the table, leaning against an empty Styrofoam take-out container was a note—two notes, really. The first from Bud and Gloria saying they'd gone to a motel, to *give the love-birds some privacy*. The second had her name at the top. *Good morning Sleepyhead, Wilson called. New information I hope will bring the case to a close. Coffee is made, just turn on the pot. I'll be home by 9:00 to pick you up for our trip to Philadelphia. Please stay put. Remember, I love you.*

Jarvis

Angie folded the paper and got up to turn on the coffee. She went to the living room and opened the heavy drapes that covered the big bay window. Brilliant sunlight flooded the room. She folded her arms and leaned her forehead against the sun-warmed glass. Across the narrow road, another house, similar to this one except it had once been bright green. The color had faded to a putrid shade of olive. The blinds, like square white eyelids, were down. Two cars were in the driveway, one a late model, the other several years old.

Remember, I love you.

What was love anyway? She guessed it was different things for each person. For her it had meant disappointment, wasted years.

Don't forget all the good times.

Angie couldn't stifle the sigh as she retraced her steps to the kitchen and poured a mug of coffee. Is there any way to tell when someone told the truth?

Take a chance.

That's what her brain said when she'd thought about going back to Will. She never could've trusted him again, Angie argued with her subconscious. So how can it be right to give Jarvis another chance?

Angie went back to the big window. A man came out the front door of the green house. He wore a sports coat and black slacks. A woman followed, wearing a pink bathrobe and a blue bandana around her head. She wrapped her arms around him. They kissed deeply. Angie turned away.

Love. L-O-V-E. A four-letter word. As a child, she'd received a mouthful of soap for saying four letter words.

Angie finished the whole pot of coffee. Now she was wired. 8:40. She thought about going for a jog, but going out meant being in the public eye. Something she'd really catch hell for when Jarvis found out.

She took the cup to the bedroom while she unpacked the

clothes she'd brought and repacked for the one-night trip to Philly. Next Angie booted up Jarvis's laptop and checked her email. A note from Mary Grayson changed her whole mood.

In the kitchen, Angie rinsed out the mug and put it in the drainer. One of his jackets hung in the tiny entryway. She put it on and went outside. The older car was gone from the neighbor's driveway.

Jarvis's yard had new shoots of green grass that reached for the warmth of the springtime sun. Not much of a landscaper; there were only two overgrown rhododendrons on either side of the cement porch, their bulging flower buds also waited for sunshine to explode them into a riot of pink. Angie walked around the house. There were no shrubs or plants at all in the back. A three-foot high picket fence in need of paint separated Jarvis' property from the abutter. A birdbath in the middle of the yard was full of raunchy brown water and slimy leaves. She tipped everything out then started into the house for a scrub brush and pail of water. Three cement steps led up to the back door. Locked. Angie cursed and went around the front. Locked. The next curse was much stronger, and not under her breath. She walked around the house. All the windows, and the bulkhead were locked.

That's when the phone started ringing. Angie stood on tiptoe and peered into the window as though by staring at the phone she could tell the identity of the caller. Who else but Jarvis checking on her? A tiny smile etched her face as she pictured him angrily slamming the phone down. "Damn her! Why can't she just once do what I tell her?"

She sat on the back stoop, elbows on thighs, chin on hands.

Had she really done all right for herself? Till a year ago, she had what she thought was a good marriage, and a good job at the hospital. One upheaval found her divorced and running a small theater with Tyson. Another upheaval brought Gloria to town. And then John had been murdered. Did she want to face another total turnaround in lifestyle and marry Jarvis?

The squeal of tires out on the main road brought her head

up. Most people would think first of a car accident. But she knew it was Jarvis. She swiped at her wet cheeks as another squeal brought the car into the driveway. She stood up, walked around the house and collided head-on with him. He grabbed her before she fell. Instead of yelling, he pulled her close, holding her so tight she couldn't breathe. "Thank God you're all right," he said, hoarsely.

She pulled back and looked up at him. "Why wouldn't I be?"

"You didn't answer the phone."

"I came out for some air and got locked out."

He pulled her to him again, burying his face in her hair. She could feel his hot breath on her scalp. After a while he led her inside.

She tapped the note he'd left. "You said you had information."

"I'll tell you on the way to the airport." And he did. "The check on the McCoy's came back." He recited the couple's history as if reading a shopping list. "They arrived in town five years ago and purchased the home they still reside in. Blake worked at the hospital until two months ago. She's worked for Monsanto almost twelve years. They're deeply in debt, to a total of four hundred and forty-three thousand dollars, not including the mortgage. The business expenses account for a little more than two hundred thousand."

Angie didn't like where this was leading.

"What it means is Trynne's got a much bigger reason to steal that three million dollar flower."

"I have some news too. Checked my email this morning. Mary Grayson heard a rumor that Pedar Sondergaard is going to reveal the red this weekend."

Sixteen

The Loews Hotel was too modern for Angie's tastes, all square edges and glass, but it was plush and shiny and spotless. Mary Grayson met them in the lobby. A shapeless string bean of a woman, the charcoal gray business suit hung limply from her hips, the jacket buckled around non-existent breasts. But rimless glasses and a welcoming smile made Angie like her immediately.

Mary and Jarvis shook hands. All business, he asked, "Do you know where Sondergaard is?"

"He went up in the elevator about twenty minutes ago. I've been sitting right here…" she indicated a long black leather sofa. "From here I can see the elevators. He hasn't come down."

"What's his room number?"

"Seven twenty-two." Mary handed Angie a red folder. "This is the intro packet given to every conference attendee. It lists the schedules of meetings and discussion groups throughout the weekend. There are name tags for you inside, that'll get you everywhere without any questions."

"Thanks." Angie tucked the folder under her arm. Jarvis was already punching the elevator button.

"You're sure you only want to talk to him?" Mary asked.

"That's all, just talk. I'll see you later, and let you know how it went. Thanks for your help."

Jarvis stepped into the elevator. He held the door for Angie. "You were going up without me, weren't you?"

"This is police business, you can't come."

Angie laughed. "Don't give me that, you don't have authority here."

"Did Ms. Grayson say anything helpful?"

"If you'd waited a minute, you would have known for yourself." The elevator slid to a stop and the doors opened. "I wish you'd stayed around. I wanted you to watch her reaction every time I mention Sondergaard's name. She's very protective of him."

"You think she knows more than she's telling?"

"I have two ideas about that. Either she knows him on a personal level or really believes he's developed the red and—"

"She wants the world to know."

Their footsteps were soundless on the colorful carpet. He knocked three times on the door of seven twenty-two. Angie couldn't hear anything from inside the room, yet the door slid open enough for Sondergaard to peek into the hallway. He was tall, six foot three or four. Olive green eyes blinked at the intrusion of light. Two parallel lines appeared at the bridge of the nose. He'd been expecting someone else.

Long, lean fingers that had recently seen a professional manicure, held the door in a no-nonsense grip. The third finger wore a gold filigree band with an emerald-cut yellow diamond. Angie couldn't discern the filigree design from where she stood.

"Good afternoon," Jarvis said in a low voice. "I'm Detective Colby Jarvis of the Alton Bay, New Hampshire, police. I wonder if I might ask you a few questions."

The nose puckered further, the nostrils widened. "What about?" The voice didn't bear the honey-like accent Judy spoke of; his words were angry. Behind him, the room was dark.

Unperturbed by Sondergaard's manner, Jarvis gave a deliberate peek up and down the hallway then lowered his voice a little more. "I'm afraid it's a rather touchy situation, sir. Could we come inside?"

"Do you have a warrant?"

A hint of humor touched Jarvis's voice. "You watch too much

American television. All we want to do is talk."

"What about?"

"I don't think you want to discuss it in the hallway."

Sondergaard gave his own glance up and down then drew back to let them in. The curtains were drawn. The light from behind illuminated only a few feet into the room, just enough for Angie to see they stood in a small hallway. To the immediate right was the bathroom. Straight ahead were two uncomfortable-looking chairs. To the right of them, a full-sized bed wearing a white spread, crumpled into a ball. Sondergaard had been napping.

He moved away from them, becoming a shadow without features or details. He bent, his arm reached down and out of sight. Angie felt herself being pressed backward into the bathroom. She began to protest then realized Jarvis was getting her out of gunshot range. She clutched at his arm. His left hand snaked back, making sure she remained behind him. The room was suddenly thrown into bright light. She couldn't see Sondergaard, but Jarvis relaxed his grip. She stepped around him to see Sondergaard approaching. He wore richly tailored slacks and a Brooks Brothers shirt, open at the collar, and no tee-shirt.

The silence stretched for several seconds. Finally Jarvis said, "We're investigating the theft of a red iris from a breeder in—"

"There is no such thing as a red iris. There cannot be, the plants lack a red color gene."

"Regardless of genes, you and I both know there is such a thing, Mr. Sondergaard. A man named John Bloom has—"

"I know no one by that name." Sondergaard crossed his arms in the classic I'm-not-talking stance.

"Think hard." Jarvis enunciated the two syllables, "John Bloom."

"I know no one by that name," Sondergaard repeated. "And I've never been to New Hampshire."

This was a losing battle. Pedar Sondergaard wasn't about to admit to, or divulge, anything. But Jarvis wasn't ready to leave.

"We know you were in New Hampshire as recently as ten

days ago, sir. We also know you've had numerous communications with Mr. Bloom regarding a specific red iris."

"I am from Holland. I have arrived for this conference only. I am to deliver a speech in—" he glanced at his watch— "one hour's time."

"We know all about it," Jarvis said. "We also know the subject of your intended speech. You are a dedicated geneticist. You—"

"I speak of genetics in general—not of one iris."

"You and Mr. Bloom were seen having a serious discussion at a local diner. You gave him three million dollars for—"

"You are mistaken." Jarvis remained firm. He mimicked Sondergaard's previous posture, legs spread, arms crossed, prepared to wait him out. More than a minute passed. Finally Sondergaard said, "Let us say I was in New Hampshire. What does it matter?"

"It matters because there *is* a red iris and it has disappeared."

Sondergaard's eyelids twitched slightly. It could have been normal blinking, it could have been surprise, Angie couldn't tell.

"Bad news, yes. But it has nothing to do with me."

Jarvis waited again.

Suddenly the man lunged forward. Jarvis thrust Angie into the bathroom. Sondergaard stopped four feet away. His voice edged almost an octave higher. "You are thinking that I have stolen this flower."

"We make no accusations. We merely want to ask you about your relationship with Mr. Bloom."

The Dane tried again, "I told you."

"Yes. You do not know this man. There is no red iris. No three million dollars." Jarvis gave an elaborate sigh. He spoke to Angie without taking his eyes from Sondergaard, "I guess we'll have to take him in for questioning."

"You have no reason. No right."

"You were seen having a serious discussion with Mr. Bloom

just days before the flower disappeared. Days before the man was murdered. Those are the only reasons we need."

"I will miss giving my speech."

"Yes."

"You have no authority here."

"Under the circumstances, even Joe Blow Citizen has the authority to bring you in."

Sondergaard frowned at Jarvis's use of slang. "I want you to leave my room."

"You are awfully calm for a man who's just lost three million dollars. Too calm."

"I know nothing of—"

"You did a good job disguising the money trail. Just not good enough. Angelina, call security."

Sondergaard looked at his watch. The exchange had eaten up almost twenty-five minutes. Sondergaard blew out a mouthful of air. Angie grinned. Jarvis the Master. She would've deemed this man unbreakable.

"All right, all right, I agree to talk with you, but first you must allow me to give my speech. We will meet afterward and I will tell you everything."

Jarvis nodded. "Fair enough."

Angie pulled open the door. Someone burst inside. "Pedar, I'm so sorry I'm late. I—"

Seeing Angie, the woman stopped talking. Angie stopped too, shock and recognition infusing her limbs. The woman's eyes widened in astonishment, the color drained from her face.

"Donna," Jarvis, Sondergaard and Angie exclaimed at the same time.

Jarvis stepped around Angie and took Donna's elbow. He led her down the corridor, leaving Angie alone with Sondergaard. In the stark light of the hallway, the pale man was almost albino-like. Intense green eyes glared at her. How could she have found him handsome?

She tilted her head in the direction Donna and Jarvis had

gone. "How do you know her?"

"I do not."

"Why then, did she apologize for being late? Why did she call you by name?"

His thin lips tightened, becoming almost invisible in the clench of his jaw. "She had the wrong room. I do not know that woman."

"Want to hear my theory?"

"Not really."

"How's this? You and Donna worked together to steal *Rhapsody in Scarlet* from John Bloom. You were planning to market it as your own."

The words were soft, but unmistakable, "The red was already mine."

Angie's mouth went dry. "Is that why you gave Bloom three million? To develop it?" He didn't reply. She continued, "Here's what I think happened. John fell in love with *Rhapsody in Scarlet*. He refused to turn her over to you. You killed him in a fit of anger."

Sondergaard backed two steps and slammed the door in Angie's face.

Damn. She hadn't meant to let Jarvis's cat out of the bag. Likely he'd deliberately neglected to mention John Bloom's death. Had her momentous announcement registered on Sondergaard's face? No, she thought not. He hadn't heard anything after she said John couldn't give up the red.

What about Sondergaard's relationship with Donna? Were perhaps he, John and Donna involved? Angie hoped Jarvis was having better success with Donna. Rather than chance disturbing them, Angie strode to the bank of elevators and pushed the button.

In the lobby, she perched on the edge of the black leather sofa, probably the way Mary Grayson had while watching for Sondergaard. Soon Jarvis, Donna and Sondergaard stepped off the elevator. The Dane and Donna turned left and disappeared through a door at the end of the corridor. Jarvis watched them then stomped to the main desk. He spoke to the clerk, who disappeared through a doorway. The man reappeared moments later followed by a uniformed guard. Jarvis talked. The man nodded and then headed toward the doorway where Donna and Sondergaard had gone.

Jarvis looked very dashing as he walked the twenty or so feet toward her. "I got security to keep an eye on them." Jarvis didn't sit. "I need a drink and something to eat."

"Good idea. Then what?"

"We talk to people."

"About him?"

"And her. Did you bring the photo?"

"As a matter of fact." Angie dug into her purse and pulled out the pictures Wilson had copied for her.

"What time is Sondergaard's speech over?"

Angie checked the event schedule. "Eleven."

"That leaves plenty of time for dinner." His fingertips grazed hers as he took the photos. She ignored the tingles that shot up her arm. A glance at Jarvis said she'd failed. He gave that patented Mona Lisa grin of his. He dangled the pictures. "I'll check us into our room while I'm there."

"Two rooms," Angie said.

Although she hadn't eaten since morning, she wasn't hungry. She allowed Jarvis to lead the way to a very plush dining room. Her order of a double-vodka on the rocks brought a lift to his brows. They didn't speak until the drinks arrived. Then Angie asked, "I suppose Donna denied having a relationship with Sondergaard?"

"No. She admitted the whole thing. They met two years ago at a conference in New Mexico and have been seeing each other off and on ever since. See also admits to 'keeping an eye' on Bloom at his request."

"I wonder how far Donna's 'keeping an eye' on John went. Remember John's neighbor said he noticed a small blue car in the driveway. I wonder if Donna began a relationship with John in order to keep on top of the situation."

"No pun intended, right?"

Angie slapped his arm. She relaxed against the back of the chair and crossed her ankles. Donna might have insinuated herself into John's life. Her love of irises would be the perfect impetus for a relationship. Things might even have progressed to the point that he confided in her about the red, showed her his creation.

"What's going on in that beautiful head of yours?"

"If John had already let the cat out of the bag with Donna, would he still feel the urge to tell Trynne and the rest of us?"

"Not sure what you mean."

"He invited us all to a gathering after the performance. He said 'I have an announcement—no, a wonderful discovery.'"

"So, you're thinking that if he'd told Donna, the cat wouldn't be so anxious to get out of the bag."

"Crudely put, but yes."

"Then again, some people want to blurt the news to everyone when they've done something special."

"Right. But as far as we know, he managed to keep it quiet for almost three years. Seems funny the urge would be that uncontrollable after so long."

"Humans are unpredictable. Jeez, where's our food? I'm starving."

She sipped her drink and set the glass down in the same ring it had left on the coaster.

"Donna swears John and Sondergaard's only relationship was that he paid John to develop the red," Jarvis said. "They met regularly to discuss the progress of the reproductive features."

"Did she meet with him while he was in Alton Bay?"

"She says no. She said she didn't even know he was there."

"You believe her?"

He nodded. "She seemed angry."

"Did she have the idea he knew about the theft of the iris?"

"She says she didn't tell him, she's been unable to reach him for almost two weeks."

"She might be telling the truth. He seemed surprised when I told him." Angie sipped again, letting the smooth clear liquid float over the ice cubes and onto her tongue. She put the glass down. "Let's say Sondergaard stole the red. He'd be able to say he never received the goods, he could demand his three million back, claiming John defaulted on their contract."

"So, why kill John?"

"Doesn't make sense, does it?"

"Think we've been barking up the wrong tree?" Jarvis asked.

"If I were John, I'd make sure to put a clause in the contract that allowed me to keep the money—or at least a generous percentage—regardless of whether I successfully developed the red. After all, the odds were so stacked against it."

"He put a big portion of his life into this project." Jarvis ran a hand through his hair and sighed. "I wonder why we haven't turned up a contract."

"Maybe the thief has it."

"If I were John, I would've stored it someplace safe."

"We've already determined he wasn't the type to do the logical thing. By the way, I stuck the three million into our conversation. He seemed genuinely surprised I knew about it." Before he could chastise her for talking about the money, she added, "I had another idea. We kind of talked about this before. What if Bloom set the whole theft up himself?"

"Motive?"

"For many years, the development of that flower has been as illusive as the cure for cancer. John finally does it. He falls in love with this plant."

Jarvis gave a sharp laugh. Angie moved her hands so the waiter could set her plate on the table. "His main focus over the past thirty or thirty-five years was that flower."

"Where do you get thirty or thirty-five years? Sondergaard only hired Bloom three years ago."

"Yes, but remember, Trynne said way back in his teens, he dedicated himself almost to the point of obsession."

Jarvis sampled the food, chewed and swallowed before nodding.

"So, what if John calls Sondergaard and says he's exhausted all possibilities and is giving up? Sondergaard takes the next flight from Amsterdam. John shows him a bunch of reddish or brownish, or whatever color flowers as the offspring. Sondergaard is devastated, or angry, or just plain depressed, doesn't matter, he demands his money back."

Jarvis aimed the fork at her. "And Bloom says no way, he's keeping the three mill as payment for what he's put into this. Sondergaard gets pissed and—"

"And what?" Angie asked. "Kills John?"

"No. I can't buy it. John's murder was well staged, no pun intended. If Sondergaard was going to do it, he would've done it right there. Crime of passion, and all that."

"You're probably right."

The scream didn't come from anywhere in the dining room, but it pierced Angie's eardrums as though the screamer stood beside her. She and Jarvis rocketed to their feet and dashed out of the room. Unable to tell where the sound had originated, they stopped. A crowd had gathered down the hall. Angie and Jarvis raced in that direction. Jarvis pushed between the onlookers and, before the opening could close up, she followed, and found herself in the entry to the main meeting room. Another scream ripped through the air.

Donna Marks stood against the back wall, hands on either side of her face. The whites of her eyes showed all around. Her mouth opened to screech again. The house lights came on, bringing the place into harsh reality. Voices murmured, then exclaimed. Another scream, this from the front of the room. Jarvis pushed through, carving a zigzag path to the front. Angie took hold of his shirt and plowed along with him, knowing she wouldn't like what she found when they finally reached the end.

Sure enough, slumped like a used dishrag beside the podium was Pedar Sondergaard. "Somebody call an ambulance," Jarvis hollered, wrenched his shirt from Angie's clutches and knelt beside the man.

Angie, adrenaline pumping like lava, stepped around Sondergaard and knelt too. He was doubled into the fetal position. His left hand clenched the hilt of a large knife protruding from the center of his chest. His white silk shirt had absorbed much blood. The excess pooled beneath him. Angie realized she was standing in it. Ridiculously she imagined throwing away another pair of shoes, the first being dinged after the trek to Bloom's greenhouses, was it only a week ago?

She closed her mind to the grisly sight and allowed her nurse's instincts to take over. She rolled him gently onto his back. Sondergaard's eyes popped open. He gazed at her without recognition. While Jarvis wadded napkins and attempted to staunch the flow of blood, Angie touched the first two fingers of her right hand to Sondergaard's carotid artery. The pulse pumped weak and thready. She counted his breaths, each more labored than the last as the fluid collected in his lungs. "More pressure," she told Jarvis, whose face was pale. She heard the desperation and futility in her voice as she encouraged Sondergaard. "Hang on, an ambulance is coming. Just hang on."

The Dane's eyes focused on her. He opened his mouth. A tiny bubble of blood popped between his lips. As she leaned down to listen for what might be his last words, the bubble grew larger and larger until gravity pulled it into the crease at the side of his mouth. It ran down, joining the ever-widening puddle on the floor. She put her ear to his lips. In the background, rejoicing voices told Angie help had arrived. Unfortunately it also obscured Sondergaard's words. "Say it again," she pleaded.

Once again his lips flattened against each other. Once again, she missed what he said.

The crowd parted and, like angels two EMTs floated in. Jarvis relinquished hold on the napkins to the first attendant, rose and turned away. "Pulse is fifteen and thready," Angie said. She'd started to rise when a flash of something in Sondergaard's hand caught her eye. Hiding her movements behind the leg of her slacks, she wedged her fingers into his and pried the object loose. As she followed Jarvis's retreat, she poked the thing into her pocket.

Jarvis would beeline for Donna, who'd obviously witnessed— or perpetrated—Sondergaard's 'accident'. Not seeing either he or Donna, she stepped into the hallway, the object she'd taken from Pedar practically burning a hole through her clothes. All she knew so far was that it was about two inches long, and shaped like a teardrop. It felt solid, but pliable at the same time. Cool air assaulted Angie and she realized how stifling the room had been.

"All right. Everyone back inside," boomed a voice from behind. A squad of uniformed officers swarmed the corridor. Angie ducked behind a huge potted palm to watch people being herded back into the meeting room; the questioning was about to begin. When the doors closed, securely locking the horror of the evening inside, Angie went back to the restaurant.

The food was cold, but she hadn't wanted it anyway. She pushed the plate away, downed the remainder of the vodka, reached once again into her pocket and pulled out the teardrop-shaped object. She laid it on the tablecloth. The waiter appeared out of nowhere and she instinctively cupped her hand to cover it.

He swept up the empty glass and spoke to her, but his eyes were focused on her right hand. "You look like you could use a refill."

"Yes, please." Instead of moving away, the young man lingered beside her. Angie turned an innocent expression upon his youthful face.

"What's going on over there? I heard somebody got killed."

Angie suppressed a smile as she realized this guy probably thought she hid the murder weapon. "A man was stabbed. He's still alive."

"I love all this cloak and dagger stuff. 'Course I hate seeing anybody get hurt. I'm an avid mystery buff, I love true crime stories. Can't get enough of them, actually. I bet they locked all the suspects in."

Angie raised her available hand to silence him. "I'm sure you'll understand when I say I can't talk about this right now. It's been very traumatic."

"Oh sure. Sure. I'm sorry." But he wouldn't let it go. "Um, did you know the person who—"

She gave him a didn't-you-hear-what-I-said look that at once brought her mother to mind. Angie thought about apologizing, but didn't have the energy. "Thank you for understanding."

He turned on a heel and left. From across the room she felt him watching, waiting for her to expose her hidden treasure. Discreetly, Angie slid it off the table and back in her pocket.

Seconds later, he returned with her drink. This time he didn't hang around. Angie sighed. How did she keep getting herself into these situations? This cloak and dagger stuff, as the waiter so succinctly put it, should be left to the professionals. Then she remembered that, this time, she wasn't here of her own accord. She'd been forced to come; her life was in danger. Someone wanted her out of the way. Jarvis had brought her to Philly so the thugs in Alton Bay couldn't find her. What a joke. The suspects were here.

Pressure on her left shoulder made her leap out of the chair. Her arm jostled the glass and she grabbed blindly before it tipped over. The pressure on her shoulder tightened, a face appeared. Jarvis's cheek brushed hers. Before Angie could turn around, he eased a very agitated looking Donna Marks into the opposite chair.

The waiter appeared again. "Can I get you something, sir? Ma'am?"

"Yes," Jarvis said. "A bloody Mary for the lady and a gin and tonic for me. Do you want yours freshened up?"

"No, I'm fine."

"Oh yes, take away these plates too, would you?"

"Would you like them reheated or something?"

Jarvis shook his head. "Just bring a plate of something we can pick at."

"Yes sir, right away."

Donna's hands, clenched in a ball on the table, were nearly lost against the stark whiteness of the cloth. Her eyes darted from Angie to Jarvis to the door, as though she expected any moment for the authorities to barge in and haul her away in handcuffs.

"Is anyone going to tell me what's going on?" Angie asked.

"You want me to tell her?" Jarvis asked.

Donna picked at something on the back of her left hand. She spoke without looking up, "I'll do it."

There was another delay as the waiter arrived with the drinks. "The hors d'hoeuvres will be right out."

Donna flattened her hands on the table on either side of her glass. "I d-don't know who did this…this awful thing." She stopped to sip the drink and clear her throat. "Pedar's talk was going so well. He hates public speaking; he gets so nervous he actually has to take a pill to relax. Most people don't realize how shy he is." She'd recovered her voice and spoke in a monotone. She had disassociated herself emotionally. As a nurse, Angie had seen this frequently in extra emotional times.

Now Jarvis cleared his throat. Donna flinched but didn't look up. "Someone behind the curtain—I only saw an arm—called to Pedar. He excused himself and went to the sideline. I couldn't see him. When he turned back to the audience—"

"How long was he gone?" Angie asked.

"Not more than a second or two. When he turned back, he was staring down at his shirtfront looking, I guess surprised is the best word. His hands were closed around something red… well, that's what I thought at first. Then I realized it was blood. And a knife."

Angie had seen the knife, buried to the handle in Pedar's chest. But try as she might, she couldn't focus her mind on it.

"What kind of knife?"

"A regular steak knife," Jarvis said.

"H-he staggered and fell. That's when I screamed. I couldn't stop myself, it just came out. Then everybody got up. I wanted to go to him, but the crowd…" Donna sobbed. Each word came out with a gasp for air. "I tried…but I couldn't get…through. I kept getting pushed back till I was…crushed against the wall."

"Did you have an impression of whether a male or female stabbed him?"

Donna closed her eyes. Tears squeezed loose and rolled down her face. "I was sitting near the back of the room. Pedar said it made him nervous if I was close." She shook her head as if trying to cast off the memory. "I saw a long sleeve. Black or navy blue. Maybe someone closer got a better look."

Jarvis put a hand on Donna's arm. "I'll tell the rest for you. Donna and Sondergaard—"

"Pedar," Donna corrected.

"—began seeing each other."

"You were still married to Paul." Angie hadn't meant the words to sound accusatory, but once they were out of her mouth, she couldn't reclaim them. Donna started picking at the back of her hand again. Jarvis reached over and pushed the drink closer. Obediently she picked up the glass and sipped.

"Since Donna was married to Paul, their meetings were restricted to conferences and such."

With a slow, lazy eye-roll Donna looked at Angie. There was apology in those eyes, and Angie knew it was for all the times she had put down Will for his cheating.

"Pedar was everything Paul wasn't," Donna said. "Considerate and thoughtful, always bringing me gifts." Angie refrained from saying that's what lovers did. "In bed, he…" Donna gave Jarvis and embarrassed glance.

"We understand," he said. "A few months later, they were having dinner at a conference. John Bloom interrupted asking if he might have a few minutes alone with Pedar. Donna went up to the room, leaving the men alone. When Pedar came up about an hour later, he was excited, but all he'd say was that he had a line on something that would make him very rich."

"For someone so very laid back," Donna said softly, "it was wonderful seeing him so animated."

"Did you know John's identity at that time?" Angie asked. "Did you know he lived right in town?"

Donna shook her head.

"Did he know you?"

"I don't think so."

"Pedar made occasional trips to New Hampshire," Jarvis continued, "nice for Donna because she saw more of him."

"Where did you meet when he visited?"

Donna answered, "The motel."

"Paul never found out?"

She gave a slow nod. "It's what broke us up."

"As I told you earlier, Pedar enlisted Donna's help keeping an eye on John."

"Did Pedar know you were sleeping with John?" Angie asked.

Donna's nod consisted of one very slow up motion of her head, and one down.

"Did John confide in you about his discovery?"

"Not until four months ago."

"You've seen *Rhapsody*?"

She smiled. "It's the most beautiful thing I've ever seen. Neither Pedar nor I had anything to do with the theft. I swear."

"Say something that'll make me believe you," Jarvis said.

"You're a cop, so there probably isn't anything I can say." Donna eyed him ruefully. "You don't know the iris world. Discovering the red is like finding the Holy Grail. It's a dedication regular people can't understand. The person who achieves it will be rich, not only in dollars and cents, not only in the iris world;

this discovery could open doors to color genetics in other plants, other fields. He'd be world famous. That's something Pedar valued above everything else. Over money." She hesitated, and added, "Over me."

Jarvis was looking at Donna, but Angie saw belief mirrored there. So, where did that leave the case?

With Trynne.

Seventeen

Angie closed the door to her room with a heavy heart. She kicked her shoes in a heap, then remembered the bloody mess she'd stepped in and gave the footwear a disdainful glance. As recently as a month ago, disposing of those shoes would have consumed her thoughts. Tonight, too little energy and too much sadness made her pull her gaze away and heave herself on the bed.

She'd wanted so badly for Trynne to be innocent. Not that she'd known Trynne for a lifetime; she'd originally been Val's friend. But Valerie was gone, and Angie and Trynne had hit it off, becoming as close as—well, as close as Angie had ever felt to anyone, besides Val. She sighed. Maybe she was just too quick to trust people. Trust came naturally for women. Trust provided the impetus to get out of bed in the mornings. Trust that things would flow smoothly, that their loved ones would be healthy and—faithful.

Faith. Another version of trust. Without that, where were people? Divorced, that's where.

At the window she looked out at the sleeping city. City skylines were beautiful; buildings in different shapes and sizes stamped across the black horizon, golden stars twinkling on the inky backdrop, the tiny sliver of moon curved upward—like a bowl. Angie was suddenly in her Gramp's lap in the creaky old rocker on the old front porch. Her parents were fighting again. Angie'd run the two miles just to be held, to hear familiar words. She and

Gramps sat in that chair long into the night. "Cast your wishes to the sky," he always said. "God will catch them and store them in that golden cup. You'll always know where to find them."

Again it came back to trust. You had to trust that's where your dreams could be found. Why did people keep going, keep dreaming, keep trusting? Why bother if life just shot you back down? She turned away from the memories. Will's cheating had made her too suspicious and judgmental, too fearful of a relationship with Jarvis. What would Grampa say about that? "Forget and forge forward, let the relationship blossom."

Where was Jarvis now? Still waiting for authorities to question Donna? Or had they gone on to the hospital to await news on Pedar's condition? If Pedar survived it would be a miracle; he'd lost so much blood. Although, Angie had seen people in far worse condition pull through.

Forge ahead.

Easy for Gramps to say, Angie's annoying little voice, interrupted. Mistrust and suspicion were the elements that made a good detective. Question everything. Weigh alternatives. Sort through lies. Construct scenarios. Angie got better at it all the time. And worse at relationships.

What did she want with her life anyway? Was it more important to satisfy her baser needs by becoming a successful detective, or her physical and emotional needs with a man who obviously cared for her? She wasn't getting any younger. Did she want to spend her waning years alone? Of course not. Nobody did. Thinking about Jarvis hurt. She forced her mind to the case—to Trynne.

Maybe Trynne had found out about Donna and, what—wanted John for herself? Couldn't stand to see him happy? Felt threatened by his intelligence? Wanted the three million? Angie couldn't imagine her friend that petty. Then again, she couldn't imagine Trynne placing those cameras.

Possibly Trynne wanted credit for producing the red. Angie shook her head. She'd already achieved immeasurable success and was renown in the woolen industry. It hadn't gone to her head. As a matter of fact, she rarely mentioned accomplishments she'd made. It was Blake who showed off her awards, and always under protest from Trynne.

But there were no other logical suspects.

Except Blake. John's understudy. He would've had plenty of time to slip away and do what needed to be done. The backs of her thighs were sore from standing so long. She flexed her legs, wanting suddenly to go jogging, to work out kinks and frustration at the same time. She jogged in place for several steps then stopped. Way past bedtime. Producing adrenaline wasn't a good idea right now. Angie's head hurt. It hurt all the way down her neck and into her spine. She undressed in the bathroom.

Possible that they were dealing with a totally unknown person. Any number of people who, if they knew about *Rhapsody in Scarlet*, might be willing to steal it. If only there were more clues, something that would break this case wide open. That would satisfy her urges. Then, she vowed, she'd leave detecting to the professionals. One clue, that's all it would take.

She slapped a palm on the sink. There *was* a clue! Angie hurried to the closet and fumbled in the pocket of her blazer, and came up with the object she'd taken from Pedar's fingers. She laid it on the table and turned on the lamp. There, swollen with impending life, ready to spring open with the least provocation, an iris bud. It had just a nub of stem still attached. The cut had been made with something sharp.

Angie squeezed the bud. Soft/solid as she'd originally noted. Dark olive green at the stem end, fading to palest, almost translucent green at the tip. Angie gently pried back one of the immature petals. Her sharp intake of breath made her dizzy and she sat on the edge of the bed cradling the flower-to-be in her palm. She let a moment pass and looked at it again, just to make sure her eyes hadn't been playing tricks on her. No doubt about it; Pedar Sondergaard had been clutching a red iris bud. Was this the reason someone tried to kill him? Or had he taken it from the potential murderer?

She needed to talk to someone. Jarvis would be still at the hospital, or the police station, or he would be here. Gloria would be asleep, but this was important. She dialed the number and waited for the connection to click through. The image from the meeting room—Pedar lying on the floor, blood puddling in the corner of his mouth—grew so strong Angie's legs buckled. Not because of the blood and horror, she'd seen enough of that through the years, but because, as she stared down at him, her own face became superimposed over his.

Angie literally shook off the vision, scrunching her eyes tight and shaking her head so hard her teeth hurt. "Come on, Mom, answer." On the fourth ring, the voice mail clicked on. Angie hung up. 2 a.m. Where was she? Angie tried again. No answer.

She began pacing, the urge to speed to the airport grew to monumental proportions. She sat in the nearest chair and crossed her legs. She turned on the television. She turned it off, then got up and paced again. Maybe Mom had returned by now, even though only twelve minutes had passed. Angie put the flower bud in her purse, got in bed and found a movie to watch.

The phone was ringing. Angie groped on the bedside table, knocking something to the floor. The clunk and thud brought her head off the pillow and eyes squinted open. The clock radio lay upside down on the carpet. The phone rang two more times before she said, "'Lo...." as she sat up. "Yeah, okay." She fumbled the phone back into the cradle.

Pounding began on the door. Angie staggered from the bed, feet tangled in the bedclothes. She flung open the door and flopped back on the bed, pulling the sheet up over her head.

Jarvis sat on the edge of the bed. "Jesus, you had me scared to death."

She lifted an edge of the sheet and peeked out. "Huh?"

"Do you have any idea how long I banged on your door? Woke two of your neighbors. I finally called downstairs to have them ring you. I swear if it had rung one more time—"

"Gimme a break, will you?" He made a sound that signified disgust. "I'm fine. What time is it?" she asked.

"Four thirty."

She sat up, pulling the bedclothes around her naked breasts. "How's Pedar?"

"He didn't make it."

"Damn." She came alert. "Did he say anything before he died?"

Jarvis shook his head. "But it looked like he was trying to say something to you last night."

"Yes, but I couldn't make it out. Too much commotion. I had the idea the word started with either a P or a B. Or maybe even an M. How is Donna?"

"Sedated. At the hospital she fell apart completely when they gave her the news."

"Not that I don't care what's happening, but why were you pounding on my door at this hour? What's so important it couldn't wait till actual daylight?"

"I was worried about you."

Jarvis's arms folded around her in an embrace that told all. She melted into him, finally able to realize he hadn't woke her to impart information. He needed to be held, just as she had earlier. She hugged him back, her right arm around his waist, left palm flat against his chest. The muscles beneath her hand were tense and tight, like thick ropes. Angie began to massage, moving her thumb in ever widening circles. She went to work on his biceps, then got to her knees and moved behind him to knead the fingertips of both hands into his back and shoulders. She worried her thumbs along his spine, feeling the knuckle-like shape of each vertebra and the sinew on either side.

Gradually he relaxed as Angie's hands worked on his shoulders. She felt the play of muscle against muscle, his head lolling from side to side as he helped work out the kinks. In total submission, Jarvis drifted onto his side. Angie lay down beside him, fitting her length along his. She put her cheek against his left shoulder blade. Her nipples grazed the cotton shirt and came erect and tingly. His buttocks nestled into the crook of her hips; delicious sexual energy shot in all directions. The tops of her thighs melded to the backs of his, her toes bent upward against the backs of his heels. This could only get better if he were naked. She settled for unbuttoning his shirt and draping her right arm around his waist and letting her fingers tangle in the dark triangle of hair just above his navel. His breathing grew deep and measured, he snored gently. Angie could feel it as a low rumble beneath her cheek. That's when she remembered the iris bud.

She lifted her head, looked at him, and decided the flower could wait. She lay there for a very long time, staring at the far wall, unable to stop seeing Pedar's pale face as his lips formed the first letter of a word. P, B or M. On television, when someone's dying, they always try to implicate their killer. Which suspects' names began with those letters? Blake, of course. And John Bloom. Well, it obviously couldn't be him since he was already dead. Blake and Trynne's last name started with M—McCoy. But if Pedar had been trying to implicate Trynne, wouldn't he use her first name?

Donna's last name was Marks. Another M. No doubt Donna's grief had been real. Angie wished she could see the police report, read the statements from witnesses. Right now, only Donna's word said she'd been seated near the back of the room. Perhaps she'd been the one to beckon him from the sidelines.

What if Pedar *hadn't* been trying to say someone's name? What if he'd been trying to tell her where *Rhapsody* was hidden? Storage facility, suitcase, hotel, airport locker, Amsterdam, vault, rental truck. Might as well have disappeared into thin air. All the places she could think where the red might be—and none of them started with those illusive three letters.

Angie squinted one eye open to see the clock—8 a.m. She reached around to pull the sheet tighter, and realized the other side of the bed was empty. The muffled roar of the shower penetrated the hotel wall. It went on for such a long time she drifted back to sleep. The squeak and thunk of the faucet being turned off roused her again. After a moment, Jarvis appeared in the doorway, thick white towel wrapped low on his waist. He raked fingers through curly hair that dripped down his neck, carving wavy rivulets along his chest, and becoming lost in the tangle of dark hair. She lost sight of the beads of water, yet let her eyes follow their imaginary path over his flat brown nipples, down the gentle swell of his pectorals, and dipping into the puckered circle of his navel and into the baby-soft downward pointing triangle.

He cleared his throat. She dragged her gaze to his face, swallowed and said, "After last night, I imagine Trynne's an even bigger suspect."

"Far as I'm concerned, she's our only suspect." Jarvis dropped the towel on the floor. This time she didn't let her eyes move south. Forge forward, she heard Gramps say.

"What about Blake?"

"Been thinking about him."

Angie rose, dragging the sheet with her, and padded past him, to the bathroom. Before she could pull the door shut, she felt it being jerked out of her hand.

"Okay, what's up?" Jarvis asked.

"Besides that?" she asked without looking down.

"Yes, besides that. What's wrong?"

"Nothing's wrong. I have to go home. I have a bad feeling about my mother. I want to go home."

"It's not safe."

"Like it's safe here?"

Jarvis sighed. "You're impossible. Our plane leaves in two and a half hours."

He took a pair of jockey shorts from the dresser top. She watched him put them on and tuck himself inside. It looked like a painful operation and was glad when he turned away to remove slacks off a coat hanger hanging on the doorknob.

"Where are you going?" Angie asked.

"Police headquarters. I'm hoping they'll share what they

found out last night." He wove a braided leather belt through the loops of his slacks.

"Hey, where did you get clean clothes?"

"Where do you think?"

"I didn't hear you leave."

"You were too busy snoring."

"I don't snore!"

Jarvis smiled indulgently and took a pale blue shirt from a second hanger.

"Well, I don't."

"Whatever."

She slammed the bathroom door.

A few minutes later, he knocked on it. "I'm leaving now. Please. *Please* stay here. I called down and had breakfast sent up."

She ate some of the breakfast while dressing. She paced and paced. And called her mother. Still no answer. Angie dried and curled her hair, put on makeup. Still no answer on Gloria's cell. Angie wished she knew Bud's number. That's it, she couldn't wait any longer. She dialed Jarvis's number and talked to his voice mail. "I can't stand it any longer. Mom's still not answering her phone. I'm going home."

She caught a cab to the airport for the 9:35 flight to Manchester. Angie dialed Gloria's number from the cab, then again as she boarded the plane. Still, no answer. The second time, Angie left a message: "I'm on the way." She sped into the Alton Bay Motel in a rented compact at quarter past noon. The clerk said they'd checked out yesterday.

Bud's black SUV was in Jarvis's driveway. Gloria's rented car wasn't there. Angie parked the rented Ford and ran into the house. Empty. Where were they? Angie made a more sedate trip through. Their luggage lay on the bed. She opened the suitcase. Still packed. She dialed Gloria's cell one last time. It rang. Angie frowned, hearing an echo. At first it seemed like a bad connection. Then she heard something. Sure enough, Mom's phone, buried beneath two pairs of Bud's slacks, was ringing.

"Shit." She flipped her phone shut. Before she got it back in her purse, it rang. Jarvis's cell number appeared on the caller ID. She poked the TALK button and spoke fast hoping to belay the expected tirade. "Look Jarvis, I'm sorry I ran out on you. You can yell at me when you get home. For now, just help me figure out what's going on. Mom and Bud checked out of the motel. I'm at your house. Their luggage is here, Bud's SUV is here. Mom's car is gone. There's no note and I have no idea where they went."

She stopped talking and prepared herself for a lecture. But all he said was, "Damn."

That single syllable sent shiver of apprehension through her. "You can't be thinking something's happened to them."

"I want you to sit there and wait for me. I'll be there in a few hours. Promise me you will." When she didn't respond right away, he said, "Promise."

"All right, I'll do it."

"I mean it," he said.

"Didn't I say I would?" She exhaled heavily and repeated after him, enunciating each word, "I promise to sit down and wait for you. Good-bye."

Angie went out to her car and drove to her apartment. From the apartment parking lot, everything looked all right. No flat tires on her Lexus. No scraped paint. No dead cats hanging on her door. No anonymous brown paper packages on the stoop. Worst of all, Gloria's car was not there. She went inside and stood in the hallway for a moment, absorbing the aura and aroma of the place. A place she'd come to love. A place that, if she married Jarvis, she'd have to give up. She chuckled. *If* he wanted to marry her after all the times she'd gone against him.

It didn't feel like anyone had been here. Still, she tiptoed through the entire place, opening closets, looking behind furniture. She even opened drawers, checking to see if her precise arrangement of things had been disturbed.

She took an orange from the refrigerator and sat at the table to eat. Angie laid the iris bud on the table. The outer skin had shriveled, the stem rippled and dry. The whole thing felt rubbery, like a butterfly cocoon. "Damn." She picked up the flower and examined it closely. Then swore again.

It had been in her possession since around 10:30 last night. At that time it had been fresh and full of life. Had Pedar, or his murderer, just cut it from the parent plant? If so, that meant one of them had brought the entire red plant to Philadelphia. The last words Mary Grayson had spoken rang in her mind: "Pedar Sondergaard is going to reveal the red this weekend."

How long did it take a bud to wilt? Angie cleaned up the orange peels, then retrieved her handbag and keys. Outside, she gave a wistful glance at her precious Lexus but got into the Ford and drove to Donna Marks'. Donna's driveway was empty. Probably the little blue car sat under a veil of frost at the airport awaiting its owner's return. Angie drove all the way into the yard and got out. A glance around told her the tall stockade fence hid her from view of the street. She tried the greenhouse door. Locked. Everyone Angie knew kept a key hidden somewhere in case of a lockout. Donna was no exception. It took Angie only a few seconds to locate it on the narrow ledge above the door. The lock and the door, opened silently. She gave one quick peek around before going inside. The air smelled damp and like soil. It didn't take long to find and pluck two young buds, about the same size as the one in her bag. The color wasn't important. Angie dropped them into her pocket and got the hell out.

At home, she put one of the flowers back in her pocket. The other she wrapped in damp paper towels and put it in a baggie. She wanted to see how long it took for each of them to wilt. It was 1:30 in the afternoon.

What to do next? Although it had been less than an hour, she couldn't help checking the iris buds. Both still looked fresh. Something niggled at the back of her mind. And it was probably important.

Less than an hour till Jarvis's ETA. She'd have to get back to his house soon. She sat in her favorite chair, leaned back and closed her eyes, letting the mental video of the suspect's faces take over. Trynne first. Tall, dark and slim. Pretty. A little domineering but that had probably developed through the years in reaction to Blake's perpetual nice-guy, agree to everything, personality. Blake, with his cocoa brown hair and baby blue eyes, made larger by thick lenses. A gentle man, friend to all. He and Trynne made a handsome couple.

Donna Marks. Blonde, a little chunky, but she carried the weight well. Angie didn't know her very well, but had the idea she would be a good friend, loyal and dependable. Had she masterminded the theft? Since Pedar was so nervous prior to speaking engagements, perhaps Donna had given him the red bud as a good luck charm.

Then there was John. The very handsome John Bloom. The possibility that he'd stolen his own flower remained. Of course, he couldn't have murdered Pedar, unless he'd been working with someone who took over after his death. Again Donna Marks' face loomed large. Sondergaard himself could have stolen the flower. The bud was clutched in his fingers after all.

Trynne's face appeared again. It hovered in the air, then zoomed closer, so close her features blurred, became larger and almost grotesque. Suddenly she wore a mustache and had an iris bud clutched between her teeth. Red teeth. Scarlet red teeth. Angie's cheekbones throbbed. Her mouth went dry as dust. Her eyes flashed open and she flew out of the chair. It couldn't be. It couldn't be that obvious.

Sure it could, her little voice said.

"But it doesn't make sense. It doesn't make any sense at all."

The hall clock chimed. She had to hurry to get to Jarvis's before he arrived home. Her mouth felt full of cotton. How in the world could a single clue—two clues really—be connected to this crime, to Alton Bay, to any number of things? Where did the pieces fit into the whole? Man, this would blow Jarvis's mind.

At his house, the light on the answering machine blinked—

two messages. Why didn't she notice before? Because she'd been racing around like a lunatic. She punched the PLAY button. The machine's mechanical voice said the first call had come at 1:33 a.m. Gloria's voice sounded clear and strong, "Angie, you didn't answer your cell phone, and you didn't say which hotel you'd be staying at, so I couldn't phone you. All I can do is hope you call home to check your messages. We've had an emergency. Bud's missing."

The machine beeped. The mechanical voice told her the second message had come an hour and a half later. Angie's heart stopped beating at her mother's next words. "I found him, we're at the hospital."

Angie leaped into the rented car and broke every speed record getting to Lakes Region General. Her heart had finally started pumping again, but now it did double-time. Things were really unraveling. Please Bud, don't die. Please.

Her cell phone rang. Angie skidded to the shoulder of Route 11A and pushed the ON button without looking at the caller ID. Jarvis's voice yelled, "Angelina, where the hell are you?"

"On the way to the hospital. Bud is there. I think I know who's responsible for this whole thing." Before the phone landed on the passenger seat, she'd squealed the tires back onto the roadway and was zooming northward. Even as she said the words to Jarvis, she wanted to scream that it just didn't make sense. How many times would she say those words before this ended?

Her growing theory still lacked a sufficient motive. Hell, it lacked any motive. But right now it had to be put on hold so she could deal with this emergency.

Angie's heart pounded so loud she thought she heard it echo in the cavernous elevator. The elevator stopped and she leaped out, then stopped herself. Tyson, she needed to tell him. She dialed—he seemed to be the only one answering his phone today. He said not to worry, he'd manage with rehearsal, and use Jarvis's understudy just in case.

Angie ran to ICU. Through the large glass wall she spotted

Gloria seated beside Bud's bed. She had her head bowed, his left hand in hers. If Jarvis didn't hurry, he'd miss this final good-bye. Her shoe made a scuffing sound as she stepped inside the door-less room. The slow blip of the heart monitor and the whoosh whoosh of the oxygen, were the only sounds.

Gloria and Angie embraced. Gloria had held together well; her face was calm, her voice steady. "He's been unconscious since we brought him in."

The elderly man looked pale and small. His eyes, surrounded by dark circles, seemed to have sunk deep in his skull. The white hair looked as though many people had run their hands through it. An IV snaked into each arm, a heart monitor sat on the side table, its yellow line zigzagging a short line. His chest rose and fell in slow motions.

"Tell me what happened," Angie said softly.

Gloria spared him a glance before taking Angie's arm and steering her into the hallway. "We got back at the house about nine. I went to take a shower. When I came out he was gone. I searched the house, and the yard. His car was there. I checked everything again, even the cellar. Even though his coat was there, I thought maybe he'd gone for a walk. You know, just in his sweater—or maybe he had a jacket—I don't know. Anyway, I took my car and went looking." She took a breath. "I didn't know what else to do. I called the police. We searched and searched—for hours. I drove up every street in town at least a dozen times. It got dark and I couldn't see a thing. Angie, I was frantic."

Angie hugged her mother.

"Then I remembered the answering machine and thought maybe he'd called. I went back to the house. And found him lying on the ground beside his car. It wasn't an awfully cold night, but too cold for a sick old man."

"Was he conscious?"

"No. He hasn't been at all."

Together they walked back down the hallway, arms around each other. Jarvis appeared in the doorway. Gloria pointed him into the room. He went in.

"Did they say how long he's got?"

Gloria shook her head gravely. "I'm just glad Jarvis got here in time. What I started to say: Bud wants to see you." She didn't say what they'd both been thinking—if he wakes up. "He asked if you'd do him a favor and go get his briefcase, first. It's at Jarvis's."

"Mom, it's a half hour each way."

"He specifically asked if you could get it."

Angie started down the hall praying there'd be enough time. She was waiting for the elevator when Gloria called to her in a loud whisper. Jarvis stood beside her. Tears glistened in his eyes. "He's gone."

Eighteen

Angie moped down the hallway leaving Gloria and Jarvis outside Bud's room. Damn, things just weren't going well at all.

Why had he wanted her to get the briefcase? Because he wanted his son and Gloria nearby? Because she drove faster? More likely something in the case that only she could, or should, see. Gloria was too emotional. On suspension or not, Jarvis was still a cop.

Gloria was surprisingly calm. Granted, she and Bud hadn't had much time together, but they'd made the most of every minute. Knowing he was dying wouldn't ease the sense of loss for her over-emotional mother. While Jarvis completed the paperwork, Angie went in to see Bud for the last time. He lay on the narrow bed, hands folded atop the white sheet. The blue veins stood out starkly on the aged flesh. His hair had been smoothed down, the tubes and monitors disconnected. The place was eerily quiet.

Gloria's voice made Angie jump. "The doctors noticed something odd about his condition." Gloria stepped up beside her and took Bud's hand. "Since he'd been out all night they expected him to be suffering from exposure, but he didn't show signs of having been outdoors more than a half hour or so."

"Is it possible he was somewhere in the house the whole time you were out looking for him? Maybe someplace you wouldn't look, like asleep on Jarvis's bed. Maybe when he woke up he went outside looking for you, passed out and fell down."

"I didn't look for him in Jarvis's room. Why would he go in there?"

"No idea. I just tried to account for the circumstances."

They drove back to Jarvis's house all in separate vehicles. What could be in the briefcase? The only logical thing was his will. And if what she'd been thinking turned out to be true, nobody would like what the document said.

She handed Gloria a sleeping pill and put her to bed. She changed her clothes and went to the kitchen where Jarvis shoved two frozen dinners into the microwave. Her first instinct was to frown, but it didn't matter, she couldn't eat much anyway. A half hour later, he headed for the shower and Angie went for the briefcase. As she tiptoed into the spare bedroom she wondered why she hadn't mentioned its existence to Jarvis. Simple, because if Bud wanted him to know, he would've told him. Gloria lay on her side, breathing slowly and rhythmically. She spotted the case, leaning against the wall near the closet. She slid two fingers through the expensive leather-clad handle, lifted and padded to the kitchen. It was extremely light. Angie set the case on the table, then used thumbs and index fingers to pop the unlocked clasps. She pushed up the lid. Wrapped in several layers of white tissue: a single gold key.

"What have you got there?"

Angie dropped the tiny key. It clattered to Jarvis's floor. They nearly bumped heads trying to grab for it. "Looks like it fits a safe deposit box." He examined the briefcase's pockets. "Funny, that's all he's got in here."

"I figured his will would be in here." She fingered the key. "I guess it's wherever the box is."

"Probably back in his home town."

"I don't think so. Bud impressed me as a logical thinking, detail-oriented guy. He knew he was dying. He wouldn't make his family go traipsing all over the country to get it. Something's missing though, the signature card so that whoever has the key can access the box. The bank won't let anyone in without proper credentials."

Angie closed the case and set it on the nearest chair. She dropped the key in her jeans pocket, went to the living room and sat on the sofa. Jarvis accompanied her, questions all over his face. He started with, "How did you know about the briefcase?"

"While you were in the room with Bud, Mom told me he'd asked me to go back and get it. That he wanted to see me."

"Why you?"

She shrugged. "All I can figure is he knew he didn't have much time and wanted to spend as much as possible with you and Mom."

Jarvis said, "Maybe," but Angie could tell he'd heard the wavering in her voice.

On the coffee table lay an envelope from a one-hour photo developer at the pharmacy. Angie scanned a few of the pictures, looking for something to talk about. Gloria had taken them during the second night's performance. Idly, Angie thumbed through, flicking them like cartoon pages. A man's face caught her eye. She went back over each, carefully searching for it. She got all the way through the pack and hadn't found him. She went through a second time, still not finding the one that had made her stop.

"What's wrong?"

"Nothing. Why?"

"You were shaking your head, like you were disagreeing with yourself."

"I'm probably just tired. I thought I saw something—someone." Angie knew better. "Seeing things" was her subconscious trying to get her attention. This time she dealt the photos across the tabletop, then studied each one closely. Many were of the sets, props and costumes. These Angie discarded. The rest were taken as the play progressed: Trynne in the wheelchair with Blake the understudy standing nearby. Trynne with her little blonde daughter in her lap. Blake and Jarvis. Jarvis holding the gun on

Blake. After the play: Trynne with a hand to her mouth, stifling a yawn. Angie smiled. Trynne had spotted Gloria with the camera and the next photo showed her laughing and wiggling a threatening finger in the air. There were four blurry figures in the background of that shot. In another, Blake listened seriously to a big bosomed lady who played a storekeeper.

A second envelope also contained pictures. About half the roll was of some tour Gloria had been on. The last half must've been taken Friday night, before the play. One showed four people—Blake, Jarvis, someone Angie didn't recognize, and John—laughing.

Angie massaged her temples with her index fingers. Jarvis nudged her hands away and took over the kneading of her flesh. She didn't let the wonderful sensation draw her attention away. Whichever photo had caught her eye didn't capture it a second time. This phenomenon had occurred before: in John's kitchen as she'd thumbed through a pile of American Iris Society Bulletins. That time, the familiar face belonged to a woman.

"Can't place it?" he asked.

"No." Men looking like women. Women looking like men. It all meant something. But what? No matter how she tried Angie couldn't tie her newfound knowledge to the man/woman 'thing'. She tipped her head up, down, left and right, working out the kinks, then gathered up the colorful prints and replaced them in envelopes.

Trynne's name begins with M, Angie's little voice reminded her. M was one of the letters Sondergaard might have been trying to communicate. No. He wouldn't refer that way to someone with whom he'd been intimate. He'd call her Trynne, or some pet name. Angie's little voice didn't reply. Damn, she told it, if you're going to plant ideas in my head, at least follow up on them.

Jarvis released her neck, rose and went to the kitchen. He returned with a can of beer and a juice glass of brandy.

"You trying to jog my memory?" she asked with a grin.

They went to bed together at eleven, but there was no hanky

panky; they lay there side by side staring at the freshly painted ceiling. Bud's death had left a void in their lives. And a whole lot of unanswered questions.

At three, Angie rose quietly so not to disturb Jarvis. He must've fallen asleep because he didn't budge. She checked on Gloria, who appeared to be sleeping, then went to sit on the couch staring at the empty television screen.

Just after seven, she heard Gloria moving around in the bedroom, Angie went to the kitchen and made toast and coffee. They sat in thoughtful silence over the strong brew. Her mother looked well rested, and pensive.

Angie set down her cup. "I opened Bud's briefcase last night. It held only a small key. Did you remember him mentioning anything about a key, a safe deposit box, or anything like that?"

Gloria thought a moment and shook her head. "No."

"Did Bud mention a will?"

"Not sure what you mean. He said one existed, that's all. I didn't ask; it was none of my business."

"What are you doing today?"

"I thought I'd help Jarvis with funeral arrangements. Try to take some of the pressure off him. For now I'm going to shower and iron some clothes. What about you?"

"I have an idea I want to follow up on."

"Is there dress rehearsal today?"

"No. We don't have rehearsal on show days. I called Tyson, he said everything went well yesterday. He sends his condolences."

After Gloria disappeared into the bedroom, Angie located the telephone book in the drawer near the kitchen phone and turned, for the second time in as many days, to the Yellow Pages, under A for airlines. Less than twenty minutes later, she dropped in the living room chair, airline passenger list clutched in a sweaty but enormously self-satisfied hand. Her 'sibling' had traveled under an alias, but it was such an obvious alias—Rap McSodie—that anyone could've tracked it down. Everything was finally falling into place.

"Whatcha doin'?" Jarvis asked, padding into the room, barefoot and wearing just flannel pajama bottoms.

She stashed the pages behind her back. Not the right time to divulge the killer. Too much happening—would be happening—over the next few days. Right now he couldn't logically assimilate what she had to say.

"Hmm?" he asked, sitting and peeking behind her.

A partial explanation was needed. She handed him the passenger list. He skimmed down the printed columns as he dropped on the couch beside her. "Damn. He's not here. I was so sure you were on to something." He tossed the pages on the coffee table.

"It's there," she said softly.

He frowned and read the list again. When his eyes reached half way down the sheet, a small smile clutched the corners of his mouth. His long index finger stabbed the page. "Him?"

Angie nodded, slowly.

Jarvis folded the pages and put them in his pocket. "Now tell me what it all means."

"I'm not sure yet," she lied. "Not even sure whether he wore a disguise."

"You mean it might be a woman?"

"Might be."

Jarvis read the papers again. "The flight to Philly left at 10:30."

Angie's laugh brought his head sharply up. His expression questioned the basis for the laugh. "You brought me here because I was in danger. The danger got on the plane with us."

"But came back on a flight that night."

"Under normal circumstances, would this be enough evidence to pick someone up?"

"It would be enough to pick them up but not enough for a conviction in court. We'd need more."

Angie went to the window to peer through the blinds. The sun shone brightly. On winter days, when it shone like this, it sparkled like millions of fireflies. Today the landscape looked dull and sad as everything turned to liquid. Mud season had begun. She hated mud, as did most everyone in the North Country, but also cheered its appearance since it meant the long winter was over. She stood for a long time, wheels churning inside her head.

"What're you thinking?" he asked.

She let the slats clink back into place. "Spring is here."

Jarvis came to hug her from behind. His crossed arms in front of her, each hand located and cupped a breast. She leaned back into him and sighed when his fingers tweaked her nipples through the material.

"Do we need a warrant to go back in John's house?"

He laughed and gave gentle squeezes to each breast before releasing them. "Fine time to change the subject."

She twisted in his embrace. "You're the one who's changing the subject."

He gave an exaggerated moan. "What are you thinking this time?"

"That we need more information, another clue. I have a suspicion it's in John's house.

"What would we be searching for?"

Angie told him about her man/woman dilemma. "Twice, as I've flipped through photographs I thought I saw someone...but when I went back through the pile, I couldn't find the person I thought I'd seen. I just have this unsettled feeling. That we've missed something." She took their glasses to the kitchen overwhelmed with guilt for not divulging the whole story.

"You ever just think you're cracking up?"

"It's crossed my mind. The old warrant isn't good any more?"

"It's expired. I'd need a damned good reason to get a judge to issue a new one. Come on, let's go."

"Where?"

"Let's just go for a ride and get away for a while."

"I'm not sure I should leave Mom alone. Maybe she could come with us." Angie walked to the door of Gloria's room and tapped lightly. No answer. She opened the door. Gloria lay on the bed, wrapped in a big brown bathrobe, curled in the fetal position. Angie watched for a rhythmic rise and fall of her body, then shut the door and went to leave a note that they'd be at the theater.

Jarvis stowed his cell phone in a pocket. "That was Wilson. There's more stuff on my desk. Man, I really hoped to leave this behind for a short while."

"It will be over soon."

As they passed the building housing the florist shop and Will's office, Angie shouted, "Stop."

Jarvis squealed the tires, the truck slid onto the shoulder a little past the building. Angie twisted in the seat. Donna's shop windows were completely filled with irises. Angie got out of the car, unable to move her gaze away.

Jarvis appeared at her side. "What's wrong?"

"Look at the window."

"Flowers. So what?"

"Irises, Jarvis, irises. Donna told me irises aren't big sellers in the shop. Why would she put them in place of everything?"

"Trying to stimulate interest in them? Jeez, I don't know."

Angie crossed the street, making an oncoming car slam on its brakes.

"Angelina!" Jarvis hollered.

She cupped her hands to see in the window. Pots and vases in all shapes, sizes and styles were lined up on shelves of differing heights, filling the plate glass window. In every color of the rainbow—including red. "It can't be."

"What can't be?" he asked.

She pointed. Six brilliant red flowers overwhelmed the center spot. They were fanned out in a plain brown cloisonné vase, one that would do nothing to detract from the beauty of the flowers. "Isn't that *Rhapsody*?"

"How would I know?"

"I'm going in."

He grabbed her sleeve. "I don't think you should."

"Don't be ridiculous, she knows everyone's looking for the red. She put them here—as an invitation."

"More like a tribute to Sondergaard. Come on, let's get out of here. We don't have much time before we have to get to the theater."

"She's already seen us." Angie waved at Donna, coming from the back room carrying an armload of irises. "Pretend you're angry with me."

"That won't be difficult."

Angie gave him a piercing look, raised her voice in an argumentative tone and added a few angry hand movements. "I'm stopping here, that's all there is to it. Go home and watch your stupid television, I'll walk home." In a low voice she added, "Storm back to the car. I want to see if I can get her to talk."

Jarvis played his part with the professionalism of a seasoned actor, raising a defiant chin and stiffening his spine. "Fine. I'll wait five minutes, then I'm leaving." He stalked across the street and got into the truck and slammed the door, hard.

Angie gave an irritated foot stomp, and jerked open the florist shop door. She stormed across the room, setting her mouth in a flat line. Donna put the vases on the counter and turned. She gave a sad smile. "Lover's tiff?"

"Bah!" Angie pretended to wave Jarvis out of her mind. "Nice flowers."

"They're a tribute to Pedar."

"Too bad he can't see them."

"I'd like to think he can."

"They're beautiful." Angie went to the nearest shelf and examined the dozen or so flowers in a large ceramic vase, deliberately staying away from the six Rhapsodies. "Why did you cut these from the parent? Won't they be ready for pollination soon?"

"I'm giving up breeding and…" Donna's voice trailed off as she looked over Angie's shoulder watching something out in the street. The squeal of Jarvis's tires punctuated the relative quiet of the neighborhood. "Your ride just left."

Angie huffed.

"I thought you two were close."

"We've been dating, that's all; two lonely people making life a little less lonely. How are you holding up?"

"Not very well." Donna pulled two folding metal chairs from a narrow space between the counter and cash register. She handed one to Angie, unfolded her own and sat down.

"I can't stay. I was just passing and saw the irises." Angie sat in the chair and crossed her legs. "Jarvis's father died."

Donna nodded. "Your mother called and ordered flowers."

Should she mention *Rhapsody*? Donna hadn't so much as looked in their direction. Instead she asked, "Who gets Pedar's money now that he's dead?"

Donna gave a derisive laugh. "Money? What money?"

"You didn't know he paid John Bloom three million dollars to develop the red?"

She looked genuinely surprised. "No way!" After a second she added, "He would've told me."

Angie unclasped her hands and wiped them on her thighs.

"Or John would've told me."

"The money is in John's bank account."

"I don't believe it." Donna flew to her feet and began arranging irises in a vase.

"Do you have any idea where either of them might have put a copy of their contract?"

"No contract. And no money." Donna came and sat down. "Angie, you didn't see what I saw. Pedar had no money."

"How can you be so sure?"

"He…" Donna sniffed. "He wanted to marry me, but he said he wouldn't until he could afford to do it right."

Poor Donna. Poor blind Donna. Possibly Donna couldn't recognize an expensive manicure or hairstyle, but could she really have missed Sondergaard's expensive clothes or that filigree ring? Didn't she know about his wife?

"Have you ever been to Amsterdam? I heard it's beautiful.

That's where he lives, right?"

Donna's eyes lit up. "Yes, in the village of Hoorn, just out-side Amsterdam. He was bringing me there for a two-week visit this summer. He said he already bought my ticket...for August 14th. I can't—couldn't—wait. Believe it or not, I had a lot of my things packed already."

"Oh my goodness," came a voice from the doorway.

Trynne wore a striped pantsuit of blue and lime green, that could've been from straight out of the sixties—and it looked great on her. Angie nearly blurted out, I thought you were arrested again.

Trynne marched to the window display. "Ooh, is this *Rhapsody*?"

Angie's adrenaline perked to life, and soared into her veins like rocket fuel. She rose and went to Trynne, bent over the vase of red irises. Trynne moved closer, tilting her head to examine each petal. "Are these really *Rhapsody*? They're very, very lovely."

Direct. Angie liked that.

"I decided to put out a display that would honor John and Pedar's work."

"Pedar?" Trynne asked, facing them.

"Pedar Sondergaard," Angie responded. "He's the one who fronted the money for John's research."

"Angie, I told you there was...no...money." Donna accented the last three words, then whirled around and went to the cen-ter shelf arrangement. She adjusted the vases three times before settling on a display similar to the original.

"Do you know who Rhapsody's parents are?" Angie asked.

She couldn't read the look Donna gave before saying, "The iris parent is *Play with Fire*."

"I'm assuming there's a genetic parent who's not an iris?" Trynne asked.

"Right. And you can believe me when I say I don't know what it is. John guarded that secret very closely."

Interesting that John hadn't trusted Donna enough to divulge the gene donor of *Rhapsody.* "Did you have suspicions?"

Donna nodded, rearranged the vases once more and then faced Angie. "I really thought it might be a tomato."

Trynne straightened up and laughed. "Makes sense."

"What makes you think It was a tomato?" Angie asked.

"Because he grew several varieties in the greenhouse."

"Didn't he sell tomatoes in the nursery?"

"Yes, he sold a lot of vegetables, in flats, as annuals," Donna said, plucking at a wilted flower petal and wadding it in a fist. "They all came from distributors. The ones I saw were in the greenhouse attached to the lab."

"What does *Play with Fire* look like?" Trynne asked.

Angie threw her a glance, but she was innocently looking at Donna, waiting for a reply. Donna picked up a potted iris from the far end of the display. One of the tall varieties, more than three feet; the flowers were deep cinnamon/maroon throughout. Under the fluorescent bulbs, it glimmered with highlights of burnt orange and gold.

"Very pretty," Trynne said.

Trynne walked the length of the exhibit. At the end, she retraced her steps. "I stopped in to see if you had some calla lilies. I thought they'd cheer up my dining room."

"I have some whites out back." Donna disappeared through the rear door.

"Some display, isn't it?" Angie said.

"Sure is. What's all this about John having a financial backer?"

"Someone paid him three million to develop *Rhapsody.*"

Air whizzed between Trynne's teeth. "Three million dollars. Damn."

"About *Rhapsody...*"

Donna returned carrying a plastic holder with bundles of callas and daisies. "How many did you want?"

Trynne met her at the counter. "A dozen. No, make it eighteen."

Donna rolled the flowers in thin green paper. Angie said good-bye to Donna and left with Trynne. Angie's intention was to restart the conversation about tomato gene donors, but Trynne now seemed in a hurry. "I'll talk to you soon. I've got some slides percolating."

Angie took a long hard look at the spot where Jarvis had been parked, then back at Trynne's car speeding away. Why the hurry, and why hadn't Angie asked for a ride? She started walking. Around the slight bend near the park, she spotted Jarvis's Jeep. It was empty.

Her heart lurched into her throat, making her choke. Even if Jarvis were to take a nap, he'd only lean his head back on the seat, he wouldn't lie down. If he was lying on the seat, he had to be…

She broke into a run.

He can't be dead. He can't be dead. Her legs pumped to the rhythm of her anxiety. What if she never saw that silly Sherlock Holmes hat again, or heard his comforting words? Jarvis had a way of knowing what she thought, knew when something was wrong. Had she and Will ever been that in tune?

She smelled everything on the air: mud, dead leaves, and that indefinable aroma of spring. She tasted the same on the air. Heard the sharp, staccato call of a blue jay, the gentle whoosh of air through the treetops. Saw no movement in Jarvis's truck. This couldn't be happening—especially not if her theory was right.

Her hand touched the damp metal fender and used it as a prop. Her shoes slipped on the gravelly shoulder, the metal provided no handhold and she went down. Pain stabbed Angie's knees. Gravel dug her palms. Panic brought her upright, feet scrabbling for traction. Her hand found the bumper again; fingers followed its length, felt the grit of road dirt on the paint, a small dent behind the passenger door, gripped the door handle, absorbed its strength.

Of their own accord, Angie's eyes closed.

She forced them open and looked inside. The truck was empty.

Despair closed her throat. Tears blurred her vision.

Behind her, gravel crunched. Fingers gripped her upper arms. Fear pulsed through her extremities. Angie twisted around and lashed out, wishing in that instant of time, for a gun. Her left fist made contact with the soft solidity of flesh.

"Ouch! For chrissake, what's the matter with you?"

She swung again.

Fingers tightened, shook her. "Angelina!"

The facial features spun, changed places. She was shaken a bit more, the features collided then finally fused into a face. Jarvis's face. Her legs buckled and she went down hard. He knelt beside her.

Anger boiled up. "Where were you?" She swung at him again. Her fist struck the side of his neck. She hit him again. And again. He gripped her wrists and pinned them tight against her thighs. She struggled, yanking and thrashing against his grip. "Where were you!"

He leaned in, putting his face close to hers. "Honey, stop."

Tears. Sobs: wracking, heaving sobs. He folded both arms around her and pulled her to his strong chest. He was alive.

"Why didn't you answer when I called you?" he asked.

"I didn't hear you."

His hands were helping her up. Her legs wobbled, wouldn't hold the weight. She let him prop her against the truck, inch her onto the seat, buckle her in. The road's low shoulder made him short, she gazed onto his balding spot. As if feeling her stare, he peered up, concern etching every line of his almost-handsome face. He laid his head on her lap. Her hand moved to the back of his neck, massaging the taut tendons. They remained that way a long time, morning light shrouding them in its embrace.

Nineteen

On the ride to John's she and Jarvis were subdued. All energy reserves had been sapped. Still, she couldn't help feeling a measure of satisfaction. She'd determined four of the five W's: who, what, when, and where. Of course, the what, when, and where had been determined at the outset. She knew the who, but the why baffled her so thoroughly she couldn't focus.

Suddenly Jarvis said, "I need a Coke," and spun the wheel left into the fast food lane.

"Question: why was Sondergaard attacked at that specific time and place?" she asked.

"I'm not sure what you mean."

"Both he and our perp were in Alton Bay for several days. Why follow Sondergaard all the way to Philadelphia to kill him? Why not do it here?"

"To throw suspicion in another direction?"

"There was no suspicion in any direction."

"Our murderer wouldn't know that," Jarvis said.

"Possibly, but I believe there's another reason." Silence a moment while they waited for the Cokes to be passed through the window.

"I want this case over," he said, steering the car back onto the main road.

"Tell me about it." It *would* be nice to get this over with. And concentrate on her theater. Her theater. What nice words. Her dream was to put the tiny place on the theatrical maps. "Poor

Donna. She really believed Sondergaard was taking her to Amsterdam."

"You don't think so?"

"He was married."

Angie couldn't help looking to see if Frank Chute's curtains moved. They didn't. John's car was parked in front of his garage. Everything looked forlorn and quiet.

"Are we going to the greenhouse or the regular house?" Jarvis asked.

"Regular house. I specifically want another look at those Iris Society Bulletins. How will we get in?"

"Try the doors and windows, I guess."

"Jarvis! Breaking and entering? You're taking up a new career?" He ignored her and began searching around the back door, lifting the mat, checking under stones near the porch. Turning up nothing, he said, "Wait here. I'm going out back to see if there're some keys there."

While he was gone, she tried the windows, first the front of the house, then around the side and back. Everything was locked up tight. She rounded the corner of the house and came up short, a hand pressed to her chest. "Jeez," she said, "You scared me about to death."

"What do you think you did to Edna? She got up to use the toilet and saw movement over here."

"And she sent you to investigate instead of phoning the police?"

Frank Chute chuckled. "I adore the wife, but even she doesn't have that much clout."

"So, why didn't you call the cops?"

"Figured you had a good reason for traipsing around here."

"How is your wife?" Angie asked.

"Nice of you to ask. Not good, poor thing."

"I'm sorry to hear that. I see you've sold your house." Angie nodded to the sign stuck in his lawn. "When are you moving?"

"About fifty year's worth of stuff to sell first. The kids try to help but they've got their own lives."

"Have you decided which one you'll move in with?"

"The youngest. She's got a big place in Colebrook with a couple extra rooms on the first floor. Edna can even bring her cats."

"That'll be very nice for her."

"Damn things," Chute said with a smile.

"You mentioned a vehicle that came down the road the night of John's death. You said by the time you looked out, you couldn't be sure if it had come out of Mr. Bloom's driveway or had just turned around here. Can you describe the car for me?"

"Near as I can recall, dark, either black or navy blue. And big, one of those SUV things. It was really shiny and clean, that tends to stand out in the winter, with all the salt on 'em."

"What time did you say you saw it?"

"'Bout nine."

She gave another nod. "Did you get a glimpse of the driver? Even a hint of the identity? A sex?"

Chute gave a firm shake to his head. "No. Too dark. I'm fairly sure the car backed out of the driveway, so when it goes past here, the driver is on the far side."

Angie smiled too then put out a hand for him to shake. "I'm happy to have met you, I hope your move north goes well."

"Thank you. You're a very nice lady to be so concerned." He reached into his pants pocket and came up with something he dangled in the air between them. It caught the bit of light and flashed gold.

A key.

He handed it to Angie. "Before all the trouble in the neighborhood, Mr. Bloom and I exchanged keys. Don't know what he woulda done with mine by now, but I kept his. Hang 'em all on a rack inside the back door."

Angie took the key and reached up to kiss his cheek. "Thank you."

"Welcome." He turned away.

"Aren't you going to ask why we want to get inside?"

"Nope. And you didn't get that key from me."

Angie thanked him again. Just then Jarvis joined them. Angie introduced them and handed him the key. "Look what I found."

In the kitchen, Angie flicked on the overhead light and bee-lined for the pile of AIS Bulletins in the stack closest to the kitchen table. The first time she'd been here, the pile had been neat and straight. Now it was haphazard. Angie pictured the forensics detectives trying to gather data in this place, stacked floor to ceiling with papers, reports, brochures and books.

She steadied the pinky finger of her right hand on top of the stack and stretched her thumb down as far as she could reach. She lifted the bulletins a couple of inches, then let them flutter down the way she had the first time. The pages flicked past like frames on a movie reel. Angie concentrated on the cover photos. A muttered word of triumph escaped her lips.

Jarvis peered over her left shoulder. "What've you got?"

Angie lifted the bulletins and let the covers flutter past a second time. Yes! She hadn't imagined it. Now to find exactly the right one.

She removed the top eight or so inches of issues and placed them on the kitchen table then sat in the chair she'd designated as John's favorite. The top issue was printed in black and white, about fifty pages in thickness. She didn't bother thumbing through it, she sought covers only. One by one Angie contemplated them. One by one they were discarded. She felt Jarvis watching and looked up. "I can't find it."

"If you're sure of what you're doing, keep looking, it'll turn up."

On the next cover were two men: one tall and thin; with cocoa brown hair and a goatee; the second man was short with white hair and a paunch. The taller man pointed at a lengthy field of blooming irises. The flowers were all light color, maybe purples, yellows and pinks, hard to tell in the black and white picture. The shorter man smiled, obviously agreeing with whatever the other man said.

"To save time, would you start looking in the dining room? Look for anybody who looks even slightly familiar."

"Okay," he said doubtfully.

Angie waited till he disappeared around the corner, then moved the bulletin closer to the light. She tilted it one way, then the other, squinting at both men. The date was August 1972. She squinted at the picture. Ho-lee shee-it. She'd found it!

Angie took a photograph—pilfered from one of Gloria's envelopes—from her handbag and laid it beside the cover. Next she tore off the cover and placed them both in the handbag. Her eyes were burning. Even after squeezing them shut for several moments, the burning continued.

"Nothing?" Jarvis asked, making her jump.

"Not really. Come on, let's go check on Mom." She spoke little all the way back to town.

"You gonna tell me what you found?" he asked as he turned into his driveway. "I know you had a specific reason for asking me to take you there. I also know you sent me out of the room because you found something. What I don't get is why you wanted me out of the way."

How could he read her so well?

"I have to check on my mother, then I'll tell you." She dialed Tyson's number. Jarvis called Sergeant Wilson. Two short phone calls went on simultaneously: "Tyson, I need a huge favor. Could you pick up my mother and keep an eye on her for about an hour? I'll explain later." And, "Wilson, Angie's figured this thing out. You want to hear it, get to my house."

Gloria was seated at Jarvis's kitchen table, telephone book spread wide. "I just ordered more flowers. I got to thinking. Except for Jarvis, Bud has no family. I wanted to make sure there were enough flowers."

Angie patted the wrinkled hand. "Good idea. I'll be back in a minute." She headed for the bathroom. As she closed the door, she heard the muted sounds of Tyson's arrival. Angie sat on the closed toilet seat and made a phone call.

Moments later she arrived in the kitchen, Tyson held out a leather gloved hand toward Gloria. "I wondered if you might have lunch with me."

Her expression became almost gleeful. Immediately it turned suspicious and aimed first at Angie, at Jarvis, then at Sergeant Wilson, just stepping through the door. He carried a stack of manila folders in his arms.

"If you wanted me out of the way, you only had to say so," Gloria said.

"The case has come to a head," Jarvis told her. "We need to talk. I'll see you in a while." Over Gloria's shoulder, she mouthed *thanks* to Tyson.

She, Wilson and Jarvis sat at the kitchen table. Wilson laid three folders in the center and pushed a fourth across to Angie. She crossed her arms protectively over it, then, atop the trio of folders, she laid the red iris bud taken from Sondergaard's dying fingers. And told the whole story—all but the *why* of it—because she didn't know. Yet.

While she spoke, she withdrew the Bulletin cover from her handbag and laid it before the men. "Check the address label."

"Jan Van Blozend Bloem," Jarvis read. "So? We already know John changed his name."

"What I don't get is, if he was hiding here, why keep the membership in his old name? Someone at the post office would've noticed."

"He has no criminal record," Wilson said. "Nobody's chasing him for money or back taxes. The name shouldn't make a difference."

"Perhaps not." She warned herself to tread gently. "Look closely at the cover."

Jarvis picked it up and gave it full attention. "What do you want us to see?"

Angie took out the photo from Gloria's stash, slipped the cover photo from his fingers and laid the two side-by-side on the table.

She watched Jarvis's face gazing at the irrefutable evidence, and realized she'd underestimated him. His professionalism would rein in whatever other emotions spilled over.

"I knew there was something fishy going on the whole time. It was just too…easy." He picked up the tiny pre-flower and chuckled. "And they say women can't keep secrets. John's not being able to keep a secret is what set this whole mess in motion."

"You need to search this storage facility." Angie reached for the notebook Jarvis always kept in his shirt pocket and wrote the company's name. She tore off the page and handed it to the sergeant. He wore a brilliant smile as he phoned headquarters and sent a pair of men to the address on the paper.

Wilson spread out the folders and picked up one with Pedar Niels Sondergaard written across the tab. Inside were several photos; one showed Sondergaard standing in front of a bank, whose name was out of the frame. The next picture depicted a sprawling country estate, high on a hill and surrounded by tall white brick walls. On the back the words: *Iridiceae. Estate of Pedar Evan Sondergaard. Photo taken 06-03-27.*

"Wow."

"Double wow," Jarvis said.

"Can you bring a case to court without knowing a motive?"

Jarvis thumped the pile of folders with his knuckles. "If we have everything else, yes. I'm hoping there's something in here that'll give us our motive."

"To make everything stick," Wilson explained, "we need to know the whole connection between Sondergaard and Bloom: how and when they first met, who introduced them, details of their business arrangement. Where did the three million come from? Is three mill a standard amount to pay a researcher?"

"I want to know what's so damned important about a red flower. And why someone's willing to kill for it. I'm still having trouble wrapping my brain around the flower thing. It's just a goddamned flower." Jarvis stood up, got two beers from the refrigerator and handed one to Wilson, who pushed it away.

"On duty."

"You want anything?" he asked Angie.

"You're looking a little pleased with yourself."

He sat, unable to stop his smirk from widening. "Sondergaard did say something on his death bed." He sipped from his can, pushing out the images that assaulted his head and replaced them with the vision of he and Angelina alone here, having dinner. Maybe not at this table. She had nice furniture at her place; nothing like this worn out stuff. Since meeting her he'd thought a lot about redecorating, even done a little painting. Liz had always taken care of curtains and furniture; he'd thought maybe sometime he could ask Angelina's help. Or maybe she'd do it after they were married.

Not much chance of that now. Not after his blunders of the past few days. He'd dumped hard on her over John's computer hard drive. Why the hell had he done that?

"Jarvis!"

He started at the sound of her raised voice.

"What...did...Sondergaard...say?"

"He said m—He said a name."

"Why you little weasel!" Angelina swung at him, landing a glancing blow on his upper arm. He assumed an injured, innocent expression. Wilson laughed as she said, "So that's why you accepted my theory without argument."

Not the only reason, but let her think that for now. Angelina pointed a copper colored fingernail at him. "Wait a minute. Wait just a cotton-picking minute. If you knew the name, why didn't *you* get the airline passenger list?" He shrugged. "You weasel!"

He laughed and patted her hand. Touching her had been a bad idea and he stood up quickly. "We already had the passenger list, my darling. FYI, Sondergaard only said the first name."

"Damn," said Angelina and Wilson together.

Jarvis flopped in the chair and picked up the photo of Sondergaard. They were right. What was the world coming to when a case was solved by a flower—a bloody, stinking flower?

A bloody, stinking, three million dollar flower.

"You're still a worm," she said.

"You said weasel."

"Same thing. Did I tell you Frank Chute is moving to Cole-brook to live with his youngest daughter?" Jarvis gave her a what-does-that-have-to-do-with-anything look, to which she replied, "That's where he'll be when you need him to testify about the vehicle being there the night of the theft."

Wilson opened another folder and took up the topmost sheet, a fax from the Danish Police. "I'll give you an encapsulated version: Sondergaard was squeaky clean. No arrests. Nothing subversive. The only blemish on his record is a ticket for loitering at the age of fifteen. Educated at the University of Amsterdam. Graduated with honors and immediately opened his iris nursery. Apparently he went to a symposium in London and met up with a number of people dedicated to developing the red. Looks like his sense of self got in the way and he spent every penny working on it."

"He told Donna he was broke," Angelina said.

"Check out the name on the picture—Pedar *Evan* Sondergaard," Wilson said. "That's our guy's father. And before you get to thinking about inheritances and all that, word around Amsterdam is that he squandered the allowance his father generously bestowed on him, and Daddy-O shut off his supply. That's when coincidence shone on him in the name of John Bloom. One, or both, of them found an investor," he gestured at the photos on the table, "willing to put up the three million."

"Might've been more," Jarvis added. "I'm thinking Sondergaard got a hefty finder's fee for putting the deal together."

"Three years ago, the three million was deposited in Bloom's account, and work began. I think we know most of what happened after that—from the Sondergaard angle anyway."

Jarvis closed the folder, slapped it on the table and then separated a third folder. One with the name of their suspect scrawled in black magic marker across the front. He withdrew several stapled sheets, scraped the chair back a couple of feet, crossed his left ankle over his right thigh and set the pages on the triangle his leg formed. He didn't read, or otherwise look at them, though. They were pretty much committed to memory by now. He handed the folder to Angelina. "This is the background check."

Her eyes lit up and he felt a giddy rush. Finally he'd surprised *her.* Jarvis popped the top on the second beer while she read. The multitude of expressions that crossed her face made him smile. Five minutes ticked off the kitchen clock.

Why had all this happened to him? Something had brought him, as a person, to the perp's attention.

"What are you grinning at?" Angelina asked. She laid the pages on top of the pile. "Do you want me to break the news to Trynne?" she said.

"I'll go with you. You can do the talking."

"She won't be happy to see you."

"She's right," Wilson said, "Angie and I will go." That moment his cell phone rang. "Hello." Wilson's eyebrows shot up, he nodded. "That's what we thought. Okay, thanks for letting us know." He set the phone on the table and ran a hand through thinning hair. "That was State Police. They've traced the loooong money trail."

"No surprises?" Jarvis asked.

Wilson shook his head. "Nope. Just the motive for drawing you in." He stood up. "What if I pick you up in about an hour? You two need time to talk."

Jarvis opened his mouth to protest, but Wilson was gone.

Twenty

Jarvis dragged the folders toward him, straightened them, re-straightened them. Pushed them away.

"He was right, you need to talk about it," Angie said.

"What's there to say? Carson Dodge isn't really my father." Angie put both hands atop his. His fingers closed around hers in a death-grip. "He's not my father. He's a lying, cheating son of a bitch who cares—cared—only for himself."

"That's not true. Yes, he was badly misguided. But he cared. I know he did."

Jarvis's leap from the chair tipped it over with a crash. "Why! Just tell me, why me?"

She stood up. "Let's go in the living room and sit down."

Jarvis spun away from her touch. "I don't want to sit down. I want to know what the fuck's going on!"

"Come sit and I'll tell you." Jarvis allowed her to lead him to the sofa. She sat beside him, but half-turned to face him. The folder Wilson had brought lay in her lap. "You were wrong when you said he only cared for himself. This whole thing was set up *because* of his daughter."

"*Daughter*?"

She nodded. "He came to Alton Bay intending to steal the iris and give it to his daughter."

"Daughter."

"Trynne."

From her folder, Angie took a folded sheet of paper, the

photocopy of a birth certificate. The name on the certificate was Trynne Bergitte Dekker. Parents: Claus Albert Dekker and Kaatje Ambian Dekker.

"Carson Dodge, AKA Claus Dekker first came to Alton Bay last summer. I think he tracked Trynne here pretty much the same way John did."

"Carson's wife, Trynne's mother, died about two years ago. Six months later he learned he had cancer. At that point I think he decided to mend some bridges."

"I don't get what that's got to do with me."

"He found you through this." Angie pulled a clipping of newspaper from the folder; the color home page of the web site he visited three times a week—for grief counseling.

Jarvis was silent. Finally he said, "Counseling?"

"You told me he went to counseling. Remember you joked that it ran in the family."

He nodded.

"I contacted the guy who runs the—"

"Greg."

"Right. He wouldn't divulge any confidences but after I named a few names, we made a connection. Was there a Mack in your group?"

After some thought, Jarvis said, "I get it now—Rap McSodie. Mack."

"Right. Did you have any contact with him outside the boundaries of the group?"

His shook his head no, then stopped and nodded slowly. "We were the only two guys in the group. We were assigned as support buddies. Like in AA? Sometimes we emailed each other off-group. We got kinda friendly; you know, talked about movies, books, fishing trips, families."

"That he used as stories about your childhood."

Jarvis dropped his head in his hands. "I started getting suspicious of him. The other day at your house, he remembered a story that happened—at least I was sure it happened—after he left us. I thought about it all night long, but figured my child's brain probably misremembered the time element."

"Did you ever mention Trynne to him?"

"No, why would I?" He peered up at her, that perplexed vee etched between his eyes. "Wait…wait. Wait. *He* mentioned her!" Jarvis thought a moment, the vee deepened further. "I can't remember the context. Doesn't matter, I guess. Somehow I let him know I knew her. That's when he decided I was so fucking gullible I'd be a great target for his con game."

"No." Angie leaned against him. "You aren't gullible." She laughed. "That's the last word I'd use to describe you."

"Right. You'd begin with jealous and suspicious."

"Intelligent, logical, caring… Sexy."

Finally the vee loosened and a crumpled grin appeared. "So, what happened? Did he tell Trynne who he was and together they set the cameras?"

"No, I'm convinced she knew nothing of his arrival in town. I think John triggered events from his end. I think the cameras were totally unrelated."

"How can you be sure?"

"I'm not, but hopefully when Wilson and I confront her with the news, we'll find out the rest."

"Why not just leave the money to her in his will?"

"To Bud, money was nothing compared to the pursuit of that flower. Remember his dedication is what got John involved in breeding in the first place."

"Okay so, he planned to give the flower to his daughter. My question is, where is it now?"

"I think the key from his briefcase is the final clue. Wilson did some checking and it fits a safety deposit box at the bank downtown." Angie wrapped a hug around him. He leaned against her. "The good news in all this is, you'll be reinstated."

He pulled away. "I've been thinking about that. I've decided to turn in my badge permanently."

If he'd struck her she wouldn't have been as surprised. Though questions peppered her brain, waiting for his explanation seemed the most prudent action.

"If I can be this blind…to be taken in by someone like him… I can't be much of a detective. A detective needs to be alert for con artists. He needs to be on the prowl. He can't be standing there with open arms, begging the guy to fuck him. Every day on the news you hear about people being scammed by someone on the Internet."

"You're being too hard on yourself."

"The simple fact is, it's not supposed to happen to someone in my position."

The sound of Wilson's return stopped the discussion. He entered the living room unbuttoning his coat. "I've been thinking. What if, instead of visiting Ms. McCoy, we invite her to the bank, to help us open the box? If she's got anything to hide about the relationship to Dodge, it might come out there."

"Good idea," Jarvis said, rising to his feet. "The connection between he and Sondergaard and Bloom is still a little vague. Why did he kill Sondergaard anyway?"

"I haven't worked that out yet," Wilson said. "All we know for sure is he sneaked away from Angie's mother, got a cab to Manchester, took the same flight as you to Philly and returned later that night."

"He must've collapsed in the yard on the way back to the house," Angie said.

"Why don't you call Trynne and tell her about the key. See if she'll meet you at the bank."

"You mean without mentioning you guys?"

"Not unless she asks."

Wilson handed her a phone. She dialed and waited, hoping Blake didn't answer. "Hi, it's Angie. How are you?"

"Like a wrung out dishrag."

"Hey, I found a key in Bud Dodge's things. I'm going to the bank to try and open his box. If you aren't too busy, can you come keep me company?"

"Busy?" she laughed sharply. "Can't keep my mind on anything. I'll be right there."

Angie handed Wilson his phone. "She's on the way."

"Okay," Jarvis said. "Wilson and I will go in the bank and see if we can get the ball rolling. You meet Trynne in the parking lot then bring her in."

"Do you want me to tell her about Bud?"

Wilson and Jarvis looked at each other. They nodded. "That might be a good idea," Wilson said. "She's beyond trusting anything we'd say."

Jarvis headed for the bathroom. Angie watched till the door closed. There was a certain gratification to having set the solution's wheels in motion, yet unease was a monster growing inside her. No good could come of this. Families would be affected. Relationships would suffer. All in the pursuit of a stupid red flower.

Wilson sat in a chair across the room. "How'd he take it?" he asked quietly.

"Not good. Thanks for leaving us alone."

"He's having a devil of a time holding things inside."

Two minutes after Jarvis and Wilson disappeared inside the bank, Trynne's little blue car turned into the parking lot, Angie got in the passenger side.

"Aren't we going in?" she asked.

"In a minute. I have to tell you something first." Angie took a breath. Words jumbled on her tongue and wouldn't come out. She took another breath. "I guess the only way to do this is to just say it. Bud Dodge is your father. Your birth father. From Oregon."

Trynne's fingers clenched higher on the steering wheel. Her pale blue eyes, so much like Carson's stared out the window as she absorbed the news. "It can't be."

"He came here last summer—after your mother died. He wanted to fix things with you."

"Angie, I know you'd never lie to me on purpose, but I truly think you're mistaken."

"It's true. I'll show you proof later. Right now, Wilson and Jarvis are waiting in the bank. We're going to open a safe deposit box we hope has all the proof inside."

"It doesn't make sense. He never contacted me. I swear he never called." When she spoke again, her voice was tinged with tears. "He said he never wanted to see me again. I believed him. Why didn't he call?"

"There's one more thing."

Trynne's laugh cut the air and made Angie wince. "One more thing. What? Are you going to tell me he's the one who killed John?"

When Angie hadn't replied after a few seconds, Trynne's head shot around. "No. No no no. He wouldn't do that. He loved John. Maybe even more than he loved me."

"I don't know what happened between them. He's also the one who stole *Rhapsody*."

Trynne's knuckles whitened on the steering wheel. Then her hands released the thick wheel and she turned and said softly. "That I *can* believe. The pursuit of that iris was his life's work. Sometimes I think the only reason I got into genetics was to be with him, work by his side. He was a genius. I don't know why he gave up breeding. He wasn't the type to ever give up anything."

"What if we go inside and see what's in that box?"

"Why did you need me here?"

"Jarvis thinks that since you're his daughter, the bank will allow you access to the box."

"I'm really pissed at Jarvis."

"Would it do any good to tell you he's sorry for the way things happened?"

"Angie, he accused me of killing John." Trynne reached into the back and took hold of her purse straps. "Accused me of killing the man I loved." She jerked open the car door and got out.

Within minutes, the parties had signed into the vault and the bank manager had placed the box on a table in the center of the room. He and Trynne twisted the pair of keys—one belonging to the bank and the one from Bud's briefcase—and opened the lid. He said, "It's all yours," and left.

A neat mass of paper lay inside the box; topmost was the original of Trynne's birth certificate. She picked it up as though it were made of fine crystal. The room was silent as a tomb while she read the written truth. Soberly, though with tears glistening in her eyes, she placed the paper on the table. Next, she removed three envelopes. In large block letters, were the names Angie Deacon, Colby Jarvis and Trynne Dekker.

They waited while Angie opened hers. The one-page letter was handwritten in a shaky script she recognized as Bud's.

"Dearest Angie," she read out loud. "If you're reading this you've figured things out. I had no doubt you wouldn't rest till you did. Consider this my confession. I took *Rhapsody in Scarlet*—my name, by the way. The flower should have been Trynne's, our family worked so hard on it, spent a fortune. When Trynne left, I was surprised when she didn't take the research with her. Then Jan moved away. That's when I lost the will to do it myself.

"It dawned on me to try and find the two of them and get them reunited. I told Kaatje my plan and she was very angry. Let sleeping dogs lie, she said. But, pigheaded me ignored her. Through the iris society, I learned Jan was living in New Hampshire under a new name. How convenient was it that he'd already found Trynne? Better still was that he still loved her. I thought all I had to do was get them together. Unfortunately, even after three years of John's gentle manipulation, she remained loyal to Blake. An admirable trait, I suppose.

"In order for my plan to succeed, Jan had to produce the red. He had the knowledge and my research. All he needed was the means—money—which I arranged for him to have through Pedar Niels Sondergaard, a man I met years ago in Amsterdam. A man equally devoted to the red." Angie stopped for a breath. Trynne was reading her own letter, sobbing openly. Jarvis's inscrutable eyes flicked back and forth between she and Trynne.

"The next part is written in a different ink, by a shakier hand,"

Angie said. "Tomorrow, Sondergaard is speaking at a conference in Philadelphia. I will go there and try to talk him into letting Trynne take over where Jan left off. Upon my death, she will be in possession of Rhapsody and all the research data.

"Angie, dear, you have my story. Under other circumstances, we might have become great friends. You are an admirable woman. When that policeman asks, marry him.

"Yours, Claus Dekker."

She wiped at some tears, folded the letter, and put it back in the envelope.

Jarvis tore open his envelope and read, "Colby. Words cannot express the depth of my sadness for what I've done to you. I joined the grief group, at the end of my rope. I'd lost everyone in my life who ever meant anything to me. You were kind and understanding and also suffering the loss of a loved one. I felt a true kinship to you. I sensed you as a man with deep emotions, a man dedicated to righting wrongs. To family." Jarvis gave a harsh snort. "When I learned you were an officer in the town where my Trynne lived, something inside me snapped, and I could not stop myself from carrying you along in my plan.

"Years ago, I did a horrible thing when I cast off my only… my precious child. Trynne accused me of being selfish and self-centered. And she was right. That is why now I cannot stop until righting what I've so thoroughly ruined.

"I feel my Kaatje watching down on me. Though she was adamant against my plan, my stubbornness persevered. I can only hope now that she sees I have finally reconnected our family.

"Colby, you are a man of tremendous vision and dedication to finishing a task. I know in the end you'll understand my ultimate need to make things right with my daughter, and be able to forgive me. Again, I apologize for hurting you. Another day, another life and," Jarvis's voice grew raspy, "I would've been proud to call you my son."

Angie groped in her pocket for a tissue, and found none. Jarvis pressed a handkerchief into her fingers then folded his arm around her shoulders. They waited for Trynne to read her letter out loud. But she resolutely clutched the pages against her chest. "May I leave now?"

"In a minute," Jarvis said. "There's one more thing in the box."

Trynne gestured at Angie who reached inside and came out with a tri-fold stack of papers that she recognized a Claus Dekker's last Will & Testament. She felt three pairs of eyes on her as she scanned the pages. The third page finally began listing bequests. "The estate is valued at just under $9 million. There are gifts to the Iris Society and other charities that amount to just under a million. He left something to the theater too. Two million dollars for 'what he put us through.' Trynne gets what's left."

"Maybe after I get out of jail."

Wilson held the door for them to pass through, saying, "I bet we can get you a suspended sentence."

Trynne ducked past him, tucking the letter back in the envelope. As they stepped out into the sunshine, she tilted her chin up and took hold of her emotions by sucking in a breath and pulling back her shoulders. Angie stepped up and hugged her. "All these years," Trynne said. "All these years I thought he didn't care about me."

"What will you do now? Are you staying with Blake?"

"We had a long talk last night. I'm going to give up my work in genetics and go into partnership with him in the business. By the way, where is *Rhapsody*?"

"In a heated storage facility in Meredith."

"What will happen to her now?"

"I don't know about wills and legal things, but since *Rhapsody*'s three owners are all deceased, I assume she's yours."

Trynne walked toward her car. She stopped at the front bumper. "It would be a shame not to follow through with her, wouldn't it?"

Angie smiled. "It sure would." She kissed Trynne on the temple and waved till the car pulled out of the parking lot. Jarvis's arms stretched around Angie from behind. He kissed her left ear. "Come on, let's go talk to your mother."

"She's not going to take this well."

"I think she'll surprise you. She's a strong lady. That's where you get yours." He eased her into his Jeep, reached across to fasten the seat belt and said softly, "And after that, we have some serious talking to do."

About Author Cindy Davis

Cindy Davis resides in the green/white/brown—depending on the season—state of New Hampshire where she spends most of her time at the computer. When she's finally released upon society, to autograph her latest book, do a talk, or research the next in the Angie Deacon series—well, heaven help the people she meets. Shutting her up becomes tantamount to stopping a volcano!

She's edited over 150 books, more than three quarters of which have been published.

Cindy is the author of ten novels and four non-fiction books. *Play with Fire* is the sequel to the first Angie Deacon novel, *A Little Murder*.

Visit Cindy on her websites:
www.cdavisnh.com
www.fiction-doctor.com

Don't miss the next novel in the Angie Deacon mystery series—

Hair of the Dog

Excerpt:

Bang bang. The damn dog was barking again. Bang bang. She clamped the pillow tight to her ears. All at once her brain registered pounding and not barking. She sat up, wadding the pillow against her chest. The hammering. It came from the back door. Angie flung off the covers and blinked the bedside clock into focus. 5:01. Now what?

She snatched up her robe from the foot of the bed, punched her arms into the sleeves and stomped down the short hallway. This was the first, and last, time she'd visit this town. Through the square window on the back door, a smallish figure stood silhouetted on the deck. The screen door propped against his left hip, right arm raised, his fist thumped on the lightweight wooden door. It was then she realized the dog really was barking, but not the inexorable woof woof of the previous nights. It was now a high-pitched, almost frantic yelping.

She twisted the lock and pulled open the door to the wide-eyed face of a boy of about twelve. His dark hair was disheveled, as though he hadn't combed it today. Given the hour, he probably hadn't. He burst into the kitchen. "Phone. I need to call…there's somebody…the dog…"

Angie put a hand on his shoulder. In a previous life she'd been an ER nurse. Touching the shocked, or bereaved, usually helped bring calmness. She guided him to a chair. He started to sit but before his rear end hit the seat he leaped up. "Phone. I need to call…"

A gentle push settled him in the chair. She knelt between a pair of new looking Nikes, one of them untied. "Tell me what's wrong."

"Mister York. He's d-dead."